ground
FICTION

Vol. 1, Number 1

Fall 2020

Editor
Seth Harwood

Managing Editor
Rich Ferri

Assistant Editor
Jennifer Fickley-Baker

Designer
Jaye Manus

Copyeditors
Chris Rhatigan
Babs Griswold

ISBN: 978-1-7356238-0-1

Visit GroundFiction.com for more info.

The characters and events in these stories are fictitious. Any similarity to real persons, living or dead, is coincidental and not intended by the author.

Cover design by Aleksandra Dabic
On the cover: *Measured and Divided*, 2017, Amy Talluto. Oil on Panel. 24" x 30". Collection of AG Rosen and Debi Sonzogni. See more at AmyTalluto.com

ground [1]

n.

1. The solid surface of the earth.
2. That on which a system, work, institution, art, or condition of things, is founded; the basis.
3. The fundamental constituent or the essential part of any thing.

v.

1. To break (new) ground, to make progress in a new direction; to gain ground: to advance, make progress.
2. To set on a firm basis, to establish (an institution, principle of action, belief, or science) on some fact, circumstance, or authority.
3. To give (something abstract) a firm theoretical or practical meaning.
4. To instruct (someone) thoroughly in a subject.

ground [2]

v.

Past tense and past participle of grind.

Table of Contents

Dear reader,

Welcome to the first issue of *Ground*. I'm very happy to introduce these sixteen entries, which, for many of these writers, represent their first published work. Please join me in congratulating them.

The writing here was developed during individual meetings and monthly workshops where we discussed and dissected stories and chapters. Our foundation, the prioritization of meaning, sense, and clarity, comes from what I learned at the Iowa Writers' Workshop under Marilynne Robinson and Frank Conroy.

Most of these writers came through my creative writing classes at Harvard, Stanford, and Lit Reactor. Afterwards, they decided to continue working with me, to stick around and dig in, keep up their practice, and build on the tools they'd learned.

I've seen great progress from every one of them, and I'm thrilled to present these stories, long and short, and excerpts from novels in progress—a few of which will be serialized in subsequent issues.

To sign up for more information about upcoming stories, audio podcasts, Zoom events, and future issues, visit groundfiction.com. To learn more about attending workshops, trying your hand at writing assignments, or jumpstarting your own work through private coaching sessions, you can find me at writewithseth.com.

Welcome to *Ground Fiction*.

Enjoy the read!
Seth Harwood

Frozen in Time

Rich Ferri

"If you're lucky, in a lifetime you get one moment in which you'd like to live forever," my father said to me. "One moment when you'd like to be frozen in time, in a landscape, a painting, a sculpture or a vase. That was my moment."

The Iowa Baseball Confederacy, W. P. Kinsella

EVERYONE ON THE PLANE groaned collectively when the flight attendant's cheery voice came over the intercom.

"Passengers, we're on hold for a few minutes to take on new passengers. Once they board, we're twenty-seventh in line for takeoff."

Perhaps sensing the surliness of the early morning crowd, she clicked on the intercom a second time, "Don't worry, we'll have you basking in that Tampa sunshine in no time!" Grumbles.

There was a commotion at the front of the plane as the flight attendant reopened the passenger door. Late passengers stumbled down the aisle like voles being led into the sunlight, looking for open seats. A dad and mom first, sporting Boston Red Sox navy tees with red lettering, a boy of about six wearing an identical tee in tow. Bringing up the rear, a girl on the cusp of her teenage years, in sensible denim shorts and a Boston windbreaker and cap.

No doubt going to the same spring training game I was but sitting on the opposite side of the field.

The girl paused for a moment in the aisle next to the vacant seat beside me. Mom scanned the remaining seats, then turned to point to the one next to me and shrugged. The freckle-faced girl plopped down in the adjacent seat and extended her hand.

"Hi, I'm Julie," she said.

I looked down at her unadorned hand and clasped it briefly, an intergenerational handshake between an old man and a young girl he'd never met.

"Hi, Julie," I said, "looks like we're going to spring training together." I touched the bill of my navy blue cap and leaned forward slightly so she could spy the stately NY logo of the New York Yankees across the bill.

"Oh," she said. "Awkward."

"Don't worry about it, it's only spring training. The games don't count yet." I shifted in my seat, reopened the book I was holding, and smiled. "Boston's real losses won't start to pile up until next month." She looked up at me, startled that I could be so impertinent about her beloved Red Sox (The 2033 World Champion Red Sox!) and when she could see that I was ribbing her, she put her head down, and giggled.

The plane started to push away, and she fiddled with the control knobs (More air! Too bright!) until everything on her side of the aisle was perfect. Within moments we were rumbling down the runway, the familiar weight of the plane pushing us back into our seats, then the moment of liftoff. The plane rumbled, grumbled, and groaned as it gained altitude, then finally broke through the fog and rain of New York City, past the clouds into the sunshine that slanted in sideways from the passenger windows. The girl turned halfway in her seat to glance at Mom and Dad behind her with a look of uncontested glee.

A true baseball fan. I immediately liked her.

She turned back to face forward in the seat, her black Chuck Taylor throwback canvas sneakers dancing with excitement. She checked the flap on the seat forward, didn't find anything to read and then craned her head to see the cover of the book I was reading. I held it out to her, so she could get a good look.

"*Frozen in Time*," she said. "What's that all about?"

"It's a baseball book. About the 2020 pandemic year."

"That was the delayed season, right? It started in July?"

"Very good," I said. "It was probably about the time you were born. The pandemic shut down everything. People were afraid to leave their homes. Families were separated. People wore masks to go grocery shopping. The economy failed, people lost their jobs. The streets were quiet—it looked like we'd never get back to normal."

"I read about it," she said, "in history class."

"The weather got warmer, spring turned to early summer, but a lot of people were afraid to go out."

"Didn't they miss being outside, around other people?"

"I think some people did. But a lot of people felt it was safer indoors and just decided not to leave."

I shifted in my chair and leaned on the arm rest so she could hear me over the din of the plane.

"Apparently on June first, President Trump called Rob Manfred, the commissioner of Major League Baseball, to the White House, and told him to start the season on July Fourth—no matter what, no matter how. It would be a national day of celebration and renewal."

She leaned closer, our heads bowed, almost touching. "So what does the book say about it, the pandemic year of baseball?"

"It was written by Tim Kurkjian. He was the lead baseball analyst for ESPN at the time. He talked to the players and umpires and the fans about what it was like to be back playing baseball."

"That first day—what was it like?"

"The first chapter is about Aaron Judge, of the Yankees."

Aaron Judge, Right Fielder, New York Yankees

I KNEW I WOULDN'T be able to sleep, the night before. My wife Kara and I had bought a small condo down in Tampa the previous season, so that she could stay with me over spring training. But when she went to sleep, I got up and went into the den. I flipped on the big screen with no sound and watched Yankee highlights from the 2019 season on MLB Network.

There was one play that stuck in my head. We were up by one, top of the ninth, the Chisox were threatening with the bases loaded and two outs. Their speedster Tim Anderson was up. Anderson fouls a couple off, then he scorches one down the third base line; I'm watching from right field and as soon as he hit it, I'm thinking it's going down the line to clear the bases. But Gio Urshela at third half turns and falls to his knees, flashes leather and snags it on one hop. Anderson tears out of the batter's box, but Gio cannons the ball over to first and Luke-ie scoops it out of the dirt a hair before Anderson stomps the bag. The umpire yanks his thumb high in the air—"He's out!"—game over. But what got to me were the fans.

They didn't leave the park after the game was over. They hung over the padded walls, slamming them with their hands, and all through the stadium you could hear it, *whomp whomp whomp*, and they're chanting, "Gio, Gio, Gio." We're all running in from the field, congratulating Gio, taking his hat, slapping five, tousling his hair. We all ran into the dugout in one big knot of Yankees, but the fans kept it up. "Gio! Gio! Gio!" They love him but he's so shy, right? Eventually we have to push him out of the dugout, onto the top step, and they won't leave until he takes a bow and waves to them.

But the thing that got to me, the thing I couldn't stop thinking about, is that it was a late August game. We were in first by a dozen games, and the Chisox couldn't find their way out of the basement with a Geiger counter and flashlight. The game didn't mean anything, and the fans didn't care.

They came to see a moment of greatness, something spontaneous, something that shocked them, something that no movie or book could ever provide. They came for that one moment when the fielder falls to his knees, the ball slaps into his glove, the runner races to first and that one quick scoop by the first baseman; the fate of the game resting in the blink of an eye. They came to see greatness.

All through the night, I sat on the couch and watched play after play wondering what would it mean, to be great. I had a monster rookie year in 2017—fifty-two homers—playing for the Yankees, living in New York. I was on the cusp of greatness. Then the next couple of seasons, injuries slowed me down. The shoulder and the wrist, then I broke a rib diving for a ball and didn't realize it until months later. My numbers fell off. There were whispers in the press that I would never live up to my potential. That I would be the new Mark Fidrych, a flash-in-the-pan who had only that one year shining in the bright sunshine and never again. I wanted to be great. I wanted to be great for the fans, that day, that afternoon. I wanted to have a Gio moment.

That morning, when my wife Kara got up, she came into the den and saw me sitting there, like that, with MLB still on.

"You been up all night, baby?" she asked me.

I just looked up at her. "We get to play today," I said.

She sat on the edge of the chair and put her hand on my shoulder.

"We get to play today," I said. "We get to play on green grass, we get to wear our gamers, the Chicago Cubs will be there, and the games will count again."

She stroked my hair and I said, "I waited so long, I just never thought this day would come."

She looked down at me and I wasn't sure she understood. I said, "It's what I do. It's what I lived my whole life for. Now the waiting is over, and I get to play again." I must have sounded like a madman to her. But I think she understood.

She made me my favorite game-day breakfast—ham and eggs and a big plate of tater tots—and I went to the field six hours early. She wasn't allowed to go to the game—there wouldn't be anyone in the stands—the first game she ever missed. Kara said she'd watch the game on TV. Then she said something to me as I left, she said, "Just be Aaron Judge."

By the time I got behind the wheel of the car, I had to take a second, my eyes were so wet. *We're playing baseball today* was all I could think of.

When I got to the stadium, I had that moment when I walked through the runway and saw the green grass again. I think every fan has had that moment once. It's like when a fan walks through the tunnel at Yankee Stadium and sees the field for the first time. It was like the first time I saw the grass, and the sprinklers going, and the perfect white lines down each base path.

I walked through the tunnel and down to the field and scanned every part of the field. It was empty; it was my field for the moment. I looked at the grass, sparkling. I looked at the expanse of right field, waiting for me. The place I belong. I walked out to the field and stood there, looking in at home plate, and the enormity of it struck me, that I get to play this game.

I knelt down. Right there in right field, I knelt down. And I kissed the grass. I never wanted to be in a place more in my life, and

I was right there, surrounded by it. A wave came over me, it shook my whole body, and I was reassured. Somehow, I knew, I was going to touch greatness, if only for an instant that day. And it would be enough.

Dannie Halloran, Umpire

I WOULD BE THE home plate umpire that day for the first game played after the pandemic. They even scheduled our game in Tampa to start at 11:59 a.m. local time to make sure we were the first. The stands would be empty, of course, but there would be a national TV audience; the Blue Angels were doing a flyover just at game time; Carrie Underwood would sing the national anthem.

It was the day we all looked forward to, the day we thought would never come.

I would be the last one out of the umpires' dressing room that day. It was my job to rub the baseballs up before the first game.

Most fans don't realize it, but there's a process a ball has to go through to be a game ball for the major leagues. The balls come to us, a dozen to a box, with the name Rawlings printed across the box. Each ball is individually wrapped in tissue paper. They're stamped with the logo of Major League Baseball; they have the current commissioner's name stamped on them—Rob Manfred.

When the balls come to us, they're pristine, but they're not ready for play. They're too slippery for the pitchers to get a good grip on them. So they have to be rubbed down with mud.

Of course, the mud has to be uniform, and it has to be just the right mud. It's even got a name—it's called Lena Blackburne Rubbing Mud. It's harvested every fall by a guy named Jim Bintliff on the New Jersey side of the Delaware River. It's a secret sauce, so to speak. The TV show *Dirty Jobs* did a piece on harvesting the mud and they had to turn the cameras off just before they got to their final location. They didn't want people dipping their own mud.

When the mud comes to us in a plastic tub, it's somewhere between the viscosity and color of used motor oil and infant poo. You dip your fingers into the goo—just a dab—and rub the ball up good to take the shine off of it but leave the white on. You have to rub it just so.

That was my job that day, to rub the balls up before the first game played. I had a few boxes of balls and a big tub of mud and was listening to Tammy Wynette and Patsy Cline on the radio, just taking my time—I wanted each ball to be perfect for its debut.

I picked one ball up, and I don't know, there was something special about it. It told me a story. It said that it would be the first baseball put in play in the pandemic year. That when Yu Darvish finished his warm-ups, that ball would get thrown out to him while he stood on the mound. He'd take off his glove and rub the ball up one last time before delivering the first pitch that would be watched by millions of Americans all over the world. That ball would be the first pitch delivered in the pandemic-shortened season, and it would be watched by the president and vice president. After that pitch, after Darvish reared back and fired that nasty slider of his, that ball would take a special trip to the Baseball Hall of Fame in Cooperstown. It would be on display for the rest of eternity as a signal that baseball, and the nation, were back on their feet.

Umpires have all kinds of compartments and bags for holding stuff. I stuffed four balls into the ball bag on my right hip. But that day I carried a second ball bag, on my left hip, and that's where the talking ball went. Ready for its Major League debut. The alarm went off, the signal that it was time to exchange lineup cards with the managers, and I hurried out for the meeting at home plate.

It was after the lineup cards, and the Blue Angels, and Carrie

Underwood, that we got down to the order of real baseball. Darvish finished his warm-ups and stood straddling the rubber. I reached into my left bag and threw him the talking ball. He rubbed it between his hands while I squatted over home plate and dusted it off one last time. I took my designated spot behind the catcher and in that instant, I looked around at the empty stands. Both teams stood on the top steps of their dugout, anticipating. The green, sparkling grass. The white foul lines down each side of the field. They say the lines go all the way to infinity.

I did my best Frank Drummond imitation, pointed right at Darvish and yelled "Play ball!"

He went into the windup and delivered—low, ball one.

I stopped the game right there and asked the catcher, Gary Sanchez, for the ball, and he handed it over his shoulder to me. And I put it back into my left bag, the talking ball. I reached in and handed him a non-talking ball to continue the game.

Right then, I don't know quite what came over me. It was my job to roll the talking ball over to the home Cubs dugout and one of the coaches would put it in a plastic baggie for its one-way trip to Cooperstown. But I couldn't do it.

Been umpiring for twenty-four years and it was the first time a ball ever spoke up. It said to me, *Give them another ball, they won't know.*

It said, *Pull the old switcheroo.*

So I did it—I pulled the old switcheroo. I left the talking ball in my left umpire bag, and slipped my hand into the right one, and rolled a silent ball over to the Cub dugout where it would be enshrined at Cooperstown for future presidents and first ladies and kids and parents and all kinds of Major-League-wannabes to ogle and remember back to the Covid year of baseball.

But it would be the wrong ball. No one would know but me and the talking ball.

So that talking ball is special. I named it Teddy Ballgame after my favorite player of all time. I wear that umpire bag with Teddy Ballgame at my side everywhere I go now to remind me how close we came to losing the national pastime.

Hannibal Delacroix Jr., superfan, Chicago Cubs

IT WAS IN EARLY June of the pandemic year when I was listening at the kitchen table to Ron Coomer—the voice of the Cubs—on the radio one afternoon. That's when he said it was official, the Cubs would be hosting the Yankees on the Fourth.

Baseball was back. The Cubbies were back.

"Myrna, Myrna, they're gonna play!" I said to my wife.

"I heard," she said, "I'm standing right here." She put my tuna on rye down on a plate in front of me.

"The Fourth of July," I said. "I got to find the cooler. Did we put it in storage?"

"Thank god," she said. "Maybe you'll get out of the house for a while."

I looked down at my plate. "What, no pickle?" I asked.

"They're playing in Tampa," she said.

"What, Tampa?"

"They're not playing in Chicago, they're playing in Tampa."

I picked up my tuna sandwich.

"No fans," she said, "they're playing in Tampa. It was in the *Chicago Sun Times* this morning."

"Tampa," I said.

She reached into the refrigerator, pulled out the jar of pickles, and put it down on the table. I liked the Polish spears with tuna.

LAST YEAR, IN 2019, I retired from the post office after thirty-five years and decided to devote my summer to the Chicago Cubs. I watched every inning of all eighty-one home games from my apartment rooftop, located directly behind left field from Wrigley Field.

This isn't as easy as it sounds.

To see every pitch, live, well, it takes preparation and dedication. Timing bathroom breaks and such. I'd get to my spot on the rooftop usually half an hour before game time with a cooler filled with ice and a dozen Rheingolds. Pacing is important. Of course, there are countless rain delays and schedule changes. One rain-delayed game took eight hours and thirteen minutes to complete, and eventually finished at 2:13 in the morning. There were a few fans left in the stands, but I was there in my poncho on the rooftop, with a few ice cubes left swimming in my cooler by game's end. Through the binoculars, I could see four relief pitchers in the bullpen, sitting side by side, asleep upright, mouths hanging open. The game ended when number twenty-four, Craig Kimbrel struck out Manny Machado in the top of the fourteenth to win the game, 8-7. Another game, April 12th, I sat silent while the snow came in sideways causing a delay between the fourth and fifth innings. I remember putting a longneck Rheingold to my lips and my teeth chattering, but I stuck it out. In early August, there was a makeup double header with the Twins in hundred-degree heat. I basked with my shirt off, but watched every inning, every pitch.

THE DAY OF THE game arrived, and I was ready. I was up on the rooftop with my filled cooler, my lawn chairs, my vintage Cubs hat signed by Ron Santo, a poncho, just in case. A local affiliate was carrying the game, so I put rabbit ears on my thirteen-inch black-and-white and set it up on the TV stand. Mrs. Barilla, from the top floor, was nice enough to let me plug an extension cord in through her kitchen window.

I always bring an extra lawn chair, where my dad used to sit to watch the games across the street. My dad, Hannibal Sr., was the true fan. He passed in 2016; he had a heart attack after game six of the World Series. A lifelong fan, he wasn't around for the final game seven, when the Cubs won their first championship in over a century. So I bring the chair like I'm watching the game with him.

I put the TV on the stand so I could face the field, and pretend they were playing right there in front of me. I stood during the national anthem. I listened to the Blue Angels and imagined them passing overhead at Wrigley Field. Then I sat down in my lawn seat, took out the first longneck, and sat back to watch the game.

Darvish was pitching a good one for so early in the season. He had those big Yankee hitters back on their heels and fooled. It was in the bottom of the fourth when Javier Báez bunted with the bases loaded with Cubbies, and Willson Contreras streaked across home with the first run of the game.

It was something, to see that ball just trickling by the outstretched glove of their pitcher, Masahiro Tanaka, and die on the infield grass, the Cubbies running the bases like a merry-go-round.

I stood and cheered, like I always do when the Cubbies score. I raised both fists in the air—"Yes, yes, yes!"—when I paused for a second, looked up from the TV, and saw an empty Wrigley Field in front of me. The stands were barren; the sprinklers were going. Not a soul in the bleachers. Not a sound. I looked over at the lawn chair beside me, also empty.

I sat back down in my lawn chair, and I reached over to the cooler, and opened a bottle of Rheingold. It would be a long season.

RIGHT THEN, THE CHIME came on and the fasten seat belts sign lit up as we started our final descent into Tampa. I slipped the book into the seatback and asked Julie, "Well, how did you like the book?"

She shrugged and said simply, "I love everything about baseball."

I said, "Really? Do you play softball somewhere?"

She wrinkled her freckled nose and shook her head. "No," she said, "I play hardball on the boys team."

I looked over at her, and she said, "Catcher. It's where all the action is."

I must have looked stunned, her at five foot two and a buck-ten soaking wet, playing hard ball with the middle school boys.

Julie said, "I got the fastest pop time in the league and threw out twelve runners at second last year." She had a wicked grin, like catchers do, like she liked to mix it up a little on the field.

I saw something special in her. A spark of something.

The plane touched down and taxied down the runway. It was mid-morning, the Florida sun whiting out the tarmac. The plane came to a stop. The seat belt light went off and everyone clamored to stand in the aisle and wait.

Julie was the first to pop into the aisle, then she looked down at me and asked if I was getting off the plane. I said that I usually just get off last.

She shrugged and said, "It was really nice talking baseball with you." She gave me a polite wave and faced forward, ready to deplane.

I looked up at her, standing there in the aisle, and I thought—we never really own the national pastime. We're just the stewards. The game is a gift. We own it for a little bit, then we just pass it on.

The crowd started to surge forward, pushing her toward the exit.

"Julie!" I yelled to her.

She turned to look at me, quizzical.

With my right hand, I reached under my coat jacket and found the umpire's ball bag, there on my left hip.

I put my fingers around the talking baseball for the last time and I flipped it to her, standing there in the aisle.

She reached for it, snagged it in midair with all the aplomb of a real athlete, a real ballplayer, one that no doubt stood in the backyard and played catch with her dad for countless hours, being connected with someone in space and time through the simple act of throwing and catching the ball, over and over.

She plucked it out of midair and looked down at it, and no doubt saw the Rawlings logo, the logo of Major League Baseball, and the stamped signature of the 2020 baseball commissioner, Rob Manfred.

Her mouth fell open and she looked at me with wide eyes.

"Take good care of Teddy," I said. "And enjoy the game."

Enjoy the game.

An excerpt from a forthcoming paranormal fantasy novel.

The Harrow

Kate M. Colby

AS THE STREETLAMPS FLICKERED to life in downtown Salem, Massachusetts, I sprawled across the black leather couch in my psychic shop's reception area. I had some time to kill before I could lock up and get on with my night. While I waited, I perused one of the *American Psychic* magazines from the coffee table. The center spread showed a curvaceous female silhouette with a pink orchid blooming in the middle of her forehead. "Third-Eye Blind: Using Crystals to Open Your Third Eye, Strengthen Your Visions, and Have Better Sex." A total crock of shit, as always.

Before I could turn to another article, a young woman entered my shop. The brass bell hung above the entrance jangled, and a chilly autumn breeze blew through the reception area. As the woman shut the door behind her, I tugged up the sleeve of my cardigan to check the time. My bulky, beat-up Seiko read 7:47. Thirteen minutes until closing, and less than thirty before I was supposed to meet my friend Carmen for dinner.

I tossed the magazine back onto the coffee table and pushed myself up from the couch.

The customer looked at me with narrowed brown eyes before hiking her Louis Vuitton purse up her shoulder and turning her gaze on the rest of the shop. Skeptics always acted like they'd entered a den of pickpockets, but when I played them right, they also left the biggest tips. Maybe this one would make working late worth the while.

"Welcome to Witch City Psychic." I stepped around the coffee table to stand before the customer. Even wearing modest heels, she was a few inches shorter than me—maybe five foot three—but she stood ramrod straight with her chin upturned. "What can I do for you this evening?"

The woman crossed her arms over her tailored blazer. "You're the psychic?"

"Guilty." I pulled back one side of my cardigan to reveal more of my faded Def Leppard T-shirt and black skinny jeans. "Were you expecting gypsy skirts and head scarves?"

"Something like that." The woman shifted her weight from one foot to the other. "I guess it doesn't matter so long as you're the real deal."

"We'll find out, won't we?" I extended my hand to her. "Now, what have you come to learn, Miss . . ."

The woman shook my outstretched hand with a cold, firm grip. "If you're psychic, shouldn't you know my name?"

I released her grasp and put my hand on my hip. "If it worked like that, I'd have bought a winning lottery ticket, and we'd be having this conversation at my Hawaiian beach house."

"Fair enough. My name is Phoebe Chou."

"Nice to meet you, Phoebe. I'm Lorena Rivera." I hooked my thumb toward the back of the shop, where the reading room rested behind velvet, wine-colored curtains. "If you're ready, we can head on back."

Phoebe nodded, so I turned and led her past the pay counter. When we reached the curtains, I pulled one aside and tucked it behind the tie-back to hold it open. "I usually keep this shut for privacy. But since it's nearly closing time, I doubt we'll be disturbed."

I motioned to the circular table at the center of the room. "Make yourself at home."

As Phoebe reached the table, she ran her hand along the black tablecloth. Then, she walked around the table, sliding her hands along the underside. Fake psychics sometimes hid wires, switches, and other aids beneath their workstations. I couldn't blame Phoebe for being suspicious, especially if she'd received phony readings in the past. When she'd completed her circle, Phoebe pointed to the table's instruments. "Do you mind?"

I shrugged. "Be my guest."

Lips pursed, Phoebe picked up the first of three cedar boxes and opened it. She slid her fingers over my runestones, slick white rocks inscribed with ancient, angular symbols, before replacing the box and moving onto the second one. It contained my scrying crystals—clear quartz, black obsidian, and turquoise labradorite with blue and black swirls. Phoebe tilted the box to and fro, examining how the crystals reflected the light. Then, she set it down and opened the box that held my tarot cards. When she saw the design—a golden pentacle centered in a starry sky—she smirked and closed the box. Last, she reached for the crystal ball. Wrapping both hands around the glossy, milky orb, she lifted it up and peeked at the base underneath. Then, she put the crystal ball back down without a single shiver or other sign of a vision. Definitely not a competing psychic come to spy then.

Seemingly satisfied, Phoebe faced me again. "Where should I sit?"

"Wherever you're most comfortable."

Phoebe pulled out the nearest chair and sat down.

I took the seat across from her and rolled up my sleeves. "Ready?"

"Give me a moment." Phoebe placed her purse in her lap and reached inside. Then, she laced her fingers and set her hands on the table. "Sorry, silencing my phone."

"Much appreciated." I tilted my head toward the ceiling, where a vintage, stained-glass chandelier hung above us. It bathed the room in a warm light, lending an ethereal, pink-gold glow to my tan skin and auburn hair. "By me and the spirits."

"Ha." Phoebe craned her neck to take in the various posters covering the walls. Carnival-style psychic advertisements, enlarged tarot cards, colored diagrams of chakras and palm lines. Most of my customers ate it up, but apparently not Phoebe. I could hear the nervous tapping of her heels against the hardwood floor.

"What kind of reading would you like?" I leaned back in my chair and rocked on its hind legs. "Crystal ball? Tarot? Palm?"

Phoebe raised an eyebrow. "What do most people request?"

"The tourists like the crystal ball. It looks coolest on social media. But you're local—came straight from the office, right?" I let my chair return to the floor with a loud clack. "Each type of reading has its pros and cons. It's more about what you want to know."

"I see." Phoebe ran a hand over her hair, smoothing a couple loose gray strands back into her otherwise sleek black bun. "You've been a psychic for a while, correct? Is there a particular style you find most accurate?"

"I've practiced my whole life, but I've only been giving professional readings for three years." I tapped my fingers on the table. "Tarot has always worked best for me."

Phoebe grinned. "Then I'll have a tarot reading."

"A fine choice." I reached across the table and removed the tarot deck from its box. I held the cards out to Phoebe. "Shuffle these, please."

Phoebe shifted in her seat, an almost imperceptible movement backward. "Why?"

"The reading will be more accurate if you transfer some of your energy to the cards." I wiggled the deck. "They won't bite."

Phoebe took the cards, turned them over, and fanned them out.

Since her gaze remained on the cards, I allowed myself an eye roll. Did she think the whole shop was boobytrapped? "They're not like regular playing cards. There'd be no point in duplicating or removing any of them."

Phoebe squinted at the cards for a moment longer then pushed them back together. "Just admiring the artwork. Don't some decks have different designs?"

Someone was full of questions—and not about her future. I tilted my head. "There's all different kinds. This is a Rider-Waite, the most traditional style."

Phoebe divided the deck in half then attempted to perform a bridge shuffle. The cards were too long, and the stacks too thick, for her petite hands. She fumbled to grip them, and the cards fell and scattered across the table. Her cheeks flushed.

"Don't feel bad. I can't do it either." I slid some of the cards back to her side of the table. "Put the deck together however you like. There'll be enough of your energy on them." Embarrassment was, after all, one of the most powerful emotions.

I waited in silence as Phoebe gathered the cards. Once finished, she straightened the deck by pressing each side against the tabletop. I picked up the crystal ball by its base and moved it aside. Then, I pointed at the center of the table, and Phoebe placed the cards there.

"Now, what do you want to know?" I asked.

Phoebe took a deep breath. "My boss passed me over for a promotion. Again. I need to know whether I have a real future at this company."

I withheld a sigh. Water cooler drama rarely made for interesting readings, but I did prefer it to telling women when they'd meet their future husbands or whether their present partners were cheating on them. If I had a dollar for all the relationships my visions had started and ended, I could close shop and retire that night.

"A three-card spread should do the trick." I cut the tarot deck about a quarter of the way down and placed the top section to the side. Pinching the first card between my fingers, I flipped it over and set it face-up on the table. It showed a knight riding a horse and carrying a large staff. In the background, five peasants cheered him on, each thrusting their own staffs into the air.

"Six of wands." I tucked my hair behind my ears. "You've been the hotshot at your job before. People respected you—or at least praised you—and you probably climbed the corporate ladder pretty quickly. Sound right so far?"

Phoebe frowned down at the card. "Yes, but only in the most general sense. I mean, I told you that I deserve a promotion, so of course you'd say I've been successful. Can't you give me more details?"

I quirked an eyebrow. "You've already lived through your past. What could I tell you that you don't know?"

"There has to be something I've missed. Something that went wrong." Deep wrinkles creased Phoebe's forehead. "Otherwise, I would have received my promotion by now."

"Not according to this card." I wiped my palms on my jeans. "Sometimes, you can do everything right and still get screwed. It's how the world works."

Phoebe huffed. When it was clear that she wasn't going to respond, I drew the second card and placed it beside the first. It depicted a nobleman riding in a chariot pulled by two sphinxes.

"The Chariot." I paused to bite the inside of my cheek. Phoebe couldn't have given me a genuine question. My tarot deck never gave inaccurate readings. "You're putting in a lot of extra work and taking charge at your job."

Phoebe scoffed. "Not that anyone notices."

"Actually, the Chariot suggests they have." I tilted my head again. "Are you sure your job's hitting a dead end?"

"Of course, it is." Phoebe glared down at her purse. "Are you certain your reading is correct?"

"Positive."

Phoebe wasn't the first person to feed me a false question. Some customers got a kick out of "tricking" a psychic, while others were too embarrassed to ask what they really wanted to know. Phoebe had an angle. I just needed to figure it out.

"Maybe the last card will clear things up." I drew the final card and placed it on the table. It featured a cloaked man with three wine goblets spilled in front of him. Two more glasses stood upright behind the man. "Five of cups. This card isn't so straightforward."

Phoebe fiddled with the straps of her purse. "How do you mean?"

"Well, look at this guy. He's so focused on the spilled wine that he doesn't realize he has two full cups behind him." I crossed my legs. "In terms of your job, this card shows that you have the wrong priorities. Whatever you're working on now will fail, but you could succeed, if you look for other options."

Phoebe shook her head. "So, I'm not getting my promotion."

"I hate to sound like a Magic 8-Ball, but 'outlook not good.'" I rubbed my chin. "If you give me more details about your job, that could help me interpret the cards better."

"No, it's fine. I got everything I needed from you." Phoebe reached into her purse.

I waved my hand. "Not here. You pay up front."

Phoebe cocked her head, then her eyes widened in recognition of what I'd said. "Oh, right." She slung her purse over her shoulder and stood.

"You can head to the counter, if you want." I rose from my seat too and scooped up the tarot cards. "I'll just be a sec putting these away."

"Of course." Phoebe smiled and walked to the counter.

I straightened the tarot cards, placed them back in their box, and closed the lid. Then, I grabbed the crystal ball, one hand on the base and the other cupped against the ball itself. A familiar warmth radiated from the crystal, sending a tingle across my palm. I stared into its milky white center, and images swirled to life beneath the surface.

The vision showed a large office space, with the words *The Salem Gazette* painted on the wall in thick black letters. Phoebe exited one of the cubicles and walked over to the office in the corner. The nameplate on the door read *Robert Bell, Chief Editor*.

Phoebe knocked on the door, waited a few seconds, then opened it and poked her head inside the office. "Hi, Bobby. I'm heading out to research my tourism piece."

Robert sat in a modern ergonomic chair behind a desk stacked with papers. He folded his hands over his round belly. "Got a headline yet?"

Phoebe wiggled her fingers. "Five Tourist Traps to Avoid in Salem."

"Punchy. Good timing, too, with the Halloween rush next week."

"My thought precisely." Phoebe nodded. "If I were visiting Salem, I'd pick it up."

Robert chuckled. "Who's the first victim?"

"The psychics." Phoebe scrunched her nose. "Then, I'll move onto the ghost tours and the so-called witch shops."

Robert chuckled. "Sounds fun. And who knows? You might find a real witch."

Phoebe snorted. "If I do, I expect to land the front page."

Robert gave a thumbs up, Phoebe shut the door, and the vision ended.

I blinked a few times, allowing the shop to return to focus, then glanced at Phoebe. During the span of my vision, she'd only made it halfway to the pay counter, about four steps. She was still walking forward, seemingly unaware of my brief vision.

My cheeks grew hot, and I realized my hands were shaking. I set the crystal ball down on the table and checked my watch again. 8:06. So, I had worked late for a journalist, who had come to my shop to lie to me and prove me a fraud. Fabulous. At least the vision lent insight into the tarot card reading—Phoebe's current work project *was* about to go terribly wrong for her.

I lifted my chin and strode toward the pay counter. Phoebe was rummaging through her purse again, as she had done before and after the reading. Maybe she recorded our session with her cell phone—that would explain why she asked me so many questions.

As I reached the counter, I removed the tablet from its drawer underneath and entered her order into the billing app. "For a fifteen-minute tarot reading, that's thirty dollars."

Phoebe pulled out her wallet and took out a fifty-dollar bill. She handed it to me. "Keep the change. I know I kept you late."

And the newspaper will expense it.

"Thanks." I folded the bill and shoved it in my back pocket. There would be time to file it in the cash box after Phoebe left. "Rivera is just 'river' with an A on the end, by the way. You wouldn't believe how many people misspell it."

"Sorry?" Phoebe frowned and dropped her wallet back into her purse.

I took a deep breath. My parents' voices echoed in the recesses of my memory, warning me to stay silent. They had worked as paranormal investigators—well, my father still did—and had taught me to navigate the supernatural world, but never speak about it. Revealing my psychic abilities, or any other aspect of the paranormal, to regular people put the safety of our family, and the newly enlightened individuals, at risk. But Phoebe intended to expose me as a fraud and discredit my business. She deserved to be put in her place.

I inclined my head toward Phoebe's purse. "Just want to make sure you get my name right for your article."

Phoebe hiked her purse strap up her shoulder the way she'd done when she first entered my shop. "I don't know—"

"You work for *The Salem Gazette*." I smiled as Phoebe's posture stiffened. "If you're writing about me, the least you can do is spell my name correctly. Free advertising is only good if the readers can find me."

Phoebe took a few steps back from the counter, and her gaze flitted around the room. No secret cameras here, honey. "How did you . . ."

"Psychic, remember?" I tapped my temple. "Can I give you some advice? Off the record?"

Phoebe's lips parted, but before she could speak, I cut her off.

"Drop this tourist trap article. Salem's economy is built on shops like mine, and I doubt the other business owners will be as forgiving as I am."

Phoebe's eyes narrowed. "Tourists read our paper too. Someone has to look out for their interests."

"I get it." I held up my palms. "Not everyone can handle knowing their future."

"Have a nice evening, Miss River with an A." Phoebe patted the side of her purse. "As I said, I have everything I need from you. Keep an eye out for my piece. I think you'll find it . . . enlightening."

As Phoebe turned and walked toward the door, my hands curled into fists. I knew I should let her go. I'd yet to say anything that she couldn't rationalize. For all she knew, I recognized her from *The Salem Gazette*'s website or social media. But I refused to let her have the last word. One little psychic revelation couldn't hurt too much, and it might be enough to scare Phoebe out of writing about me.

My lips curled into a smile. "I know you and Bobby were joking earlier today, but I think you do deserve the front page."

Phoebe turned around. Her eyes were wide, and the color drained from her face. "Excuse me?"

"You might not have found a real witch, but a real psychic is still rare." I wiggled my fingers in a goodbye wave. "Come back when you have a true question for me."

WITH MY SHOP LOCKED up for the night, I strolled out onto Essex Street to meet Carmen for dinner. Even with half the stores closed for the evening, a steady stream of tourists ambled down the cobblestone avenue, creased city maps and black shopping bags clutched in their hands. The pedestrian-only street would be even more crowded the next weekend, as tourists flocked to Salem for Halloween, hoping to glimpse a Puritan ghost or catch a witch coven worshiping in the woods outside of town.

For most people, Salem was one of the few places they could believe in the paranormal. I wondered how they'd feel to learn that supernatural beings rarely visited the town—monsters either despised its cheesy tourist trappings or feared the mobs of easily spooked humans it attracted. It was exactly why I'd chosen to move to Salem when I left my parents' paranormal investigation business. But who was I to spoil the fun?

Although I still felt flushed from the encounter with Phoebe, the crisp autumn wind nipped at my skin. I checked my crossbody purse for gloves—no luck. So, I stuffed my hands into the pockets of my leather jacket and fell into step behind a ghost tour group, hoping the mass of bodies would shield me from the cold. The tour guide strode ahead, waving a red light-up pitchfork and barking out summons to the spirits of the 1692 witch trials. The tourists followed behind, thumbs posed over the shutter buttons of their camera apps.

"Hey, Mom. I think I got something at Old Burying Point." A teenage boy held his phone up to a middle-aged woman. As he zoomed in on the image, I noticed his nails were painted black. Emo never went out of style in Salem. I chuckled and quickened my pace to walk beside the pair.

The mom took the phone from her son. As she squinted at the screen, her mouth puckered. "You mean that fuzzy spot next to Judge Hathorne's headstone?"

"It has to be his ghost. The camera on this phone is the best they make—it wouldn't show a smudge like that unless something was there." The boy grabbed the phone back and opened a town map. As he examined it, his lips puckered in an exact mirror of his mom's. "The guide said Giles Corey haunts the Howard Street Cemetery. He was pressed to death in it."

"Sure was." I checked over my shoulder, then lowered my voice to a whisper. "I've seen his specter there."

The mom startled and put a protective arm around her son. The boy shrugged her arm off and stared at me with bright, round eyes. "Really?"

"Sure," I lied. "Try recording a video near the historical marker. Sometimes, you can hear him groaning, 'More weight.'"

"Wicked." The boy held his hand up for a high five, and I slapped it. "Thanks for the tip."

"No problem." When the boy turned back to his phone, I winked at his mom. Her cautious frown softened into a smile, and she gave me a conspiratorial nod. I saluted them as they turned south toward Old Town Hall.

Continuing down Essex Street, I glanced at my watch. It wasn't quite eight thirty yet, so I was still in the realm of acceptable lateness. Hopefully, Carmen had already ordered us drinks.

At the intersection of Essex and Washington streets, another group of tourists gathered around the famous *Bewitched* sculpture, one of Salem's most popular photo ops. Tourists loved to pose with Samantha, the famous TV witch, pretending to ride on her broom with her as she flew in front of a crescent moon. As I walked toward them, a loud scraping sound filled the air. The tourists jumped back from the sculpture, some screaming and others shouting, "Watch out!" Over their cries, I heard a metallic crash.

I couldn't see what had happened from the crosswalk, so like many other bystanders, I jogged over to the intersection and weaved my way through the crowd. When I reached the front, I gasped.

Someone had beheaded Samantha. Her bronze body still perched side-saddle on her broom, but a clean, straight line cut across the top of her neck and shoulders. Her head rested upright on the stone sidewalk, as if the witch were buried to her neck. It sat next to the Hollywood-Walk-of-Fame-style star that was inset into the sidewalk and listed the sculpture's formal name, sculptor, and dedication date.

I squatted down to get a better look at the statue's head. The sculpture's curled hair and smiling face remained intact, but her eyes had been indented, as if a giant had pressed his thumbs into the sockets. Samantha's iconic nose, which she wiggled to make her TV magic, had been removed. But there was no sign of a cut. The bronze surface in the center of her face was perfectly smooth, as though the nose had never been there at all.

My legs trembled as I stood up. I didn't know much about power tools or metalworking, but I couldn't image how someone could have beheaded the sculpture so cleanly, let alone made the nose disappear. I scanned the crowd for someone who looked guilty or suspicious, but was met with bewildered, wide-eyed faces and the flashes of phones documenting the vandalism. A siren blared in the distance. One of the bystanders must have called the police.

I balled my hands into fists inside my jacket pockets. More than anything, I wanted to bend back down and touch Samantha's head to produce a vision about the sculpture's destruction. But I couldn't risk going into a trance, even for a few seconds, with so many witnesses around and the police on the way. Not to mention, I didn't want my fingerprints on the crime scene.

The middle-aged woman next to me squeezed my elbow, and I flinched. "Ope, I didn't mean to scare you, honey." She released my arm and smiled. Her pudgy cheeks were flushed. "Ain't this the damnedest thing?"

I nodded. "Did you see it happen?"

"Sure did." The woman fidgeted with the zipper of her puffy North Face jacket. "Got my selfie with Samantha right before her head came off."

I frowned. "What do you mean, 'came off'?"

"Exactly that. I took my photo with the sculpture, and as I stepped away, her head fell clean off. If I'd walked right instead of left, it would have hit me." The woman shuddered. "My husband says I'm crazy, but I swear I sensed it coming. Like when you feel the electricity in the air before a thunderstorm."

I cupped my hand around the base of my throat. My heartbeat pulsed against my fingers in fast, hard throbs. If the woman felt static in the air, that could mean that the sculpture was destroyed through magic. Magical energy could create a prickly sensation, not unlike the tingling feeling I received when crystals or other objects transmitted psychic energy to me for visions.

"What about the face?" I asked.

"Creepy, huh? The eyes and nose looked like that when it landed.

They must have been damaged in the fall." The woman shook her head. Then, she glanced around at the other people, before leaning closer. She whispered, "Between you and me, it kinda feels like an episode of *The X-Files*. Unnatural. We *are* in Salem, y'know?"

"Trust me, I know." That was why it was so damn wrong. I'd been living in Salem for five years, and nothing even remotely supernatural had happened in that time. Salem was supposed to be normal, safe.

The woman removed her hands from her pockets and wrung them. "Lord, please say I didn't break it when I leaned on the broom."

"You didn't." The sirens had grown louder, and the police would arrive any minute. I took out my phone and snapped photos of the vandalism. "Maybe the sculpture had a structural weakness that finally gave out. Or it could be a prank—someone cut the head off, but left it balanced there to fall later." I put my phone away. "They could have put something on the face too—a chemical, maybe—that damaged the metal."

My own voice rang hollow in my ears, but the woman nodded as though I had said something wise. She bounced on her heels. "I hope the cops figure out who done it before we leave. We fly out on—" The woman looked to her other side, then stood up on tiptoe and craned her neck. "Where did my husband run off to?"

Before the woman could turn back to me, I walked into the crowd. More people had come to check out the statue, and the bystanders were packed shoulder to shoulder. As I squeezed past them, the gaps I left behind filled in with people moving closer to the sculpture.

Once free from the crowd, I headed across the Lappin Park square behind the *Bewitched* statue. It was lined on two sides by streets, with the other two sides containing various businesses, including the restaurant where Carmen and I were meeting. There wasn't anything else I could do about the sculpture, and when the police arrived, they'd tape off the whole area for their investigation. Maybe Carmen would have a theory about what had happened—she was a prominent figure in a local Wiccan coven and believed in the human convention of magic. Of course, we humans couldn't practice magic, only psychism. True magic belonged to monsters, and only particular species at that.

As I reached the middle of the square, a crow swept down between the trees, nearly hitting me in the head. It dipped low to the ground, and I realized that it carried something in both its beak and talons. The crow dropped the two objects on the brick pathway. Then, it cawed and soared out of sight.

I hurried over to examine what the crow had dropped. The larger object was the body of a doll, wearing a long-sleeved black dress, stilettos, and a cape. Its hand held a tiny broom. The other object was the doll's head. Though the pointy witch hat and curled blond hair remained intact, the eyes had been pressed in, and the nose had been sliced off. The doll was, unmistakably, Mattel's rendition of Samantha from *Bewitched*, and had been brutalized in the exact same fashion as the statue. A classic example of what Salem Puritans would have called a poppet, or what modern-day Americans would call a voodoo doll. And there was only one kind of monster with the magical ability to perform poppetry or voodoo.

"It can't be." I raked my fingers through my hair. "This isn't your problem, Lorena. You don't mess with this shit anymore."

Blue and red light flashed against the brick walkway, and I glanced over my shoulder. The police had arrived to inspect the sculpture. The other people were busy watching the police work, and it seemed that no one had noticed the crow or its delivery. And even if they did see it, why would they care? Sure, the doll implied that the statue was intentionally vandalized. But I was probably the only person in Salem who knew that poppetry was real magic. I could walk away right then, and maybe, just maybe, everything would be fine, and the tourists would be none the wiser.

My phone buzzed. Carmen had texted to ask if I was still coming to dinner. I looked between her message, the poppet, and the restaurant. The pieces had landed only a few yards away from where Carmen waited for me. And only a few yards beyond that, the sculpture the doll represented had been destroyed. That nice woman nearly got hurt. What if she *had* been hurt? What if Carmen, or someone else I cared about, had stood in her place?

Cursing under my breath, I texted Carmen that I had a family emergency and had to cancel. It was, in a sense, the truth.

I pulled the sleeves of my jacket over my palms, then crouched down and picked up the doll and its head. I was careful not to let either object come into contact with my skin, for risk of sparking a vision while in public. Then, I tucked the pieces into my purse and zipped it shut. Before I could talk myself out of it, I rose and started walking to my apartment as casually as I could manage.

I still had a lot of questions about what had happened in the last few minutes. Why had the *Bewitched* sculpture been targeted? From where had it been attacked? And how did a crow deliver the poppet to the scene of the crime? But two things I knew for certain.

The Samantha sculpture had been vandalized—harrowed, technically—through a magical practice known as poppetry.

And there was a real witch in Salem.

Ladies First

Nell Porter Brown

I'M ON SHAWN'S BED with his sister Kim. Next to it, baseball trophies line a shelf. Striped wallpaper matches the bedspread. His St. Peter's School uniform, navy jacket, white shirt, clip-on yellow tie, hangs over a desk chair. He won't need his mother to press it all again until Sunday.

I've only been in girls' rooms before. Shawn and Timmy, his best friend, go into the closet and pull out a couple of quarts of Colt 45 malt liquor.

"Ladies first," Shawn says, passing one to me.

They must have just got it from Jimmy Coughlin because the bottle's cold. I take a sip, trying to swallow without tasting. But it's sour and cutting. I give it to Kim. She likes beer. And Parliament cigarettes. There's a fresh pack outlined in her blue jean jacket pocket, but she'd never smoke in the house. We're on the top floor of their brownstone at the end of the street, and Shawn's door is shut. This bent-over Irish lady with brown spots on her legs who lives around the corner is downstairs watching the little ones. She can't even climb the stairs to where we are. But if Kim's mom comes home from the company where she works and smells cigarette smoke, she'll ground Kim for a week. That's the rule.

There are a lot more rules since Kim's father died. Feed the baby.

Vacuum the living room. Sweep the stoop. Kim's mother is bird-thin and wears business suits with straight skirts and high heels to work. She likes things in order. Every other Saturday Kim has to polish the brass railings and knocker on the front door. I sit on the stoop and play solitaire or jacks as she furiously rubs the metal. Once, when I was sleeping over, we were talking in the dark and she told me she wished her mother was dead, too. Then Kim could go to California and be an actress, like she wants. She could do it, too. She's prettier than me. With blue eyes and black wavy hair she wears in a side part with a barrette over her ear.

Most of the time she's mad at something—her mother, Shawn, the nuns at school. Then she stomps around in her work boots, eyes blazing, or we walk up to the park so she can smoke. We love the park. The best times are when Kim and me are there playing dodge ball, red rover, manhunt—whatever. When we're on the same team we always win. But most of the time the old lady who runs after-school games for girls separates us. Then we whack the ball at each other as hard as we can. If one of us goes down, the game's pretty much over. Manhunt in the winter is the best because we play in the hills on the far end of the park, running through trees and rocks when it's getting dark, being chased by boys. Most of the time me and Kim can outrun even them.

All the grown-ups on our block say Kim's mother is doing a re-markable job, under the circumstances. My mother had picked up the phone as soon as she heard about Mike Hanlon's heart attack. "He was only thirty-six," she told her best friend Sharon, across the street. "What's Carol going to do? She's full time at the company, with those four kids—and Kim's a handful! She must be going out of her mind."

My dad says Carol Hanlon looks just like Jackie Kennedy. Pale skin, black hair, and round golden-brown eyes. She wears pantyhose that make her legs look tan, shiny black heels without a single scuff. And red lipstick. Nothing like my mom, who sometimes has a hard time getting out of bed in the morning because her head hurts.

But I've seen Kim's mother in a sweatshirt and jeans and looking all bony. She's not so great then, I want to tell my dad. When she yells at Kim, her lips disappear; she shakes her hands like sticks poking all over, and once she threatened to go get the hanger. Kim can shout a lot louder than her, but instead she just stares back with her blue marble-hard eyes, cheeks steaming red. Then she runs up to her room and bangs the door. I'm sent home.

But today we're on our own. Kim's mom won't be home for hours and we're going up to the park when we're done with the bottle, I guess. Shawn and Timmy drink beer a lot. They're sixteen, two years older than us. But this is the first time they've invited me and Kim along.

"You take that one," Shawn says, nodding at the whole bottle. "We got more, right Timmy?"

Both are named for their fathers. Timmy's is a stock broker, goes into the city every day, works late. His mother takes care of the nine kids; comes around in a track suit with a whistle on her neck, blowing it, yelling, "Timmy! Johnny! Kevin!" to round them up for dinner.

Kim takes a slug and passes the bottle back to me. It's foaming up.

"Just lick that off." Shawn laughs. He looks like Kim, but with brown eyes and a harder face.

Tipping the brown glass to my mouth, I open wide and let the icy bubbles slide down. A grizzly burn. I've tasted my dad's martini; he lets me at their parties. I like martinis. Like I like the smell of gasoline when he fills the car up.

"Uuuuuuurp!" I try to cover my mouth, but the burp escapes.

The boys laugh again.

"Andrea likes it. Right?" says Shawn, watching me even after Kim takes the beer and chugs it, wiping her mouth on her denim sleeve. I want more, but I don't want to ask for it.

I've heard that Jimmy Coughlin will buy it for anyone for an extra three bucks. I stay away from him. Last winter when I was walking home from the bus after school, he pushed me down and crammed my face in a snow bank until I could hardly breathe. I tried to punch him or kick him in the balls, but he just kept on grinding my nose in the ice. I grabbed at his neck and wriggled around and finally he let me go. In the bathroom when I got home, I found his skin underneath my fingernails.

He lives in an apartment around the corner, down by the avenue. One of his sisters is humongous. Maddie. The fattest girl in the neighborhood—probably in all of Brooklyn. She must need special pants, and her sneakers are always squashed flat on the inside heels because she rocks side to side when she comes down the block. Shawn yells, "Earthquake!" and shakes his body, spazzing out when he sees her. It's mean, but everyone laughs.

She can't play stickball or handball with us. So, she stands in the corner and calls "Heads up" when a car's coming down the street. Everyone knows her because, how could you not? She's so big. Even my mother. One time at dinner when I reached for more rice, she slapped my hand, right in front of my brother and sister. "Do you want to look like that fat girl?" Sometimes now I sneak Snickers bars in the downstairs bathroom; the chocolate tastes sweeter in the dark.

I'm hungry now. My head feels tingly, and it's like my eyeballs are swimming in a fish tank. I want to lie on the bed. Kim is next to me, leaning on my shoulder, her head heavy and warm, humming some song. Shawn and Timmy are on the floor cross-legged, slapping each other on the back, burping and gulping the malt liquor. Shawn's a big boy. The Hanlons moved in down the block two years ago. I noticed their dog first, a giant German shepherd, Shawn swagging around with this wolfish animal on the streets of Brooklyn. But once he gets to know you, Pepper is the sweetest.

Shawn asks do we want to play a game.

I'm seeing freckles on his flushed cheeks even though he has that black hair. His eyes are brown with specks of copper pennies. He sees me looking at him and holds my look so I want to stay. "Timmy," he nods over, "I think we could use some tunes."

His friend scrambles to the record player by the window that overlooks the backyards of the people on our block, and the yards that meet them along a row of mismatched fences and walls from the brownstones on DeGraw Street. I know that because my own room is on the top floor, too, same place as Shawn's, but in the middle of the block, not the end.

At night I can lie in my bed by the window and watch the rooms light up across the yards. Like dollhouses. Sometimes the guy on the first floor walks around naked. He has a thick body with a hairy back, and his thing swings between his legs when he walks from the kitchen to the couch.

Timmy's swaying to The Cars. *I don't mind you coming here . . . and wastin' all my time, TIME! 'Cause when you're standing oh so near, I kinda lose my mind—Yeah!* Shawn lurches up to hit the air guitar, and his arm flings out and knocks down a baseball trophy that bounces off the carpet. I laugh. So does he.

"Watch this!" He picks up the trophy, opens his window, and throws it out. I rush to see it land on the cement in their backyard, pieces of fake gold spit through the air catching the late afternoon sunlight. I stick my head out, looking down the rear outsides of the houses, toward my room, and I see our empty yard. The crabapple tree my mother planted last year, not doing too well. The blue plastic pool my sister plays in with her Barbies still has water from last weekend.

"Hey—don't hang out the window!" Kim's pulling my arm.

"Oh, she's all right," Shawn says, "Andrea, come here."

He sits on the bed and pats the spot next to him. His face looks different up this close: long eyelashes and a jagged chipped front tooth. Soft pudding lips smiling at me.

I kissed a boy at a party last summer, the first boy-girl party I went to, during Seven Minutes in Heaven. I got Anthony Russo. His lips were velvety, then his tongue like a little worm exploring a cave. It went on forever, his body pushed up against mine in the dark coat closet. His small hands rubbed my hips.

Shawn pulls another bottle out of a bag and flips the top, the liquid making his throat bob up and down. I smell the beer, like sour yeasty bread, and something else coming from Shawn.

"You know why girls wear lipstick?" he asks. "Because it makes their lips look red, like, uhm, like, you know—down there. Is that true, Andrea?"

"Don't ask her that." Kim jets across the room, The Cars singing, *I needed someone to bleed* . . . She jabs his chest. "You don't even know what you're talking about."

"Yes, I do. It's in the book, right Timmy?"

Timmy's fiddling with the records. He's a good kid, not like his brother Donnie. Their mother has had it up to *here* with him—I heard her telling my parents when they were out having their cocktails and she came around with her whistle. She tells them about how Donnie's going to Long Island Military Academy 'cause she can't take it anymore. Timmy looks like his mother. Same flat pan pale face. He looks up at us on the bed, his eyes shining, a little zig-zaggy.

"Hey—DJ! Timmy!"

"What?"

"I'm telling them about the book. Saying that girls put out a smell when they want a guy." Shawn juts the beer bottle out, so it fizzes up. "The book says it's all natural, *biological*. It's not bad—see? Not like Father Ryan says."

My head feels like a fuzzy blanket, and I giggle at him. "That's funny."

I heard a girl in my class went to third base and they did it in a movie theater. Maddie the fat girl says a boy has to burst a sack in there, and the first time it hurts. The record bangs out: *I needed someone to feed.* God, I love this song.

"If it's so great, why was that girl in *Saturday Night Fever* crying in the back of the car? Right?" Kim looks at me. "Remember that part, Andrea?"

Last year we snuck into the movie theater, put on a lot of makeup, acted like we were eighteen, didn't tell our parents. I *really* love John Travolta. I thought about the girl and her mascara running down her face.

"I don't know," I say. I'm not sure what really happened. But I know my dad's whole family is in Bay Ridge—I know all the streets where they filmed the movie, and the Verrazzano-Narrows Bridge where the guy who got the girl pregnant jumps, even though John Travolta tries to save him. The girl's really crying then.

"Andrea? Earth to Andrea!" Kim's warm beside me.

"Hey, leave her alone," Shawn says.

"*You* leave her alone." She whirls around to hit him and he grabs her fist.

"She's having a good time!"

"What do you know anyway? All you do is read dirty books. Timmy couldn't get a girl if he paid her a million dollars!" She wheeled to him. "Everyone knows you're Shawn's little retarded sidekick."

"Wait—what'd I do?" Timmy had been picking through the record collection in a crate on the floor.

"Andrea—come on—we don't need them."

"She doesn't want to go." Shawn throws his hand out at me. "Right? Aren't I right?"

"Andrea! We're going to the park. Now." She turns to leave.

I squint 'cause things are a little swimmy. I look at the ceiling where a gray airplane model is hanging that I didn't see before. "I don't know." The Cars pounding in my ears. "I want to hear this song."

"Fine." She's firing her eyes at me, but she runs out. Down the hall, her bedroom door slams.

The boys look at me. Timmy raises his pale eyebrows, face like the moon. "What she so mad about?"

"She's always like that—just ignore it." Shawn turns. "What do you think, Andrea? We do want to know—about kissing. Isn't kissing normal?"

"I guess so."

"Do you like it?"

I thought of Anthony Russo in the closet. How he smelled of something soft and baking, a cake. "Yes," I say, without really meaning to, or maybe I do. My mouth is dry, my tongue feels too big in there, but another jolt of beer helps.

"You're not as square we thought." He's still on the bed, his leg almost touching mine. "You're not bad!"

"Where's Kim? Do you think she's all right?"

"Yeah, she has to cool off."

Shawn's single bed has sheets with rocket ships and moons in space. My head's floating like that above my body. I put the bottle on the floor and stand, my legs shaky, and I move a little to The Cars. The words are like mumbling, but the beat drums through me. Me and Kim dance all the time in her room. But I don't care who sees me now. My arms up, I swing my hips, close my eyes, and spin around—and bump into the stereo; the needle screeches crazily across the record.

"Whoa! Watch it!" Timmy inspects the vinyl.

Shawn's right there, grinning. "You're a really good dancer, Andrea." He reaches out.

"Put on Le Chic—'Freak Out,'" I tell Timmy.

"We don't have that girl stuff." Then he stumbles over my bottle, and it foams out across the carpet. "Oops! Okay—what I—?" He grabs a bed pillow and mops at the wet stuff; that sour smell fills the room. Then he grabs Shawn's bottle off the bedside shelf, and shoves the whole top of it in his mouth, jerking it to the ceiling, sputtering when beer streams down his chin. "Yahhh! Getting this party started!"

I don't want anymore. I just want to dance—and jump, and fly around, like a birthday balloon—because I feel soooo good. Waving my fingers in the air, I see them there, wriggling and curling like they belong to some other girl.

"Billy Joel's the man!" Timmy says, slipping "The Stranger" out of that weird album cover with Billy Joel staring at a mask in bed. Timmy's yelping like a puppy, "'Come out, Virginia, don't make me wait!'"

Shawn slides in. "Hey. Come over here. I want to tell you something." He's reaching for my hand. "Come on. Come here."

His freckled arms encircle my knees and move me to the bed. "I like you."

He holds me as I tumble. Then his mouth is on mine, open wide, our teeth clash. I close my eyes. And we find our lips and get lost in the silvery floatingness of each other. I cup the back of his warm head, his shiny black hair, and it feels like cradling a baby. And then I am down; he's on top of me, kissing my jawbone, my neck. Making a sucking sound. His back is hot and strong under my hands. He's pushing up my shirt, pulling my breast, putting his wet mouth on it. I squint up and see the plastic airplane hanging there, over his shoulder. His black hair tickling against my white skin.

The door whips open with a smack and Kim walks in. She sees me underneath her brother. Timmy's standing with his big mouth open, holding the bottle. Her cheeks shine, her lips pinched shut in a straight line—she's furious.

"Get off her, Shawn. She's my friend!"

"It's all right, Kim. She was dancing and they started kissing," Timmy says, "Nobody—" She kicks him hard, where it hurts. He howls.

Shawn rolls off me, ducking away from her lunge, and clunks onto the floor. I jump up, yanking my shirt to cover the sloppy red blotches. Kim smacks Shawn's head, then puts her arm around me and pushes me to the door.

IN HER ROOM DOWN the hall the sun is still streaming through windows that overlook our street. I find my jacket, numbly fumbling.

"Got everything? Coat? Keys?"

Yes, I nod, trying hard to focus on her pretty face.

Up in the park, the sun is setting. I reel along the tree-lined concrete paths, through the fields where we play the games after school, up a hill where the boys chase us in the woods in the winter, remembering that we can usually beat them back to our team's home base, and if we do, we're free. We win.

We walk until I can see clearly again. It's dark by the time we stop on a bench so Kim can have one last cigarette and chew enough gum on the way back so her mom won't suspect anything.

Kim takes a drag and lets go these beautiful, thick smoke rings, her mouth in a perfect O. They drift toward the lamppost that's shining a circle of light around us. High above, the huge old trees are rustling, their branches strung with glowing orange and yellow leaves that haven't fallen yet. I know these trees will soon be bare. Her cheeks are flaming from the chilly evening air. She crosses her arms against it. And I lean my head on her shoulder. I want to turn and kiss the faded, feathery cloth of her jean jacket.

The Haunting at Darlington Boardwalk

Jennifer Fickley-Baker

MONDAY

SIX DAYS BEFORE Roscoe Sterling was arrested for burning the carousel on Darlington Boardwalk to cinders—a feat that took the local fire company four hours to put out—he'd stood back, cigar in hand, and waited with greedy delight for the trucks to deliver what was supposed to be the masterpiece of the boardwalk: Darlington Boardwalk's first-ever carousel.

The weather was shit the day it arrived. A heavy fog had parked itself over the lapping gray Atlantic and only a handful of stragglers huddled along the beach, picking at shells. Roscoe shuffled his feet on the sandy boardwalk, antsy that his best shoes were getting soaked, and annoyed to the hilt that the mid-May storm was keeping the crowds away. Only half of the businesses on the boardwalk had even bothered to turn their lights on today.

Roscoe checked the time as raindrops fell on his wristwatch.

A dog barked somewhere in the distance.

Darlington Boardwalk had been built fifteen years ago out of an old fish cannery that sat smack on the New Jersey coastline. The first floor of the brick building had been divided up into shops and boardwalk attractions. Apartments lined the second floor, where most of the shop proprietors lived. An electric sign on the roof pulled it all together: DARLINGTON BOARDWALK.

Roscoe was the second owner of the place. The market crash of '29 had put nearly everyone, including Elmer Helmsley, the property tycoon who'd built Darlington Boardwalk, on the bread line. Helmsley, not wanting to count himself among the fellows who couldn't afford aftershave let alone soap, had put a pistol in his mouth. Roscoe had bought the ugly stretch of wood for a song at auction six months ago.

At the time, the boardwalk had come stocked with a semi-permanent string of subpar circus-like acts. There was a strongest man exhibit, a woman who played the violin with her feet, three magicians (in rotation), a Hall of Mirrors, a poorly done haunted house, a flea circus (but everybody had one of those), and Mel's Taffy Emporium—each of which had to pay monthly storefront and apartment rent to Roscoe. In addition to attractions, there were shops where patrons could purchase shells or wind-up toys, and games of chance like Fish Pond, where children would fish with tiny poles for wooden fish with numbers etched on their bellies. Catch the winning number and get a prize.

And of course, the beach itself was a big draw, but Roscoe didn't see a dime from that.

"Got it here as fast as I could sir," the driver of the first of six trucks said when the shipment finally arrived an hour late. He was a shaky man with a bony face and nervous eyes. Behind him, a handful of delivery men heaved crates off the truck's flatbed at breakneck speed.

Roscoe dropped his umbrella and tossed it aside. Rain soaked his perfectly slicked-back black hair, but he paid little mind. The attraction that would bring the crowd back—and then some—was finally here.

"Never mind that, never mind!" he said, climbing in between the growing stacks of crates. He'd purchased the carousel and its calliope used from a park in New York state whose owner had gotten into some kind of trouble and had to sell fast. Roscoe pulled a list from his pocket and checked each crate had a label matching every precious item. "One carousel turntable . . . one . . . two . . . three horses . . . one traction engine . . . a fourth horse . . . a fifth . . . ."

"How many more?" Roscoe asked a pair of shabbily dressed men who lugged a crate toward the growing pile. One horse packed in each.

One of them shrugged. "'Bout thirty total."

"Crack one open!" Roscoe directed.

"Now?" the other man looked annoyed as they set the crate down. The man nodded out toward the sea. "There's lightning coming."

"I want to see the beauty!" Roscoe pulled a damp cigar out of his pocket. "Open her up!"

Within minutes, one of the delivery men had located a crowbar and the top of the nearest crate was pried loose. Inside lay a white carousel horse whose black mane appeared blown back in the wind, frozen in time. A gold saddle with tassels lay across its back and pink roses wound through its tail, all hand-carved and hand-painted, just like the ad promised.

"Ahh, if that isn't a derby winner, I don't know what is!" Then Roscoe spotted black streaks on the horse's back hooves. "What's that there? Damage from transport?"

The man who'd retrieved the crowbar crouched down and ran a thumb over it. "You bought it used, didn't you?"

"Fine." Roscoe placed the cigar in his mouth, grinding down on it with his back molars. "I'll have it painted."

"What's this?" a female voice asked.

Roscoe looked behind him to find Julia, or Madame Julia as she called herself, standing a few feet away. Her arms were crossed over the dozen necklaces she was never seen without, glaring up at him from her tiny, five-foot-tall frame. Instead of an umbrella, she'd wrapped a rain hood over her head, covering her solid gray hair and showing only her wrinkled face, which was caked with too much makeup. The combination made her look like the old Russian woman she really was.

"Afternoon, Julia," he managed, then tipped his hat and forced a smile. "This is going to be our new masterpiece. A carousel."

She narrowed one eye at him and his smile disappeared. Julia had never been fond of Roscoe, but she had grown even more disapproving after catching him in bed with her only daughter, Simone, a twenty-year-old clairvoyant-in-training.

Julia narrowed her eyes at the pile.

"You know, a carousel," Roscoe said, searching for any sign of anticipation. "You get to ride beautiful horses to happy music. Children will love it." Carousels were a showpiece for sure. What little girl wouldn't love to take a ride on a fancy pony painted with flower crowns and feathered headpieces? Children would be delighted, and their parents would empty their pockets of every extra penny they could muster. Depression be damned.

"Something is wrong," Julia said, turning away as two delivery men angled in an especially large crate.

"What's that now?"

She shook one finger in the air, her back to him now as she retreated up the boardwalk toward Fortunes, her storefront. "It will be the end of you."

Roscoe glared at the back of her head. He was certain that Madame Julia was a hack, but her business attracted a lot of single women eager to ask about beaus, so he tolerated her.

He was thinking of a retort when the lead driver interrupted him.

"We need to drive the truck closer to unload the calliope," the driver said, wiping the rain from his brow. "Damn thing weighs a ton. Where do you want it?"

"On the very end here," Roscoe said, walking him around the far-left end of the boardwalk. "We're adding the whole carousel on right here. It will be our first expansion." Expansion. He loved the sound of the word coming out of his mouth. If the carousel netted enough profits, maybe he'd buy the accompanying lot. Even build a hotel there someday.

"Alright, I'll go tell the fellas to bring it around." The man disappeared around the pile of crates.

As Roscoe watched the truck back in and unload a tarp-covered calliope, he glanced at the darkening sky above and prayed that the weather would be better tomorrow. And that this would all work.

TUESDAY

"Hold your ears if you know what's good for ya," Mudd Thompson said, chewing on a toothpick. He stood in the center of the carousel platform hovering over the calliope's system of levers and pointed a thumb up to its pipes.

Roscoe slapped his hands over his ears.

The rain had dissipated by early Tuesday morning, which Roscoe was thankful for. It meant his investment in this fellow named Mudd Thompson wouldn't go to waste. Mudd was known as the best amusement ride serviceman of anyone in the business. Roscoe had first mistaken him that morning as a jobless bum panhandling the boardwalk for work, what with his patched overalls and Southern drawl. But after spending ten minutes with the fellow, Roscoe could see why he had a great reputation. Any tool Mudd needed, he produced from one of his many pockets, and although he was tall and sinewy in stature, Mudd was strong as hell. Smart, too. He could make any type of electronic gadget spin, whirl, move backwards or forwards, light up or go dark with the flip of a switch. And he charged as such. A whopping six dollars a day!

Roscoe had already spent two hours with Mudd working behind a construction tarp they'd set up around the carousel platform that concealed his great purchase from nosy patrons (and Madame Julia) walking the boardwalk.

So far, Mudd had helped Roscoe set up its steel center pole and the mirrored casing (to conceal the center engine and calliope), and hung up three of the horses. Now with two black-maned white steeds and a tan horse poised at the ready, they were set to give the carousel a test run.

Roscoe nodded, giddy, and with that, Mudd—who didn't bother holding his ears—pushed up two levers. The carousel lurched forward and began to swirl slowly around them. The trio of horses pumped lightly up and down. The calliope's silver pipes blasted a minor chord at an ear-splitting level, the tune charging forward at an equally loud volume. The music sounded haunting and dark.

Mudd switched it off.

"That's 'The Midnight Waltzers' Ball'! The old ragtime tune! I've only heard it in maybe one other carousel in my time, and that was years ago!" Mudd yelled, even though the music had stopped. He pulled a second lever back. The carousel swirled to a stop.

"Why's it so loud?" Roscoe asked. "Can you turn it down?"

"No. See here?" Mudd pointed up at the pipes. "Your calliope was made from old steam engine pipes. With them, there's no such thing as volume. Where'd you say you got this thing?"

"An ad in the paper," Roscoe said, immediately afraid he'd been swindled. "A company called Sunrise Amusements."

"Ah," Mudd nodded, then cracked a smile and punched Roscoe in the shoulder. "Heck, that could be to your benefit. Everyone within five miles will have 'The Midnight Waltzers' Ball' stuck in their heads and wonder where the music's coming from."

Roscoe nodded, hoping that the mirrored center casing would block a bit of the sound.

The two worked until dusk, sweating as they opened crate after crate, hauling horses over to the platform, sliding them up onto their hanger rods and securing them in place. Roscoe grew gleeful with the addition of each one, picturing how many people would line up to take a spin on his carousel.

Finally he stood back, his shirt run through with sweat and grease. He looked at the nearly full carousel the two of them managed to piece together in just a day.

"Mudd." He pointed toward the hooves of the horse closest to him. "The discoloration on some of the horses. Any idea what it's from?"

Mudd ducked down, squinting at spots on the horse's hind legs. Roscoe searched the others. Here and there, brownish-black stains marked their hooves.

Mudd leaned in and sniffed.

"Smells burnt."

"Burnt?" Roscoe stared at the marks, his blood pressure rising. The salesman hadn't mentioned anything faulty with the ride. "How?"

"Got me," Mudd wiped a handkerchief across his brow. "Though I've seen all kinds of oddities in this business. It's possible some electrical wiring shorted out. See here, some of the glaze has melted away. I know a lady who does touch ups. I can have her called in if it really bothers you."

Roscoe tilted his head as if considering it, when in reality, his bank account had dwindled down to a few dollars and cents after the cost of the carousel and Mudd himself.

"Eh, maybe." He shrugged.

They called it quits at seven thirty with Mudd promising to be back at dawn the next morning. Roscoe headed upstairs to his one-room apartment above Boardwalk Souvenirs, a shop at the very end of the boardwalk that overlooked the carousel site. As he ditched his filthy button-down for a clean undershirt, he gazed at the slice of the Atlantic he could see from his window. Every time Roscoe glimpsed his oceanfront view, he felt like a big deal—and that's exactly what he'd always wanted.

Roscoe had grown up determined to be somebody, ever since he dropped out of eighth grade for a job in a haberdashery in downtown Albany. There, he'd sized and sold hats to every businessman in town, bewildered by their shiny shoes, golden cufflinks, pert top hats, coattails, and fat billfolds. It wasn't just the way they dressed, it was the way they spoke, their words flowed easy and clean and unbroken. They certainly smelled different than his own father, who worked in a mill and was in a constant state of crabby exhaustion. Roscoe saw the customers at the haberdashery and knew what kind of man he wanted to grow up to be. Rich.

Roscoe's surprise unveiling of the carousel on Memorial Day, just a week away, was the key to bringing the boardwalk back to life. And by God, he needed the thing up and running perfectly before the bills came due at the end of the month. Buying the carousel had nearly drained his savings, but businessmen had to take risks, right?

Roscoe sat down and poured himself a tall glass of whiskey to toast to his own success, then downed a dinner of Heinz baked beans and bread.

He finished his drink and then passed out in bed, unable to remember the last time he'd worked that hard.

ROSCOE SAW HER FOR the first time that night. Or at least, swears he did.

He'd jolted awake in the dark, alarmed at first why his own body had made such a rapid jerk. Then his hands flew up to his ears as the piped notes of "The Midnight Waltzers' Ball" blasted outside. Yellow lights, too, the lights from the carousel, flooded in through his shadeless window.

He scrambled out of bed. Had someone turned the damned thing on?

He stepped to the window and peered down. The volume rattled the glass pane. Mudd wasn't kidding about hearing this thing for miles.

Below, Roscoe could see the carousel begin to turn in its clockwise motion. The calliope blared away, its notes hollow and relentlessly loud.

"Goddamn it!" he said, but just as he stepped away from the window, he saw the figure of a lone woman standing on the inside of the construction tarp.

"Hey!" Roscoe banged a fist on the windowpane, then unlatched and lifted it. The blare of "The Midnight Waltzers' Ball" filled his apartment. "Hey, doll! You can't be in there! Whatcha turn it on for?"

But as the words came out of his mouth, he noticed something strange about her as the speckled yellow light of the carousel flashed over her. Light, then dark, then light again. Her wavy hair stopped just above her shoulders, and the neck of her dress was tied in a bow at her collarbone—but when the light flashed on her, she became a blur, like he was holding up a glass of ice water, trying to see her through the distortions of the glass.

The woman took no notice of his words, so he tried again as the song finally came to a pause.

"Hey lady, scram! I said you can't be in there!"

The figure just stood there, staring at the spinning carousel.

A sudden pounding on his apartment door behind him made Roscoe jump.

Wonderful. Tenants.

Roscoe slammed the window shut, just as "The Midnight Waltzers' Ball" started up again a second time. He shoved his feet into his shoes as he pulled the door open. Before him stood Madame Julia, her gray hair pinned up in curlers. She held her threadbare nightdress closed with one white-knuckled fist.

"Mr. Sterling! It. Is. Three. A.M.!" She enunciated every word.

"There's an intruder!" he mumbled as he brushed past her. He dashed down the double stairs, out onto the boardwalk, nearly slipping on the slick wood, and ducked under the construction tarp. Before him, the carousel spun, empty. He headed for the spot he'd seen her. "Miss?"

But there was no sign of her—or anyone.

Roscoe hopped onto the carousel, squeezed between the horses, folded back the mirrored wall, and jumped inside. He yanked all the levers down, shutting off the power. The carousel's lights went dark and the turntable eased to a slow stop, the platform empty except for the shadow of horses swirling around him.

"Hello?"

Whoever she was, she'd gone.

WEDNESDAY

"I need you to check the calliope again," Roscoe said, getting to his feet as Mudd made his way into the construction site the next morning. Roscoe had spent the night on guard, half-sleeping against the boardwalk wall just in case the woman came back or the carousel turned on again. And to avoid any tenant complaints.

Mudd held his hands up. "I already told ya, pal. It only came with one song. That's not up to me. Take it up with the guy you bought it from."

"It's not that," Roscoe said. And the guy hadn't swindled him. He'd known the calliope only came with one working song, that's why it was the right price. "Something's wrong with the gadgetry. Thing turned itself on last night."

Mudd screwed up his face. "The carousel?"

"Yeah. Round three a.m., too. Upset a buncha neighbors," Roscoe said.

"Well, I'll look," Mudd said, weaving his way through the horses toward the mirrored center pole. Roscoe followed. Mudd popped it open, stepped inside, and jiggled each lever, one by one. "Everything looks fine here. There's no real way to turn it on but to push these all the way up."

Mudd ducked down and peered underneath the console. "Something could've fell and hit it, or bumped it."

Roscoe searched the ground inside the tiny space. "I don't see anything."

So it had to have been that woman. She turned it on.

Mudd shrugged. "Some kind of fluke then? Let me know if it happens again."

Roscoe nodded and told himself he'd secure the construction site with tie-downs tonight.

"Oh, and I wanted to ask about your lead horse," Mudd said, leading Roscoe back out onto the platform and resting an elbow on the rear of a black horse with a chocolate mane.

"My what?"

"Your lead horse," Mudd repeated. "Every carousel has one."

Roscoe looked at him blankly.

"A carousel is supposed to be a team of horses running on a wild stampede," Mudd explained. "All of the horses are decorated differently, and yours are, 'cept you've got no lead horse."

"Is that bad?"

"Well, the lead horse is the fanciest." Mudd absently scratched at the stubble growing on his neck. "It's the one the designer throws all their time into decorating. It's the horse all the others follow, see?"

"Which means it's the most expensive one," Roscoe reasoned.

Mudd popped a toothpick into his mouth. "Might want to call the fella you bought it from. Ask about its whereabouts, just in case you ever want to resell this thing, you know?"

Roscoe nodded. Damned newspaper ad.

By lunchtime, Mudd had crawled underneath the platform to oil some gears and recheck some of the wiring. Roscoe excused himself, hoping to recoup some lost sleep from last night, but instead found his feet turning toward Fortunes, three doors down. Something about the woman he'd seen itched in the back of his brain. Something about the way she looked in the light. There and then gone.

The weather was fair today and a few dozen patrons were strolling the boardwalk—a decent showing for midday Wednesday. The doors to Mel's Taffy Emporium were propped open and the sweet smell of sugar blew on the breeze.

Roscoe stuck his head inside Fortunes, a bell clanging over the door. He was relieved to see it was Simone sitting in the fortune-teller's chair and not her mother, Madame Julia. Simone was doing a palm read for a woman with a gray bun and tiny spectacles, tracing the lines on her hand and whispering when he popped his head in.

"Simone," Roscoe hissed. He hated coming in here. Everything was dark, from the maroon carpet to the black curtains, to the vases constantly filled with blood-red roses. The place felt like a permanent funeral. "I need to talk to you outside."

Her eyebrows raised. "Now?"

Roscoe had never interrupted her in the middle of a session, but still, he wanted answers. The closest he could get to anyone with experience with ghosts was, well, Simone or Madame Julia.

"This will just take a minute, ma'am," Roscoe said to the teary-eyed woman, and nodded outside.

"What's this about?" Simone asked once they were clear of the door. Simone was a shadow of her mother. The same sharp jaw and glaring dark eyes, only hers were framed with long lashes. She also didn't have the ugly Russian accent her mother did, although she was fluent, a fact Roscoe had found out when Madame Julia had caught them together.

He realized just then that he'd been avoiding Simone since that morning. He hadn't spoken to her about that night yet.

Roscoe cleared his throat and nodded back toward Fortunes. "Ghosts. Are they real?"

Simone's brow furrowed. Clearly this was not what she was expecting.

"Are ghosts real? Are you really asking me this?"

"I saw something last night. Or thought I did."

She crossed her arms over her chest. "Alright. What did you see?"

"A woman."

"Ah, of course it was," Simone shook her head and took a step away, but Roscoe grabbed her arm, pulling her back.

"No. It's the carousel, really. It somehow started up in the middle of the night," he said. "When I looked out the window, there was a woman standing there, but not. I could sort of, I dunno, see through her. When I went downstairs, she was gone."

She narrowed her eyes at him. "Have you been up all night?"

"Just tell me," he said, suddenly exhausted. "How does this ghost thing work?"

"Well, first a person dies, and then—"

"I'm serious!"

Simone's expression softened. "You really think you saw something?"

"I'm not sure what I saw," he mumbled.

"Well . . ." Simone sighed. "If she is a ghost, you'll know."

"How?"

"She'll come back." She shrugged. "Most ghosts have unfinished business. They feel like they can't move on until it's done. Did you try talking to her?"

"Talking to her? I guess I yelled at her to get away."

Simone rolled her eyes. "No, talking to her nicely. You know, asking what she wants, why she's here. That's what I spend a lot of my time doing, Lord knows."

Roscoe nodded. "Okay. Alright."

"That way she can move on." Simone took a step back toward Fortunes. "And remember, be nice. And Roscoe, try to get some sleep. You look like shit and you stink like whiskey."

With that, Simone pivoted and walked back to Fortunes, where Madame Julia stood glaring at both of them from the doorway.

After his conversation with Simone, Roscoe headed back upstairs where he left two urgent messages for the salesman at Sunshine Amusements inquiring about the lead horse, then walked back down the hall to his apartment, where he downed three glasses of whiskey on an empty stomach, washing away all thoughts of ghosts. Twenty minutes later, he passed out cold, barely noticing the sound of Mudd hammering away at the carousel below his window.

When he woke, it was dusk. The hammering had stopped and the sky outside showed an eerie purple. He sat up, realizing that his undershirt had been soaked through with sweat. He wiped his face. He wished for a second that he'd slept the night through, that there was no chance of the carousel turning on again, or the woman appearing.

Roscoe pulled off his shirt and pushed himself up onto his feet, instantly feeling nauseous and dizzy at the same time. He stepped over to his kitchenette to grab a slice of bread to settle his stomach when someone else pounded on his door.

"Mr. Sterling?" A deep voice on the other side of the door yelled. It was Mel, of Mel's Taffy Emporium.

Roscoe grabbed a fresh shirt from a stack on his dresser, yanked it on, and pulled the door open.

"Sorry to wake you, Mr. Sterling," Mel said. He was wearing a shirt the color of strawberry taffy and a white apron over white pants. His pudgy face looked stricken for a second. Roscoe realized how terrible he must look. He hadn't shaved for at least two days and could probably count the hours of sleep he'd gotten on one hand.

Mel nudged a thumb back over his shoulder. "You got a call earlier. I tried knocking before, but there was no answer."

"Oh, sorry." Roscoe was puzzled. Mel was a loud guy. Why hadn't he woken up?

"I took a message for you the second time they called." He held out a paper to him. "Some guy from Sunshine Amusements called about a . . . missing horse? Promised they'd bring it around tomorrow morning."

"Thanks." Roscoe nodded, plucking the note from Mel's meaty fingers. He made a mental note to call Sunshine Amusements again tomorrow and ball them out anyway.

That night, Roscoe showered and sat down to eat a full meal. As he did, he stared out the window that overlooked the carousel. He felt on edge. Simone had said the woman would return if she really was some kind of ghost. What would he do if she did? If he wanted the carousel—hell, the boardwalk—to be a success, he certainly couldn't have a ghost wrecking things.

He took another swig of whiskey, then another, until he'd finished his dinner, curled up in bed with the bottle, and drank until he fell asleep.

Around three a.m., Roscoe was blasted from sleep by the piped sounds of "The Midnight Waltzers' Ball." He turned over on his back, listening and hoping this was some sort of nightmare. It wasn't. Same song. Same time. Same damn yellow electric lights shining into his window.

He placed the whiskey bottle he'd fallen asleep with onto his nightstand and stood up carefully. He kicked himself for not asking Simone to stay the night, even though he knew that would've been completely unrealistic. He slid open the window, the calliope's pipes blaring.

Roscoe saw her immediately. The fear of what she might be—the idea that he was actually seeing a ghost—made him cling to the windowsill, unable to tear himself away. She was standing in the exact same place as the night before, a few feet left of the carousel, watching as it whirled in front of her. Her face was visible in the light and then gone again, her very being wavering where she stood. A sudden chill gripped him by the spine. The woman had to be a ghost. There was no other explanation.

Roscoe thought again about his conversation with Simone. Talk to her. Ask her what she wants.

He waited until the tune ended.

"Hey, 'scuse me!" He said, not in a yell, but certainly loud enough to hear from one story below.

But the woman only continued to stare forward as the horses spun.

"Ma'am?" He tried again. "Is there a reason you're here?"

The song started up again. Roscoe cupped his hands around his mouth. "Is there something that you need? Something . . . I can help you with?"

With that she looked up at him, as if noticing him for the first time. Her head first, then her shoulders, then her full body.

She took a step toward his window and held her wrists up. They were stained with something dark.

Roscoe squinted. "That blood?"

The woman didn't respond. She only stared at him for a few more seconds, the light from the carousel brushing her entire being into and out of existence. She turned her head completely to the side, as if showing him something.

He froze.

The entire side of her head, from her ear back, was a bloody mess.

He recoiled. "You hurt? Should I call a doctor?" Roscoe felt ridiculous. What ghost would need a doctor?

But the woman made no reply. Instead, she turned back toward the carousel. Then all at once, she moved forward, took a step up onto the platform and disappeared into the horses.

"Shit!"

Roscoe backed away from the window, horrified. "The Midnight Waltzers' Ball" continued as he slammed his window shut. He had to shut it off. Again. His heart rattled against his ribs. Last night he'd been certain she was an intruder, but now . . . .

Best get it over with. He slipped on his shoes and threw open his door. The hallway outside was empty. Its sole lightbulb flickered midway down the hall, just over the telephone.

As Roscoe descended the stairs, the music stopped. He froze in the dim stairwell. Maybe she had turned it off? He waited a few seconds, standing stock still on the stairs.

A few seconds passed.

Silence.

He pivoted to go back up the stairs . . . then— "Damn it!" he shouted, hearing the song started up again. The notes of "The Midnight Waltzers' Ball" reverberated through the wall.

He wanted the music to stop. He wanted everything to stop.

Roscoe rushed down the last few steps, pushed through the door that let out onto the boardwalk, rounded the corner, and slipped under the construction tarp. The carousel whirled before him, lit up bright as day, just as he'd seen it from his window. But the woman was nowhere to be seen.

He jumped up on the platform and slipped through the carousel horses toward the section of the mirrored door in the center, then hesitated. What if she was inside?

He glanced up at the boardwalk's building as the carousel spun him round. Lights were popping on in the second-floor windows. Tenants were awake and were no doubt lining up to complain.

On his next rotation, Roscoe lurched forward and yanked open the mirrored door. The tiny space was empty. He jumped inside and slapped his hands over his ears. The pipes were almost intolerable. He studied the series of levers in the light of the carousel. Each one was switched to the OFF position.

It made no sense. He jiggled the controls. How would he turn it off if it wasn't . . . on?

The fuse box.

Roscoe stepped back out onto the platform, rushed through the horses again, and jumped down. He ran back inside the building and ducked underneath the staircase to the fuse box. Roscoe squinted. He could barely see the labels next to the switch and certainly hadn't paid attention when Mudd told him which was which.

Outside, "The Midnight Waltzers' Ball" started up again. In a panic, Roscoe yanked out each fuse one by one, until the carousel fell silent. Roscoe waited a few seconds, hearing muffled complaints from the tenants standing in the dark upstairs hallway.

He thrust the fuses back into place, except for the last one, the one that powered the carousel. A stream of light from the upstairs hallway leaked down through the stairwell. He returned to the boardwalk door, which he'd left open, and poked his head out, listening. The carousel was silent. Roscoe yanked the door shut and bolted it, then turned to walk back up the stairs.

But as he did, he came face-to-face with her.

The woman stood inches away. Half her face and her golden hair were beautiful, half ruined and bloody. The expression on her face was blank, save for her eyes, which were not of this world. They were a faint shade of milky white, not like they were damaged . . . more like they'd been replaced by some sort of soft light lit from within. She held her gashed wrists out toward him, her arms shaking as blood dripped off.

"Wh . . . wha . . . whadda you want?" Roscoe stammered. He backed up against the stairs as she moved closer.

She swept toward him.

"No! Wait!" He threw his hands up and jumped back, bracing himself, but she didn't stop. The ghost rushed through him in what felt like a cold blast of air from an icebox.

The sensation passed in seconds, and suddenly finding himself alone again, Roscoe scrambled up the stairs and ran back into his room. He slammed his door shut and bolted it, then propped his kitchen chair under the doorknob for good measure—even though the ghost had just passed through, well, him and could probably just as easily pass through a door. He stepped backward in his room, his whole body quaking. He ran his hands over his shirt, looking for evidence of the blood from her wrists, but nothing was there.

Whiskey. He had whiskey in his top cabinet. He'd just grabbed the cabinet knob when he noticed that his bedroom window was open. He was certain he'd closed it before running downstairs to shut the carousel off. Dead certain.

He stepped over to the window and slammed it shut, flipping its latch into place and holding his thumb over the lock for a second. He grabbed his liquor and climbed into bed, both eyes on the window and an ear on the door. He drank and drank, and stared at it until the sun came up.

THURSDAY

Morning arrived with a thud of a fist on Roscoe's door.

"Mr. Sterling? You in there?" It was Mel's voice again, sounding annoyed this time. "Delivery out back!"

"Okay! Okay!" Roscoe waved his hand at the door as if he could stop Mel's pounding. Roscoe's entire head felt like it was in a bubble. His mouth was so dry it was painful. Damned whiskey.

He rolled over to see rain pelting the windowpane. What the hell had happened last night? If he closed his eyes, he could still see every detail of that woman. Her awful transparency. And that blood. And the dreadful icy feeling he'd felt as she'd swept through him. Was that how death felt? He shivered thinking about it.

He stumbled out of bed and his empty whiskey bottle tumbled to the floor, rolling over a stack of bills scattered on the floor. He stepped to the window and glanced down at the carousel through the rain. It sat there like an innocent bystander as Mudd rushed around, pulling a tarp over the thing.

Roscoe jogged down to meet the delivery truck still wearing the pants and undershirt he'd slept in. Each step shook his brain. He wanted to get this over with as soon as possible and crawl back into bed.

At the bottom of the stairs, he turned away from the boardwalk door and continued walking straight into the warehouse that ran behind all the boardwalk storefronts. He passed an enormous stack of sugar bags for Mel's Taffy Emporium and an overflowing box of stuffed panda bears (Fish Pond prizes), then turned left out the warehouse's back door and into the employee parking lot, where it was pissing rain.

To call it a parking lot was a bit of a stretch. Only three tenants even owned cars. Most of the space was occupied by a small shed where Roscoe kept extra planks, tools, paint, and gas cans.

A single delivery truck hovered just beyond the shed, lights on and wipers flicking back and forth. The driver stepped out, popping open an umbrella. Roscoe recognized him as the shaky fellow who'd originally transported the carousel.

"Mr. Sterling," the driver said. "I have that crate that belongs to you. One of the delivery men thought it might've been damaged. He was going to take it back to Sunshine Amusements, which is why it wasn't delivered with the rest of the bunch."

"Damaged?" Roscoe followed him around back, shading his eyes from the rain.

The driver stopped at the back of the truck. He glanced up at the tarp-covered crate stacked in the flatbed of his truck with the side of his eye. His mannerisms were bizarre, just like last time.

"My guy said something seemed to be leaking from it." The driver's eyes flitted from the crate to Roscoe and back. "Didn't want to get the blame for it, especially since it came from Avonberry Park and all. Shame what happened up there. Real shame."

The driver collapsed the umbrella and tossed it aside, rain soaking him instantly.

Roscoe stepped closer. "What do you mean?"

"Avonberry Park," he said, pulling at one of the crate's tethers. "Up in Newburgh. New York."

"I don't understand. What happened there?"

The driver's lips parted in genuine surprise. He stared down at the knot pinched in his fingers. "I . . . I should get this down. Don't want to keep you in the rain and all."

"Tell me! What happened in Avonberry Park?" Roscoe shouted through the rain as the driver climbed up onto the flatbed of the truck.

"You'd need to ask Sunshine Amusements, sir. Ain't none of my business what they sell," the man said, turning his back to Roscoe, his fingers now working double-time on the tethers.

"But—"

Roscoe stood there, dumbfounded. What had they sold him? Had they known there was something wrong with the carousel? Something to do with the ghost? They couldn't have known about her, could they?

Roscoe turned back toward the warehouse door. He needed to get Sunshine Amusements on the telephone. Now.

Just then Mudd ran around the back of the construction site end of the warehouse, holding a scrap of tarp over his head.

"This weather!" he yelled.

"Mudd, can you help him?" Roscoe pointed toward the truck.

Mudd nodded.

Roscoe ducked back inside, wiping the rain from his brow. He headed back upstairs to the telephone, where he left a furious message with a flustered secretary at Sunshine Amusements for their sales rep to phone him as soon as possible. Roscoe's face flushed red as he slammed the earpiece back down on the telephone.

"And up your nose with a rubber hose, lady!" he mumbled. He

stared at the phone a few seconds, then picked it up again. The operator popped on the line.

"Get me the Darlington Bus Station. It's urgent," he said. He drummed his thumb on the side of the telephone box.

Within minutes it was arranged. It would be a three-hour bus ride from Darlington Bus Station to Newburgh, New York. He'd go to Avonberry Park himself and speak to the park's owner. He and Mudd would likely get little-to-no progress done on the carousel in this weather anyway.

Roscoe checked his wristwatch. Nine forty-seven a.m. His bus was scheduled to leave in just under an hour.

THE BUS, WHICH SMELLED faintly of old roast beef, pulled into Newburgh three hours later. Before today, Roscoe had never heard of the place. It was a little town on the west bank of the Hudson, the type with a Main Street and pleasant homes with big front porches, flowerbeds and American flags. The pelting rain hadn't followed Roscoe, but the gray misty sky had. It hovered over him as he disembarked and studied the street outside the bus station, wondering which direction to go. Walking in such weather was foolish, he decided, so he followed the others to a town bus waiting at the corner.

"You go past Avonberry Park?" he asked the driver as the door snapped shut behind him.

"Avonberry Park you said?" The driver studied his face for a second. "Sorry to tell you, sir, but the park closed."

"Closed?"

"Yessir. About two months ago."

"Two months?" Roscoe repeated. It made no sense. He'd only just purchased the carousel from them. Perhaps the owner was still at the park working in the main office or preparing more items for sale.

"Just stop there," he said and dropped a nickel into the slot.

"Yessir." The bus driver shook his head and pulled away from the curb.

Roscoe watched as they passed a handful of mom-and-pop-owned shops, hardware stores, and a few sandwich places buzzing with a decent lunchtime crowd.

About five minutes later, the bus paused next to a luscious green park sprinkled with white picnic pavilions. Its lawn sloped down toward a small pond where a group of swans lay huddled together under a weeping willow.

"This it?" Roscoe stood, walking to the front.

"Heck no. That's Hawthorne Picnic Pavilion," the driver said, then thumbed out his side window. "Avonberry Park's on this side of the street."

Roscoe ducked down and peered out the other side of the bus. For a minute he had to try to decipher what he was seeing. But no, there it was: a burnt-down skeleton of an amusement park that teetered behind a wood fence that had been burned black as ash.

"I . . . I don't understand," Roscoe said as he hurried off the bus. He crossed the street and walked along the sidewalk, his shoes crunching over burnt paint flakes. The entire place smelled like a campfire.

Over the fence and ruined hedges, Roscoe could pick out the framework of fire-torn food stands and game booths. He continued on, walking slack-jawed along the front of the park. Further down, a white wooden roller coaster named THE WHIZZLER had collapsed spectacularly in on itself, its track and support beams toppled into a heap like a pile of match sticks. At the far end of the park, Roscoe could see a small Ferris wheel. Its metal wheel framework still stood upright, but fire had torn away the seats inside each car.

There had to be thousands, possibly hundreds of thousands, of dollars of damage.

Roscoe paused at what had been the park's entrance. Its glass-and-metal AVONBERRY PARK marquee lay on the ground partially smashed. A pile of glass shards had been swept back from the sidewalk, but not picked up. A hastily made closed sign was taped inside one ticket booth window. The glass inside was cracked like a spiderweb.

Roscoe stood, horrified, taking it all in. He'd expected a scaled down, even picked-apart park with some attractions sold off, but nothing like this. Some of his horses had burn marks, but how could his carousel have survived any of this?

"I don't understand," he mumbled.

"Nobody does," a deep voice called from behind him.

Roscoe turned to see a white-haired old man with a face full of wrinkles crossing the street toward him from a drugstore that stood kitty-corner to the park's entrance.

"I'm Bill Hapford, the druggist," he nudged his head back toward the shop. "You another newspaper man?"

"No. I was asked to buy some attractions from this park," Roscoe fibbed. "Thought I'd come up here and check it out myself. Do you know what happened here?"

Mr. Hapford raised his eyebrows. "Yes. Most of it, at least. I was the one who phoned the fire brigade." He looked past Roscoe, shaking his head. "The whole thing was ablaze. It was terrifying for me, you see, owning a shop so close. And so peculiar how everything burned at once."

The druggist was silent a second as he rubbed his chin, remembering. "It's a shame. It really was a nice park. And they were a nice couple."

"You mean the owners? You know them? Because I was wanting to speak to them specifically—"

"I said I *knew* them," Mr. Hapford corrected softly. "The Schwartz-es. Of course we only ever talked business. They were much younger than me. Oscar was a big idea man, always talking about expanding and such. And Madeline had lovely blonde hair."

"Blonde hair." Roscoe repeated. His stomach clenched. "The way you talk of them. Are they dead?"

The druggist pursed his lips and was quiet a moment. "Mr. Schwartz . . . is in the hospital. He won't be coming home."

"He was injured in the fire?"

"No," the druggist shook his head. "He's . . . in the kind of hospital you don't come out of. An asylum." He looked back over the park again. "I think part of it was the fire. And then losing Madeline . . ."

"She died?"

Mr. Hapford shifted his jaw, eyeing Roscoe as if making a decision to speak more.

"She disappeared," he said, finally. "The firefighters looked for her, you know, afterward, but they never found her. Some think she ran off and left him that day, but I doubt it. I think that's what drove Mr. Schwartz mad. The not knowing."

Roscoe turned back to the rubble. The body of Madeline Schwartz could still be somewhere in there, burned to bones, ash among the kindling, the same mist falling on her remains that fell on Roscoe at this very instant.

"How did the fire start?"

"They don't think it was a question of how, but a question of who."

"Someone did it intentionally? Who?"

The old man looked away for a long second. "I overhear things in my shop. Rumors. Gossip. As nice as they were to me, the Schwartz-es had tempers. Both of them. Oscar was known to solve a problem with a fist from time to time. And Madeline was a fiery one."

Roscoe pointed to the wreckage. "They think one of the Schwartzes did this to their own park?"

"It's just a theory." Mr. Hapford glanced back at his shop where a heavyset woman waved to him from the door. "I must get back. Besides, I shouldn't give rise to rumors. As for buying anything, like I said, I doubt they have anything to sell."

The druggist nodded to him, then turned and crossed the street.

"Mr. Hapford?" Roscoe called. "Did this park have a carousel? A wooden one?"

"Oh yes. A lovely one," he called, continuing across the intersection. "I'd take my little granddaughter there whenever she'd visit." He shrugged. "Sad for such a beautiful thing to be destroyed."

Roscoe watched as old Mr. Hapford held the door for his customer, then disappeared inside his drugstore.

But the carousel hadn't been destroyed. Roscoe knew right where it was.

It and Madeline Schwartz.

ROSCOE HAD PLANNED ON catching up on his sleep on the ride home, but instead found himself staring at rain droplets sluicing down the windows as the bus sped back to Darlington. He slipped the bottle of gin he'd bought back in Newburgh out of his pocket and took three deep chugs from it, making no attempt to hide it from the white-haired old lady glaring at him from the seat across the aisle. The burn of the liquor on his empty stomach sent beads of sweat to his forehead. He sat back, the bottle balanced on his knee.

Questions ate away at his brain in one continuous circle. He may be the only person in the world who knew for certain that Madeline Schwartz was dead. What had happened to her? Why had she followed the carousel all the way to his boardwalk? What was her unfinished business, as Simone had put it? And how could he get Madeline Schwartz to go away?

He sighed, laying his head against the seat back. He usually dealt with problems by buying his way out of them, but this time, that wasn't an option. Maybe he could sell the carousel and she'd follow it, but still, he'd never find a buyer overnight, and he'd still be in the hole after paying the shipping.

He took another swig. What was he to do? And how was he to get Madeline's ghost to go away?

THE ONLY LIGHTS ON at Darlington Boardwalk when Roscoe finally made it home were the lampposts that ran along the sea, plus one upstairs light in Mel's apartment. One of his five kids was always up making a racket.

Roscoe wavered there in the employee parking lot looking up at the building. Dread hung on him like a heavy cloak. He should've sprung for a motel in Newburgh for the night.

Roscoe swallowed and staggered ahead. He'd nearly finished off the entire bottle of gin on the bus. His steps felt sloppy and his feet felt heavy shuffling through the wet sand lot and into the warehouse.

It was eerily quiet in the warehouse at this time of night. He dodged through the aisles of supplies and headed upstairs to his room. Someone had slipped the month's electric bill under his door, as well as a note from Mudd. Roscoe tried to make sense of it, but everything was blurred by alcohol. Something about a problem with the delivery. Phone him ASAP. Roscoe tossed them aside, adding to the stack of bills on the floor.

His legs had felt especially wobbly on the stairs, so he decided he should have something to eat before bed. Roscoe opened his icebox to find only some pastrami and pickles, so he made a poor excuse for a sandwich by wrapping his last slice of bread around them, then washed it down with more gin.

That's it, he decided as the gin hit the back of his throat, warm and familiar. That would be his answer, for tonight at least. He'd drink himself to sleep. That way he wouldn't see or hear or feel Madeline's ghost even if she paraded through his room with a full brass band. He took another swig. Then another longer one to wash it down.

The last thing he remembered was the hollow sound of the bottle hitting the floor next to his bed.

AT THREE A.M. ROSCOE bolted upright in bed, oddly enough, to darkness and silence. He sat in bed, feeling as if his head was underwater. Lack of sleep tore at his eyes as he peered around the dark room. What had woken him up? Everything was still.

Seconds later, the music began—but it wasn't the blaring notes of the calliope. He cocked his head, alarmed. It was the swelling sound of an orchestra. Then a voice! A male voice, and he was singing. The voice sounded faraway and tinny, like a record playing on one of those old phonographs.

> *There'll be a waltz or two, for me and you,*
> *I'll hold you tight, later tonight,*
> *At the Midnight Waltzers' Ball!*

The voice paused as the orchestra rolled on. Roscoe threw back his cover and stumbled to the window. He squinted down at the carousel, his senses dulled by so much liquor. The horses were dark and still. Where was the music coming from? He pulled on shoes, tore downstairs, and out onto the boardwalk.

Outside the rain had stopped. The ocean beyond was a solid

black. Roscoe was still so heavy with gin that the salty fish smell of the night air brought him dangerously close to retching.

He glanced at the other apartments above the shops. The windows were dark. Could no one hear the music but him? It was definitely louder out here.

The song came to an end. Roscoe spun in a circle.

"What do you want?" Roscoe yelled. His voice echoed back from the boardwalk shopfronts. "Madeline? Madeline Schwartz?"

No response.

The orchestra started up again, then the singer, the tone of his voice was disturbingly cheerful.

Wear your best perfume, honey,
Tonight's the night we'll waltz 'til dawn . . .

Roscoe turned, looking down toward the center of the boardwalk in the direction of the music. There she was, the shadowed edge of her, disappearing into a darkened door among the shops. Her blonde hair glinted in the lamplight for an instant, then disappeared as the door fell closed behind her.

"Hey! Stop!" Roscoe ran after her, past Magician's Palace, past Fish Pond, past Fortunes.

He felt a horrible twist in his gut as his steps slowed where she'd disappeared.

The Hall of Mirrors.

The Hall of Mirrors was owned by a decent enough guy named Al, but the attraction was so gimmicky—people scaring themselves out of their own stupidity—that Roscoe had never bothered to venture past the lobby where he collected Al's rent each month.

He took a deep breath and yanked the door open. The music was louder in here.

"Al?" he yelled. "Al, you in here?"

No response.

"Madeline?"

But the only voice he heard was the singer's, whose jolly crooning didn't cease. Roscoe pulled the door shut behind him, quietly. Past the cashier's counter, a black curtained doorway marked with an ENTER IF YOU DARE! sign that led into the tunnel of mirrors rippled as if someone had just stepped through it.

"Madeline? Mrs. Schwartz?" Roscoe took a breath, then charged inside. The curtain swept shut behind him and suddenly he was surrounded by an army of men—all reflections of himself—in dozens of mirrors. His silhouettes were dark and featureless. The music continued, drawing him deeper into the maze. He moved forward, resisting the urge to jump at every reflection of his own movement. Roscoe squeezed his eyes shut, reached out, and grabbed onto the mirror next to him, deciding to feel his way through. He slid his hands along the edge until he felt it come to a corner, then stepped around it.

"Madeline?" He paused. He opened his eyes slowly, taking in the reflections in the mirrors around him. Could he see her? Would a ghost have a reflection?

"I saw your park. I saw what happened."

At this, one shadowed reflection separated from his, jolting forward, shooting off deeper into the maze. He felt as if all his drunkenness had run off with it.

"Madeline?" Roscoe yelled, stepping forward, his back and hands now gliding along the mirrors. One turn, another, a turn back again. "Can you tell me what you want?"

No response.

He followed the mirrors deeper, but something felt off. The Hall of Mirrors obviously circled back at some point to let patrons out through a curtain next to the one he'd entered through. But Roscoe only felt he was being drawn deeper and deeper inside.

Somewhere ahead of him he heard the record reset with a series of clicks. The orchestra began again.

"Madeline, if you can't tell me what you want, I can't help you!"

He rounded another corner and the mirrors came to a sudden end. He stood there, facing total darkness, and waved one hand out, his fingers catching on nothing. The record played on from somewhere ahead of him.

He took a blind step forward and felt the hall's slick tile flooring end underneath his feet. He waved his arm to the right and his knuckle tapped against something wooden, not glass. He took another step and reached both hands out, feeling a door frame around him. It must be the doorway to the Hall of Mirrors' warehouse space. Roscoe moved ahead and pulled his lighter out of his pocket. He flicked it on and jumped back, nearly knocking over a crate of sugar at the sight of a horribly sunken face hovering just inches from his. It was his own reflection in a shard of a cracked mirror that sat propped behind Al's place.

He straightened himself and held the lighter up. He peered through the warehouse. No sign of anyone, no sign of a phonograph, although the music was even louder back here. So was the sound of rain, which didn't make any sense, unless . . .

The warehouse back door.

Roscoe hurried to the rear of the building. He was right. The warehouse's back door, which he'd walked through just a few hours ago after returning from Newburgh, sat propped open. The music was coming from outside.

He stepped out into the parking lot where it was raining lightly and glanced right to left. Next to the shed sat the lone crate for the lead horse that had been dropped off just before he'd left for Newburgh. Mudd had left him a note about it. What had the note said? There was some sort of problem . . .

Roscoe rounded the crate moving toward the carousel construction site, then stopped and turned back. He flicked on his lighter, cupping a hand around the flame and examining the crate's seams. Heavy industrial nails held it together. Not just that, but they seemed to be nailed in by bunches, haphazardly. It made no sense. One of the first crates off the truck had been opened so he could see it, and it had taken only a crowbar to pop it open. He ran his forefinger over the nails. Each nailhead was as thick as a man's thumb. Who the hell would pack a crate like this? No wonder Mudd had left a note. Prying this open would be a nightmare.

Just then the singer started up again. The carousel's lights snapped on around the corner.

Roscoe walked the few yards to the end of the boardwalk building. He could see through the construction tarp that the carousel was spinning. Shadows of horses rolled past on the inside of the construction tarp. The record played on from somewhere inside.

Roscoe stepped softly through the wet sand lot and lifted the tarp.

The flickering figure of Madeline Schwartz stood there, staring at the carousel, swaying back and forth to the music, and watching the horses spin round and round. A phonograph lay between the carousel and the boardwalk building behind her.

Roscoe pocketed the lighter and lowered the tarp behind him softly, as if any sound would scare her off.

"Madeline?"

She turned and reached out a hand toward him. Her eyes glowed white.

"Dance with me."

Her words came out like a whisper.

She raised her left hand up and cocked her right elbow, readying for a waltz. It wasn't a question.

Roscoe furrowed his brow. Was this her unfinished business, having one last dance? If so, would it get her to go away?

His jaw clenched as he stepped closer to her, Madeline's arms still poised and waiting. He took another step. How would this even work? She'd rushed straight through him last night. How would he hold onto her for a dance? Still, the very idea of going near her, let alone touching her, made the gin in his stomach roil.

Roscoe's feet crunched over the gravel. He raised his hands to meet hers. They shook in the light of the carousel. He touched his fingers to hers, Madeline's feeling like cold wet flesh against his warm skin, but she didn't pass through him like she had last night. She stank, too, like something rotten. The smell climbed into his nose and hung there. Roscoe held his breath as he wrapped his arm around her waist. He pursed his lips and closed his eyes so that he wouldn't have to look at her pale face, her mashed-in head, her bizarrely lit eyes, just inches away.

"You need to see," she said, leaning her head toward his. Her clammy forehead touched his and the instant it did, it was as if Roscoe had stuck his head and hands into a pond of freezing water. Roscoe's eyes went blurry, as if water had been dashed upon them. When they cleared, he was standing in Avonberry Park—a flawlessly intact Avonberry Park—surrounded by the Ferris wheel, a hotdog shop, and a kiddie ride with a roof shaped like a miniature castle. It was night, very late at night, and the park was empty. Roscoe looked around.

Everything was standing. Nothing was burnt.

Why would she bring him here?

Then Roscoe heard screaming. Arguing. He turned toward the sound. A thick-boned man with slicked-back black hair and a mustache was dragging a blonde woman by the forearm in front of the carousel. Roscoe blinked. It was Madeline Schwartz, and it was *his* carousel, but in its old home at Avonberry Park.

Neither of them seemed to notice him.

"Where do you think you're gonna go, Maddie?" The man screamed in the dark. "Where?"

"It doesn't matter! I'm not spending another minute with you, you—" But before Madeline could even get the last word out, Mr. Schwartz pushed her from behind. Madeline fell down against the carousel, knocking her head on the edge of the platform.

"You unholy bastard!" Her eyes widened as she rolled over on the ground, holding the side of her head.

He hovered over her. "No woman leaves me, do you understand me? You are my wife!" Mr. Schwartz yanked her to her feet by the collar of her dress. He pinned her against one horse and shook a thick loop of rope loose from around his elbow.

Madeline screamed. Roscoe struggled to move his feet to the right or left or any direction to see what Mr. Schwartz was doing, but couldn't. It was as if he was tethered to one place.

With the man's back turned toward him, Roscoe caught only a word here and there.

Destroyed everything . . .

. . . love . . .

. . . watch from here . . .

Watch it burn . . .

"No!" Madeline screamed over and over.

Mr. Schwartz finally backed away. Madeline had been tied to a carousel horse, her wrists bound together with the end of the rope.

Mr. Schwartz stormed away, retrieving a gas can from a little green shed hidden behind the bushes nearby. He dumped its contents out just a few feet away from Madeline, sloshing it along the ground as

Madeline yanked her wrists against the ropes, both of them bleeding now. The gash on the side of her head had grown dark. Blood from it had spilled down past her shoulder now.

Mr. Schwartz turned and walked directly toward Roscoe, his face flushed red and an angry line etched between his eyes. As he came closer, he pulled a lighter from his pocket and flicked it open.

Behind him, Madeline screamed.

Roscoe didn't want to see what happened next. He released Madeline's cold hand and waist, pushing himself back away from her, falling onto the ground. He scooted back a few feet, his heart racing, and opened his eyes looking up at where she'd stood just moments ago.

She was gone.

Roscoe scrambled to his feet, scanning the lot for any sign of her. So Madeline had been murdered, her tortured soul tethered to the carousel just as her body had been when she died. She wanted justice (why else would she have shown Roscoe her death?) but what was he to do about it? Mr. Schwartz was already locked up in the nuthouse. The firefighters never found a body. There was no way to prove that Madeline had been murdered.

Roscoe wiped a hand over his brow. He was sweating. So how was he to get her ghost to leave? Memorial Day was just four days away—but he couldn't have a ghost wandering about, forcing him to relive her death over and over again. He took a step toward the carousel. Even if he could pull it down and pack it up again, it would sit here until he could find a buyer, and even then he'd have to pay to ship the damn thing.

No. He needed to get rid of it now. He could make up the money. Raise rent on all the tenants or something in the meantime.

Almost in a trance, Roscoe tore back out into the employee parking lot and into the tool shed. He threw open the doors, grabbed the flashlight he kept inside, and shined its light over the contents. Four gas cans. He tucked the flashlight under his chin and grabbed them, two by two, and set them outside the shed. Then he went back inside and snatched up every can that read WARNING: *Flammable!* He made a basket out of his shirt, then carried out three cans of paint thinner, grabbed one of the gas cans, and walked back to the carousel.

There was no sign of Madeline's ghost.

Roscoe uncapped the paint thinner and tossed it onto the platform as it spun.

He stepped over to the phonograph, yanked the record off, and smashed it against the side of the building. He stooped down, scooped up the parts, and threw them onto the carousel. He glanced around. Would she show herself again? He didn't wait to find out. He turned and ran back for the rest of the gas.

He tore the caps off and emptied each one onto the platform as the horses spun by, shaking out every drop.

Once all the gas and paint thinner had been emptied, Roscoe backed up and tore off his shirt, just in case anything had spilled, and tossed it onto the ride. Then he ran around the carousel, tearing down the entire construction tarp, so the fire wouldn't spread to the main building.

He stood before the carousel and read his watch in its light. Four sixteen a.m. No one would wake until at least six to get their shops ready. That would give the thing two hours to burn good and well before anyone would be awake to call the fire brigade.

Roscoe pulled out his lighter and snapped it open, a tiny flame flickering. He stared at it, the risk of what he was doing played through his mind again.

All the money spent.

No body, no proof. No way to help.

This was the only way to help himself.

Roscoe tossed the lighter deep into the carousel platform, fire snapping to life. He jumped back, the sudden pop of heat singeing the hair of his forearms. The spin of the carousel drew in just enough air to sweep the fire back through the platform and within a minute, a burning stampede of horses circled in fire before him. He backed up, staring at the sight as the flames grew higher: the platform's gold paint cracked and peeled away like frail bark. A mirror from the center casing crashed to the ground revealing a glimpse of the calliope within, and one of its pipes let out a low howl through the smoke. Roscoe stared at the burning horses, not moving, not breathing, and felt an uneasy shake move through him—their carved black eyes now appeared to bulge with terror, their wavy manes blown back by their own smoke and ash, and their mouths frozen open with inaudible screams as flames devoured galloping forelegs that would do nothing to save them. For an instant they looked too real.

What was left of the mirrored casing reflected it all, turning one fiery horse into dozens.

Roscoe backed away and slumped down against the building. The smell of burning gas was nearly overwhelming. The wood of the structure groaned and cracked before him as the fire pulled it apart. He'd sit here and watch it, watch it until it was nothing but cinders, he promised himself.

FRIDAY

It was Mel who called the fire department. He'd worked in kitchens long enough to recognize the difference between something *burning* and something *on fire*. He'd followed the smell only far enough to see smoke before running for the telephone.

By six thirty-two, the trucks had arrived, sirens blaring. Within minutes a firefighter carried Roscoe Sterling out of the smoke over his shoulder. He'd been found covered with ash and slumped against the building, unconscious and overcome with smoke. After a medic treated him onsite, Roscoe saw the firefighters trying to dampen the flames on the charred carousel and attempted to run back, screaming nonsense and threatening to set fire to it again—all in front of the tenants, who'd gathered in their pajamas on the boardwalk. After he punched two firefighters, the police had to be called. Roscoe was arrested and taken away, mumbling and pounding on the back window of a police car, clawing at the window, trying to get out.

TWO MONTHS LATER

Within two months, the Darlington Boardwalk was sold, again at auction for a low price. It was snapped up by the Allens, a young couple who came from old money and wanted a life on the shore where they met. Part of the deal of the purchase was that they were responsible for repairing any damage the fire had caused, which they did, before moving into the one-bedroom apartment that overlooked the charred but cleared-out space.

It was August when they reopened and business was grand. They'd tried to make enhancements to each of the shops to delight the visitors upon their return. New flavors at Mel's, a shiny new cotton candy station, and a roaming clown brigade with a fleet of poodles that did tricks on command.

Especially popular was a lucky find Mr. Allen had come upon out behind the boardwalk warehouse—a heavy crate containing a purchase likely made by the previous owner, but unopened before he'd departed. Mr. Allen had to use a sledgehammer to crack it open, as the fixtures were impossibly tight. Inside he'd found something perfectly creepy for the boardwalk's haunted house, which, in his wife's opinion, needed "a little something" anyway. Customers gazed at their find, which they'd placed outside the haunted house to draw people in, in astonishment, amazement, and grotesque curiosity. And no one could blame them. Nearly everyone's steps slowed at the sight of a black skeleton tethered by the wrists to a charred black carousel horse. It was gruesomely clever, a spooky sight that enticed patrons to enter the haunted house—or at least inspired each passing young rascal to dare his friends to do so. Adults, too, would pause and remark on the craftsman's morbid intricacy in carving every single bone in detail, from the tiniest bones in each individual finger to the small gap between the skeleton's front teeth to the crack in the side of its skull. Even the remnants of a burned gown that clung to the skeleton like a sinewy tissue was cause for remarks.

One could say that the skeleton almost looked real.

An excerpt from *The Cold Warrior's Guide to Medicine.*

Deborah and the Corpse

Lynn Bemiller

THE AUTOMATED DOUBLE DOORS leading from the Acute Care Department to the ambulance bay swished open. I stood on the air-conditioned side of the door and caught the cloud of hot, heavy night air that blew in. The department was quiet at this very late hour, and I had nothing better to do than to watch the two junior corpsmen leave the building and become shadows. Their summer white uniforms glowed faintly against the dark wall of Sewells Point Branch Clinic. Their faces reemerged in the sudden flare of a Bic lighter, then disappeared leaving only the glowing points of two cigarettes as clues to their presence.

I turned and paced back down the short, darkened hallway, wishing away the remaining four hours until the first shift of my first real doctor job ended. On my right, I passed the main four-bed treatment room, empty, and lit only by the bluish light of X-ray view boxes lining the back wall. Across the hall behind me, the door to the radio room stood open, spilling static and tinny voices out into the passageway.

"Doc? Base police on the radio, requesting an ambulance. They got a man down over by the air station."

I turned around as a figure on a rickety chair propelled itself out the door and into a patch of light on the white rolled-vinyl floor.

"Coming," I said. I checked my watch again, and followed Matthew Jenkins, hospitalman second-class, as he rolled himself back into the room. He pulled up to the desk and resumed a radio conversation laced with police and EMT jargon.

Through the static, I thought I caught the word "dead." I stepped closer to the radio and tapped Jenkins on the shoulder. "Wait, what was that?"

Jenkins paused, took his thumb off the transmit button, and looked up.

"Patient appears to be dead, ma'am." He put the handset down and rode his chair over to a tattered map of the Naval Operations Base. "Right here," he pointed to the top of the map, "in the parking lot by Gate 23."

"Dead? Really?" I said, suddenly awake and interested. A dead body would certainly start this new job off on a dramatic note. "I'll ride along, okay? In case he's not?"

Jenkins shrugged. "Sure, if you want." He turned back to the radio and activated the microphone. "On my way with the doc, in ambulance ninety-five. ETA 0315." He dropped the handset and stood up.

I watched him put on his regulation cap, then looked down at the surgical scrubs and sneakers I had on under my white lab coat. I wondered if I should be in proper Navy uniform too, but the idea of climbing back into polyester and pantyhose was not at all appealing. I decided if scrubs were good enough for the medical center, they'd be good enough for visiting a dead body here in Norfolk, Virginia, aka "Shit City," at 0300 hours. "Right," I said, and stepped back out into the hallway.

"Hey, Doc," Jenkins called from behind me. "Might want this."

He handed me a bright red fishing tackle box, with M.O.O.D. JUMP BOX lettered on it in white.

"What is it?" I took it from him. It was surprisingly heavy and clanked a little when I lifted it.

"Stuff the docs like to take when they go out in the field with us." He frowned, looking skeptical. "Didn't you get some orientation or something?"

"Nope. They said they were really short-staffed over here and needed someone to take call. I get the whole tour tomorrow, I guess." He followed right behind me as I headed down the hall and through the double doors to the ambulance bay. "So, hey, we're just winging it tonight." At the sound of the door, the two junior corpsmen flicked their cigarettes onto the pavement and ducked back inside before it slid closed. "You guys hold the fort, okay?" I called after them.

Ambulance ninety-five sat parked between two other vehicles. Jenkins pulled the door open on the driver's side and climbed up, adjusting lights and flipping switches as he settled into his seat. When the headlights came on, I pulled the passenger-side door open and tossed the jump box into the cab. The cab sat higher than I expected, and I'm pretty tall. I looked around for a handle of some sort but didn't see anything, so I put one foot up on the running board, grabbed the door frame with both hands, swung up onto the seat. As I buckled my seatbelt, I surveyed the interior of the vehicle by the glare of the dome light. "Pretty cool," I said, as Jenkins backed us out.

His gaze flipped from the rearview mirror to me, and back to the mirror. "First ambulance trip, ma'am?" He looked just about my age, one of those guys who joined up after high school instead of hassling with college or waiting to see what happened with the draft.

I smiled at him. "Yep. As interns they only let us hang out at the back end, and then only when it was in park and some disaster was getting unloaded."

Jenkins flicked me a skeptical glance as he put the ambulance in drive and pulled out into the road. He drove the speed limit through the maze of gray industrial buildings, stopping dutifully for stop signs at deserted intersections. I watched out the side window as the narrow street we were on suddenly became an empty parking lot, then reemerged as a one-way alley. Small blue signs with gold numbers tagged the corners of the buildings, in no apparent order.

"You'd think building ten would be next to building eleven, wouldn't you?" I said, pointing to a sign that read "36." "Not that signs like that one make navigation any easier." I pointed the other way, at a large blue that read, FASOTRAGRULANT. "Is that even in English?"

Jenkins pulled out into an empty intersection. "No, it's in 'Navy.' As in, you know, 'there's the right way, there's the wrong way, and then there's the Navy way.'"

"Never heard that one back at Oak Knoll," I said, still puzzling over the sign. LANT probably was short for "Atlantic," but that's as far as I could make out.

His look said that he wasn't surprised. "They also say there's no one less military than a military doctor."

I laughed out loud. "Glad to hear it." I reached up and re-pinned the heavy knot of blonde hair that was sliding awkwardly down the back of my neck. "Being a doctor is hard enough without being military too."

We stopped at a stop sign where the narrow road we were on crossed a wider well-marked one. Jenkins pointed to his left. "See that?"

About a block to the left, the low buildings opened up to the waterfront. Two blocks farther on, the spotlit bow of an aircraft carrier loomed several stories up out of Hampton Roads harbor.

"*USS Nimitz,*" Jenkins said. "Nuclear carrier. Medical department has operating rooms, ICU capabilities, full dental department, the works. Now that's the real Navy." I watched the massive ship disappear behind a gray warehouse as Jenkins executed a right turn. "Just left her two months back. Shore duty is starting to suck already. I can't wait to get back out there."

I pictured an operating room with a floor that tilted back and forth. "How many people does it have on it?"

"Crew," he emphasized the word slightly, "of around five thousand."

"Wow," I said, and wondered how it would be to live twenty-four seven with five thousand of your patients all around you. I was still watching the ship through the rearview mirror when Jenkins announced, "Arrived" into the radio, and put the ambulance in park.

I jumped down and looked around. The base police's van, haze-gray and a little rusty along its edges, was parked at the back of the lot. On my left, a World War II-era guard shack stood empty, and the double gate separating the shack from the neglected stretch of road on the far side of the fence didn't appear to have been opened in recent memory. Pines choked with Virginia creeper hemmed the other three sides of the lot. The white lines had chipped with weather and time, and dandelions poked through cracks in the asphalt. In the middle of the lot, the two policemen stood with their backs to us, smoking and looking at something on the ground. I grabbed the jump box and jogged over to where they stood.

The younger of the two guards acknowledged us with a nod. "Just like we found him, Doc." He took a big draw on his cigarette, held it a moment, and exhaled through his nose.

I knelt on the ground next to the corpse. He was past middle age, smallish but with the look of someone used to physical labor. He lay on his back with his knees drawn up in a stiff fetal position. His dull half-open eyes had receded in their sockets, and in his gaping mouth, a set of top dentures still stuck to his palate. He was dressed in snagged double-knit brown slacks, and a faded short-sleeved plaid shirt. A wedding band seemed trapped on a thin finger by knobby knuckles. His feet were bare, swollen, and discolored in a way that hinted at chronic heart disease.

I sat back on my heels for a moment, deciding what to do with him. Sensing that the three men watching expected something of me, I pulled a stethoscope from my coat pocket and, feeling vaguely foolish, bent my cheek to the man's face, feeling for breathing. I put the scope on his chest and listened in vain for heart sounds. In spite of the heat, his pale skin felt unpleasantly clammy and cool.

I shoved the stethoscope back into my pocket, stood up. "Odd position for him to be in, curled up like this, don't you think?" I walked all the way around him once, then bent down and pressed lightly against his bent knees. They didn't budge. I turned my head sideways and looked again. "Maybe he was lying on his side when he died."

Jenkins shook his head and shrugged. "Couldn't tell ya."

I stood up. "Let's get the poor guy up off the ground at least."

I watched as he opened up the back of the ambulance. He reappeared a minute later, pushing a gurney that he rolled up next to the body. He motioned to the nearest cop, who ground out his cigarette with his shoe and ambled over. The two of them hoisted the corpse onto the gurney, and lay him on his side, facing away from them. I pulled up his shirt and inspected his back: no blood, no sign of trauma, just the livid marks that blood makes when it settles after death. His unwashed trousers were faintly damp and smelled of urine. Something about that smell made him seem sadly human. I looked down at him for a minute more, feeling helpless and sorry as Jenkins pulled a sheet over him.

I turned and paced slowly toward the honeysuckle-wrapped fence. Through the vines, the main runway of the Breezy Point air station stretched away from me at a diagonal. I could hear a prop plane idling in the distance. Nearby among the pines, a nightjar called, *chuck-wills-widow*. A second one, farther away, replied, *chuck-wills-widow*. My Southern grandmother used to say that nightjars call like that when they sense a soul departing. The superstition made me shiver in spite of the heat. I fanned it away with the open edges of my lab coat. After a moment, I straightened my scrub top, retied the baggy pants, and walked back to the others.

The headlights of an unmarked blue sedan blinded me for a moment as the driver pulled into the lot and parked next to the ambulance. I shielded my eyes with my hand and watched the driver's shadow approach across the cracked asphalt until its owner stood in front of us. He was about Jenkins's height, but leaner, dark-haired and neatly groomed. A 35mm camera with a large telephoto lens hung from a strap over his left shoulder. His eyes moved slowly in a methodical visual inventory of the scene. I wondered what sort of man wore a white shirt and a tie to do field work at three a.m.

He checked the time on a large diver's watch that emerged from his neatly rolled cuffs and extended his other hand to me with the practiced air of a politician.

"Bill Whitley, Naval Investigative Service." He gave my hand one short, sharp shake.

"Lieutenant Deborah Slater," I said. "Navy Medical Corps." I glanced around hoping for guidance, but the others had strolled a respectful few paces out of earshot and were chatting in low voices.

Bill's eyes scanned my sneakers and hospital scrubs. "You're one of the new general medical officers."

"First night on duty," I said. Still not clear who he was or what respect I owed him, I added, "Sir," and held my breath, expecting to be barked at.

Instead, his tanned face relaxed into a wry smile. "Relax, Doc. I'm a civilian. Now, what's happened here?"

I cleared my throat. "Well. Base police called the clinic at about 0255 and said that they'd found a man down and probably dead. HM2 Jenkins and I arrived at about 0315, and found that man," I nodded at the corpse under the sheet, "on the ground. I did a quick assessment, but I didn't find any obvious cause of death. It looks like the poor guy's been dead a little while too." I reached down and held up a corner of the sheet for a moment so he could see for himself.

Bill's eyes made another circuit, from the corpse to the parking lot, the vehicles, and the surrounding trees.

"Did you search him when you moved him?" he called over his shoulder to Jenkins.

Jenkins shook his head. "Not our role, sir. Doc just wanted him up off the ground."

Bill looked amused at my concern for the dead man's welfare.

I exhaled a little louder than I intended to. "He's my first corpse. I honestly don't know what the procedure is here."

"Pretty simple, really. I'll get some photos and talk to the guards who found him. Since he's a civilian, the city medical examiner will take over his remains. They should be here shortly to pick him up."

"Will they do an autopsy, or some kind of investigation? Find his family, stuff like that?"

Bill shrugged. "Usually, a postmortem gets done on any unexplained death. But it depends on the coroner. Guy like this, they may just attribute to natural causes."

He pulled the camera off his shoulder, removed the lens cap and tucked it into his shirt pocket. He snapped a couple of shots of the scene. Then, kneeling down, he twitched back the sheet and took two or three close-ups of the corpse before looking up. "Have you pronounced him?"

I folded my arms. "Are you serious? He's clearly dead."

"Correct. But the instruction specifies that a medical officer needs to pronounce him, date and time, before his remains can be released from a government facility."

"Fine," I said. I looked down and swallowed. "Is there some prescribed official language I'm supposed to use?" I laughed a little, to hide the tears in my eyes. "Back at the medical center, they kicked us interns out of the room before they got to this part."

Bill shook his head and gave me half a smile. "I'm sure whatever you want to say to him will be fine with the Navy."

I nodded, knelt down, and looked into the corpse's half-closed eyes.

"My friend," I said, and stopped, feeling small and lonely. A nightjar called again. The prop plane revved, and I heard Bill's shutter click.

"My friend," I found my voice and began again a little more loudly, "I, Lieutenant Deborah Ann Slater, Medical Corps, United States Navy, pronounce that at 0329 on Monday, 16 August, 1982, you are dead."

Someone's son, someone's beloved, maybe someone's father, dead and abandoned in a parking lot in the middle of the night in godforsaken Norfolk, Virginia. Dust you are—something I hadn't thought of since Sunday school—and to dust we all return.

"Done here?" I asked Bill, blinking back tears.

"Yep," he replied. His camera continued to click.

I replaced the sheet as gently as though he were a sleeping child and patted his lifeless shoulder. As I stood up, I heard the crunching sound of another vehicle arriving.

"There's the city guys," said Bill. "I'll leave you to it then." He capped his camera and walked back to his car. He opened the door and hesitated a moment before getting in, giving the scene one more look. Then he waved to me and drove off.

Jenkins and the two officers lifted the corpse off the ambulance gurney and onto one in the back of the city's mortuary van. It looked uncomfortable, I thought, as if that still mattered. The rear doors slammed shut, and the city van pulled away. The base police followed behind, leaving Jenkins and me alone in the empty lot.

I could find nothing useful to say during the short ride back to the clinic. The acute care area was still dark and quiet when Jenkins pulled in and parked ambulance ninety-five. He resumed his spot at the dispatch radio: feet on the desk, hands folded on the top of his head, eyes closed. I stowed the jump box in the radio room and checked my watch again: 0350. Still time to get a couple of hours sleep before muster at 0700.

"In the call room if you need me," I said.

"Aye aye, ma'am," he said, without opening his eyes.

I crossed the hall to the tiny cinder-block on-call room just off the main treatment area. I took off my lab coat and sneakers and switched off the light. It was pitch dark except for a thin band of bluish light under the door, and the small bed had the comfortingly familiar smell of bleached hospital sheets. I pulled the covers up over my head and was immediately asleep.

THE DEPARTMENT WAS STILL quiet when my Timex chirped at 0600. The only clue that it was really morning was the bright daylight seeping under the door. I got up, made the bed, and spent fifteen minutes in the tiny attached bathroom, taking a hot shower and steaming the wrinkles out of the uniform I'd stuffed in my on-call bag. I wiped the steam from the mirror, brushed out my unruly hair, and pinned it into a fair approximation of a regulation bun. The pantyhose and white polyester uniform blouse felt sticky as I wrestled them on over my damp skin. After a little foundation and blush, the face in the mirror looked only minimally the worse for wear.

I stepped out into the hallway and looked around. An HM3 that I hadn't met yet sat at the check-in desk. The ambulance dispatch radio in the room behind the desk was quiet. Lights were on in the main treatment room, where the night crew had spent the last hour of their shift putting the department into some semblance of order.

I caught a whiff of coffee. I scooped up my on-call bag, tossed it into the converted supply closet that was my new office, and followed the scent around the corner and two doors down, to the staff lounge, where a half-full pot sitting on an industrial hotplate emitted a slightly scorched smell. It didn't deter me from pouring a paper cupful and admiring the oily scum that floated to the surface.

A baby-faced sailor came into the room just behind me, carrying a chipped mug that read "Virginia is for Lovers." He smiled at me as he picked up the pot and poured.

"Careful, ma'am," he squeaked, "that stuff'll put hair on your chest."

I looked at the front of my blouse, and then grinned at the sailor whose name tag read "Seaman Apprentice Mayhart." "Yikes! Thanks for the warning!"

Mayhart, who couldn't have been over nineteen, blushed. "No offense meant, ma'am." He poured a heavy dose of granulated sugar into his mug and stirred it with a wooden tongue depressor from a box next to the coffee pot.

I set my coffee down on one of three round tables that filled the center of the room. In the middle of the table someone had placed a box of Krispy Kreme donuts and, next to it, a Styrofoam cup with "donations" engraved into it with black ballpoint. I put a quarter in the cup and picked out a glazed one, pinched it to verify that it had been fresh in the recent past, dunked it in the thick coffee, and consumed it in three bites. I had to admit that a doughnut and coffee made sometime this morning surpassed most of what could be scavenged on a hospital ward at this hour.

As I stood up to leave, the door swung open to let in the department's senior enlisted man, Chief Petty Officer Don Babcock. He was probably close to forty but looked older—paunchy, red-eyed and smelling of last night's booze. He headed straight for the coffee pot, poured a mug emblazoned with the chief petty officer insignia, and stacked two doughnuts on top of it.

"Hear you caught yourselves a floater last night." He gave me a quick glance. "Some old gomer, Jenkins said."

"Well, he wasn't floating exactly," I said. "But I can safely say he's done his last swim."

Babcock cackled and stepped back to let me pass, keeping the doughnuts expertly balanced. "You know what they say, Doc. 'The Navy: it's not just a job, it's a blow job.'" He followed me through the open door and as far as my office, then continued on through the treatment room, cackling to himself. I watched him disappear out the ambulance bay doors before I opened my office door.

On the desk, someone had left a hand-drawn cartoon. AROUND HERE, the caption read, IT'S JUST ONE F***ING THING AFTER ANOTHER. Below it, a determined-looking anthropomorphic penis chased a frightened-looking vulva that was sprinting away from him. I had to admire the detail: she even had a Minnie Mouse bow tied in her thick curly hair. I put down my coffee and rummaged through the desk drawers until I found a fresh manila file folder and a black Sharpie marker. On the tab of the folder, I wrote "Navy Instructions" and slipped the cartoon inside.

"Didn't like your welcome present?"

I looked up to see (according to his name tag) Lieutenant Commander Howard Schwartz, Medical Corps, standing in the hall. He was freshly shaved, his curly dark hair neatly combed, and he smelled of expensive cologne. A smile that seemed genuine enough crinkled the dark eyes behind his horn-rims. He exuded confidence.

I pulled the cartoon out of the file and handed it to him. "Points for ingenuity, I guess. Can't say I've seen a cartoon quite like this one before."

"Looks like something from Babcock's bag of tricks." Schwartz snickered and handed the paper back. "Don't take it personally: the man's been a pain in the ass since he got passed over for senior chief, but his bark is worse than his bite. Usually."

"Good to know." I put the cartoon back in the folder and put it in one of the file trays on the desk.

"I'm Howie, by the way. I work sick call." He pointed over his shoulder to another corner of the building. "I've been volunteered to give you a little tour and introduce you to the boss." He looked at my half-empty paper cup. "For that, you're gonna need more coffee. Follow me."

He headed past the lounge and out into a back hallway that ran the length of the clinic building. Walking briskly, he turned right into the first cross hallway, pointing at doorways as he walked.

"Radiology," he pointed left, "Optometry," pointing across the hall, then, "Lab's here," as he reached the end of the hall. I hustled after him as he turned right again into a long front hall. Through an open doorway I could see into the spacious, battleship-gray-colored front lobby. Although it wasn't yet 0700, the space was filled with uniformed patients lining up at the check-in window.

"This way." Schwartz turned left, heading back the way we'd come, in an identical parallel hall. "Sick call: vital signs, nurse's office, physician assistant office—ever worked with PAs? They're one of the Navy's best-kept secrets. Ah, my office."

He ducked into a doorway on his right. Several patient charts already bulged from a rack on the door. He closed the doors to two adjoining exam rooms, then the one to the hall. Without slowing his pace, he scooped up a Thermos from his desk and a small mug from the top of his bookcase, poured something fragrant and handed it to me.

"We have to work here," he said. "We don't have to drink that swill they call coffee."

I accepted the mug, sniffed, then tasted. Espresso, perfectly sweetened. Made me a little homesick for my favorite North Beach café. "Much better," I said. Thanks a lot."

"Most welcome. My New Yorker wife makes it. Never lets me leave home without it. Now sit." He gestured to a hard plastic chair facing his immaculate desk.

I dutifully sat, admiring Schwartz's tidy, well-furnished office. "How long have you been here?"

"Starting my third year. By July, my obligation will be paid up and God willing I'll be home in Pittsburgh in a nice psychiatry residency."

"Three years?" I looked down into my espresso cup, disappointed. "I had been hoping to be out of here in a year."

Schwartz, seated now behind his desk, made a clucking sound and shook his head. "Well, there's always hope—but take my advice, and don't count on it. Politics are fierce around here. Not like what you're used to, back in sunny California."

I nodded. "I've heard that about the East Coast. I'm hoping for a residency at Bethesda, and then a fellowship at the National Cancer Institute, so I thought coming out here might help my chances."

Schwartz looked at his watch and stood up. "Almost seven. Let's try to catch Captain Roughner." He walked to the door. "He's one of a kind. General medical officer with thirty years of operational experience and likes to say he's as rough as his name. Our goal is not to piss him off between now and the time he retires, which is rumored to be soon." He held the door open for me, looking me over as I passed him. "Wait." He put a hand on my arm. "Fix the wispies."

"The what?" Another new term to learn.

"All the loose stuff," he said, pointing to my hair.

I walked over to a sink in the corner of the room and checked my hair in the mirror over it. It had slipped into its usual lopsided snarl. I took it down, raked it with my fingers, and rerolled a bun, doing my best to catch all the stray ends. "Did I get them all?" He gave me a quick look and a thumbs-up, and preceded me through the door.

We traversed the clinic and arrived at the front office in less than a minute. In the anteroom, Howie nodded to the captain's assistant, then knocked at the senior medical officer's half-open door.

Captain Roughner sat at his desk, with one foot on the desktop, hands folded on top of his head, gazing out the big windows that occupied one wall. As he looked up, Schwartz murmured, "See you later," and left me standing alone in the captain's doorway.

His jowly, creased face reminded me of a pet bulldog. "Christ," he said, "They've sent me another one. Can't get a good man these days; the fleet gets them all." He surveyed me head-to-toe with an air of exasperated amusement. "Well, what's your story, Slater? And yes, I know who you are. Fresh out of internship at Oak Knoll, God help us."

"Yes, sir."

"What's the rest of it? Joined up to follow your sailor sweetheart around the world? Or to please Daddy, who was hoping you'd been a boy?" He pointed at me with one accusing finger, "You better not say 'for the adventure.'"

I smiled, remembering Babcock's version of the recruiting slogan. "For the money, I guess you could say. I had an Armed Forces scholarship for medical school."

He raised his eyebrows another millimeter and seemed to be studying me. "Know why they call California the granola state?"

"No, sir."

"Granola," he repeated, "what's not fruits and nuts is all flakes. And you look to me like one of the flakes."

Something told me it would be safest to say as little as possible. I bit my lip.

His look clearly said that I'd confirmed his suspicions. He waved his hand up and down a couple of times, gesturing at my appearance. "Those uniforms are a hazard, did you know that? Fire aboard ship, the damn polyester stuff melts right onto to your skin. Guaranteed third-degree burns." He pulled at his own shirt front. "Find yourself some cotton khakis like these. And lose the high heels, sister. This isn't a fashion show."

I looked at my feet, and back at Roughner. "They are regulation Bates pumps, sir."

He shook his head, hissing his disapproval. "Well go on, get out of here. You've got work to do."

I gave him two quick nods. "Good to meet you, Captain Roughner. Thanks for your time." I hustled out the door and closed it behind me.

IT DIDN'T TAKE LONG to pick up the department routine in the Acute Care Clinic: quick briefing with the previous night's medical officer on duty at 0700, then a quiet couple of hours while business on the base got started for the day. By lunchtime, the bays were usually filled with patients complaining of back strain, lacerations, or the occasional asthma flare-up. Once or twice a day, though, a truly urgent case came in; something that should by all rights go to a hospital emergency department but for the sake of convenience wound up here instead. It made me uneasy, to say the least, but I didn't want to get a reputation as a whiner, so I tried to concentrate on doing what I could.

On Friday morning at 0645, it was already ninety degrees and ninety percent humidity when I pulled my robin's-egg blue VW beetle into officers' parking, across from the clinic's emergency entrance. Despite the short commute, my uniform was already sticking to my skin and sweat had collected under the band of my "bucket" hat. I flapped the neck of the blouse to generate a little breeze, trying not to picture the stiff fabric bursting into flame and melting.

I locked up the car and walked smartly, heels clacking, across the parking lot to the automatic doors. Once inside, chilled and Betadine-scented air raised goosebumps on my arms. I already disliked East Coast summers: too hot outside and too cold inside.

I dropped my on-call bag on top of one of the large cardboard supply boxes that took up the majority of the cubic footage in my small office, grabbed a lab coat from a hook behind the door, and replaced it with my sweaty cover. When I reopened the door, Babcock, just back from muster, was standing outside his own office across the hall.

He stood with his thumbs in his belt loops, rocking back and forth.

"Full moon," he said. "Day shift will be quiet, then get ready to grab your ass." He looked intently at me, as though daring me to contradict him.

I gave him my most reasonable smile. "Thanks, Chief. I appreciate the heads-up."

He stopped rocking and grunted, then went into his own office and shut the door. Taped to the outside was a sign that read, "Complaint Department. Take a Number." Beneath the lettering was a drawing of a large hand grenade. On a tag tied to the firing pin was the number "1."

I snickered. Even though I'd only known him a week, I didn't doubt for a minute that the cartoon was a true reflection of Babcock's preferred method of conflict management. The temptation was too much to resist. Seeing no one around, I carefully peeled the sign off the door and tucked it into my "Navy Instructions" file.

JUST AFTER SUNSET, I snipped a tail of black suture and set the needle and driver on the instrument stand at my elbow. I smiled at the man in front of me. "All done but the Band-Aid," I said.

"Hear that, bud?" The man loosened his hold on a small grubby boy sitting in his lap. Five neat stitches now tracked across his forehead like a tiny black caterpillar.

Anticipating the kid's next move, I grabbed the boy's small hand just as he reached up to feel what I'd had done. "No touching yet." With my other hand, I picked up a small piece of gauze and folded it over the laceration, then looked around for the corpsman who'd been assisting me.

"Hughes," I said, "please hand me the one-inch silk tape."

HM3 Hughes didn't seem to hear me the first time. She was leaning against a row of supply shelves at the end of the bay, talking to someone around the end of the privacy curtain. Her short, dark blonde hair had been aggressively frosted, and her small green eyes seemed even smaller behind their rings of black eyeliner. Her white uniform strained in all the wrong places, and she had avoided panty lines by eliminating panties altogether. Something in her smile told me she wasn't talking patient care with whoever was in the next bay.

"Hughes?"

She reluctantly turned and picked up a roll of tape from the shelf behind her. She winked at the boy's dad before pulling a length of silk tape off a roll and taping down the gauze.

I looked down at the squirming child. "Come back and see me on

Wednesday, okay? And stay off that Big Wheel for a couple of days." I pulled off my gloves, patted the boy's head, and walked across the room to wash up.

"Hey, Doc?" Hughes peered over my shoulder at the mirror above the sink, licked a pinkie finger, and dabbed at her eyeliner. "Jenkins needs you in bay one." She nodded her head toward the closed curtain.

"Thanks." I dried my hands and walked back across the room.

A short man in a pale blue guayabera shirt, tan trousers, and polished black shoes sat on the gurney in the first bay. He held his right hand in the air, but otherwise looked enough at ease to nod a hello when I came in. Jenkins stood in front of the patient, one foot in front of the other in a stance that suggested exertion. Both of his hands gripped the man's upraised one.

Jenkins motioned me over with a sideways nod. "Got a problem here." When I moved in close to get a good look, he loosened his grip on the man's hand. As he let go, the thumb fell loosely away from the rest of the hand like a disarticulated chicken leg, and a little jet of arterial blood spurted straight up. He clenched the hand again, but not before I saw a long, clean slice through the flesh between the thumb and first finger.

"What happened?" I asked. Feeling a little faint at the sight of the spurting blood, I leaned against the gurney and folded my arms.

"Well, Doc," the man said, as calm as if he were discussing the weather, "she came at me with a butcher knife, and I tried to grab it from her."

I pictured the man's hand grabbing a knife blade and tried not to wince. I wondered who "she" was and why she was brandishing a knife but decided it was more than I really wanted to know.

"You'll need a surgeon to fix that." I ducked around the curtain and grabbed the sleeve of the first corpsman to walk by. "Tell the LPO we have a transport, and then get right back here."

While my heart rate rose, Jenkins stood quietly conversing with the patient. Something he'd said that I couldn't hear made the man laugh. I sorted through supplies on the shelves behind the bed, and came up with some packets of sterile gauze, a couple of Ace wraps, sterile gloves, and a portable blood pressure cuff.

"Not much to work with," I said to Jenkins, "but I think we can—"

"Wing it?" He raised one eyebrow at me.

"You catch on quick, HM2," I said. "Just keep pressure for another minute, okay?"

"Yep," he said.

I wrapped the cuff around the man's upper arm and inflated it partway, then pulled apart the gauze packets and put on a pair of sterile gloves.

"Okay," I told Jenkins. "Let go." As Jenkins relaxed his grip I folded a thick pad of gauze, packed it between the man's thumb and first finger, and squeezed his hand in both of mine. "Okay, Jenkins, now wrap those Aces around, good and snug."

He started just below where I was holding pressure, wrapping the compression bandages around the man's hand. I inched my hands up as he wrapped, and finally let go. Once he clipped the end of the wrap in place, I deflated the cuff and pulled it off the man's arm. For a moment, all three of us stared at the bandage. I pinched a fingertip; it blanched for a second, then turned pink with normal blood flow. After a long-seeming minute, no blood had leaked up through the gauze. I gave Jenkins a thumbs-up, and slid back the curtains. "Cool. Now let's move."

There were too many people huddled around the front desk, none of whom needed to know the details of the man's injury, so I detoured to my office to call a consultant.

The office door was already open when I arrived. On a large cardboard box labeled, "Tubes, paper, drinking, disposable," in black letters sat Bill Whitley, the agent from NIS. He had taken off his blue blazer and had set it neatly folded on the box next to him. He stood up, and I slid around him to get to my desk.

I picked up the phone. "Agent Whitley, right? What's up?" I asked, as I dialed the paging operator at Portsmouth Naval Hospital. When the operator answered, I requested the duty orthopedist. I put my hand over the mouthpiece while I waited.

"Bill," he said. "Just making my rounds, so to speak."

The surgeon came on the line. I held up a hand to Bill while I gave a quick summary of the patient's injury, thanked the listener in advance for seeing the patient, and hung up.

"Sorry, what did you say?"

Bill handed me a manila envelope. "I wanted to drop these off."

I took the envelope, opened it, and glanced at the contents. Inside were three eight-by-ten color crime scene photos with Bill's business card clipped to them. "Morbid," I muttered under my breath, and shoved them back into the envelope. "So, what did you find out about the dead guy?"

Bill shrugged. "Nothing. Not in my job description to investigate civilians. Felonies against government personnel," he added, preempting my question about what his job was. He rummaged in the pockets of his blazer and pulled out a battered paper bag. "Found these. I gave the city the info, but I thought you'd like a souvenir."

I hesitated for a moment before taking the bag and pulling out the contents one at a time. Inside were three plastic medicine bottles labeled "digoxin," "procainamide," and "furosemide," and a small brown glass vial of nitroglycerin tablets. Each was down to the last few pills. According to the label, they had been filled three months ago at Main Street Drug in Le Claire, Iowa.

"Mr. Freddy Martin," I read. "If that was him, it looks like he had heart disease." I remembered his swollen, shoeless feet and couldn't help adding, "As I suspected."

I thought about the man as I stuffed the bottles back in the bag and handed it back to Bill. "So weird. How do you suppose he ended up here from Iowa?"

Bill shrugged again. "Who knows? Probably just some bum."

I pulled out the top photo and stared at it for a moment. "But look. His shirt is clean, fingernails too, and he's had a haircut recently. Doesn't seem like a derelict, does it? Somebody might be looking for him, or missing him, or—" I stopped and looked at the photo again. "And, he must've been military, right? How else could he have gotten on base?"

"Well, Doc, I'll tell you from experience," he said, standing up and slinging his jacket over his shoulder, "cases like this are dead-ends. You'll be hard-pressed to find anyone who gives a hoot in hell about these washed up old geezers, military or no."

Including you, apparently, I thought. His cavalier tone bothered me. I tossed the photos on the desk.

"Hey, Doc," a voice called from the main room. "Got a brawler out here for ya."

"Duty calls," I said. "Thanks for coming by."

Bill rose, draped his blazer over his arm, and pushed the box he'd been sitting on back into its previous position as a doorstop. He stood back against the door and gave me a small smile.

"After you, Doc."

Release

Jane Boulden

BILLY'S WHOLE PLAN WAS predicated on the assumption that the guy he'd seen coming out the back door for a smoke yesterday would do the same thing again tonight, at roughly the same time. By sheer chance he'd seen the guy exit the evening before, and it had given him the idea of getting into the building using that door, rather than trying to slip past the front desk. Billy worked with smokers you could set your clock by. If he looked out across the room and saw Aaron pushing back his desk chair, he knew it was between ten fifteen and ten thirty in the morning.

Last night he'd sat in the parking lot of the senior care home and watched from his car while the back door opened, and a guy in an orderly's uniform had leaned down to pick up a stick to jam in the door to keep it just a bit ajar. The guy then straightened up, his lighter in hand, and flicked the flame to light the cigarette already in his mouth. He slipped around the corner of the building to go and sit somewhere out back, probably on the picnic table none of the residents ever used.

Billy sat in his car and went over the plan in his head. All that he could think of were the million ways it could go wrong. He looked at his phone: 7:16 p.m. He could just turn the keys, pull out of the parking lot, and head home. No one would be the wiser. He leaned back against the seat and looked into the rearview mirror, reaching up to adjust it a little so he had a better view of the metal door in the building behind him. If the plan was going to work, he had to be out of the car before the guy appeared so that he could get into the building quickly.

He picked up the plastic bag from the passenger's seat and pulled out a mask and a pair of latex gloves. His sister Suzie had dropped off six medical masks a few weeks ago, just as the virus was arriving. Even then she'd stayed outside to talk to him, backing up halfway down the front path when he came to the door. She'd left the masks in a white plastic bag on the front step. The kind they give you at the hospital to put your clothes in when you have to change into a gown. He put the mask and gloves on, flexing his fingers to make sure the gloves were snug, and looked in the mirror to check the mask. He then dropped the bag behind the console on the floor of the back seat, pulled the keys from the ignition, and got out of the car. Standing at the front of the car with his back to the building, he crossed his legs and leaned back against the hood. If anyone passed by or asked him what he was up to he'd say he was waiting for someone inside the building. Staring at his phone, he rolled his shoulders back and forth a little to ease his tension.

He froze when he heard the squeak of the metal door opening. He heard someone shuffle a few steps and then what sounded like the flick of a lighter. After counting to three he turned to look. There was no one in sight. He shoved his phone in the back pocket of his jeans as he stepped quickly past the car to the door. He grabbed the outer edge of the door with his right hand and the stick that was jammed in the opening with his left. In one movement he pulled the door open and stepped inside, then whipped around to place the stick back where it had been, guiding the door closed to avoid any extra sounds.

On the second floor he stopped at the door to the hallway. He should have waited to put the mask on. The fabric flapped back and forth against his mouth and nose as he breathed. He fought a wave of claustrophobia. Resisting the urge to pull the mask off his face, he closed his eyes for a second and tried to slow his breath while he rehearsed what he would say if he opened the door and met a staff member. Opening his eyes, he put his hand on the bar of the door handle and pushed down and forward. There was no one in the hall. He strode to the second door on the right: 207, the plaque said. Below it was a slot where a resident's name could be slid in and out easily. "James Murray." No one had called his father James his whole life. He'd always been known as Pat, short for Patrick, his middle name.

Billy could hear the TV blaring through the door. He turned the handle and walked in. The room was dark except for the weak twilight coming through the window straight ahead of him, and the beam of the television screen that stretched sideways across the room. His father was sitting in the middle of the room about six feet away from the TV, in the Lay-Z-Boy chair that was one of the few things they'd brought from home when they moved him here after Billy's mother died. His father continued staring at the screen, his left hand resting on the top of the cane propped up against the side of the chair. Someone on the television was shouting about the prices of cars at a dealership in Plattsburgh.

"Dad," Billy called. His father didn't move. "Dad." Billy raised his voice but still got no response.

He walked further into the room and stood behind the TV, shuffling his feet to avoid the wires. Even then, his father's eyes remained focused on the salesman's animated pitch about the virtues of zero financing during the time of covid. Billy waved his hands back and forth in front of himself. All of a sudden, his father saw him and erupted with sound and motion. "Ahhhhh," he screamed, lifting his cane and shaking it, fluttering his feet back and forth as if he was swimming, his toothless mouth wide open, his lower jaw working furiously. "Ahhhh."

"Dad, Dad, Dad." Billy raised his voice with each word. "It's me. It's Billy." He reached up and pulled the elastic off his ear so that the mask dropped down to one side. He leaned over the screen and pointed at his face. "It's Billy." He shouted this time. His father paused for a second as comprehension flashed across his face. And then just like that his response shifted.

"Amn . . . damn . . . damn," His voice got louder as he went. He shoved the tip of his cane against the floor. "Ou," he sputtered out. He tried to lift the cane as if to point it at Billy but the gesture faltered when his hand couldn't sustain the weight of it. He stared hard at Billy, rubbing his gums together and moving his lips as if he was trying to get them in shape enough to say something.

"I'm sorry, Dad. I didn't mean to startle you." Billy stepped around the TV and turned it off. The screen went black. His father erupted again. "Final," he said urgently, pointing at the screen with a long finger. "Final," he worked his mouth hard and shook his finger at the TV again. Then he reached down next to his right leg and pulled out the remote control from the crevice between his leg and the arm of the chair. He hit the power button and the screen came back to life. "Final," he said again.

"Right, right. Final Jeopardy. Okay." Billy raised his hands in surrender, and turned away. "God forbid we should miss that," he said under his breath as he reached down and pulled the elastic from the dropped side of the mask back over his ear.

He went to the little kitchen area to look for a bag to put things in. The so-called kitchenette was little more than a short counter with a sink, a mini-fridge underneath, and a microwave on top. A beige plastic tray sat on the counter with foil-covered plastic dishes. Billy touched the top of the largest foil covers and pulled the foil off from the corner. The dim light made it hard to see. He reached to the wall and flicked on the switch. The fluorescent light under the counter hummed into action and revealed three piles of pureed mush, one gray, one white, and one green. Billy swallowed down a gag reflex, and turned back toward his father.

"Is this your dinner, Dad?" He shouted to be heard over the television. His father glanced up at him and Billy pointed to the tray. "Your dinner?"

"Cold," his father responded. Alex Trebek was reading the answer to Final Jeopardy.

"You're supposed to warm it up in the microwave," Billy called back to him.

"Cold," his father said again.

"When was the last time you ate, Dad?"

His father shook his head without moving his gaze.

"Can't say I blame you," Billy said to himself.

He opened the cupboard above the sink. There were three white mugs, a jar of instant coffee, and a clear plastic container with some tea bags. When he opened the second of the three drawers next to the mini-fridge he found a pile of ketchup, mustard, and mayo packets. But in the bottom drawer he found a bright green cloth Dollar Store bag.

He turned back toward the middle of the room as Alex Trebek began revealing the contestants' responses. His father shifted in his seat. Billy walked past him and headed into the bedroom. Four pill bottles and some silver blister packs lay on the bedside table. Billy scooped them all up and dropped them into the dollar store bag. His father's dentures were in the bathroom, sitting on a piece of tissue encrusted onto a plastic shelf. He shuddered. At least it was unlikely that anyone else had touched them in the last few days. He picked up the dentures, holding them at the very ends of his thumb and index finger, and took them to his father. "Here, put these in." Alex Trebek was congratulating the winner as the closing theme music played. His father took the dentures and pushed the bottom teeth into his mouth first, stretching his mouth wide to get them in. The top set went in more easily. Suddenly his face had structure and form. He shook his head and started to spit them out again, reaching his hand up toward his mouth to grab them.

"No, no, no," Billy said, reaching down to stop him. "Leave them in, Dad." Billy opened his mouth and pointed to his own teeth, forgetting the mask was still there. "Leave them in for now. I can't understand you without them in." His father paused with the bottom teeth half out his mouth. "Please, Dad, just leave them in for now. You can take them out when we get home."

His father lifted his head and sucked the teeth back into his mouth, grimacing a little as he worked them back into place. He looked at Billy. "Home?" He spoke the word carefully, moving his lips as if he didn't want them to touch his teeth.

"Yes," Billy said. "Home. You're coming home with me. I'm getting you out of here." Until he heard the words leave his mouth, Billy himself did not quite believe it.

His father shook his head. "No," he said.

"Yes," Billy said. "It's too dangerous for you here. The virus is here. Do you understand?" His father nodded, his eyes focused on Billy's face. Billy continued, "The virus is here. In the building." He pointed a finger to the ceiling and circled it around. "There are three residents with it now. And if they're saying there's three, there's probably more. That's why I'm wearing a mask. And gloves." He pointed to the mask and held up his hands to show his gloved hands.

His father shook his head. "Home?"

"My home," Billy replied. "You're coming to my home. Your home is gone, remember?" Billy wished he hadn't said it. His father looked away.

"Look," Billy tried again. He squatted down in front of his father. "Because of the virus they're not letting anyone in. I'm not supposed to be here even. And in lots of places like this, staff aren't even showing up to work. If we leave you here you're just going to get the virus, and if you get the virus you're probably . . ." Billy stopped. He wondered if his father was even listening.

His father turned back toward him. "Suzie," he said.

Billy shook his head. "Suzie is working at the hospital. She can't do anything. She can't see anyone until all of this is over. We'll call her when we get to my place."

His father slumped a little in the chair and stared at his hands. He rubbed his right thumb back and forth across the top of his left hand as if there was a spot there. Billy stared at the veins showing through the parchment skin. He reached over and took the remote control from the chair and turned the TV off, robbing the room of its strongest light. His father didn't react. For Billy, the silence was a relief. He put his hand on the arm of the chair.

"Look, Dad," he spoke slowly. "We need to get you out of here so that you don't get sick. Really sick." He waited. "Dad?" His father's thumb continued to travel back and forth across the back of his hand. Billy's knees were beginning to ache, so he stood up and straightened his back for a moment, then squatted down again. He reached up and pulled the elastic off his ear so the mask dropped down.

"Dad." His father looked at him this time. Billy realized he hadn't been this close to his father's face in a meaningful way in a very long time, perhaps ever. Even in the gray light of the room the view was jarring. His father's skin was loose, and the stubble above his lips and around his chin was white and thin. His lips were pale and dry, and the bottom lip was cracked. But the nose was as straight and strong as it had always been, and above it, his father's hazel eyes stared back at him with full attention. Billy blinked. He shifted his weight, and started again. "Here's the situation, Dad. There's really only two choices. You can stay here on your own. Really on your own—no visitors, no staff except them bringing your meals to the door." He gestured toward the tray in the kitchen. "If you get sick, you'll stay here unless they need to take you to a hospital. And if you go to a hospital none of us can come and be there with you." His knees were starting to ache again. He rolled his shoulders but stayed where he was, meeting his father's gaze.

"Or," he said, "or, you can come home with me and stay with me until it's safe to come back." He dropped his eyes, and then raised them again. "I know being with me is not your first choice, but it's really your only choice other than staying here." There was still no reaction from his father. Billy put his hand on the arm of the chair and pushed on it to ease himself back into a standing position. He looked at his father. "The thing is, you have to decide right now. Once I leave, I can't come back." He reached for the elastic loop of the mask and pulled it back over his face. "Take a minute to think about it. I'm going to do a last check to make sure I have all your meds."

His father reached his hand over to the cane and looked up at Billy. "Yes," he said.

"Yes?"

"Yes, I'll come with you." His father's voice was thin somehow, but firm, and he spoke every word. His hand gripped the cane, and he started to shift himself forward in the chair.

Billy stood motionless for a moment, taken aback by the clarity of the decision. "Right. Okay. Great," he said. "Just hang on and let me find your walker, then I think we're ready to go."

"Under the window," his father said, scooting his body forward again on the chair.

Even with his walker, it took Billy's father longer than Billy would have thought possible to get out into the corridor and through the door to the stairway. The whole time Billy worried that someone would appear and ask what they were up to. And it was only as his father passed the door of the room next to his that Billy thought about the possibility of cameras monitoring the halls. But there was nothing to do but keep going, one slow step after the other, one push of the walker after the other. Once they reached the top of the stairs, the challenge of what was ahead hit them both. They stood together looking down the cement stairs to the first landing.

"Can't do it," his father said. "Have to take the elevator."

"We can't. I'm not supposed to be here. Someone will stop us."

His father sighed. "Can't," he said, shaking his head.

"Yes, you can, Dad. Look I'll help you. Leave the cane and walker here and I'll come back for them later." Billy slid the walker away from his father and wheeled it behind him. "I'll walk one step ahead of you and you put your hand on my shoulder for balance. It will be fine."

At that moment, Billy heard a metal door click shut, followed by footsteps on the stairs. "Can't," his father says again.

The footsteps paused, then came quickly. Billy watched an arm grab the stair railing at the landing, and a body round the turn. It was the smoker. He stopped short and stared up at Billy and his father.

"What's going on?" he asked. Billy stared at the smoker, unable to formulate a response. The smoker looked about the same age as Billy. He had dark hair cropped short enough to look like a buzz cut. His name tag said Gerry. "I said, what's going on?" Gerry climbed a few more of the stairs. He reached a hand to his back pocket and pulled out a phone.

"This is my father," Billy said. "I'm taking him home."

Gerry looked at Billy's father. "Is this your son, Mr. Murray?"

There was a pause. Long enough for Billy to wonder what kind of answer his father might be contemplating. Then finally his father spoke. "Yes, it is," he said. "He's taking me home."

The three of them stood looking at each other for a moment.

"I know I'm not supposed to be here," Billy said, "but I decided my father would be better off with me now that the virus is here, and the hands-on care here is limited." Gerry didn't move, his phone still in his hand. "No offense," Billy added quickly. "I know you all mean well here, but you're totally overstretched."

Gerry gave Billy a long look and put the phone back into his back pocket. "Where's your car?"

Billy licked his lips and swallowed, unsure of the intent of the question. "Right near that door," he said, nodding down the stairs.

Gerry reached around to the back pocket on his other side and pulled out a yellow folded-up mask and some gloves. He put on the gloves and mask, then trotted up the remaining stairs to stand next to Billy and his father. "Right," he said to Billy. "Do you know where the sunroom is on the other side of the building?"

Billy shook his head. "No, but I'll find it."

"Drive around there and meet me at the door. I'll take your father down the elevator and out that end of the building." He looked at his watch. "I'm already late, we'll have to be fast."

He stepped behind Billy to grab his father's walker.

"Okay, Mr. Murray. You and I are going to go for a ride. Got it?"

"Okay."

"Chop, chop," Gerry said, looking at Billy. "As long as he can keep his feet off the ground while I push him on the walker, we'll be quick." He handed Billy his father's cane. "Here, you take this."

Billy grabbed the cane and took two steps down before Gerry called back to him. "Hey!"

Billy turned to look over his shoulder, his hand on the steel bannister.

"If we get caught . . ." Gerry paused. "If we get caught, I'll just make something up and take him back to his room."

"Okay," said Billy. Instead of heading down the stairs, he turned fully around to face them. Gerry had already turned and was carefully guiding Billy's father back a step so he could sit on the seat of the walker.

"Why are you doing this?" Billy asked. Gerry didn't respond. He had his hand locked under Billy's father's arm for support, and was watching as Billy's father dropped onto the seat of the walker. He straightened up and leaned in to Billy's father's face. "Okay, Mr. Murray?" His father nodded. Gerry stepped behind the walker and looked over Billy's father's head at Billy.

"If it was my father in here, I'd be doing the same." Before Billy had time to reply, Gerry began turning the walker. "Keep your feet off the ground, Mr. Murray. That's super important."

IT TOOK A VERY long time for Billy to get his father up the three steps from the garage into the house. Billy stood behind his father, his hands ready to catch him if needed, ducking out of the way occasionally when his father swatted his hand behind himself and grumbled at Billy to "leave me alone." When his father reached the top of the stairs, Billy hopped up to stand behind him. His father put his hand on the wall and looked down the hall toward the bathroom at the end.

"That's it, Dad. Just straight ahead now into the bathroom."

His father reached for his walker, which Billy had placed in the hall for him. His shoulders slumped forward as he gripped its handles. "Why?"

"Because you're going to have a shower."

"No." His father rattled the walker a little.

"Yes." Billy stepped out from behind his father and turned his back against the wall so that he could slide past his father and stand in front of him. "Sorry, Dad, but it has to happen. First, because you may be carrying the virus." Billy put his hand on the black strap stretched across the front of the walker and pulled it gently forward so that the wheels started turning. "And second, because, sorry to say it Dad, but you smell. I think it's been a while since they've helped you with a shower at the home, right?"

His father gripped the brake handles to stop the walker. He raised his head and looked at Billy. Billy hoped the feeling of fear he had every time he was this close to his father was going to fade over time. All he could think about was the possibility that his father was shedding the virus with every move, and spreading it with every breath. Billy stared back at him.

"Really, Dad, it's not optional. You have to have a shower."

"No."

"It's a walk-in shower. And I put a chair in there for you. And there's a plastic bin for your clothes. I'm going to put them right into the laundry. I've got some clean clothes and a robe ready for you." Billy felt like he was babbling. His father remained in place. "Just straight down the hall now and into the bathroom," Billy continued.

"No," his father said in the direction of the bathroom. "Don't want to."

"I know you don't. But you have to. You're going to have a shower, Dad. You might have the virus on you. We have to get rid of it. Start fresh. It's why I'm still wearing the mask, and the gloves." He lifted his hands and spread them wide in front of his father's face to emphasize the gloves. "As soon as you have a shower, I can take them off. Then you can sit in the big chair in the living room and watch TV while I have a shower." As he talked, he gently pulled the front of the walker forward again, prompting his father to take a step, then another. "After that I'll make pancakes and we'll have them with Gilbert's maple syrup." At the mention of food his father stopped the walker again and looked at Billy. Billy smiled. "Sounds good, doesn't it? Like you used to make us on Sundays, when we were kids. I still make them for the girls sometimes." His father didn't respond but shuffled forward slowly. Billy kept his hand on the front of the walker to maintain the momentum.

At the bathroom door, Billy took the walker from his father and gave him his cane. "Just a few steps more, Dad," he said. His father held his cane in his right hand and stepped into the bathroom, putting his left hand on the vanity for support. Billy stepped in behind him and suddenly realized he hadn't thought through how he was going to make this work.

The bathroom was small. The two of them standing together made it difficult to maneuver. Billy stood behind his father and reached up to his shoulders. "Let's get this off you first."

His father straightened his back to allow Billy to pull the fleece jacket back and down. They were standing one behind the other, only a few inches apart. As Billy lifted the fleece jacket off his father's shoulders, he saw their reflection in the mirror over the sink on his left. He saw how alike they were. The same length of neck rising from a long back. The same round shaped ears, the same high forehead. The fabric of the fleece his father was wearing was thin, and his trousers hung loosely off his hips. Under the fleece his father wore a short-sleeved shirt buttoned up with the holes mismatched to the buttons so that it hung slightly skewed. Billy tossed the fleece into the sink and reached around his father from behind to unbutton the shirt while his father leaned heavily against the vanity. Billy had trouble with the buttons. They slipped this way and that as he tried to maneuver them with his gloved fingers. His father dropped his cane and swiped his hand at him.

"Stop doing that, Dad, I'm doing my best." Billy managed the buttons finally and slid the shirt off. He reached around again to the top of his father's trousers. When he undid the button, the trousers dropped straight to the ground.

"Have to sit." His father suddenly shuffled forward and swayed. The loose pants at his ankles slid around his feet. The cane on the floor was in the way. Billy grabbed at his father's arms from behind. His father kept moving forward. The two of them jostled and shifted together, his father's body moving with a momentum neither of them could control.

"Okay, okay. Here, sit on the toilet." Billy let go of one of his father's arms and shoved his hand forward to flip the lid down just before his father's body twisted and landed heavily on the toilet seat. His body continued to tilt to the side. Billy grabbed his father's arm and pulled back.

"Ow!" His father turned his head to glare at Billy.

"Sorry, I was just trying to stop you from falling."

"Leave me alone." His father kicked his feet forward but the pants were still tangled around them. He lost his balance and tilted sideways again. Billy grabbed his father's arm to steady him. This time he noticed how little muscle was there and how easy it was to feel the bone.

"Stop it!" His father swatted at Billy and kicked his legs back and forth.

"Dad, this is going to happen. If you just let it happen it will go a lot easier."

"Hah."

The air in the bathroom felt thick, and Billy's mask made him feel like he couldn't take a deep breath. "Honestly, Dad, I was hoping not to have a fight." Billy paused. He tried to force his breath to slow down. "But I want to be clear. You have to have a shower. I'll try to make it as easy for you as possible."

"Forget it." His father's words were getting clearer. It was as if his lips had remembered how to work around the dentures. Or maybe Billy was just getting the hang of how his father talked. Billy sighed. He scooped the clothes out of the sink and dumped them in the plastic bin. He stood up straight and looked at his father.

"Is there something you're worried about, Dad? Some problem about having a shower you're not telling me?"

"No."

"Okay, then, let's get it done."

"No."

Billy fought an urge to threaten his father with a time out, and start counting backwards from three, techniques they used when the girls were little. He wondered what Gerry would think if he showed up at the front door of the care home this evening, pushed his father and his walker through the sliding doors, and walked away.

His father stirred. "Didn't ask for this, you know."

Billy responded without thinking. "Hey! You think I did? I'm just trying to do the right thing here."

His father turned his head toward Billy, but didn't lift it. "No, you're not!" His father's voice was louder this time. The words traveled sideways out of his mouth. For a split-second Billy wasn't sure he heard correctly. But even before that possibility fully registered, Billy felt his blood rise from his chest and rush to his head. He yanked the mask off his face and dumped it into the sink.

"What do you think I'm doing here? What gives you the right

to say what I think? When did you ever once pay attention to what I thought?" Billy felt like the blood in his head was gathered into a ball and was pulsing deep in his brain. "Never. That's the answer to that question. Never."

His father shook his head back and forth, staring at the floor. He was visibly taking a breath as if in an effort to get words. Billy kept going. He had never in his life raised his voice to his father, but now he stood over him and yelled.

"I'm trying to help you. Help. You. Do you get that? And all you can do is criticize. Nothing I do is ever good enough for you. Nothing."

"Not true. Not true." His father shook his head while he spoke.

"You can keep shaking your head but I'm telling you, this is us, Dad. Right here. Me trying to do what I think you want, and you carping on about how it's not good enough somehow."

His father raised his hand to point at Billy and moved his lips as if to say something, but no words came. He shook his head again, his eyes not leaving Billy's face. Billy stared back at his father parked on the toilet seat in his underwear, his hands clasped between his knees. A red mark was forming on his father's arm where he had grabbed him, and he could see an old yellowed bruise below that. Billy felt his heart rate drop and his head clear. He squatted down next to his father. "I'm sorry, Dad. I didn't mean to yell. It just all came pouring out, you know?" His father kept his gaze on Billy and nodded slowly. Billy sighed. "You're tired, aren't you?" He reached out his hand and clasped his father's. Their thumbs curved over each other. Billy gave his father's hand a squeeze for a moment.

"Okay," he said. "Okay." He stood up and stretched his back. "Let's get that shower over with."

They managed the rest in near silence. His father followed Billy's instructions and used the toilet while Billy was out of the room, then he let Billy move him onto the chair in the shower and wash him, then towel him dry. Billy dressed him in one of his T-shirts and a pair of sweatpants. They shuffled out of the bathroom together, Billy's father holding Billy's arm with one hand and his cane with the other.

Billy settled his father into the recliner in the living room and found a channel that was playing *America's Funniest Home Videos*. He left his father there and went back to the bathroom to get the clothes for the laundry. It was only then that he noticed the mask in the sink where he had tossed it earlier and realized he'd forgotten to put it back on while he helped his father with the shower.

When Billy made the pancakes they were light and fluffy and golden brown. Their smell filled the kitchen and drifted across the counter into the living room. For his father, Billy cut two of the pancakes into small squares, then trailed maple syrup in lines back and forth over the resulting pile. They sat in front of the TV, Billy on the couch eating off the coffee table, his father in the recliner with a TV table in front of him. His father ate every little pancake square, stabbing his fork into one after the other and pushing them around the plate to get all the maple syrup. After Billy took the plate and the folding table away, his father fell asleep in the chair, his head turned to the side, his arms tucked up against his chest.

Green River

Andrew C. Peterson

I STOOD AT THE counter of a gas station mini-mart across from a snow-covered field in the middle of nowhere, Illinois. A bottle of seltzer, a bag of chips, and a Slim Jim were in a basket slung over my arm. Leaning on my hickory heartwood cane, I looked out through a large picture window that was once the bay door of an auto shop. When I was a kid I had a summer job in a garage. Now I made my living as a private investigator. Both jobs required me to get my hands dirty fixing things.

The slate gray sky churned overhead. Snow fell at a moderate clip, slowly turning the landscape featureless. I glanced at my watch, reckoning that I still had miles to go. I wasn't sure that the weather would cooperate, even though no one else knew I was coming, and the dead are not concerned with punctuality.

The woman behind the counter was short with ample hips. She had a tattoo on her right hand, pink-tinted hair, and two different-colored eyes, like David Bowie. The nametag on her denim, button-up shirt read "Mandy."

"Will this be all for you today?"

"This'll do," I replied, placing the basket on the counter and resting my hand on the curved top of my cane.

Mandy scanned the items, then placed them in a thin plastic bag.

The basket disappeared behind the counter. The snow fell faster. The wind blew harder. "Storm's picking up," she said.

"Yeah," I said. "The roads are wicked icy right now."

"You're here for the funeral." It wasn't a question.

"What makes you say that?"

"Your accent. Boston. You talk like Mark Wahlberg."

This offended me slightly. "Fair enough," I said, handing her a twenty.

"Did you know him?" asked Mandy.

"Mark Wahlberg? No. We've never met," I replied casually as my shoulders tensed up under my barn coat.

"No, Jimmy Reardon. You served together, I bet," she said.

We met on my second tour of duty. Like me, he joined the Marines after the towers fell. Like any war, combat action was rare. During the quiet, Jimmy and I would talk about everything and nothing. Jimmy grew up here, the son of a Vietnam vet and grandson of a decorated World War II vet. He punctuated sentences with words like "duty" and "honor." The shadow cast over Jimmy by the men in his family loomed large. I was never sure if he meant it or if he was merely parroting the words that he had heard at their knees.

We both loved to read. He'd read Homer in English class. A dog-eared copy of *The Iliad* was with him wherever he went. It was his bible. I preferred *The Odyssey*. Sometimes you had to go to war. Sometimes you just wanted to go home.

"Mister?"

I looked at Mandy again. "We did, yes. We served together."

She considered me more closely. "Which place?"

"The sand." I shifted my weight from one leg to the other and glanced toward the door, my hand held out for the change.

She counted each bill slowly, then placed the bag on the counter.

"Did you see a lot of combat?" Her eyes widened just a bit, like I was going to tell her a great secret.

I didn't. I thought of the roadside bomb that flipped our Humvee. I softened my stance, forcing my shoulders down, releasing the tension in my neck. "I'm guessing that you didn't know Jimmy personally?"

"Nah, I didn't," she said. "I read about him in the local papers," her voice dropping in volume, like she realized she was talking too loud in church. "I guess he was kinda a hermit, although his mama wanted him buried like a hero. It's kinda sad."

"Kinda," I said, grabbing the bag. "Thank you, miss."

"Have a nice day," she replied. "And thank you for your service."

I nodded, hating this platitude more and more every day.

The wind blew strong as I pushed the door open and squinted into the gale. On a rare good day I was able to walk without the cane with only minimal hurt. Today was not a good day. I limped across the parking lot using my cane, armed now with the lunch of champions.

At the car, I threw the bag and my cane on the passenger seat, and fell in behind the wheel. I was grateful for the heat that blasted through the car. The rental car radio was playing Vivaldi. Or maybe it was Bach? I let the notes wash over me.

We were on patrol in 2008. I was in the lead vehicle with Jimmy, Faust, and Dewclaw, who was driving. I was sitting shotgun next to him. Jimmy was on the gunner platform. Faust was in the seat behind Dewclaw, telling some joke about hookers in Fallujah. At least I think it was a joke? You never really knew with Faust.

We had scored a carton of cigarettes. I was smoking. So was Dewclaw, who was laughing loudly at Faust's story. Faust was reaching for his lighter, a cigarette dangled from his bottom lip. He was yelling something.

Noise swallowed me whole.

The hot desert sand rose up to greet me. I focused. The Humvee was upside down. Fire engulfed the wreck. I heard shouts through the thick, black, smoky haze. I tried to stand. I couldn't. I tried again. I howled in pain. Cries from inside the Humvee filled my ears. I smelled barbeque mixed with nicotine. Jimmy stood over me, staring at the vehicle, not moving. We listened to Faust and Dewclaw scream as they burned.

"Help them!" I yelled. My hand was stretched out toward the Humvee in vain, my fingers spread wide.

Shapes ran behind Jimmy. My squad tried to pry the doors open. Jimmy stood there, mute and staring. There wasn't a scratch on him. He just stood there. I blinked through the smoke and gritted my teeth at the pain. "God damn it, soldier! Help your men!" My eyes burned, the pain in my leg was blinding. I couldn't stand. I raised my voice. "Fucking coward! Help your men! That's an order, Sergeant! HELP THEM!"

Jimmy looked at me one last time, turned, and started walking into the desert.

The car jostled as a gust of wind slammed into it. Now back in Illinois, wipers set to high, I drove to the edge of the parking lot that opened onto I-57. Snow swept across the highway from the fields and toward the gas pumps in giant, unrelenting bursts as if shot out of a turbine. The white cloud layer had merged with the snowy surface. The copse of trees had disappeared. The field was gone. For that matter, so was I-57. I couldn't see the road or the lane markers or the road signs. I couldn't see anything. Whiteout.

After a few more seconds only the neon lights in the windows were visible in my rearview mirror. I put the car into reverse and inched toward the store's bright lights. Thankfully mine was the only car in the small lot. I pushed the car door open against the shrieking wind. I stood up, put my head down, dropped my keys in my coat pocket, and walked toward the store, the thin layer of frost on the asphalt forcing measured steps. Mandy was on the other side of the picture window, standing at the counter, watching my progress. Another gust of wind gave me a shove from behind, pushing me toward the door with a stutter step. I planted my feet to pull the door open against the wind.

"Looks like I'll be here for a few," I said, stumbling inside and stamping my cowboy boots on the rubber mat, brushing snow from my shoulders, coat, and blue jeans.

"Looks like."

"Do you have any hot coffee?" I asked while removing my knit cap and shoving it into one of my coat pockets.

"Machine's broken."

"Seriously?"

She arched an eyebrow like a Vulcan. "Seriously."

"Would you like me to take a look at it for you?"

"I know how to fix the machine, mister. It needs a new part. Supposed to be delivered today." She sighed. "Probably tomorrow, though."

Mandy turned to restock the cigarette racks behind the counter while I pulled my phone from my pocket and tapped at the screen, hoping to get a weather update. No signal. I walked closer to the plate-glass window. No signal. I put my phone away. The now-monochrome landscape filled my view. Where once two gas pumps stood underneath an aging metal canopy there was now only relentless and sometimes sideways-flying snow. I watched the storm. My mind wandered.

Later, much later, in a hospital in Germany I learned that some of the guys suffered serious burns trying to get into the Humvee, but it wasn't enough. Faust and Dewclaw burned to death. Jimmy was found hours later, walking through the endless terrain, ripping pages from *The Iliad* and leaving them in his wake. He never went back to the war. Although, truth be told, he never really left it. My left knee took the brunt of the shrapnel that lodged in my body. I never went back to the war, either.

During the long months of my convalescence, the reality of what happened came to me in waves only after I was done assessing the damage, and counting the dead. The horror came after I realized that I somehow survived. The loathing washed over me in my darkest moments when I realized I was grateful to be the one doing the counting and not being counted.

Jimmy was never the same after he came back home. His guilt consumed him. So did mine. I needed him to know that I had misspoken. That it wasn't his fault. My letters were returned unopened. My emails went unanswered. I came here to Illinois to see him. Once. I knocked on his door every day for a week. His mother said he didn't want to see anyone. I left.

My wounds were physical. Mostly. Jimmy's wounds ran much, much deeper. In the end, his wounds ran so deep that no amount of pills or alcohol could touch them anymore. A bullet touches everything.

My hand went into the pocket of my barn coat. I wrapped my hand around my keys and squeezed until the edge of the keys dug into my flesh. I imagined putting my fist through the glass, hoping that my blood and bruises offered in supplication might let me put Jimmy's ghost to rest. I turned back toward the store's interior. Except for the darkened hallway that led to a steel door that was a holdover from when this place was a garage it looked like any other forgettable convenience store.

"Oh my God!"

I turned quickly and followed her gaze outside. I made out the lines of an SUV that fishtailed wildly and slid directly toward the horseshoe that protected the gas pumps. It slammed into the horseshoe with a bang, crumpled the hood, and stopped. The car horn blared into frozen oblivion.

"Wait here," I commanded. I took three long steps and pushed against the door. The wind pushed it back. I pushed harder. I raised my arm to my face against the wind and snow. The horn stopped. All I could see of the SUV were the headlights trying in vain to cut a wedge through the raging snow. Leaning heavily on my cane, I pushed myself toward the headlights. The driver's door was closed but I could see him through the window. He wore a flannel shirt and a baseball hat.

The wind nearly took the door off its hinges as I opened it.

"Hang on!" I yelled over the howling wind, reaching inside. The smell of stale cigarette smoke filled the car. Blood poured from a gash on his forehead into his eyes. He fumbled for the seatbelt. I put my cane over the crook of my left arm, reached inside, and unclipped the buckle with my right hand. It slid away from him slowly. I reached under his arms and guided him to the ground. I steadied him, then reached in and turned the engine off. The wind howled now like a pack of wolves chasing down prey. If he said anything I couldn't hear it.

I put his keys in my pocket and threw his left arm over my right shoulder. My cane dangled from my left arm. The door slammed shut. The wind hurled snow at us from all directions. It stung. I leaned into the storm. We walked slowly, my right arm was around his waist. We were like contestants in a glacial three-legged race. My right leg supported most of my weight, so I leaned on the stranger for added support. Even so, my left leg slipped once, forcing us to stop briefly. We soldiered on. The squall picked up, landing a punch right in the middle of my back. Mandy pushed the door open against the wind. She stepped onto the sidewalk and held it in place. We squeezed by her. The door slammed behind her as she followed us inside. I set the stranger down in a folding chair that she had placed near the counter.

I stamped my feet to get the blood flowing through my leg while I tried to ignore the throbbing in my knee. I simply nodded at her while she unrolled some paper towels. Jimmy once told me that when the wind blew across Lake Michigan, it sliced through you like a cold blade between your ribs. I believed him now.

Mandy opened a bottle of spring water and wet down the paper towels. She removed his baseball hat with one hand and let it drop to the floor next to him. The stranger held the damp clump against his forehead and wiped the blood away, leaving red streaks of war paint across his pale cheekbones. "Keep that there," she said, repositioning his hand over the wound.

He dabbed at it. The skin was torn, but not separated by much. Every time he eased up on the pressure, it bled more. It was a superficial wound that looked much worse than it actually was.

"Hey! Keep pressure on that," Mandy said as she rubbed her wet hands on her pants. "Don't make me tell you again."

"Okay," he muttered. His eyes darted around, trying to get his bearings. "Thanks," he said, glancing at me while red-tinted water streaked down his face.

"Don't mention it." He seemed off-kilter. I would be too, if I just rammed a vehicle into a concrete barrier.

Mandy announced, "I'm going to call 9-1-1. Get an ambulance."

The stranger glanced up. "There's no need to call them. I'm fine."

She retreated behind the counter. "You might be hurt," she said as she picked up the receiver on a wall phone.

"I'm not concussed, if that's what you mean." He laughed unsteadily. "I done worse to myself playing high school football. Been hit lots of times."

He said this with pride, like being knocked around was a badge of honor. I examined him closer. His nose had been broken at some point and never set properly. His red hair poked out at odd angles. He looked at me the same way—from an odd angle.

"It's just a precaution," I said. "That gash is probably nothing but you never can tell."

The stranger eyed Mandy as she dialed. I stepped into his gaze. He glanced away from me, back over his shoulder straight to the SUV.

"My name's Tannhauser. Adrian Tannhauser," I said, as I extended my hand.

He turned back to me and stared for a long second. "Um, I'm Nate. Nate Gibbons." He shook my hand. "Isn't Adrian a girl's name?"

"Haven't heard that since junior high," I replied coolly.

Nate cocked his head slightly and considered my cane. "How'd you hurt yourself?"

"Bowling accident."

"Must've been some accident." Nate snickered. "Does it hurt much?"

"Enough to need the cane," I said, then noticed that the outline of a tear was inked at the corner of Nate's eye. "Nice ink," I said. "Any significance?"

"Uh, yeah, my mama died," he said, squinting out the window. "I remember her this way."

His mama might be dead but I recognized jailhouse ink when I saw it.

"Dammit all," Mandy said, placing the receiver back on its cradle.

"What's the matter?"

"Emergency services closed down. No one's comin' until the storm passes."

Nate exhaled, shifting in his chair, turning it a little back toward the window.

"Makes sense," I said. "They usually won't put first responders at risk out when conditions become unsafe." I turned back to Nate. "No one should be driving in this mess."

"These whiteouts don't last too long," Mandy said. "I've never seen one longer than a half hour or so."

"Thirty minutes isn't long," I said.

Nate repositioned the paper towels on his head. "Can I get a little more water for this?"

"Actually, I have a first aid kit back here. It has some Band-Aids in it." Mandy grabbed the white metal kit from under the counter, opened it, and rummaged through it for a few seconds. She grabbed a couple of bandages and unwrapped the first one as she walked out from behind the counter.

"Will you let me do it?" she asked Nate, holding the bandage up for him to see.

"Much obliged," Nate said.

"That was some quick thinking back there," Mandy said to me as she stuck the first bandage to Nate's forehead.

"All instinct," I replied.

"Still," she said, smiling, "good work."

"Thanks." Mandy worked quickly, like she'd applied a few bandages in her day. Nate fidgeted a bit as she did so. "You smell nice," he said. She ignored him and went a bit faster. Two Band-Aids were firmly in place as Mandy gathered up the bandage wrappers and shoved them in her shirt pocket.

Nate stood up. He had three inches and at least twenty pounds on me. A pretty old scar ran across his neck, and he was wearing a timeworn pair of work boots. I would have bet even money that they were steel-tipped.

Snow and wind slammed into the little building, shaking it fiercely. Nate started to pace. "You got anything to drink? Any coffee?" He glanced outside again.

"No coffee," I replied.

"Really?"

"Really."

"Everybody wants coffee," Mandy muttered as she walked down back toward the refrigerated section. Meanwhile, Nate sat back down in the chair near the door. I leaned with my back against the counter and watched the snow fall behind him. Nate's eyes darted around the store, taking it in, but his gaze always turned back to the SUV.

Mandy returned and handed each of us a soda. Nate grabbed his. After taking mine, I noticed that his chair was now a bit closer to the door.

He opened the bottle, took a big swig, and gagged. "God damn, what is this stuff?"

Mandy laughed. "You aren't from around here, are you?"

"What makes you say that?" he asked quickly.

"Everyone in Illinois knows what Green River soda is," she replied. "In the 1950s only Coca-Cola sold more bottles than Green River. It's a Chicago staple."

"I'm just passing through," he said. "Visitin'."

I twisted the cap off and took a sip. I swallowed and pointed at the bottle. "Like Polar back home but really sweet."

"Yeah it is." Mandy laughed.

I gulped it down, the lime taste washed down my throat easily. Nate took a few more sips in silence.

"What do you do back in Boston, Adrian?" Mandy asked. "It's Adrian, right?"

I nodded. "I'm an insurance adjuster."

"Sounds boring," Nate added, rolling his eyes.

"It is, but it pays the bills," I replied. "What do you do, Nate? Anything exciting?"

"Nothin' much. Landscaping, mostly."

"Not looking to make that first million by the time you're thirty, Nate?" I asked.

"Funny guy, for an insurance adjuster," he said with a snort.

"Do you guys mind if I smoke?" Mandy said, peering at the weather and frowning. "I can't head outside right now."

"I'd prefer you didn't," I replied. "Nate?"

"Filthy habit," he grunted.

"You don't smoke?" I asked, as I finished off my bottle of Green River and placed it on the counter.

"Nope. Causes cancer, you know." Nate placed his mostly full bottle on the floor next to his chair. He stood up again and shrugged as he held the red, damp paper towel in his hand. Mandy gestured to a small trash barrel. He dumped it there.

"Snow sure is takin' its sweet time blowin' over," Nate said to no one in particular. His fingers drummed against his leg.

"It's been near a quarter of an hour now, maybe a bit more," Mandy said. "Can't last much longer."

Nate had his back to me. "What type of car is that you're driving, Nate?"

"It's an SUV."

"I can see that. Who makes it?"

His nostrils flared with his reply. "What difference does it make?"

"None. Just making conversation."

"Snow's letting up," Mandy interjected.

The whiteout ended as suddenly as it had started, like someone had turned off the snow machine on an old movie set.

"Who has my car keys?"

"I have them here," I said, pulling the heavy jumble of metal from my coat pocket. Hanging from the key ring was a miniature TARDIS.

"Can I have 'em back now?"

"Sure." I smiled. "You're a fan of the Doctor?"

"What doctor?"

"*Doctor Who*. The TV show. You're a fan?"

"Oh, I am," Mandy said. "I go to the conventions."

"Yeah, sure," Nate said. "Big fan."

I stepped closer to him, slipping the keys back into my pocket, leaning on my cane. "Who's your favorite character, Nate?"

For the first time he stared directly at me with a hateful gaze that should have had a blade attached to it. He reached fast and pulled a handgun from his waist under his shirt. "Give me my fucking keys," he said as he aimed the Smith & Wesson M&P Shield 9mm at me.

"Uh . . . give him his keys, Adrian," Mandy said, and in a rather off-the-cuff way, like she saw this all the time.

Nate jerked the gun toward her. She shrank back slightly, like a puppy faced with a rolled-up newspaper. She never took her eyes off him, though. Tough girl. I rushed forward. I wanted his eyes on me, not her.

Nate targeted me again. I raised my arms. He smirked. I didn't.

"No one wants any trouble, Nate," I lied. I grabbed the set of keys from my pocket and tossed them to him.

He caught them with his other hand. His eyes filled with manic energy. "I just want to leave, okay?" Nate said. "I don't want any trouble with you people." He took a few slow steps back toward the door.

"You won't get any. Not from us," Mandy said.

"I damn well better not," he said, throwing the door open.

Outside, the landscape was white. My thoughts were black and I saw red. The door closed behind him.

I whipped around, pointed to Mandy, and said, "Get into the back room and barricade the door."

"Why? What are—?"

"Do it, Mandy. NOW!"

She jumped and sprinted toward the back of the store.

"Is there a phone back there?" I yelled after her.

"Yes," she yelled back.

"Call the police again. And don't come out!"

I turned to the door and watched Nate run across the parking lot. He slipped once, going down on one knee but never coming to a stop. He kept a tight grip on his gun as he scrambled up again, but he moved a bit slower now. Nate passed in front of the SUV, barely noticing the damage to the front end. He yanked the door open and climbed into the driver's seat, slamming the door behind him. He dropped the gun on the passenger seat and gripped the steering wheel with his left hand. His right hand worked the keys into the ignition with a quick jerk. The wipers struggled to clear away the heavy snow. Nothing else happened. His arm moved again. The lights dimmed briefly, the wipers moved slowly. The engine stayed quiet.

Nate screamed and pounded on the steering wheel with both hands. His head jerked up with a start. His murderous gaze fell on me. The door to the SUV flew open. Nate got out, his face bright scarlet. The gun was back in his right hand; his left was clenched into a fist. He walked stiffly toward the mini-mart door.

I locked it with a quick flick of the deadbolt. Nate's hate-filled face was separated from my own by only a quarter inch of Plexiglas as he yanked fruitlessly on the door.

"My car won't start!"

"I figured."

"Give me your god damn keys!"

"No." I leaned on my cane.

He looked back at the SUV. As he did I turned the lock again. He turned back to me, pointing the gun level with my gut.

"Give me your god damn keys," he said slowly, raising the gun for emphasis. "I will fucking end you, man, if you don't—"

I shoved the door open, smashing it into his face.

He staggered back, blood falling down from his forehead again. He stumbled on the snowy surface. I followed him, slamming the head of my cane into his stomach, popping the air from his lungs. He bent over in surprise while I knocked the gun from his hand to the ground. He had two choices here: attack me directly or reach for the gun. He reached for the gun. A quick crack from my cane smashed into his teeth. A second crack to his throat meant it would hurt if he swallowed any of those teeth. His hands went to his face to protect it from any more blows. He fell down on the snowy asphalt, moaning in pain.

Tossing my cane aside, I reached down and snatched his gun. I rolled him over onto his stomach and planted my knee firmly on his back.

He strained his head in the direction of the SUV. I did, too, confirming my suspicion that it had Illinois plates.

"Forget it, Nate. Whatever's in there is no longer your concern."

"I'll fucking kill you," he groaned with labored breath through clenched teeth.

I nestled the gun to the back of his head. "Give me just one good reason, Nate, and I will spray your brains all over the snow."

He stopped squirming.

"I know the car is stolen, but what else?"

"Stolen?" he cried. "That's my—"

I nudged the gun again. "Go ahead. Lie to me." I pressed my knee into his back a bit harder. "Illinois plates but you're just passing through," I said. "You don't smoke but the car reeks of cigarettes. And you don't know who the Doctor is but his spaceship is on your key ring."

A muffled banging was coming from somewhere.

I stood up, painfully, with Nate's gun in my hand. My leg throbbed in protest. Another bang. I turned and looked across the parking lot. Another bang. A few solid strikes. The SUV.

I yanked Nate to his feet by his shirt collar and dragged him stumbling across the parking lot to the back of the vehicle. Without the use of my cane I felt each step across the pavement. I gritted my teeth. The banging got louder. I shoved Nate up against the rear door.

I handed Nate the keys. "Open it," I said, my voice barely above a whisper.

He trembled beneath my hand as the door slowly lifted open.

Inside, a young woman, dressed in jeans and a T-shirt with duct tape wrapped around her wrists, was crumpled on the floor, partially obscured by a tarp and blankets. She stared at us through tangled hair, wide-eyed like a caged animal. Tape was also wrapped tight over her mouth and around her head. She screamed into it.

Her cry swallowed me whole. I slammed Nate's head into the doorframe with two quick strokes. He slipped on the ice and fell to the ground. I followed him down and dropped the gun. I landed on his chest, my legs pinning his arms to his side. I rained blow after savage blow into his face.

For this girl.

Jimmy is dead.

For Dewclaw.

I survived.

For Faust.

I was grateful to be the one doing the counting.

For Jimmy.

And not being counted.

For me.

And I hated myself for thinking it.

I stopped only after I heard the satisfying crack of the cartilage in his nose smashing to pieces beneath my fist warmed by his blood. Sirens that wailed in the near distance, getting closer, smothered Nate's pitiful groan.

I stood up and reached for the army knife on my belt to cut the duct tape. My hand was covered in blood and snot as I reached toward the woman in the SUV, my fingers spread wide. "Please, let me help you."

Top of the World

Victoria Ferenbach

"HONEY, CAN I HAVE the binoculars?" Joan asked from the rear seat of the Range Rover.

Ted unlooped the strap from around his neck and passed the binoculars back over his shoulder to his wife. "You don't really need them," he said." Look at those big guys. Almost close enough to touch."

No more than twenty feet away, a pair of enormous tusked elephants padded across the savanna with ponderous grace. Everyone in the vehicle watched in rapt silence. Only the repetitive clicking of a camera shutter broke the stillness.

"For God sakes, Bunny," Ted said. "Knock it off."

Bunny lowered her Nikon with its long lens. She inclined her head a fraction of an inch toward Ted on the seat next to her. "Anyone else have a problem?" she asked. When no one replied, she raised the camera again.

Ted glared at her then turned back toward the elephants.

There were five of them traveling together, longtime friends from summers on Fire Island. They had come to Kenya for the annual wildebeest migration and only that morning had witnessed hundreds of the shaggy brown creatures wading across a shallow river, tripping and falling and splashing their way to the other side.

Now their vehicle was parked in the middle of the Maasai Mara, a vast plain that seemed to go on forever. As they watched the elephants amble toward the horizon, they could also see in the distance a line of humpbacked wildebeests moving slowly along the far ridge, silhouetted against the blue sky like paper cutouts.

"Wow," Bunny said. "That's a shot." She focused the lens and the shutter clicked.

Joan reached forward and patted her husband on the shoulder. He shrugged her hand away but didn't say anything.

Once the elephants were well out of sight, their jovial guide Sam called from behind the wheel. "Ready to roll, folks?"

"Ready," they answered.

Sam put the Land Rover in gear. "Okay, let's go find ourselves a leopard."

They bumped along over the uneven terrain heading toward the wooded edge of the plain. The Mara surrounded them, green and vast. "It feels like the top of the world," Natalie said from her seat in the back next to Joan. As they drove past a herd of grazing impala, the lithe copper-colored animals began to disperse. "Look at them run," she said. "Graceful as ballerinas."

Sam pulled the vehicle into a clearing surrounded by dense green bushes and a cluster of trees. He cut the engine and signaled for them to be quiet. Nothing moved as they sat watching in silence. Suddenly a flock of small birds burst out of the tallest tree, soaring up and away, their iridescent blue-green wings dazzling against the azure sky.

"Gorgeous," Bunny said. "What are they?"

"Starlings," Sam said. "Superb starlings to be exact. Their wings and orange bodies make them hard to miss."

As the brilliantly colored birds disappeared over the grassy plain, the travelers trained their attention back toward the undergrowth.

A small silvery-grey monkey with a black face scrambled up a tree, chattering all the way. Then everything went still.

"You're sure there's a leopard in there?" Natalie asked, peering toward the bushes.

"Be patient," Sam said.

Brian, who was sitting in front with Sam, saw it first. He pointed to a tree on the left. "Look up," he whispered.

"Oh my God," Bunny said.

Sam put a finger to his lips.

The large spotted cat was draped along a high branch like an oversized beanbag. His handsome, triangular face was turned toward them. His eyes were closed and his tail hung down, thick as a rope.

Bunny glanced sideways at Ted, holding her camera still in her lap.

After a few minutes, the animal stretched a paw forward and shifted his position. His tail twitched and began to swing back and forth in a lazy cadence. Then in one swift movement, he rose to his feet, balancing his sinewy body on the branch as easily as if he was standing on the ground. He arched his back and yawned.

Sam held up a hand.

After several seconds, without ever looking in their direction, the big cat leapt to the ground and sprang off into the woods.

They sat staring at the opening in the brush where he had vanished.

"That leopard was huge," Brian finally said. "What if he had charged us?"

Sam grinned. "Not a chance. The animals only see the vehicle. That's why we don't move or talk. That big guy was probably heading down to the river to shop for dinner." He looked at his watch. "Speaking of dinner, time to head back to camp."

He turned the key in the ignition.

"Thanks, Sam," Joan said. "That was awesome."

"Just doing my job," he said with a broad smile as he backed into the clearing and turned the vehicle around.

It had grown dark by the time they arrived at the mobile camp set up by the outfitter for the migration. A dozen staff members, many of them Maasai wearing red patterned shawls and beaded belts, stood at the side of the parking area holding lighted torches. The five travelers clambered out of the vehicle with packs and hats and water bottles in tow. Sam helped the women maneuver the long drop to the ground.

The camp manager, a tall black Kenyan wearing khaki shorts and a matching shirt with the outfitter's logo on the pocket, stepped forward from the group. "Welcome back," he said, bowing slightly. "I can see by your faces that you've had an exciting day. Dinner is at seven. That should give you time to shower and change. Drinks first by the fire whenever you're ready."

Several of the young Maasai stood waiting to accompany them to their tents. As animals were known to wander into the camp at night, they had been advised not to walk alone after dark.

Bunny was the first to move. "See you in a few," she said as she turned to the closest of the men. He raised his torch and they set off together down the path toward her tent at the far end of the campsite. Although nervous at first about the remote location, once she learned that Sam would be staying in the tent just beyond hers, she relaxed. He had laughingly told her not to worry about any strange night noises unless she heard him screaming.

A tall thin Maasai youth in black sandals and a large square of red-and-white checked fabric thrown over his shoulder stepped forward with a flashlight.

Natalie looked over at Joan and Ted. "After you," she said.

"We're in the first tent," Joan said. "We don't need an escort. You two go ahead."

"Okay thanks," Natalie said. "See you at the campfire."

She and Brian fell in beside the young Maasai and they headed off toward their tent in the middle of the camp. Torches had been placed at intervals along the edges of the path as guideposts although the sky that night was clear and starry and a half moon floated almost directly above them.

The tents were set up to allow for maximum privacy, not too close to one another and facing in different directions. In front of each, two chairs and a table were placed under a canvas canopy. Lights glimmered around the edges of the tent flaps and as Natalie and Brian strolled along with their escort they could hear the sounds of murmured conversation and the splash of bucket showers coming from within.

"Let's just drop our stuff," Natalie said when they reached their tent. "We can shower after dinner."

"Good idea," Brian said. He tapped his watch then held up three fingers. "Three minutes?" The slim Maasai nodded.

Joan and Ted's tent was near the head of the sandy footpath that wove through the campsite. At this early hour, with the torches lit, they could walk to it on their own. When they got there, Ted unzipped the canvas flap and they ducked inside.

Two battery lamps, one on either side of the bed, illuminated the cozy interior. Another lit the bathroom and shower area that was curtained off at the back. Their duffle bags rested on folding stands opposite the bed. Plastic hangers for shirts and jackets hung from a dowel up in the corner alongside a canvas panel with pockets for shoes.

Ted kicked off his sneakers, stretched out on his side of the bed, and closed his eyes.

"You okay?" Joan asked.

"Yup."

"Sure?"

"Yup."

Joan unzipped her khaki vest and tossed it on top of her duffle. She took a small plastic container from the bedside table, opened it, and tipped two yellow tablets into her palm. She poured water into a glass from a bottle with a band of red-and-green Maasai beads around its neck, then popped the pills into her mouth, took a drink, and swallowed.

She looked over at Ted who had rolled onto his side facing away from her. She sighed and began to unbutton her shirt. "I'll shower first."

Standing under the gush of hot water falling unevenly from a bucket overhead, she let herself cry for the first time all day. The words her doctor had spoken only three weeks before rang in her ears. When she had told Ted the news he didn't want to believe it. It was obvious to her that he was still denying the truth. His crankiness gave him away.

She stepped out of the shower and took a towel from a nearby hook. After drying herself, she tiptoed naked back into the main area of the tent and rummaged around in her duffle for clean underwear and a new set of clothes. Once she was dressed, she ran a comb through her damp hair and pulled it back into a ponytail.

"Ted," she said.

The only answer was a muttered groan.

"If you want a shower you have to get up now."

He groaned again but didn't move.

Taking her journal and a pen from the table, she sat down on the bed. She flipped the notebook open to a new page and began to write, letting Ted lie motionless next to her until it was time to go to dinner.

A PORTABLE BAR HAD been set up near the entrance to the clearing where folding canvas chairs were arranged in an arc on the far side of the campfire.

Brian fixed two gin and tonics and handed one to Natalie. "Cheers, darling." He draped his arm over her shoulders as they walked around the fire to the empty row of chairs.

"I'm worried about Ted," he said as they sat down in the middle two chairs.

Natalie frowned. "He seems so angry."

Brian reached for her hand. "Listen, if you ever got a diagnosis like that, I'd be angry too."

They sipped their drinks and watched the flickering fire. Muffled voices and the occasional clang of a pot drifted toward them from the cook tent nearby. A skinny Maasai boy poked at a log with a stick sending a spray of sparks into the night sky. He looked over at them and grinned.

"If it was me," Natalie said, "you might be angry but you would still be sweet and caring, not a pain in the ass like Ted."

Brian set his glass into the chair's canvas pocket and leaned forward, elbows on knees, clasping his hands together. He looked down at the ground. "Ted's hurting. He needs our support as much as Joan does. I'll try to have a talk with him."

Bunny appeared on the other side of the campfire, stopping at the bar to pour herself a vodka. She had changed out of her day clothes into skinny black pants and a white shirt. A turquoise pashmina was draped over one shoulder.

"You're looking very elegant tonight," Natalie said. She peered down at her own rumpled tan pants and shirt. "What can I say, we wanted a drink."

"No excuses required," Bunny said. "Especially from you, miss fashion editor lady."

"I have to admit it's a relief to be away from all that," Natalie said.

Brian raised his glass. "To being on safari."

Bunny made her way around the fire and sat down next to him. "Wasn't that leopard gorgeous? I was dying to get a shot of him but I thought Ted might explode."

"I think we need to cut him some slack," Brian said.

"You're probably right," Bunny said. "But how come he never barks at you two?"

Brian chuckled. "Hah. Not with our little point-and-shoots."

"I'm still glad they didn't cancel," Bunny said. "It's good for Joan to be here with us. She's very brave."

The fire had settled into a ripple of low flames that warmed the evening air and lit up the small open space like a stage. The surrounding foliage was dark and dense and mostly silent except for the occasional rustle of some small animal in the bush or a waft of breeze through the trees.

"Sam is such an amazing guide," Natalie said. "He knew just where to find that sleeping leopard."

"I wonder if those people in the other vehicle got to see him," Bunny said.

"We did, as a matter of fact," a man said from the far side of the fire. He was tall and thin with blond hair almost to his shoulders. He stopped at the bar then strolled around toward them carrying a glass of red wine.

"I'm Jeremy," he said smiling down at them. "Didn't get here until this morning." He held his glass up to the firelight then took a drink. "Flight complications."

After introductions and handshakes he lowered himself into the chair next to Bunny and stretched out his long legs.

Bunny eyed him from the side. "Are you here alone?" she asked, running a hand through her curly blonde hair.

"I'm with my partner," he said. He craned around to look at them. "Is it just the three of you?"

"We're five actually," Natalie said. "Our friends Joan and Ted should be along soon."

Jeremy looked at his watch. "Almost dinner time." He sniffed the air. "Something smells wonderful."

A few minutes later, Sam appeared over near the bar. "Dinner's on, folks," he said. "Bring your drinks if you want but watch your step. The path to the dining tent's a bit uneven. I'll go ahead and meet you up there."

They finished their drinks then Jeremy led the way up the slope with Bunny, Natalie and Brian picking their way in single file behind him. When they reached the dining tent, Jeremy moved aside.

"Ladies," he said sweeping his arm toward the entrance.

Bunny went in first. "I've just died and gone to heaven," she squealed as soon as she got inside.

"I'll second that," Natalie said, one step behind her. "Wow."

The inside of the tent glowed with the flickering light from a row of votive candles placed along the center of a long narrow table set for eleven. Interspersed at random between the candles were a large ostrich egg, a convoluted fragment of bone, and a spiky bit of wood resembling a bird. Red cotton napkins were twisted into tall cones and plates of beet salad waited at each place.

A serving table, also lit with candles, was set against the rear wall. Bottles of wine and pitchers of water stood at one end, extra glasses and serving utensils on the other. On both sides of the tent, canvas flaps had been unrolled and lowered over the horizontal screened panels to keep out the increasingly cool night air.

Joan and Ted were already seated at the table in the two chairs closest to the entrance.

"Sorry we missed drinks," Joan said, turning to look up at her friends. "Somebody took a little nap." She winked and tilted her head toward Ted.

"Have a seat anywhere you like, folks," Sam said.

Natalie and Brian sat down across from Joan and Ted. Bunny pulled out the chair next to him.

"Good evening all," Sam said from his seat at the far end of the table. A short, robust Kenyan with a broad smile and dark twinkling eyes, he radiated warmth and good humor. "For those of you who just arrived today, I'm Sam." He extended his hand toward a heavy-set dark man with a mustache at the opposite end. "And this is J.P., my esteemed colleague."

"Hello everyone," J.P. said. "Greetings to Sam's people and welcome again to my group. We saw some awesome animals today but I guarantee there will be plenty more tomorrow. Now please relax and enjoy your dinner."

Bunny turned to her left and looked at Ted. His shirt was rumpled and a wayward cowlick of brown hair stuck up at an angle on the top of his head.

"We missed you at drinks," she said.

"I dozed off while Joan was in the shower," he said. "She didn't wake me until five minutes ago." He leaned toward her. "Had a few nips from my flask though."

"Is Joan feeling okay?" she whispered.

"Absolutely," he said. "She has more energy than I do." He looked into the distance for a moment and started to say something then waved his hand in the air as if brushing away the thought.

Bunny picked up a bottle of South African chardonnay from the table in front of her and held it up to him. "May I?" she asked.

He nodded. "Fill her up."

After pouring wine into both their glasses she turned and offered the bottle to the person on her right, a grey-haired man with a boyish face. "White wine?"

"Thanks," he said, taking the bottle from her. "I'm Jay."

"Bunny," she said lifting her glass. "Cheers."

Natalie caught her eye from across the narrow table and pointed to the ostrich egg. "You should take a picture," she said.

Bunny's mouth turned down. "No camera." She leaned toward Natalie and whispered. "Need to keep the peace."

"I heard that," Ted said.

Bunny laughed. "Okay, mister grumpy, what if we negotiate a truce?"

"I'll drink to that," he said. He looked down the table. "Pass me that bottle."

Joan was sitting on the other side of her husband. She watched as he refilled his glass to the brim then leaned close and said something in his ear.

"Mind your own goddamn business," he said, lifting the glass to his lips and gulping down half its contents.

Bunny turned to Jay. "So where are you and your friends from?"

"Jeremy and I are based in London right now. We're working on a show in the West End."

The tall blond man next to him leaned forward and smiled. "Hello again."

Jay pointed to the couple across the table. "Those two run a restaurant in San Francisco. We just met them today. They're newlyweds."

He took a sip of wine. "You?"

"We're all from New York," she said. "I'm in the city. The other four live in Brooklyn."

The clinking of a spoon on glass interrupted them. "Before I forget," Sam said. "A quick heads up for tomorrow morning. Five thirty wake-up. If you want earlier, tell us tonight. Coffee and tea available here at six. Vehicles loaded and rolling at six thirty." He looked around. "Any questions?"

No one spoke and Sam continued. "We'll stop around nine for a picnic breakfast and plan to get back to camp for lunch sometime around noon." He looked down the table. "What'd I miss?"

J.P. shook his head. "Not a thing."

Two young waiters in khaki pants and white T-shirts made their way around the table, removing the salad plates before placing dishes of grilled chicken in front of each diner. A third man checked the wine bottles and replaced the empties with fresh ones.

"Is there any red?" Ted asked.

The waiter brought a bottle of pinot noir from the serving table and set it in front of him. Before he could pick it up, Joan reached over and grabbed it.

Ted flushed. "What the hell?"

"Hey buddy," Brian said from across the table. "Early call tomorrow. Don't want to be hung over for those animals, do we?"

Ted glared at him. "You and Joan on the same fucking team or something?"

Joan put her hand on Ted's arm but he shook it off. "If I want another glass of wine," he said, "I'll damn well have another glass of wine." He lunged for the bottle.

Joan slid it farther away from him toward the end of the table.

Ted pushed himself halfway up out of his chair and lurched sideways across his wife. She raised both hands and tried to shove him away but he kept straining past her toward the bottle, nearly collapsing in her lap.

"Back off, Ted," Brian said. "You're going to hurt her."

"Sit down," Joan said still pushing at him. "You're being ridiculous."

Ted ignored them both as he struggled to stay upright, bracing himself with one hand on the arm of Joan's chair and one on the table.

J.P. stood up. He looked over at the tallest of the waiters. "Give me a hand here, Batu."

As the two men moved toward Ted, a trumpeting roar thundered through the tent. Seconds later, the whole side of the canvas behind Brian and Natalie billowed inward as though something heavy rested against it.

At the same moment, Ted lost his balance and fell forward, landing facedown on the table, pinning Joan in her chair.

"Oh, my God," Bunny shrieked.

Brian was on his feet. "What the hell?"

Jeremy jumped up so fast that his chair fell over backwards.

Sam raised a hand. "Sit down and stay calm," he said. "It's just an inquisitive elephant paying us an evening visit."

"Elephant!" Jeremy croaked.

"Do you have a plan?" Brian asked, looking over his shoulder at the bulging canvas.

"Yes," Sam said. "The plan is to stay right where we are. We are perfectly safe inside the tent. Our visitor will move on in a few minutes and the night men will let us know when he's left the camp." He looked over at Ted, whose upper body was still folded over the table with his face pressed into the surface. "Meanwhile," Sam said nodding to J.P. "Let's take care of our friend there."

J.P. and the waiter lifted Ted off of Joan's lap and set him on the ground behind the table. His nose was bloody and there were several small cuts and scratches on his face. One of the other waiters brought over a first aid kit. He crouched by Ted's side and began to carefully wipe away the blood and debris.

Jay and Jeremy and the honeymoon couple huddled together at the far end of the tent next to the serving table. Brian and Natalie remained frozen in their chairs holding hands.

Bunny slid over next to Joan and put an arm around her. When Joan attempted to brush away the crushed pieces of chicken and bits of broken china on the table in front of her, Bunny reached over and pulled her hand back.

"Don't," Bunny said. "You'll cut yourself."

The tent continued to buckle inward and they could hear the big animal's labored breathing and the rasp of his hide chafing against the canvas. Then very gradually the side of the tent began to flatten out. The breathy grunts diminished and were soon replaced by the heavy crunch of retreating footfall and the snapping of twigs and branches as the elephant heaved off into the night.

It took a minute before anyone moved. Then Jeremy and Jay returned to their places and the honeymoon couple sat down.

Brian leaned across the table. "Joan, are you okay?"

She nodded.

"Are you sure?" Natalie asked. "I'll get you some water."

"Just sit for a minute," Bunny said.

Joan looked at each of her friends. "I'm fine," she said. "It's my husband who's not."

She pushed back her chair and stood up, brushing a stray piece of chicken off her pants. She turned away from the table and took a step over to where Ted lay on the ground.

She remained standing while the young waiter kneeling next to Ted finished cleaning his face and neck. After he had gathered the bloodied bits of cotton and gauze into a plastic bag, he rose to his feet.

"Thank you," she said.

She knelt down next to her husband and reached for his hand. He opened his eyes and looked up at her for a long moment. "I'm so sorry," he whispered.

"I know," Joan said. She kissed the top of his head.

The others remained sitting at the table and gradually began talking quietly to each other. Sam and J.P. had moved to the front corner of the tent and at the sound of approaching footsteps, Sam unzipped the flap. He peered through the opening and motioned for J.P. to follow him.

"We'll be right back," he said over his shoulder. "The night guards are here."

The two men slipped through the opening and out into the dark. After several minutes of muted and animated conversation, unintelligible to those waiting inside, Sam stuck his head back in the tent.

"All clear, folks. Everything is okay."

An excerpt from the novel-in-progress, *Vengeance*.

Under Pressure

Alyce Werdel

JEFF FOLLOWS THE GERMAN uphill through the cool, dense forest. Pine needles crunch under his boots. He glances up at the trees silhouetted in murky gray against the phosphorous green night vision lenses. Narrow slices of dark sky appear between the branches. They're closing in on the peak.

At the top, where the woodland abruptly ends, the German veers left and leads them north along the crest of the mountain. Jeff slips his thumbs under the padded straps on his backpack and lifts them a few inches off his aching shoulders, providing temporary relief. They've been hiking through these rugged mountains in southwestern Albania most of the night. According to Uwe—former East German Stasi, now German military with a side gig as hacker extraordinaire—they have less than an hour remaining. Jeff has to admit, Uwe seems to know what he's doing. And as former CIA Special Ops and current head of the Agency's Cyberwarfare Division, Jeff recognizes competence when he sees it.

But that's not his primary focus. He slips his fingertips under his goggles and presses them against his eyelids for just a moment. He can't get that photo of his kids out of his mind's eye. Clara and Evan sitting cross-legged on a dirty wooden floor, hands bound behind their backs. White rags stuffed in their mouths and held in place with duct tape. Both are leaning forward, holding their hands away from the splintering wall behind them. Clara's chin is thrust upwards, her eyes glowering into the camera. And Evan. His eyes are as big as saucers, staring above the lens at the person holding it. It was all the motivation Jeff needed. He'd comply with Uwe's demands and install the CIA malware. But he'll figure out what this group is planning. And a way to screw it up.

Jeff slides his fingers out and readjusts his goggles. The kids are still alive, he reminds himself. All is not lost.

But then he stiffens. Horror seeps into his thoughts, clouding his vision. If those assholes do anything to Clara . . . he'll fucking kill them, slowly and painfully. Jeff glares at Uwe's back. He fantasizes about lunging at the German, grabbing him by his wide shoulders, and shoving him over the side. Then watching his tall, thin frame roll and bump over thorny bushes and jagged rocks until it lands in a crumpled, twisted heap at the base of the mountain. The potential satisfaction is almost too much to resist. But then he remembers the terms: if the mission isn't successful, regardless of reason or fault, his kids die. And he's seen what this group is capable of. They'll follow through. So he trudges on, following Uwe under the tree line along the ridge.

Sounds of night surround them: chirping, hooting, howling. But when Jeff hears light footfalls scamper through scrub brush on the right, he freezes. He turns and scans the hillside, searching for a four-legged predator. Or a pack of them. All he sees are low-lying bushes on a steep slope lined with vertical crevices. The mountainside descends a hundred yards to a valley divided into neat strips of crops. A third of the way across, the quiet farmland is interrupted by fifty well-lit acres of fenced cement buildings and steel pipes, burning an eerie green through his goggles. Their target. A compressor station on the Trans Adriatic Pipeline that transports natural gas originating in Azerbaijan and shoots it downstream through Albania, under the Adriatic, and into Italy. And from there, further into Western Europe.

"Over here." Uwe gestures toward a large, smooth boulder firmly embedded in the earth under a clump of fir trees. It faces east, down the mountainside and over the valley below. "This is a good vantage point to review our plan of attack."

"You mean *explain*, not review, and it's *your* plan of attack. It'd better be good. Fucking good. I don't intend to spend the rest of my days in an Albanian jail because of your sloppiness." Jeff swings his pack off and rolls his shoulders.

Uwe sits on the rock and lets his pack slide off behind him. "This will be the best-planned mission you have ever been part of." He cracks his neck from side to side.

"Doubtful." Jeff takes a seat on Uwe's right and looks out to the compressor station. The goggles illuminate two hundred yards into the distance. Beyond that the night sky and everything under it is swallowed in complete darkness.

Jeff sets his pack on his lap. He catches a glimpse of their legs draped over the side of the boulder. He realizes it would be difficult for someone to tell them apart from behind. Close in age, mid-forties, they share a similar tall, athletic build. Both are wearing the same black tactical pants, black waterproof jacket, black knit cap, and black Salomon hiking boots. They're even carrying the same black backpack.

But from the front they are easily distinguishable. Uwe raises his goggles and wipes the sweat off his forehead with the neckline of his shirt, pushing aside loose strands of white blond hair, which could never be mistaken for Jeff's wavy brown hair. A jagged scar runs from Uwe's right temple to his jawline. And frown lines firmly embedded between his brows give the impression that he's perpetually pissed off.

"You see the mouth of that crevice over there?" Uwe points to his left. "That is our path down."

"The one that looks like a luge track without any turns?"

"Correct. It is deep and narrow. Provides excellent coverage from prying eyes."

"What prying eyes? Seems like we're alone out here." Jeff examines the area below for lights or homes, but the only sign of life is the compressor station.

"The main town, Bilisht, is on the other side of the valley. You cannot see it from here. But below us, near the foot of the mountain, there are small clusters of homes. See that grouping of evergreen trees? In there."

Jeff adjusts his lenses and zooms in on the crevice. He traces it down the mountainside into the thicket, where he makes out roof shingles between the branches. He loses sight of the crevice amongst the trees, but picks it up again below the thicket where it continues down the hillside another fifteen yards. It ends at a dirt road running along the base of the mountain.

Uwe continues. "We cross that dirt road. From there we have no cover. We must run through two grain fields. About 120 meters. When we reach the fruit orchard bordering the west side of the station, we stop and regroup."

Jeff rests his elbows on his knees and holds his head in his hands. His gaze slides from the wood shingled rooftops, across the dirt road, over the grain fields, and to the orchard.

Uwe wags his finger. "No speaking. No rustling the bushes. Absolute quiet the entire way."

Jeff peers at the target. Like the fields, it's laid out on a north-south axis. A narrow road cuts through the orchard providing the only access to the facility. Tall floodlights are spaced evenly outside the perimeter.

"They'll have cameras surrounding the station," Jeff says.

Uwe nods. "They are mounted on the light poles outside the fence line."

"I assume you have a plan to deal with that?"

"Naturally."

Jeff studies the site, committing it to memory. Five large windowless cement buildings housing the compressors run north to south through the midline of the station. Behind them, on the eastern side, the station yard houses pipes transporting natural gas through filters, coolers, and other heavy machinery on its way into and out of the compressors. A mobile home, storage shed, and entrance gate border the western side of the facility.

"Where's the industrial control center? In one of the compressor buildings?"

"No. It is in the technical and control building, which is the caravan, to the west of the compressors. The engineer on duty also sits in there."

"And you're certain they have a Siemens ICS? That's the system I've got the login info for. If we get in there and find they've got an Emerson, for example, we're shit outta luck."

"Positive. It is Siemens." Uwe pauses. And then decides to continue. "How did the CIA acquire Siemens's top secret login information for techs who service the system?"

"Our hackers are the best." Jeff examines the beige trailer situated across from the southernmost compressor. Its front window, assuming it has one, would provide a clear view of all five buildings. Jeff's gaze moves south to the storage shed that lies between the trailer and the entry gate. He maps the path to their target. "So we pass through the gate, which I hope you also have a plan for. Then we head to the storage shed on the left and scoot along its western wall, where we're fully covered. The engineer cannot see us there. But we'll have to dash through that open area between the shed and the trailer—looks to be about thirty yards?"

Uwe nods. "Correct."

"How'll we break into the trailer *and* evade the engineer?"

Out of the corner of his eye, Jeff detects Uwe's gloved hand lightly pass over the gun holstered to his leg.

Jeff flips up his lenses and turns to face the German. "No. Don't say you're going to take him out. That's like ringing an alarm in the main control center, announcing we're planning a cyber attack. They'll know exactly why someone would break into a compressor station. It'll be shut down immediately." Jeff rubs the heel of his hand against his forehead. "Please, no killing."

Uwe rolls his icy blue eyes and presses his thin lips together. "Calm down. We enter the caravan through the back door after the engineer leaves through the front. On his rounds."

"When's that?"

"Every two hours on the half hour, he inspects the facility for any malfunction the sensors do not pick up. We hit the 2:30 a.m. patrol." Uwe pulls his jacket sleeve up and glances at his left wrist. "It's 1:33 now."

"How long does the patrol take?"

"Thirty minutes."

"Does he always follow the same route?"

"Yes. He walks straight out the front door and starts at the southernmost building. He makes his way north. Then he walks around back to the station yard and inspects the piping, filtering, and cooling systems behind each building. He works his way south and then returns to the caravan."

"So we have twenty-five minutes to get in, find the industrial control panel, unlock it, let the software update run, and get the hell out?"

Uwe holds his hand out and rotates it side to side. "Meh. Twenty is better."

"Of course it is. Doesn't mean it's doable."

"I have faith in you."

"You going to tell me what this is all about? Germany needs natural gas. Why would you take out a source?"

"As I have said several times, you are on a need-to-know basis. And you don't need to know."

Jeff lowers his goggles. He didn't expect a forthcoming response. But he'll keep prodding and needling. Hoping to goad Uwe into proving how much smarter he is than the CIA man. And giving up some useful information in the process.

"Please tell me we don't return the way we came." Jeff slides down the boulder. His boots land on damp mulch.

"No. Our driver meets us afterwards at preset GPS coordinates. Besides, backtracking would be dangerous. If we trip an alarm, we must get far away." He unzips his pack and pulls out a black nylon balaclava. He shakes it in front of Jeff's face. "Gear time. Put yours on, too. There could be cameras inside that are not connected to the exterior system."

Jeff takes off his goggles and knit cap. "What do you mean, *could be*? You don't know?" He retrieves his mask from his pack and tugs it over his head. Then he puts on the cap and straps the goggles over it.

"I could not find any evidence of interior cameras. But I prepare for surprises."

"That's the difference between you and me. I don't leave room for surprises." Jeff pulls on his tactical gloves and flexes his fingers a few times. The stretch nylon grips his fingers perfectly, allowing for maximum dexterity.

"And it's time to put our equipment in place. You'll need shoe covers and your tools." Uwe removes a pair of blue disposable shoe covers, a white plastic card-key, computer cables, and his phone. He deposits each item into a different pocket lining his pant legs.

Jeff follows suit. He retrieves a black case from his backpack about the size of a paperback novel. He unzips it and removes a penlight, tension wrench, various lock needles, and the battery-operated lock pick. He zips the shoe liners, the pick lock tools, and the penlight into separate pockets.

Uwe swings his pack over his shoulders and buckles the waist and chest straps. He stretches his arms overhead, twisting from side to side as though he's warming up for a track meet. Then he turns around to face Jeff. He jabs his finger in Jeff's chest and says, "*Keep your shit together*, as you Americans like to say. Remember the consequences of failure."

Jeff swipes Uwe's hand away. "*He who eats fire shits sparks*, as you Germans like to say. Remember, this is your plan and it presents risks beyond my control."

Uwe mutters something unintelligible under his breath and turns toward the crevice. Jeff follows him into the opening, about ten feet deep and four feet wide. Low-lying thorny shrubs and tall grasses scrape against their tear-resistant pants as they tread downhill. Once they get their bearings, they pick up their speed.

About halfway down, the tip of Jeff's right boot catches on the pointed edge of a rock, propelling him downhill. Instinctively he folds at the waist to lower his center of gravity. Heat flashes through body. His hands reach toward the walls on either side, searching for something to grip onto. But all he finds is soft dirt. He digs his gloved fingers in and drags them along the edge, trying to slow his downward momentum.

His feet thrash through the bushes, catching on branches and further throwing him off-balance. He's tumbling headfirst toward Uwe's back, when the German spins around and throws his arms in front to catch him.

"Shit," Jeff mumbles, as he slides into Uwe's outstretched hands.

"Idiot. Pay attention!" Uwe snaps, shoving Jeff off him.

"Prick. Fuck off," Jeff replies. After nearly ten years of sitting behind a desk, he is far from the peak physical condition he was in when he was Special Ops. Mountain biking and yoga don't cut it. He wipes the back of his sleeve across his forehead. For the sake of his family, he hopes the more specific technical skills required for the task ahead aren't stale as well.

They continue downhill, a little slower now. About two-thirds of the way, the shrubbery and grass underfoot give way to loose rocks and dirt. And the crevice walls gradually erode to shoulder height, no longer providing adequate cover. When they reach the cluster of homes, they crouch over to keep their bodies below the line of sight.

The ground becomes less and less stable with each step. Jeff rises up and peers through the trees to the quiet stucco houses set back thirty yards on both sides. Fissures run at odd angles along the exterior walls, revealing the original stone underneath. He studies the windows for faces and light but sees only thin white curtains over wood-framed glass.

"Uwe," Jeff whispers, "let's climb out of this crevice. It's steep and filled with loose dirt. There's more ground cover above. We'll have better footing."

"*Nein!*" Uwe hisses, continuing downhill. "Sidestep and hold onto the walls if you must, *Fräulein*. We can't risk—"

The ground below Uwe gives way. "*Scheiß!*" His feet slip out from under him. He lands on his back. With his arms glued to his sides and his head propped up, he slides on his backpack like a tobogganer on bumpy ice. He digs his boot heels into the earth, kicking up dust.

Eventually he skids to a halt twenty-five feet below. An avalanche of rocks and dirt cascade down around him and land in a heap on the road below.

Jeff peers over the crevice wall, searching the windows to see whether Uwe's slip and slide drew any attention. But they remain dark and empty. So he reaches over the top and grabs hold of thick tree roots jutting from the earth. He digs the toe of his boot into the wall's soft dirt and boosts himself up and over the four-foot ledge. Squatting behind the tree trunk, he glances at the surrounding area one more time. All clear.

Jeff scurries downhill to Uwe, still lying on his back with his heels firmly implanted in the earth.

A bitter smile spreads across Jeff's face. "You okay *Frau* Uwe?"

"Piss off," Uwe mumbles.

"We should keep a lower profile."

"Shut your mouth. Pull me out of here." Uwe holds up his arms.

Jeff reaches into the crevice, grabs Uwe's hands, and yanks him up to standing.

Uwe clambers over the ledge onto the hillside. He looks at his watch. "2:02. We must hurry."

Now that they are on firmer ground, they quickly descend the mountainside. When they reach the dirt road, Uwe swipes his boots across the pile of debris, dispersing the rocks and shrubbery. Jeff examines the houses one last time, but finds no sign that anyone heard the commotion.

"Let's go." Uwe takes off, running through the harvested fields.

Jeff follows, flexing his ankles and running flat-footed over the sticky, uneven ground.

When they reach the grove of apple trees bordering the station, they slow to a walk. Jeff inhales through his nose and mouth, trying to steady his breathing. At the edge of the orchard closest to the entrance, they sit and lean against a tree trunk. Ten yards in front of them a floodlight beams on an iron rod security fence topped with razor sharp points, like the tips of spears. A camera is bolted to the side of the light pole facing the entrance. Jeff estimates the entry gate is fifteen yards to their left.

They slide off their goggles and stash them in their packs. Uwe pulls out a Panasonic Toughbook, a small rugged notebook computer. He opens the display and sets it on the dirt while it wakes up. Then he creates a hotspot with his phone.

Jeff knows cyber security experts are well-acquainted with the vulnerabilities of camera systems. If sophisticated hackers, like Uwe, know the manufacturer, they can find chinks in the armor without much difficulty.

In a matter of minutes Uwe breaks into the camera network and frequency. As Jeff watches him maneuver through the system, he realizes there may be an easier way to access the industrial control system. One that requires much less risk.

"Are the camera and the industrial control system on the same network? If so, once you're in, I can pivot to the ICS and install the bug from here."

"Give me some credit." Uwe hands his open computer to Jeff and stands. He wipes off the dirt and rocks off the back of his pants. "The security cameras are on a separate network. The ICS is air-gapped. We cannot access it via internet or Wi-Fi. That is why we have to physically infiltrate the plant." He turns to face the tree closest to the camera. Then he grabs hold of opposing limbs, places his foot on the fork in the trunk, and hoists himself up.

"Just thought I'd check. I'm not familiar with your work."

Uwe climbs from limb to limb, until he's nearly ten feet off the ground. Then he carefully lowers himself into a seated position astride a thick branch and scoots out until he has an unobstructed view of the fence. He snaps his fingers. "Computer."

Jeff rises on his tiptoes and hands it over. The smell of rain hangs in the air, and he hopes it will hold off for a couple hours.

Uwe scooches out a few more inches until he's nearly in line with the security camera. From there, he adjusts the computer's camera and records a short video clip. When he's finished, he drops the device into Jeff's outstretched hands.

Uwe swings his leg up and around the limb, grips the branch with both hands, and drops lightly to the ground. He takes back his computer and kneels on the dirt. Jeff stands behind him, peering over the German's shoulder, watching him drop the video clip into a program that he previously created. The scrolling clock in the lower right corner gives the impression that the projected image is live, not a recorded clip. It reads 2:26:17. Uwe blocks the actual live feed from the camera's image sensor and replaces it with his program.

Jeff nods. "Hmm. Should work. There's no change in shadows at this hour. Especially on an overcast night like this."

"Glad you approve." Uwe packs up his gear and slings his pack over his shoulders.

Having disabled the camera covering the entrance, they jog under the bright floodlight to the pedestrian gate, located just before the automobile entrance.

Uwe checks his watch. "2:28. We wait until the engineer leaves the caravan for his patrol. Otherwise he sees when someone enters the premises."

Uwe bends over to unzip a pocket on his lower pant leg. Jeff takes the opportunity to inspect the station. Ahead on the left, the industrial storage shed faces the main road. It's an uninspired flat-roof concrete building. Delivery trucks can easily pull up to one of the five corrugated metal garage doors, slide it up, and unload. Beyond the shed are the eighty-foot-tall compressor buildings. The gas-fired turbine engines powering the indoor compressors emit a steady muffled whine. Behind these buildings, steel pipes four feet in diameter bring low pressure gas into the station and, after traveling through the compressor, send high pressure gas down the main pipeline to the next station.

Uwe holds a white plastic key card in one hand and taps it against the other.

"Whose name and photo pops up on the security system's screen when you wave that thing over the card reader?" Jeff asks.

"An employee who frequents B'liss Bar in Bilisht. After every shift, he stops there for a beer. Says his wife likes him better after he's had a drink."

"And you bellied up to the bar with him? Got close enough to clone his card?"

"Even bought him a second drink."

"Such a guy." Jeff rubs his thumb back and forth along his pack's ridged nylon strap, eyeing the brightly lit surroundings. He feels completely exposed under the lights, like he's standing stark-naked in a public square. "So when you did the recon, you not only mapped the path through the mountains, but you also replicated the security card and scouted the camera system."

Uwe nods. "I am the security guy, after all."

In the distance a door slams shut.

Uwe straightens. "That was the engineer. He left the caravan." He waves the card over the reader. When the lock clicks, he pushes open the iron gate. Jeff follows him inside the facility and quietly shuts the door behind him.

Uwe takes the lead, jogging across loose dirt and weeds to the storage shed. They creep in tandem along the west wall. When they reach the edge, Jeff rises above Uwe and peeks around the corner.

He sees the trailer located behind the shed. A thick heavyset man is crossing the road that separates the trailer from the compressor building. He unlocks the door to the southernmost building and disappears inside.

Jeff dips back behind the wall.

Uwe scoots behind Jeff. "I got us in here. The rest is up to you."

"Thank God." Jeff removes the tubular lock pick from his thigh pocket. He rolls it over in his hand and runs his thumb along the metal until it lands on deep grooved grip lines. It's already fitted with the appropriate needle for a standard door handle.

He takes a moment. If the circumstances were different, he'd enjoy the adrenaline rush of being back in the field. His heightened senses and sharpened mind humming at full speed. He has missed this feeling. And the excitement of facing a life-or-death challenge. He closes his eyes and envisions successfully completing the tasks in front of him. And getting the hell out.

He cranes his neck around the corner one more time. The engineer is not in sight.

"Now." Jeff bolts across the open space to the trailer. He leaps up three steps to the back door. He tests the knob. Locked. With still hands, he works the tension wrench into the top of the lock. Then he glides the pointed pick needle inside and presses his thumb against the power button. After only a few seconds of vibration, the lock clicks open. He drops the tools back in the pocket.

Jeff slides on the shoe covers and opens the door. When he steps into the darkness, he stifles a gag. The stagnant interior reeks of foul-smelling over-cooked vegetables mixed with a healthy dose of onions and garlic.

Uwe steps in behind him and shuts the door.

Jeff lets his eyes adjust. On his left he makes out a narrow galley kitchen with green vinyl tile floors. Despite the smell, the space is tidy. Clean dishes and a frying pan are propped up in a drying rack next to the sink. The counters are wiped clean. A folded blue dish towel hangs on the oven door handle. At the opposite end, the galley opens to a dining area where a plate holding a brown lump and a few florets of something green, probably broccoli, sits on a round wooden table.

Jeff steps past the kitchen and onto the brown wall-to-wall rug. On his right he glances down a short hallway with two wooden doors opposite each other. He continues straight, passing the partition separating the kitchen and the front room. Uwe follows behind.

The living room, now a converted work space, is saturated in a deep blue glow. A ten-foot plywood folding table is pushed against the front wall to the left of the main door. Two gray vinyl folding chairs are pushed under it. A computer, printer, and scanner are set up on the end closest to the door. On the far side, an ultrawide curved forty-inch monitor projects blue-tinted feed from the cameras surrounding the station. Above the table, mounted on the faux wood-paneled wall, are chrome wire shelves holding labeled plastic bins of tools, electronics, and wiring.

Jeff's eyes slide over the table and land on a steel cabinet about the size of a freestanding oven. It's mounted on a sturdy stand and bolted to the wall. He breathes a sigh of relief. This is where he'll find the industrial control system that sends the station's data, like flow rates, operational pressures, and temperature, to the main control center in Italy. From there engineers analyze the data. If they detect any deviations outside of normal operating range, they'll remotely make adjustments through the supervisory control and data acquisition system (SCADA), which practically every industrial machinery system has.

Jeff whispers over his shoulder, "Keep an eye out. If you see the engineer heading this way, give me a heads up." Then he makes a beeline to the cabinet.

"Okay." Uwe crosses the room to the only window gracing the front wall, wedged in the space between the cabinet and the plywood table. He removes the Toughbook and cables that will connect the computer to the ICS and sets them on the floor next to Jeff. Then he stands and pulls the metal slats on the shade back a few inches, just enough to have a clear view of the compressor buildings.

Jeff slides his palms over the sides of the cabinet. He finds a latch on the right and flips it open. But when he tugs on the edge of front panel, it doesn't budge. He leans around the side and sees it's secured by an aluminum cam lock.

"Damn," he mutters. He pulls the penlight out of his pocket and clamps it between his teeth. Then he removes the lock pick. This time he changes the needle, attaching a tubular pick about seven millimeters wide. He slips five pick wires into place so that they protrude evenly from the tube. Then he aligns the pick needles with the pin stacks and inserts it. Gently he applies pressure and twists. He only has to jiggle it a few times before the lock slides back.

He opens the front panel and sits back on his knees. Color-coded cables connect input and output modules. He shines the flashlight over neat rows of switches, dials, and gauges until he finds a row of unused ethernet ports. His shoulders loosen just a little. He might actually get this done and get out of here in under fifteen minutes.

But when he runs his gloved fingers over the ports, he realizes that won't happen. "Fuck me," he mutters.

"What?" Uwe spins around. The metal shade jingles against the window frame.

Jeff examines the flashing LED lights next to each ethernet port. "The unused ports are plugged with epoxy. And all the others are in use, registering current activity."

"USB port available?" Uwe returns to his post at the window.

Jeff continues to inspect the ports. "Searching. Usually one is left open for a printer or some other peripheral device."

"The engineer is leaving building three and entering building two," Uwe says.

"How much time do we have?"

Uwe glances at his wrist. "Twelve minutes."

Jeff puffs out a breath. "Found one." He picks up the USB to firewire cable and connects the computer to the ICS. When the network login prompt appears, he enters the stolen ID and password. The one that Siemens reserves for techs servicing the field.

"He's walking around the back. To the station yard. And it just started sprinkling."

Jeff opens the malware and prepares to upload it. "Thirty seconds."

"Damn you write efficient code."

"Only way to avoid antiviral detection."

Light rain taps the sheet metal roof. They wait in silence while the SCADA system is updated with Jeff's worm, programming a series of events on Sunday at midnight, when the flow rate will increase and the valves downstream will shut off so that the pressure builds beyond what the pipes can handle. At the same time, the SCADA system will send a steady stream of fake data to the main control center in Italy, ensuring no one is alerted to the dangerous increase in pressure. Only after the explosion will those monitoring the station realize what's happened. And it will require months, if not more, to repair the damage.

Uwe's breath catches in his throat. "He comes this way. Between buildings one and two. He cut the patrol short. Probably the rain." He drops the shade and picks up the unused cords on the floor. Then he scoots past Jeff, running toward the dining table.

"Just a few more seconds," Jeff says, standing over the ICS, drumming his fingers on top of the cabinet. They're too close to walk away now.

Uwe's footsteps thud across the vinyl tiles. He opens the back door. "You coming?"

"Shut that! He'll notice the cold air." The malware finishes uploading to the host. Jeff disconnects the cable from the port.

Uwe steps outside and shuts the door.

Jeff clips the cover panel in place. Then he glides the pick in the lock to bolt it shut. But the mechanism sticks.

The engineer's keys jingle outside the front door.

"Fucking kidding me?" Jeff closes his eyes and wriggles the pick from side to side with loose hands, finessing it into position. When the lock turns and the bolt slides in place, he yanks the pick out and drops it in the open thigh pocket. Then he picks up the computer and cable. He takes elongated strides through the living room on the pads of his feet.

The sound of metal grating against metal passes through the thin aluminum door. The latch clicks just as Jeff reaches the intersection to the hallway. No time to get out the back door.

He continues straight down the carpeted hall and darts through the open door on the left. Inside he scans the dim, dingy space set up as a second office. A steel-framed desk with side wood panels is backed up against the opposite wall. An aluminum-framed swivel chair on wheels is pushed under it. Dust particles float in the stream of light passing through the window. He starts to make his way toward the desk when the front door slams shut.

Jeff stands stock-still. He gently swings his backpack around to his front and slides the computer and cable inside. When the engineer stomps his heavy boots on the plastic door mat, the entire trailer quakes.

Jeff closes his eyes, allowing his other senses to inform him of the engineer's movements. The heavy man grunts with each step. The floor joists under the carpet creak when he transfers his weight from foot to foot. He passes the hallway and continues toward the kitchen. Jeff decides the engineer plans to finish his dinner, which means he can escape out the sliding glass window above the desk.

He leans a knee on the desktop and heaves himself up. Just as he releases the latch on the window frame, the engineer's footsteps stop short. No more creaking floors. No more grunts. Jeff envisions the engineer standing next to the back door, sensing the cooler air.

He holds his breath, praying Uwe locked the door. As though reading his mind, the Albanian tests the handle on the rear entrance, rattling it back and forth. Jeff exhales when it doesn't click open.

The engineer begins moving again, albeit slowly. His rubber-soled boots squeak across the kitchen's vinyl tiles. He pauses every few paces. Jeff detects hesitation. And suspicion. He lets go of the window latch. Too risky.

As the footsteps move further down the galley, Jeff gently climbs off the desktop and rolls the chair back over the laminate flooring. He crawls under the desk and scrunches between the wood panels. His knees are hugged in tight. Dust bunnies holding clumps of hair, lint, and other debris float through the air. He waves them away and reaches for the chair's center leg. Slowly he inches it over the floor until it's tucked under the desk. Once again, he is completely still, straining to hear to the engineer's footfalls.

The man is walking on the carpet again. He's moving continuously now. The right side of the trailer vibrates as he lumbers through the work space. Jeff senses neither urgency nor reluctance in the footsteps. Just confidence. Perhaps even a little relief.

The engineer comes closer, down the carpeted hallway. Jeff slows his breathing until it's inaudible, five counts in, five counts out. He turns his head toward the door and lays his cheek on his knees.

A rush of body odor and stale cigarette smoke sweeps into the room. Jeff holds his breath, not wanting to so much as shift the air. The engineer's thick-soled work boots approach the desk. His lower pant legs, soiled with grease and dirt, are just inches away. His keys clank onto an aluminum tray above Jeff's head.

Jeff buries his head between his knees. He squeezes his nose and mouth shut, stifling a sneeze as the engineer shakes out his wet coat. Jeff waits agonizing, anxious seconds to see whether the engineer detected the hitch in his breath. But the Albanian simply drapes his jacket over the back of the chair and turns on his heels, heading out of the room.

He crosses the carpeted hallway into the bathroom. When he pushes the door behind him, the latch bounces off the metal plating. Then the plastic toilet seat hits the rim.

Jeff slowly pushes the chair back and crawls out from under the desk. He rocks onto his feet and straightens to standing. The toilet seat squeaks against the base when the big man sits down.

Jeff rolls the chair back under the desk and tiptoes across the room to the threshold. Directly across the hall, the cheap door to the bathroom is several inches ajar. The engineer's hairy knees are partially visible through the opening. The Albanian hums and rustles through pages of a magazine. Jeff steps into the hallway. The engineer can't see him from where's he's sitting.

The rain intensifies, ricocheting off the metal. Jeff slinks down the hallway, gently shifting his weight from one footpad to the other. Outside the water flows down the roof drain and splashes onto the cement, providing some noise cover for any squeaky joists. When he reaches the main room, he veers left and lightly treads toward the back door. Then he waits for the Albanian to move.

The toilet flushes. Water rushes through the pipes overhead and between the thin walls. Jeff rotates the door handle. When he opens it, Uwe is standing in the pouring rain, pointing a suppressor at Jeff's chest.

He drops it to his side. "Thank God," Uwe says, "I thought I was going to have rescue you."

"You're a lame knight in shining armor," Jeff whispers. He turns the door handle and softly pushes the door into place. "You panicked. Vamoosed before the job was finished." He gently lets the lock turn into the plate.

Jeff lets the stifled sneeze rip, though not too loudly, and waves for Uwe to go ahead. They sprint to the gate. Uwe gets there first and swings the door wide, giving Jeff enough time to get through. His blood pumps through his veins as he runs along the fence line to the orchard. Uwe cuts in close to the camera and collapses behind a tree trunk. "Too close," he says.

"No shit." Jeff open his pack and hands Uwe the computer. Then he slides on his goggles, takes off the shoe covers, and stuffs them in the pack.

With swift keystrokes, Uwe disables his program and reinstates the live camera feed. "Let's get out of here." He stuffs the computer inside, slides on his goggles, and pulls out the GPS. He holds it out in front of him. "Follow me."

They tear through the orchard and the grain fields, heading west away from the station and its lights. It's raining hard now. Fat drops soak through Jeff's balaclava, sticking it to the sides of his face. His chest burns.

At the dirt road, they turn left and run south. Jeff's boots splash through mud puddles that have filled the potholes. Eventually they come to a clump of trees bordering the road on the right. They use their hands and feet to climb the ridge line and hide in the thicket.

"This is where our driver meets us," Uwe says, sitting on the wet ground.

Jeff leans over, resting his hands on his knees. He's gasping for air. His skin and clothes are sticky with rain, sweat, and mud. He reaches back and grabs a water bottle from his side pocket. He guzzles it in a single draft. Uwe does the same.

Before long, Jeff recognizes the same mud-splatted silver pickup with a shot suspension rambling up the road. The windshield wipers pump at full speed, pushing streams of water over the sides. The driver stops below them and climbs out. He peers into the trees as he walks toward the truck bed.

Jeff and Uwe emerge from their hiding place and slide down the ridge. Jeff catches the driver's eye and gives him a curt nod. The Albanian returns the greeting as he yanks the straps securing the farm equipment in place, like a wrangler checking his cinches.

Uwe opens the passenger side and slides onto the stained upholstered bench seat. Jeff crawls in after him and shuts the door. The stifling combination of heat and dead cigarette smoke is enough to suffocate him. He cracks the window and lets in air and a little rain.

The driver climbs in. Without a word, he shifts into drive. They bounce and splash over the uneven road, heading south.

Uwe exhales. "Not bad for two middle-aged guys. Once we got our feet under us."

"Where now?" Jeff flops his head back against the head rest.

"The Ionian National Airport. There's a plane waiting for us."

An excerpt from the novel-in-progress, *City of Sevens*.

The Interview

Elizabeth Coleman

MYST'S HEADQUARTERS WERE LOCATED on the San Francisco Bay in an industrial warehouse on Pier 70. The enormous brick front of the building, punctuated by several arched windows, rose up to meet the pitched roof. Despite the hustle and bustle surrounding it, the massive, multistory brick-and-steel warehouse with its large, reflective glass window siding—some broken and covered in soot, grime, and graffiti—looked abandoned. It definitely didn't look like the type of building to house a tech startup run by Numinals, supernatural and mythical beings who lived among unsuspecting humans.

Nadia stood in front of the building and glanced about herself. Moms jogged on the sidewalk as they pushed baby strollers. People walked their dogs down the street. No one gave the building a second glance. Nadia realized that the building was magically glamoured and warded to not draw attention to itself and to keep people away. Even the squawking seagulls overhead seemed to give the building a wide berth. If Nadia squinted and turned her head slightly, she could see the wards. They looked similar to the ones around her grandmother Marina's house, but far more complex. Golden alchemical symbols, shimmering in the light of the late morning sun, sat in a faint fractal web around the building like a geodesic dome.

Even though it seemed to repel people, Nadia didn't have a problem crossing the boundary line once she sensed where it was.

Only two days ago, Nadia had sent her resume in to Myst. The next morning, she had received a response inviting her in for an aptitude test and interview. The HR manager had been thrilled with her art history background and cataloging experience. The director in charge of Myst's antiquities and library collection was leaving soon, and they were eager to find a replacement, even temporarily, to carry on day-to-day activities. The position would focus on maintaining Myst's charitable foundation's extensive collection, as well as working with other departments to help them use the antiquities and knowledge from the library in their projects. The HR manager had also subtly asked about Nadia's powers as a witch—part of the initial screening process. Myst only hired humans who had Sixer abilities—the sixth sense to pierce through the glamours that Numinals cast to hide themselves in plain sight and pass as human. Nadia hadn't told the woman about her Septer abilities—the ability to cast spells, practice magic, and bend reality to her will. She was too new to it all, too unsure about her newfound skills to broadcast those powers to a potential employer.

After her Lyft had dropped her at Pier 70, it had taken Nadia about ten minutes to find Myst's headquarters. The building was entirely devoid of signage apart from a strange sacred geometry symbol etched into the wall above the door: a circle with a blossoming, fractal center similar to the one on Marina's front door and the one that had been above the doorway to the Mortal Coil bookstore. Nadia suspected that it was a symbol for the Numinous, the God power of the universe. A secret glyph to tell people that the building was a Numinal-safe zone. The only indication that she was at the right place was Myst's mountain logo painted on the front door below the symbol.

Nadia rang the buzzer. A short, gruff security guard answered. He peered out from behind the heavy metal door, and she sensed he was a Numinal. His glamour shimmered in her vision. He looked like a bridge troll, his face wrinkling, his nose changing shape into something looking like a lumpy potato. His name tag, pinned to the front of his rumpled uniform, read "Arne." It was not visible unless you pierced through his glamour.

He stared at her, without expression.

"Is this Myst?" Nadia asked. "I'm here for a test and an interview."

"ID," he demanded. Nadia fished out her wallet from her bag, and handed him her driver's license. He inspected it as he checked something on his phone. Apparently satisfied that she had an appointment, he pushed the door open and let her enter.

Nadia walked into an antechamber. A security desk sat in the corner of an otherwise bare part of the industrial warehouse. Nadia followed the guard to a small, plain room off to the side.

A test packet and pencil were lying on a small elementary school desk in the center of the room. The guard ushered her inside, grunted at the packet, and slammed the door, leaving her alone in the windowless space. Nadia looked around, feeling like this was some sort of *Men in Black* scenario. She was sure they were watching her.

Nadia was no stranger to standardized testing. Her academic career was liberally sprinkled with all sorts of exams, ranging from admissions test to get into prep schools, the SATs, various APs, and even the LSAT, when she briefly considered going to law school before she decided that was a horrible idea. She took a seat at the desk and picked up the paper, scanning the questions. It appeared to be a logic or IQ test, mixed with a personality test, focusing on game theory, critical thinking, and psychological assessment. She picked up the pencil and started answering the questions.

There was only one question that appeared to measure Sixer ability. *What was the security guard's name?* She wrote Arne on the line provided.

After about thirty minutes, she reached the last question, filled in the bubble, and put down her pencil. She wondered if she should somehow signal she was finished. After a few moments, Arne returned, furthering her impression they had been watching her. He grabbed the test and left again. Nadia waited patiently at the small school desk, her hands clasped in front of her, until he came back several minutes later.

"Okay, you pass. Come with me." He beckoned her with a lumpy hand. She grabbed her purse and quickly walked after him. Her heels clicked on the concrete as she hurried to catch up. He led her back through the antechamber to a secure door next to the security guard station, scanned his keycard, and opened the door to the lobby.

A woman looked up from behind a large desk. The Myst sign and logo were prominently displayed behind her on a partition with blue and purple lights. Over the sound system, an electronic downtempo song played. The strong beat thumped out in time to the pulsing, multicolored LED light canopy on the ceiling. Arne led Nadia through the waiting area around mid-century modern leather couches and chairs and past eclectic, abstract art on the walls. Next to the front desk was a magnolia tree in a large pot, the blossoms giving the room a pungent, floral smell.

"She pass," said Arne gruffly as they stopped in front of the desk. He handed the striking blonde receptionist the test. Nadia sensed she was a Numinal as well—a type of sexy nymph creature if Nadia had to guess. Normal humans definitely weren't born with those Kate Moss cheekbones.

"Wonderful! I'll let Vega know. Thanks Arne," said the nymph.

Arne turned to Nadia, grunted, and walked away.

The receptionist pushed a button on her Bluetooth headset.

"Vega? It's Anya. I have," she paused, reading Nadia's name from the top of the test, "a Nadia Winters here. Yes. She passed. Okay. Great. I'll bring her to you."

Anya handed Nadia a guest badge and walked around the desk, revealing golden tan legs in a red leather mini skirt. She showed off a dazzling smile. "Ready?" She motioned for Nadia to follow her around the partition and down the hall.

Nadia gasped as they entered the main floor.

The space was huge, even bigger than it had looked from the outside. There was definitely some spatial trickery going on to make the inside larger than the outside. About sixty or so employees—mostly magical creatures interspersed with a few Sixer humans—bustled around the floor, holding team meetings and going over specs. A troupe of tiny green faeries trailing green pixie dust flew over Nadia's head, startling her. A garden gnome in a pointy red hat argued with a banshee with long white hair that floated up around her face like she was underwater, the banshee's voice rising to shrieking levels as they debated something about the WishSeed app. Some Numinals still had their glamours on, but many of them were freely exposed, revealing their true form. Nadia was surrounded by faeries with bright, translucent wings, squat goblins with large pointy ears, shifters that were half-changed into animals, sprites and elementals with bodies that dissolved into the air as they moved, and centaurs with mohawks and dreadlocks wearing Hawaiian shirts. Nadia fought the urge to stare and tried to keep her face impassive like it was every day she saw this many supernatural creatures in an office environment, battling copy machines, playing foosball, and typing away at laptops.

Anya led Nadia around the perimeter of the first floor, which consisted of a minimalistic, open coworking space. Glass-encased conference rooms and offices lined the sides, adjacent to the main area. In the back, a giant steel staircase wound up from the first floor to the second-floor balcony that lined the perimeter of the space.

One corner of the main floor had a café and lounge area next to a huge indoor oak tree that was crawling with goblin-like creatures serving up snacks and drinks. Employees sat at tables and on bean bag chairs eating lunch, while others played foosball and ping pong in a gaming area lined with retro arcade machines. On the wall, giant flat-screen TVs alternated news broadcasts with calming images of nature and sacred geometry. Over the sound system, the music changed. Nadia recognized a song by Nora En Pure. Several employees started dancing to the DJ's music as they worked at stand-up desks. Others bobbed their heads as they sat in front of their laptops.

A giant mural covered an entire wall on the ground floor, and Nadia stopped for a second to admire it. It was like a Hieronymus Bosch, street art mashup, complete with graffiti goddesses, immortal deities, and the battle between good and evil playing out in a vibrant tapestry of reds, purples, golds, and blues.

Anya noticed Nadia's head swiveling about as she tried to look at everything. She chuckled. "Sixers always lose their minds the first time they come here."

"How big is this place? It doesn't look like all this could fit in here from the outside."

"Bigger than you would think. There are several floors underneath this one as well, where the innovation lab and vaults are located."

Nadia hurried to catch up with Anya's long strides. "Do non-Sixers ever come inside? I think they might notice this isn't exactly your normal work environment."

"Oh sure. But we warn all the employees over the Godspeaker so they can put their glamours on before a muggle enters."

"You actually call them muggles?" Nadia asked.

She laughed, nodding. "We screen movies every Thursday night in the lounge, by the way. Last week was *The Last Unicorn.* Not a dry eye in the room."

They climbed the giant metal staircase to the second floor, and Anya led Nadia to one of the glass-walled conference rooms that lined the perimeter.

A kind-looking woman in her fifties, with a mane of dark, unruly curls loosely pinned up on top of her head, rose to her feet when they entered, a set of tiny translucent wings vibrating behind her. She was wearing a pink pantsuit and floral neck scarf, which made her look vaguely like a real estate agent. She floated over and shook Nadia's hand warmly, giving off a distinct "house mom" vibe.

"You must be Nadia. Please, take a seat," she said with a benevolent fairy godmother smile, gesturing at one of the chairs around the conference room table. "I'm Vega, the HR manager." Tattoos peeked out from under her jacket sleeves as the woman sat down and clasped her hands. Nadia took a seat, poised on the edge of the chair with perfect posture, and folded her hands in her lap.

"Well, to start off," said Vega, "I'd like to congratulate you on passing Myst's aptitude test. We know it wasn't easy. But as I'm sure you're aware, we only hire humans for full-time positions if they have Sixer abilities and we think they would be a good fit for the unique personality of the company."

Vega shifted around some papers in front of her. She held up a pair of gold-rimmed spectacles to her face as she read from one of the sheets. "As I told you on the phone, your background is exactly what we are looking for at the moment. Imogen McKenna, the director of Myst Foundation, is returning to Dublin at the end of summer. We're planning on finding a long-term replacement, but for now, we need someone to oversee the daily functions of the collection."

"As I noted in my resume, I have extensive cataloging experience with various museums and auction houses including the Smithsonian and Christie's."

Vega nodded approvingly. "Your most recent position after you graduated wasn't in the arts, though. Why the shift?"

Nadia took a deep breath. "My experience in the arts was all unpaid internships. There aren't a lot of paid positions, and most of the time you have to continue as an intern until a position opens. I would have loved to get a job working for a museum or gallery, but with student loans and bills to pay, I didn't have that option. I always intended to pivot back." Nadia didn't mention that she could have continued as an intern, taking the money her father had offered her when she graduated. But she had wanted to prove that she didn't need him and could make it without his help or the strings that came with it.

"Understandable. I myself took many strange jobs over the years until I found a career at Myst. Are you familiar with Myst's onboarding structure? New employees come on as 'Unassigned.' After working on several projects and with different departments, we develop a position and title that is customized to their interests and skills. It looks like you have some experience interacting with artists?" Vega picked up her glasses again and squinted at the resume.

"Yes, that's correct. I interned one semester during school for a gallery in Virginia Beach. The owner had a very collaborative approach to running the gallery. I helped a lot with artist management and cultivating relationships with not only the clients, but with the artists as well."

Vega's tiny wings fluttered behind her. "Excellent. Our VP of Talent Management is looking for an assistant on some upcoming projects and that could be a good fit for you as well as with the Foundation."

Nadia leaned forward slightly, trying to look eager. "I'm definitely interested in that area."

Vega nodded. "Hobbies include horseback riding, sailing, field hockey, reading, chess, and volunteering. Sounds like you're pretty active. Myst actually has a few sports teams that play other startups in local leagues. If you are picked for the position, you should look into those."

"That would be great. I played on several intramural teams in college."

"Wonderful." Vega shuffled her papers together, collecting them into a folder. "Well that's it for me. I think you're very qualified and would be a good fit here. Our CEO, Rune Christiansen, interviews all candidates, though, before we extend any formal offers. Normally, you would have to come back for a second interview with him, but since Imogen is leaving, I want to expedite this process. I'll go see if he's available right now."

Vega flitted out, leaving Nadia in the conference room.

Alone, Nadia started to grow nervous. The Myst Psionic smartwatch on her wrist beeped at her change in mood. She smoothed down her blouse and slacks, and ran a hand over the top of her dark hair, pulled back into a neat bun. Nadia squared her shoulders and took deep breaths, willing her racing heart to calm. In her mind, she practiced her interview smile and handshake, imagining how the encounter would go.

After a few minutes, the door opened. Nadia rose to her feet. Her mother had always said you only get one chance to make a good impression, and Nadia wanted to win over the CEO. This job was going to be hers.

A tall man with broad shoulders walked in. He wore jeans and a gray Henley shirt and held a two-pronged manila folder. He looked up from the papers he was reading. Nadia flushed.

He was the most beautiful man that she had ever seen.

He looked to be in his early thirties, with dark hair swept back from his face and piercing sapphire eyes. Nadia's own eyes roamed freely over his chiseled jawline and wide, sensual mouth. Everything about him screamed sex, from the way he moved with a casual, primal grace, to the way he looked at her, like he was a predator assessing his prey. Without thinking, Nadia stood up straighter, pushed her shoulders back and her chest out. He flashed a smile, revealing a row of perfectly white teeth that contrasted sharply with his tanned skin. He was a Numinal, most likely High Fae, but his glamour was too strong for her to see through. He was powerful, brimming with strong magic in a dark, dangerous way.

"You must be Ms. Winters," he said in a deep, silky voice. He held out his hand and Nadia somehow had the sense of mind to reach over and shake it. "I'm Rune Christiansen." His touch was electric. Her fingers tingled at the contact. "I've reviewed your resume and test scores. Very impressive."

Nadia had a momentary flash, a rogue fantasy, of Mr. Christiansen pulling her to him and grabbing her like he owned her, dipping his mouth to hers in a possessive, claiming kiss.

Nadia gave herself a shake. What the hell was that? She tried to push all inappropriate thoughts about Mr. Christiansen from her mind. He was ridiculously, unfairly attractive, but she had to focus on the interview. They took a seat at the conference table kitty-corner from each other. Their knees brushed as they sat down. Nadia's breath hitched. She quickly pulled her legs away. The room suddenly seemed too warm, her conservative, high-necked blouse too constricting. A trickle of sweat slid down between her breasts.

Nadia cleared her throat. "You can call me Nadia." It came out a little harsher than she had intended.

He looked up at her from under long lashes. Nadia's heart did a little flip flop.

"Nadia it is, then. So, tell me a bit about yourself."

Nadia launched into her background in art history and experience working at museums and auction houses, highlighting her cataloging skills and business experience. She mentioned the various classes she had taken in college that related to ancient myths and artifacts and told him about the passion she felt for antiquities. She also worked in her experience managing artists while she had worked for an art dealer. Nadia could tell he was impressed, nodding as he took notes on her resume.

Nadia knew that she had nailed the interview, but as Mr. Christiansen walked her down the hall, he stopped at the top of the stairs.

Regret tinged his deep voice. "Ms. Winters, I have to be frank with you. While I appreciate your interest in Myst, I'm going to have to pass."

Nadia's heart leapt into her throat. "What? Why?"

Mr. Christiansen studied her for a few seconds. "I can tell you have a lot of relevant experience and a certain—" he paused, searching for the right word, "—*zest* for antiquities, but I'm afraid you're just not a good fit for Myst."

Nadia felt like she'd been kicked in the stomach. This was *not* how this was supposed to go. Panic started rising, but she squashed it down and steeled her composure.

"Listen, Mr. Christensen. I'm perfect for this position. I have experience with both ancient artifacts and with talent management. You aren't going to find another Sixer with my unique qualifications. I know I'll fit in here. I'm adaptable. Like a chameleon." She glanced over the balcony at the scene below, the Myst employees busy and unaware of the conversation above them.

Mr. Christiansen smiled slightly, pityingly. He shook his head. "I'm sorry, but my mind is made up. I'll walk you out."

Nadia needed to get this job. She wanted it. And not only because her vampire overlord was forcing her to get a job at Myst to pass along insider magic and tech secrets. She actually thought she could be happy at Myst and make a difference. She needed an anchor. Something to tether her down and give her life direction. Everything had gone so unexpectedly wrong the last few weeks. Completely gone to shit. And suddenly, Myst had come into her life, a shiny carrot dangling in front of her. The ring she was reaching for on the merry-go-round of life. She needed a rudder, something to guide her and give her something to work toward, or she was going to implode.

He started heading down the stairs. "Wait!" she cried out as she held up her palm. A blast of reddish pink energy shot from her hand and wrapped itself around his bicep like a vise made of lightning. It was a pathetic attempt. Not at all like the djinn's two-headed snake that had tortured Thomas. Mr. Christiansen froze, stunned. Slowly, he looked down at the thin ribbon of energy before he flexed his bicep, his hand tightening in a fist. The vise disintegrated into the air like wisps of cotton candy. Nadia's measly little attempt at casting a spell was clearly nothing he couldn't handle.

"You're a Septer?" His face was a mask of anger and disbelief at her lame attempt to bind him.

"I think so? I'm not really sure."

He shot her an incredulous look. "An untrained Septer, at your age?"

"I'm new to the whole Sixer and Septer thing. It's kind of a long story, but I just found out about Numinals and magic." The words came out rushed. The Myst Psionic pinged, and she held up her wrist. "See? I'm trying to learn. I have the smartwatch and everything. My grandmother is a witch too, and she and her Seelie roommate are teaching me about my powers."

His eyes flicked back and forth over her face. She could tell he was trying to calculate the risk she brought to the table.

"Where did you get the Myst Psionic?" He gestured at the smart-watch. "We only released a limited number."

She shrugged, trying to look nonchalant. "A friend gave it to me to help with my training. I promise, I'm doing everything I can to control my powers."

The seconds crawled by. Nadia held her breath, waiting. Mr. Christiansen's dark, sapphire eyes assessed her.

Finally he spoke, his voice cold and matter-of-fact. "You have issues with emotional control. This is extremely dangerous for a Septer. To control your magic, you need to be able to control your emotions and tap into them at will."

She gaped at him, shocked at his overly familiar evaluation of her mental state.

He continued, not breaking eye contact with her. "The moment you saw me, you lit up like a disco ball. Your scent, the pheromones you were emitting, were palpable. I can't have that sort of—" he paused, a nerve in his temple fluttering, "—*distraction* in my company. For any of my employees. It's hard enough balancing out all the strong personalities here without worrying about some human who can't control her magic interfering with productivity and employee safety. Half the demons in the city would be at our doorstep the second you lost control, trying to get to you."

"What do you mean?"

He stepped in closer to her, his head dipping down. "When you light up like that," he said, his voice low, "it's like a beacon for de-mons to come feed. You are basically pulsing, glowing like a little star, *leaking* energy and emotion all over the place. It makes you an easy and attractive target."

Nadia paled. Suddenly, he seemed menacing, looming over her like that. She stood her ground and jutted her chin, not wanting to show him that he intimidated her. She was tired of men using their power and position to threaten her.

"I didn't know that. Listen, if you give me the job, I'll work extra hard to control my magic. Already I'm getting better. I know I'm the right person for this job. Please, just let me prove myself. You won't regret it. Please."

Mr. Christiansen closed his eyes, considering her words. In her mind, she cast a spell, silently mouthing *say yes, say yes* and throwing the full weight of her desire to get the job behind it. If she had any real magical ability to bend reality to her will and sway the outcome of events through manifesting intention, now was the time to try.

After what felt like an eternity, he opened his eyes and stared intently at her, his dark eyes boring into hers. She couldn't look away, knowing that if she did, she would lose this chance.

"Alright," he said, a tinge of uncertainty still in his voice.

"Alright?" she asked, hopefully.

"I don't like this, but we could use someone with both Sixer and Septer powers. It's rare, and you could be very useful if you actually learn to master your abilities. Plus, Imogen *is* leaving soon and I do need someone with experience to temporarily manage the vault. You can have the job. On a test basis."

A grin broke out over her face. A warm feeling of excitement and relief flooded her body. The Myst smartwatch pinged at her change in mood.

He frowned at the watch. "But only on the condition that you agree to training with me to learn to control your abilities. I can't have you lighting up like that again and attracting half of the demon scum of the city here."

"Absolutely. When do I start?"

"Monday."

She'd done it. The job was hers.

Dad

Jeannie Hua

DAD HOLDS HIS ARM up for me to put his jacket on. I can see his scalp through his gray hair as his thin pale arms slide easily through the sleeves. He smells like old sweat. His sunken eyes look straight ahead at framed baby pictures on the piano as I zip his jacket up. More photographs in mismatched frames over the wall behind the piano. A feng shui money tree sits to the right of the piano, both resting upon bright green carpet.

"He needs his shoes," Anton says in a subdued voice. He's standing by the door, wanting to be out of the way. He's trying to look casual with his hands in his pockets, rumpling the bottom of his suit jacket and leaning against the wall, yet he's anything but. His very presence denotes our somber purpose. Anton almost never takes off from work. But today he has, because he recognizes that my dad is dying.

A voice from the adjacent master bedroom floats out. "*Ta de xie zi zai chian men.*" Anton tilts his head and looks at me. From habit, I automatically interpret without prompting.

"Mom said his shoes are by the front door." My heels clack on the cream tiles with orange, yellow, and brown flowers lining the hallway. Adjusting my eyes from the sun-filled family room to the darkness, I see a pair of faded blue canvas shoes. There's a hole in the toe of the left shoe. I bend down and the back of my shirt untucks. I tuck my shirt back in with one hand as I carry his shoes with the other. Clacking back to Dad on the black leather couch, I crouch down before him. This must be how shoes salespeople feel, subservient all the time.

I pick up his left foot, straining my suit jacket.

"*Ai ya! Nur er, tong ah!*" My dad croaks. I drop his foot. "*Ai ya!*"

"What's wrong?" Anton asks, straining his neck to see.

"He told me I hurt him," I say. "Sorry, Dad." I steady myself with one hand on the carpet and look up at Anton, who's still standing by the family room door. "Mom told me his cancer has probably spread to his bones."

Anton winces. "Honey, you need to be careful, I think that really hurts."

I snap, "Tell me something I don't know." I regret my words instantly. I need him here. I cradle my dad's left foot, place his toes into the opening of the shoe, then his heel. I do the same with his right foot. "I need to buy him another pair of shoes. This pair has a hole and is all stained. I didn't see any other shoes by the door." My heart aches, picturing the rows of designer shoes in my closet.

I'm four years old, I pull my hand from Dad's and run to the monkey exhibit. I sit on the ledge by the fence and look down into the pit at the monkeys. Dangling my legs, a flip-flop dislodges and falls onto the netting covering the top of the pit. Monkeys hoot and holler at the intrusion. Dad calls me a bad little monkey and carries me for the rest of our visit.

"Okay, honey," Anton replies. As I stand up, Anton strolls from the family room door to the couch. We each take an arm to help Dad up. Anton pushes the coffee table from the couch with his foot. We all turn in a line toward the hallway like community theater Rockettes, one step, then two. I watch my dad's face, his features still in silent concentration.

It's twenty-two steps to the family room door leading to the hall-way. We walk the pace of a New Orleans funeral march.

I'm in fifth grade; Dad just bought me a blue-and-white bike. Mom thought he spent too much money. We're in front of our old house on the sidewalk. I'm afraid and excited. Cars whiz by as Dad pushes me off, telling me I can do it. I veer to the left and crash. We laugh.

It's thirty-four more steps along the hall to the front door. I open the door and get a whiff of grass. A female voice is calling for some-one named Bobby and a car screeches a block away. I shuffle through the front door, still clenching Dad's elbow. He clears the door with Anton clasping his other arm.

"Should we tell your mom we're leaving?" Anton asks while the three of us are still on the front porch.

I glare at him, grit my teeth, and admit to myself that he's right. Just because she chooses to ignore Dad doesn't mean I should ignore her. It's so annoying to be the better person. Without responding, I stomp around Dad and yell into the house, "Mom, we're taking Dad to the doctor's." I shut the door without waiting for a reply.

It's twelve steps from the porch to the driveway.

I open the front passenger door of Anton's beloved gold Altima, the first new car he's ever owned. Anton treads the last couple of steps with Dad, still clasping his elbow. Dad surprises me by drawing his arm away. From supporting himself with his right hand on top of the car door, he walks around the door. I grab dad's left elbow as he stumbles.

I'm three years old and I'm at the beach with my parents. My dad picks me up, walks a few feet through the swirling water, and steadies me on a big rock. My mom gasps as Dad points the camera at me. As the camera clicks, I give him a smile so wide my eyes close. We both laugh at Mom's nervousness as sea water laps around the rock.

"*Wo ke yi*," my dad says to the dashboard and tugs his arm from me.

I put my hands up and say, "Alright, Dad, you're right, I know you can do it." He bends his legs, angles his torso into the car, and sits down. The smell of Anton's sweaty basketball gear assails me as I get into the back seat. As I cup a hand over my nose, Anton gets into the driver's seat.

He starts to back out the driveway and asks, "What's the doctor's address?" I lean forward and hand him a piece of paper. As he enters the address on Google Maps, I wait and stare at the back of my dad's head. His hair didn't start graying until his mid-forties.

"Dr. Burr, good man," Dad says to his house in front of the car. "Like him. Old like me." He wheezes out a laugh as Anton backs out of the driveway.

McDonald's, Pizza Hut, Carl's Jr., and Del Taco flash by my window as Dad acknowledges with a bend of the head to every building. The delicious smell of fried foods seeps through the windows.

I'm seven years old and it's Thanksgiving. The smell of roast duck has been torturing me for the past hour. Dad had hung the duck to dry for a day. He then braised and marinated the duck for another day. Finally, after roasting it at a low temperature for hours, he pulls the duck out of the oven and cuts it expertly. I'm filled with pride. There's nothing my daddy can't do. I take a bite of the duck. Perfection.

Dad mumbles something in the direction of Kentucky Fried Chicken outside of the car window.

"Did you say something, Dad?" I angle forward and ask.

"Alvin, did you say something?" Anton asks. I listen to Dad's muttering for a bit. I can feel the weight of my gut.

"I think he's talking to someone about the Bible." Dad hesitates, tilts his head, and resumes rambling.

I'm eight years old, in my blue bedroom in Taipei. I can't seem to wake up from a bad dream. I'm babbling to Dad. Tears mingle with strands of sweaty hair as I feel the weight of my Dad's warm hand on my chest. He's singing a lullaby and patting my chest to the beat. I quiet down, that hand protects me from everything.

"You think the cancer spread to his brain?" Anton asks.

"I don't know. If it's spread to his bones, it could've also spread to his brain. He's been talking to the air." I don't want to admit to Anton that it feels like he's talking to God. Anton doesn't believe in God. And I thought I didn't either. But here is Dad talking to Him. Maybe He is real. I want Him to be real so that Dad has some place to go to after this. So that he never really goes away.

After fifteen minutes, Anton pulls into a parking lot and to the front of a pink stucco building. I sneer and wonder how good can the doctors be if they're housed in a giant melting birthday cake. I hasten out of the car and the acrid smells of asphalt, smog, and grease from the Denny's across the street greet my nose. I catch my reflection in the car window. Lipstick intact, some volume left in my hair, but the side of my silk hot pink shirt is untucked. Tucking my shirt back in, I help Dad to the vestibule. I gaze down at the gray mats, sniff, and grimace. It smells like feet.

I'm nineteen years old, in college. My parents have been visiting me every weekend since my suicide attempt. They enter my dorm room just as my boyfriend leaves from the adjoining room. My dad's nose crinkles at the smell of sex. I hug him. He doesn't hug back.

Anton parks the car and with a lanky stride, hurries to the vestibule. He reaches us and opens the door. The door swings shut and traffic sounds from the outside stop. I find Dr. Burr's suite number on the black plastic board.

"Suite one fifty-seven."

Anton looks around, "It's that way."

We reach a frosted glass door framed in black metal with Dr.

Burr's name painted on it. Anton pushes the door open and ambles to the orange reception desk.

I point to the nearest chair to the door. "Sit here, Dad." We sit side by side in a row of red plastic chairs lined along a yellow wall. The floor is covered with blue-and-green tiles. Orange, red, yellow, blue, and green, it's as if illness and death can be conquered by Crayola. With nothing to do, I look down at my feet. My polished black heels are next to Dad's old canvas shoes, both pairs in wide.

Anton's still at the desk when a nurse opens the purple door next to it and calls out, "Alvin Gou?" Her voice is deep and melodious.

She leads us down the hall, lined with photos of families pinned on bulletin boards. We round the corner, and the nurse stops by an examination room.

"Dr. Burr will be right with you." She grins at my dad as he pushes his walker past her and enters the room. He nods and grunts at the examination table. She pats him on the shoulder and leaves.

Dad walks to a chair directly opposite to the door, pushes the walker away and half collapses into a chair. Almost immediately, a man in his sixties bustles in. What hair he lacks on top of his head is made up by his bushy, pepper-colored mustache. "Hello Alvin, good to see you again!" His voice is casual but his eyes stay on Dad. His lab coat parts to show a potbelly as he sinks down on his swivel chair by the salmon pink counter. Salmon? As if after the reception area, they've run out of the popular colors and were left to using colors neglected in the crayon box. He scoots the chair to my dad. My dad grumbles back. Dr. Burr turns to me.

"Hi, I'm Dr. Burr. So, you're Alvin's daughter?" His gruffness comforts me.

I half raise my hand in greeting and say, "Hi, I'm Melissa and this is my husband Anton."

"So, what do you do?" Dr. Burr asks while eyeing our suits.

I'm twenty-eight and I'm at my law school graduation. Mom and Dad had flown in, first time since we immigrated to this country, just for the event. Finding them afterwards, I walk up to them. Dad takes a picture of me. I go up to hug him. He doesn't hug back.

"I'm a lawyer, but no worries, I don't practice medical malpractice."

Dr. Burr snorts. "So, what's been going on, Alvin?" he says as he cups the top of dad's head and gently pulls up the lid of dad's right eye with his thumb, then left. Dad nods mutely.

I clear my throat. "I just found out today that Dad has been skipping the appointments I made for him at the Nevada Cancer Institute."

Dr. Burr flashes a light into Dad's eyes.

"That place is awesome," I say. "Not only do they take his crappy insurance, they even supply taxi service for him when he has his appointments." I pause. "When I ask him how treatment's going, he tells me everything is fine."

"Melissa previously got a call from Dr. Goodman's office that he was missing appointments," Anton says. "So, she took the earliest appointment they had and took him herself."

Dr. Burr taps his stethoscope, then puts it to Dad's chest. He listens and nods to himself.

"That ended up being the last appointment he kept," I say. "He kept turning down taxi service and canceling appointments after that."

Dr. Burr's seat creaks as he turns away from Dad and tilts his head toward me.

"Why was he missing appointments?" Dr. Burr asks.

"I'm not sure. I'm guessing it's because Dr. Goodman's staff wanted him to enter some study for prostate cancer. He kept telling them he didn't want to be experimented on. They kept assuring him that by the time the FDA allows studies on humans, it's been rigorously tested on animals. I just couldn't explain it to him sufficiently for him to understand." My voice catches. Anton puts a hand on my shoulder. I find my voice again. "So, I got a call just this morning from Dr. Goodman's staff telling me that he's been skipping appointments again and they're worried."

"Dr. Goodman couldn't see him today so my dad suggested you. He told me he likes you and he usually doesn't like anyone." The corners of Dr. Burr's mouth curl up slightly. "So, thank you for squeezing us in today. I know how busy you doctors are."

Dr. Burr swivels away from Dad and sighs. A nurse in purple scrubs leads a man and a preschooler past our room. The little girl's teary and her arm has a pink Band-Aid on it. The man pats her on the head and murmurs something about a lollipop.

"Paste, asparagus, good for prostate," Dad says. Everyone turns and stares at dad.

It's Thanksgiving again and I'm thirty-two now. I just divorced my first husband and am seeing a Latinx. I go downstairs, wondering why the delicious smell of Peking duck isn't roaming in the air like it always does this time of year. When I sit down at the dining table, my mother plops a ready-made duck breast still in its microwavable packaging from the local grocery store with a packet of orange sauce. "Baba doesn't feel like cooking this Thanksgiving." I take a bite. The duck breast is still cold. They didn't microwave it enough. I chew dejectedly.

"He told me he's been eating asparagus paste during one conversation we had on the phone a couple weeks back," I say. "I thought he was eating asparagus on top of getting treatment."

"With this being the third time the cancer has come back, maybe he's just tired," Anton says.

"I should've asked more about the asparagus paste," I say. "I should've pressed him further."

I'm thirty-four years old. I'm with Anton at our wedding reception.

The DJ tells Dad it's time for the father-daughter dance. Dad shakes his head and walks away. The DJ tugs at his collar and gives me a side glance.

"You didn't know," Dr. Burr says. "And even if you did, you can't make him do what he doesn't want to do."

I'm thirty-five years old. I'm at Santa Rosa Hospital. I call Dad to tell him he has a grandson and that labor was thirty-seven hours. He tells me it's my fault; I didn't exercise enough during my pregnancy.

"I could've tried harder. I had so many trials coming up and I was behind on my jail visits, the house is still a mess and Stevie needed help with his project . . . ." I say and dig my nails into my palms.

"Doctor Burr's right," Anton says. "He's a grown man. And a stubborn one at that."

Dr. Burr presses on both sides of dad's neck, pivots back to me and speaks.

"I don't know if your dad told you, but he's been coming regularly to see me. I keep telling him that I'm a general practitioner and not an oncologist, but he keeps coming back." Dr. Burr hesitates then continues. "Your dad's prostate cancer has spread to his bones and most likely his brain. Again, I'm just his GP but he's brought his test results for me to look at. He seems to want to get radiation, but I told him that his cancer has spread too much to be adequately addressed by radiation."

I nod dumbly. I can hear Anton's knees crack as he shifts his weight from one leg to another.

"Radiation therapy is good for isolated spots. When your dad's cancer was just in his prostate, radiation took care of business. But now his cancer has spread so far, if he wants treatment, chemotherapy is the way to go." I cringe at the mention of chemotherapy as Dr. Burris continues.

"And like I said, I had discussed your dad's cancer prognosis and his choices before. I'm not sure if he understands—"

A worrying thought occurs to me. "Do you guys have taxi service?" I ask.

Dr. Burr shakes his head. "No. At that point, your dad was still driving himself." I shudder at the thought of Dad driving himself. Dr. Burr continues, "He's declined pretty quickly in the past few weeks. Your dad is elderly, and he's frail. With his health, I'm not sure his body can handle chemotherapy. It's a rough process." He pauses and with a softer voice says, "I've been trying to convince him to go into hospice but I'm not sure if he's understanding me."

My face is tingling. I shake my head as if the word "hospice" can be knocked out of my brain. I lower my head as my heart drops to my stomach. Is this really happening?

I'm thirty-nine years old and eight months pregnant. Back from a long day at court, I limp through my parents' front door in heels too small for my swollen feet. Dad hands me my five-year-old as my three-year-old hugs my legs. He looks up and down at my suit and asks me how can I enjoy my new house while the house I bought for them was so old.

I straighten up and turn to him. "*Baba, you yao dao hospice chu hai shi yao dao yi yuan zuo* chemotherapy?" I'm disgusted with not knowing how to say the most important words in Chinese. Dad looks past me at something above my right shoulder and shakes his head.

"*Baba, Dr. Burr yao yi dao hospice chu,*" I say.

"Hospital?" Dad asks.

"No, hospice," I say.

"Hospice *shi she me?*" Dad asks.

"He just asked me what hospice is." I glance at Dr. Burr.

"Alvin, a hospice has medical staff to attend to your needs. They'll have the right pain medication for you to keep you comfortable."

Dad doesn't answer. Dr. Burr shrugs. I gulp and soldier on.

"Hospice *xian yi yuan yi yang. Ke shi shi gai bing ren mai you yuan wang de.*" Dad's eyes get big and he shakes his head. I turn from Dad to Dr. Burr. "I just told him hospice is like a hospital but it's where you go to die in comfort and peace."

Dr. Burr presses. "Alvin, they have some really nice hospices in town. They'll make sure you'll be comfortable. With the cancer spread into your bones, you must be in so much pain right now." His forehead wrinkles. "That's your dad's generation. They never complain."

Dad shakes his head vehemently.

"Or you can get chemotherapy," I say.

"Radiation," Dad says.

"Radiation *mai yo yong. Zhi shi yi ge di fang. Ni su yao* chemotherapy," I say as Dad continues to shake his head. Frustrated, I repeat my words, but louder. His eyes get big when I say "chemo."

"Chemo? Chemotherapy ah? Good!" He nods emphatically. Dr. Burr's sigh fills the room.

"Alvin, I really recommend hospice. I don't know if your body can take chemo. Chemo is very rough, you're going to be nauseous. The side effects will do more harm than the chemo itself will do you any good." Dr. Burr's voice remains steady but an almost imperceptible quiver at the end.

I'm six years old. Mom has swaddled me up in a hat, scarf, and heavy coat. I'm standing by the pool with her watching Dad swim. His arms slice through the water with surgical precision. He stops and tells the waiter unhappily standing by that the water isn't cold enough and to get some ice. While the waiter gapes at Dad, Mom tells Dad I need to go inside. It's twenty degrees and my lips are turning blue. I giggle. Dad is invincible.

I look at Anton and scratch the back of my ear. He shrugs and gawks at me. Do I do what's right for Dad regardless of what he wants, or do I respect his wishes? Which is more humane? As a lawyer, after informing clients of their rights and the possible outcomes of each choice, I have to respect their decisions, even if I disagree with them. "I guess I have to respect my dad's wishes."

Dr. Burr sits still and silent for a minute, staring at Dad. "Alright." Dr. Burr gets up and grabs his pad as if both acts took Herculean effort. "Do you need me to set it up or are you going to continue treatment with Dr. Goodman?" Dr. Burr asks.

"I made an appointment with Dr. Goodman for tomorrow already. We'll set up chemo with him." Dr. Burr nods. Lines on his forehead and along the crease of his mouth deepen as he shakes our hands and leaves.

Anton brings the walker to him and holds it steady as Dad braces himself up from the chair. I walk out the door Dr. Burr left open, turn around, and watch Anton and Dad. Dad, teetering on his walker, wheels through the door. Anton follows with his head down. Families in photographs smile at us and staff clad in scrubs rush pass as we scuffle our way out of the building and to the car.

We drive home in silence, interrupted by Dad's occasional comments to the passing commerce. Then it's snail's pace from the car, to the house, then the sanctuary of the family room. Dad pushes the walker to the piano and sits at the bench. The cushions make a whoosh noise as I sink into the couch. Anton excuses himself to go to the bathroom. My feet hurt. I look at my dad. My eyelids feel heavy. The day weighs upon me. Dad looks out the glass door to the backyard and nods at the sunlight streaming through and illuminating his face.

In a dry crackling voice he says, "*Ta shi haw nu er. Zuo shemi dou shi gei fumu.*" My eyes widen and I stop breathing. The anvil in my stomach is gone. He continues, "*Ta shi haw nu er. Zuo shemi dou shi gei fumu.*" I blink at him. Did I hear correctly? Could he be talking about someone else? I hear a door open and the click of a light switch. Anton returns from the bathroom.

"Honey, my dad just told the screen door that I'm a good girl, that everything I did, I did for my parents."

"That's great, honey!"

I beam at Anton through my tears. I've been starving for those words. I've been swinging a sword at the windmill for so long, until my arms grew sore, my shoulders near dislocation. That sword just met the flesh of the giant and sprayed a warm gush of blood against my skin, staining the family room carpet red. Thank you Dad for that crispy, sweet Peking duck of acceptance you've been dangling before my dog-like gaze. I'm going to put down that sword carefully in a corner, rub my sore arms, wash the blood off my hands, grab a plate, nestle that chunk of duck in bing, smear it with hoisin sauce, baptize it with scallions, swaddle it all up, and sink my teeth into it, let the juice flow down my chin, savor its richness, and allow it to nourish me.

"Honey I have to go back to work," Anton says, glancing at his watch.

"Alright, let's go."

I hug Dad. His arms remain limply by his sides. I kiss him on the cheek. Back to work.

Shield Monkeys

B. R. Welch

THERE'S NOTHING BEYOND MY toes but two klicks of empty air.

I'm about to entrust my life to some ropes that are barely as thick as my finger. I'm two hundred pounds Earth standard. I'm not sure what that translates to on this planet, but I do know that if I fall from this height, I'm definitely going to die.

The parachute pack I'm wearing might work, but I can't be sure because I didn't pack it. And who the hell rides a zipline with a goddamn parachute?

This "mystery date" was a mistake.

I tighten my grip on the two contraptions that connect me to the zipline cable: the roller and the brake. The two devices fit neatly over the cable. The roller has a hinged chassis with embedded wheels that run over the top of the wire, while I, in theory, hang underneath. The entire chassis clips around the wire for "safety." The brake is a separate device slotted on behind it, with two buttons you squeeze to work it. My fingers already ache from squeezing.

I peer over the edge in an attempt to steel my nerves, staring down the sheer side of Central Tower. It looks like a dark vertical highway, broad and long, scattered windows flaring in the red sun, going down and down and down. At the base of the tower the rooftops of the well-heeled inner sectors make a shining circuit board of red and gold spanning outward.

The dark vertical road blurs and splits into two. I feel myself being pulled toward the edge as the distant rooftops slowly rotate. My knees almost buckle as dizziness washes through me. I don't want to puke in my helmet but I'm not sure I get a choice. My chest tightens and every muscle in my body seems to contract with it, and the world narrows down to me and one long, inevitable fall. I keep trying to suck down more air to calm myself, but I can't seem to get enough oxygen with each breath, so I breathe faster, and faster, and faster—

"Bard, I can hear you hyperventilating," Trin speaks in calming tones, drawing out the vowels. "Big, long breaths. Concentrate on the feelings in your hands and feet."

My date's voice is solid and calm. Easy for her; she's already on the other side.

I close my eyes and take her advice, feeling for the solid ground under my boots and the hard surfaces under my gloves. I wait for the world to stop spinning, wondering what I've gotten myself into.

The zipline is at the mouth of an open-ended maintenance corridor at the top of Central Tower. It is, according to Trin, the highest accessible point inside this city's Habitat Shield, the vast honeycombed blister-bubble that protects Sankar City from the intense summers of a tide-locked planet. The tower's full name is Sankar City Central Shield Support Tower, which tells you everything you'd ever want to know about its location and function. The other eight Shield Support Towers encircling Central have similarly creative names.

Sankar folk have no sense of subtlety.

I open my eyes again, this time looking upward, away from the massive drop below. Being here makes me feel like a flea inside a giant transparent umbrella. Just above my head, past the steel cable I'm attached to, the metallic ceiling of the corridor ends and the Habitat Shield begins with a single glass-like hexagon revealing a pale green sky. It is one of millions of such hexagons, exactly the same in shape and structure, tiled off in every direction into the distance, each one framed by red-tinged native steel, together creating a single curved surface arcing gently down and away before touching down on red soil some tens of kilometers away at the outskirts of the city. This Shield is a luxury for Sankar's citizens. Back in Stormside, we have to stay underground during the summer.

Where Sankar folk would say we belong.

Far below, a distant chime of morning bells marks eight a.m.

Trin's voice pipes into my earpiece. She speaks softly. "Bard, I can't come back there. If we're going to make it to Tower Six and not get caught in the process, you need to come down here."

This is not a place I'd normally choose to be. Not this high up, not in this city. But my date is the adventurous type and I have—or perhaps now, had—a carefully constructed image to maintain. When she suggested a "mystery date" I had images of a new chow joint or a secret underground bar. Maybe a slick band. I'd just said yes without thinking, probably because she's the only girl I've really had a thing for since I arrived on this forsaken planet.

I should have said something when she handed me the harness and chute pack.

Trin calls me again. "Bard?"

"Yes," I say, "I hear you."

I scan down the zipline, willing myself to believe that I can do this. The cable gently slants down to the other platform before curving up and into a steely black column that attaches to the underside of the Shield, bristling with ziplines and support cables.

There is Trin. Standing beside the cable I'm supposed to be flying down right now. She's wearing a form-fitting exosuit, temperature controlled and pressurized, helmet clipped into the collar, chute pack over her shoulders and fastened to her zipline harness. Same thing I'm wearing, but she looks good doing it.

"How illegal is this again?" I ask.

"It's only illegal if you get caught," Trin says, then laughs. The earpiece layers the sound with a slight digital shimmer. I decide that her laugh is my new favorite sound. Something inside me melts.

I shake my head. I've been single way too long.

"Listen, you need to chill," Trin says, "I've done this many times. And I like you too much to put you in danger."

The butterflies in my stomach go wild.

She continues, "Just keep one hand on your brake. The roller is clipped around to the wire so you can't fall. What's to worry about?"

"The wire could snap," I say, attempting to sound calm and reasonable.

"It won't. These wires are actually for the maintenance teams. They're secure."

"And yet we are wearing parachute packs."

She clicks her tongue. "An abundance of caution."

A moment passes in silence. I can tell her patience is running thin.

"Hey," Trin says. "I'm just going to count you in. Don't think. Just go. On my one."

I just nod. As good a plan as any. My heart thumps in my ears. I wonder if she can hear it through the earpiece.

"Three."

I tug on the rope. I tell myself to focus on the process, not the heights. I check the connections like I'm doing the holy cross—roller knot, harness knot, waist cinch, thigh cinches. All points secure.

"Two."

I slowly release the brake buttons and the roller inches forward, pulling my torso over the precipice. My feet feel like they're glued to the edge. The drop below me is insane and I squeeze the brake and close my eyes. My gut twists and I think I'm going to shit myself.

"One."

It's like someone else does it for me: they let go of the buttons on the brake and the roller pulls my toes off the edge. It's suddenly too late to do anything about it as I swing down, dropping off the edge and under the wire, hanging completely from the roller. I keep my eyes shut. The wire bows under my weight and the harness bites around my crotch.

I start to roll down the wire.

I am not falling.

I am hanging from the zipline.

Everything seems to be working: gravity drawing me downward, the roller's wheels zipping against the cable, sound growing in frequency. I lift up my knees and lean back, partly 'cause I know that's how I should do it, and partly 'cause I want to open my eyes but I don't want to see the gaping void below me.

I open my eyes. Air rushes past, roaring around my helmet, tugging on my pack and chute. Above, the trusses of the Shield whip by in blurring streaks of steel and glass. The speed picks up and the adrenaline courses through me.

Something in my brain clicks, a switch turns on, and I grin like an idiot.

I'm flying.

"YEEAAAAAAHHHHHHH!"

Trin whoops through the static. "We have lift off! That's it, man!"

I'm still accelerating. I look ahead, down the wire, and see Trin waving at me from the platform.

Trin saves me. "You should think about braking."

I forgot to count the seconds. I squeeze the two brake buttons. "Thanks."

My speed bleeds off. I can see why her advice was to brake early. If I needed to stop suddenly, I don't think this would work. It's a gradual slowing. The honeycomb structure of the Shield again becomes distinct, sliding above my head.

I snatch a glance to the left. Sankar City is awash with the blush of morning as the Shield's glass plates allow a greater flow of light from outside, a luxury for the biorhythms of the locals.

Everything seems to glow. Below, the Inner Sector alleyways etch around tiny glittering rooftops of red, purple, and gold. Arterial boulevards radiate from Central Tower, evenly spaced like spokes in a wheel, terminating at the base of each Shield Support Tower. The Support Towers rise up, majestic man-made trees, metallic branches fusing into the downward slope of the Shield holding the superstructure aloft. Past the towers, the Outer Sectors stand in a grid of faceless concrete towers separated by deep, trench-like streets cutting between them.

Even from this height, the city buzzes with activity. Cigar-shaped Antigravs slide through the air between the Support Towers, circling the city in preprogrammed lanes, bussing food, water, or people to their jobs and homes. Rainbow-colored birds—cloned from Earth-stock, no doubt—wheel and dip around the towers in loose flocks, singing as they chase each other in the red sun.

It's so far removed from where I usually spend my days. My heart swells up and I think it's going to burst with gratitude.

Trin's voice cuts in. "Eyes front, soldier. Platform coming up."

I do as I'm told. Ahead, the platform is a black hexagon that'd be more than large enough to land a chopper on. Taut cables run from each corner and up to vertices in the Shield, distributing its weight. The steel column at the center of the platform is the nexus of ziplines, ascending up into the Shield, with four more zipline cables sloping away from the pillar in different directions.

"Alright. Now land it, nice and slow," she says when I'm right above the platform.

I ease in, sitting up straight, helmet next to the rope. My feet hit the platform one after the other, which sways slightly as it takes my weight. I stand up and the rope to my roller goes slack, my harness releasing its grip on my thighs. It feels good to be standing again, at least several meters away from an edge.

"That was . . . something." I reach up and carefully unhook myself, heaving down with my left hand so I can take the roller off the wire. I keep a hold of the wire, trying to look casual.

"Fun, right?" she asks.

"Wow. And not so scary once you get going. Say what you want about this city, but . . . ." I trail off, looking out at the rainbow-colored birds flying higher now, dancing past thin clouds of vapor hanging from the gentle curvature of the Shield.

I shake my head, looking away. "It's gorgeous."

A gust of wind tugs at my pack and suddenly I'm glad I'm still holding the wire.

Trin squints at me through her faceplate. "I didn't think you'd be scared of heights."

I cock an eyebrow and nod at the edge. "This isn't height. It's altitude."

Trin looks off into the distance, eyes narrowing. She looks back to me and grins.

"Good news. We can take it easy. My guy just confirmed there's no planned maintenance works today."

"Nice. And how do you know your 'guy'?" I ask, clawing the air with two fingers.

"Kind of a long story."

"And you just said we can take it easy. We got time."

"Yeah," she says as she breaks eye contact, looking over the edge. She takes a breath. "So, I used to work up here."

I blink a few times. "You worked? Up here?"

She nods, lips pursed. "Yep. You're looking at an ex-Shield Monkey. Got caught hanging out up here for fun, and they didn't like that. I was arrested. They planned to send me to the mines."

I exhale heavily, fogging my faceplate for an instant. "And?"

"My grandma got me out. Pulled some strings, or bribed someone, I don't know. She had me smuggled out to Stormside."

My mind does backflips as I reassemble the pieces I know about Trin. Living in Sankar, having a city-funded job, being smuggled out—this meant serious money and connections. Not the street-savvy, woe-is-me orphan she played herself up to be out in Stormside. More like an aristocrat with a trust fund on the city's wanted list.

"Are you on the watchlist?" I hear my voice rising as questions stack up. "Why are you back here?"

"I am," she replies, grinning playfully. "I just can't stay away. Too much fun."

This is insane. And now I'm pulled into it.

"Fuck, Trin," I look down at my boots, shaking my head. "Can they track you? I thought Sankar citizens got chipped."

Trin's voice goes quiet, tentative. "Gran had the implants removed when I left."

I look back up at Trin. Her smile is gone. She frowns, uncertain.

"Those black-market surgeries cost a bomb! I'm still paying off my retina implants. Your family must be goddamn loaded. And you're probably being hunted by the city." I hear my voice rising. "Anything else you want to tell me while we're two klicks in the air engaged in flagrant criminal behavior?"

Hers was so far from the life I'd built using my savings from Earth supplemented by petty criminal endeavors like brewing contraband beer. Even being able to live here was a sign of privilege. I didn't mind the wealth itself, that was just a surprise. It was the stupidity of coming here while knowing she was being watched, then bringing me into it, knowing I have my own responsibilities, that was just careless.

My body tenses as my blind infatuation shatters. I see it now, like when they turn on the lights in a dance club and everyone looks tired, drunk, or ugly.

I want to get out of there.

I force a smile. "Right. Well, shall we get moving?"

The breeze tugs at our suits and I renew my grip on the wire.

She studies my face for a moment, brow furrowed. "I really didn't think you'd judge me—"

"I'm not judging," I interrupt, "I just feel like this is a serious thing and you're treating it like it's a fucking game. It's one thing to run a little booze in from Stormside, it's another to be up here, literally hanging from the roof—"

"If you want to get moving, let's get moving," she cuts me off, slicing the air with her hand. "I'm ready to go. You were freaking out, taking your sweet time. You said you'd done this stuff before."

"I was *conscripted*, Trin. They had to boot me out of the airplane. Literally."

Her face goes blank and she looks away. "There's only two more lines to run down, then a short run into the maintenance corridor on Tower Six." She points over the edge to her left, down to one of the towers. "Right there. That's Tower Six. I'll see you there."

She turns away, heading toward another long, sloping cable running toward the tower she just pointed out.

"We should stick together," I say.

Her brake is already attached to the wire. She doesn't look back as she clips the roller on behind it.

"So keep up."

Hands on the roller and brake, she steps off the edge and sits back into the harness, lifting her knees to her chest as she accelerates away. I scan down the wire. It follows the descending curvature of the Shield, long enough that it's hard to make out where the next platform is. Trin seems to be flying into a rosy haze of light that clings to the underside of the Shield.

I click my tongue, realizing I still had questions about the mechanics of the zipline.

"Trin, how long should I wait before—"

A violent clap fills the air, reverberating through my helmet and echoing in my earpiece. I wince, ducking involuntarily, arms up around my head.

"*Kao!*" Trin swears. Her breath comes fast with fear, and in the background is a sharp ticking, loud and staccato, accelerating, then breaking into a chorus of cracks.

Her scream rips through my earpiece as the sky shatters above her.

Falling pieces of Shield-glass tumble down, seemingly right on top of her; dagger-shaped shards flashing with the bright, unfiltered sunlight bursting through the hole above. A sudden differential in pressure and temperature creates a gale that snatches at Trin and then, moments later, me, pulling toward the hole. I grip the wire with both hands and plant my feet wide, holding on. Trin's dwindling figure—still on the wire, thankfully—sways and bobs with the gyrations of the wind. She seems to be struggling to stay on.

"Trin! Are you okay!"

I hear heavy breathing.

From far below, distant sounds of a sharp-edged commotion filter upward, from what must be a massive crowd. My chest tightens as I think of how deadly those man-sized shards of glass would be.

"Trin," I try again, "are you okay? Were you hurt?"

"I got cut but I'm okay," she replies. I exhale with relief. She continues, "We really need to get out of here. I don't know what happened. Something bad. The plates are not supposed to shatter like that. Someone will be coming, and fast."

I look at the hole in the Shield. Nothing still falling that I can make out.

The tugging gusts stabilize into a steady wind, sucking the atmosphere out. The wire undulates like a snake.

I attach my brake to the wire, squeezing the buttons hard. I check my knots and harness and clip on my roller.

"Okay, I'm coming."

I take a huge breath, pushing away the waves of anxiety. I push off the edge. I tuck my knees up but the air is pulling at me, trying to twist my body away from the direction I'm facing. Light floods through the hole in the Shield ahead, so bright I can't see anything beyond it.

Wind rushes past my helmet as I gather speed. As I approach the hole, the currents of air swirl, jostling me side to side and up and down. I grip the roller chassis like a demon, jaw clenched as I accelerate, speeding right under the broken hexagon. The swirling intensifies, pulling me up and sideways. The wire rotates like a skipping rope, throwing me upward. The wheels of my roller clack and clatter as they lose and regain contact with the wire. I put both hands on the chassis of the roller, trying to weight it down and keep it on the cable.

Big mistake.

The brake slips off the wire. It swings down behind my back. The howling around my helmet intensifies as my speed increases.

"I've lost my brake."

Trin replies instantly. "Reach behind you. Get it back on."

"But I'm holding my roller to keep it on the wire."

The wind rushes faster around me, tugging at my legs.

"Bad idea. That'll make you go faster. You need your brake."

She's right. The line tosses me around like a doll but I'm barreling down the wire, still accelerating.

I force myself to take one hand off the roller. I reach behind my body, palm wide open, searching for the brake. The shift in weight pulls my legs sideways and the oncoming air catches at my legs, pushing them back, causing my body to rotate.

"Shit, I'm coming down ass first."

I can't see where I'm going, how close the platform is. I remember the thick steel column in the middle of the platform and my throat tightens.

"You're too close to bail," she says quickly. "You need to twist back around. Keep trying to get the brake on. Your speed is reduced by the wire bucking; it might be okay."

I continue to accelerate, my feet pointing back toward the red hole in the sky.

I try again for the brake, this time tracing my harness until I hit the brake's dangling rope. I grab it and flick it upward, letting the rope run through my hand until I can catch it.

"Got it!" I crow, victorious.

"Turn around. Put it on the wire behind the roller."

I try to twist around but the fierce wind holds me backward. I tense my arms and core, kicking in the air, trying to twist my hips and shoulders to make my body turn around. Nothing works.

Brake in hand, I try to fold at the waist like I'm doing a sit-up, reaching toward my toes and past the roller, trying to slot the brake over the wire. I misjudge the angle and the speeding wire catches the edge of the brake housing. The brake flies out of my hand.

"Fuck! Lost it!"

"Okay," Trin says, fast, low, and urgent. "I can't safely catch you at this speed. You're going to hit the central pillar. Try to relax. Your suit and helmet give some protection. We need to count on that. Tuck your knees up high. Relax your back, neck, and shoulders. Good luck. I'll be here."

I close my eyes and breathe hard. Trying to relax makes me clench my teeth. I feel the roller pass through a dip in the wire. I rocket upward.

Then it all happens at once: I open my eyes to see a blur of black under me. My back slams into the steel pillar. Air rushes out of my lungs. My head cracks against something and my vision simmers with white flecks. Someone shouts. Hands grip my harness. A voice floats nearby. The sky, blurred pink, hangs still for a moment, then recedes into the far distance, dissolving into a purple-tinged blackness.

A DARK PILLAR STANDS above my head like a tombstone.

I groan as pain floods in. My back, shoulders, and head throb.

"Hello?" I say.

No response.

I try to lift my head but pain flashes behind my eyes. I lie still, taking stock of what I can see through my visor: a metal pillar rising several meters above me, connecting into the honeycomb trusses of the Shield. Thick cables run into the pillar. A red hexagon glows at the edge of my vision. The wind rushes around me. Far away, a klaxon wails, rising and falling. I run my tongue over my teeth and taste metal.

I remember ziplining. The Shield shattering. Above Trin.

"Trin? Where are you?"

Nothing but static wash.

I remember our argument. Trin said she was an ex-Shield Monkey on the city's watchlist. A rich girl bankrolled by her grandma. Who has now left me, apparently, injured and alone.

I force myself to roll onto my side. The intense pain in my skull reports that this was a bad idea. I lie there for a second, breathing steadily before I push again, clenching my teeth as I lever myself into a sitting position. I think I'm going to puke. I need medicine.

I have medicine. I packed two painsticks and two stimsticks. They're stowed in my chute pack. I slowly unclip the pack from my harness, sucking in small, deliberate breaths to work through the pain. I gingerly move onto my knees and unzip the left, then right side pockets, reaching in each to feel for the small hard-case medikit. I find it on the right side and pull it out.

Inside the case are four sticks: two red, two brown.

I remember Doc holding these up under the fluorescent Earth-spectrum lights of his lab. *Remember,* he said, *pink for pain, green to go.* Under red sunlight, the colors don't work like that and the mnemonic fails. I try to recall the rules of color math but I'm in no state to do the addition.

But it doesn't really matter. I need both.

I unclip my helmet. The temperature-controlled atmosphere inside hisses out. I lift my helmet off and my face and neck feel scalded with heat. I pull down a breath, but the air is thick and too hot, like swallowing fire. I'm light-headed. My stomach clenches once, then twice, and I know I'm going to vomit. I lean to the left just in time to avoid my helmet. A rush of bile and breakfast streams out. I retch again, and again.

A thought drifts in as my retching turns to dry convulsions: the Shield is broken. Intensely hot, not-quite-breathable air has rushed in. I'm being cooked.

I snatch up two different-colored sticks and shove them into the side of my neck, clicking the tops of both at once. They pierce and sting for a breath or two and I blink and grit my teeth.

Another breath and my nausea and dizziness wash away.

My heart thumps in my chest. The pain becomes muffled, wrapped in thick blankets and buried deep. Energy floods my limbs and I feel invincible. I can take on anything and anyone with my bare hands. I am alive, a beast, full of raw energy and ability, I am so fucking powerful, I am—

—really high.

I'd felt this before: the force gave us go-pills before a drop. Go pills made minimally trained men feel great about leaping out of a high-altitude cruiser with nothing but a secondhand rifle and a parachute.

I tug my helmet down over my head and clip it back on at the collar. The suit quickly repressurizes, pumping in cooled, balanced air from the exosuit's filter membranes, and I gasp with pleasure; it feels like I stuck my face in a refrigerator. The medikit goes back into a side pocket, then I shoulder the pack and clip it to my harness.

I take a deep breath, trying to make a plan. That klaxon means someone is coming soon. I need to get out of here, and fast.

"Aimy: run health check."

The glow of warmth at the base of my skull is almost comforting. Time for that implant to earn its keep. Emergency health readouts flip down into my retinal display from the top of my vision in red flashing letters:

→ Major injuries detected. Head trauma. Two broken ribs. SEEK MEDICAL ATTENTION.

→ Blood analysis detects controlled substances. High concentrations of synthetic amphetamines and lipsomic nano-anesthetics. DO NOT OPERATE HEAVY MACHINERY.

"Thanks for the insights, Aimy. Clear warnings. Display Location Lens."

The text scrolls off screen as I orient myself back toward the one landmark I'm sure of: the huge metallic trunk and branches of Central Tower. Superimposed in the air, a glowing blue line appears, connecting the tower to a blue rectangle containing letters and numbers that tumble then resolve:

SANKAR CENTRAL TOWER, Distance: 1.32km, Altitude: +200m.

I turn back, toward the circle of Support Towers. Blue signs spring up around every building like a chaotic field of antennae. The amount of data is almost overwhelming, but I keep scanning the sky until I find the one I'm looking for.

SHIELD SUPPORT TOWER SIX. Distance: 1.64 km, Altitude: -400m.

Only one wire heads in that direction, sloping down and into its branches.

I blink several times to turn the AI off. The warmth behind my neck seems to be growing. I blink faster. Still doesn't turn off.

"Aimy, power down!"

The buggy implant finally complies. The warmth at the base of my skull dissipates and the rectangles disappear. I'm glad to be left with my own naked eyesight.

I try one more time. In case she truly didn't just fucking leave me. "Trin. This is Bard. Not dead. Where the fuck are you?"

I strain to hear, focusing to catch even a distant murmur. In the earpiece all I get is a subtle buzz, the artifacts of digital silence. Outside, muffled by my helmet, is the sound of wind, the klaxon, and a clanging, jangling noise. Coming from behind me. I turn around to see that the line I just came down is moving, jostling around and clanging against the pole.

Up the line, past the red glow of the broken Shield plate, I see a dark gray shape running down the wire. The zip of the cable hits my ears. I squint to see who it is, but the clothes don't look right for it to be Trin. Suddenly there's someone else on the line, not far behind the first figure, and a few moments later another.

The earpiece crackles violently. I nearly jump out of my skin. The crackle resolves into a pattern of bass tones, then a deep, commanding voice booms at me.

"Stop. You are violating city law and will be arrested."

Shield Monkeys.

I turn back, looking toward Tower Six and calculating the odds. They're bad no matter which way I cut it. If I run and get caught, I get sent to the mines. If I stay and get arrested, I get sent to the mines.

Might as well give them a chase.

I move fast, attaching my brake and clipping the roller onto the wire. I step off the platform. The harness bites into my thighs. I lean back and swing my feet up and forward, trying to make my body straight like a missile, legs straight, pointing toward the descending wire. The wind jostles me, tugging my feet. I keep my core tight and focus straight ahead, tensing my arms as I grip the brake and the roller to hold position.

The Shield Monkey speaks. "Bad decision, kid."

I continue to accelerate, zipping down the wire.

Moments pass. The air whistles around me and the zipping of the line reaches higher and higher pitches. A panorama of Sankar City's superstructures rushes by, tempting me to turn my head, to slow down and drink it in. I'm far enough away from Central Tower now.

All eight of the Support Towers are visible, circling Central Tower, each one a vast and majestic tree of steel glowing red in the sun. Air-trains and Passenger Skimmers carve through the sky.

I force myself to focus. I'm hesitant to brake; I can't risk losing speed. The wind continually gusts and tugs and it takes all my concentration to stay facing forward.

Support Tower Six looms large below. My feet are pointing at the tower's top-most branch. The hexagonal black platform hangs a couple hundred meters up the slope of the Shield. Its dark pillar sits amid a web of cables, growing rapidly in size as I approach at breakneck speed.

I have to slow down. I squeeze the brake. My speed barely changes. Ahead, the cable I'm riding scoops down then arcs up and over the edge of the platform. I lean forward, dropping my legs to catch more air resistance. That helps, but I'm still moving way too fast as I hit the lowest point of the wire and start zooming upward. I lift my knees again to clear the edge of the platform, still squeezing the brake hard as I ride up and over the edge, still too fast. I put a foot down and it bounces off the rubbery surface and twists me to the left, right shoulder facing the pillar. Just before I smash into it, I lift my right leg up as if I'm going to kick the pillar, hoping to cushion the impact.

I catch the pillar with one leg, my foot connects first and my leg takes most of the shock. The rest of my body thrashes around the column in a hollow clanging jangle of ropes and metal. I grab hold of the pillar to steady myself. Pain echoes through my body, from my hips to my chest to my skull, blessedly muffled by the strong painkillers. Both feet on the ground, I steady myself and unclip.

The wire bounces against the pillar and the zipline buzzes. I snatch a glance up the wire and there they are, the Shield Monkeys, closer this time. All three wear fitted gray flightsuits—some type of exosuit, probably—with black boots and gloves. Their helmets are black too, with faceplates of reflective silver that flash as they glide down the wire, moving with smooth and practiced ease. It's clear how they get their name; they look like monkeys on a wire.

I flip them the bird.

"Fucking show ponies."

The Monkeys are silent. Maybe they've never seen a pony on this planet.

I turn away, moving across the platform to the cable running down into Tower Six. The cable is short. It runs down in between two branches that angle up and into the Shield. The wire scoops down then up into a large, shadowed opening, probably a maintenance corridor like the one we started in.

I get connected to the wire, grip both handles tight and push off the edge. I start accelerating downward, toward the corridor, and then . . .

. . . I realize I don't know what's next. My drug-fueled bravado has pushed me into action and tamped down my fears. But now it's not clear there'll be an elevator waiting for me, or that Trin is there, or what I will need to do except perhaps jump.

The earpiece comes to life. A different voice this time. "We have Trin. Surrender when you dismount."

My hackles rise. I take a deep breath. I'm halfway down the wire, picking up speed. It's a short wire so I squeeze the brakes. The shadowed corridor comes into clearer view as I zip between the two branches.

I see Trin.

She is on her knees, facing away and into the corridor, hands tied behind her back. Her helmet is off and lying on the floor next to her. The atmosphere must be less harsh this far from the hole in the Shield. Her captor stands next to her, wearing a blood red exosuit and helmet with a bronzed reflective visor facing out, looking at me. I tense up in alarm, wondering if he is a Guardian. But Guardians usually wear black and look ready for anything. This one stands at the end of the wire, waiting. He is tall and weedy, shoulders rounded and arms crossed, feet too close together. He doesn't look like someone who knows how to tangle. I figure he's just a red-suited Shield Monkey.

I slow steadily and consider what to do. I glance over my shoulder. The Gray Monkeys come into the platform behind me. Soon I'll be hemmed in.

A plan forms. No way to go but through. I'm suddenly glad I brought my belt knife.

I move fast, hoping the Red Monkey won't figure out what I'm doing. I lift the brake off the wire and drop it behind me. I feel the tug as it hits the end of its rope and swings. The roller increases its pitch as I accelerate.

I grab the roller with my right as my left hand comes off the chassis, reaching for my belt knife. I unlock the blade near the hilt and start sawing at the rope running down from the roller. The rope frays quickly and I tense my right arm, lifting my weight out of the harness, and finish sawing through the rope. Suddenly my entire weight is hanging from my right hand. I grunt with exertion, elbow screaming.

The Red Monkey speaks again. "Slow down, fool. Guardians are below. You are under arrest for damaging the Shield."

I throw my knife in his direction. He swears and ducks. Left hand now free, I reach up and grab the roller in both hands. The wire curves, bottoming out before running uphill and into the roof of the corridor. I bring my feet up and straighten my body like a missile to gather speed. The Red Monkey looks up, still standing at the terminus of the wire. Just where I want him. Trin is watching over her shoulder. She sees my plan and starts to shuffle sideways to get out of the way.

I start speeding upward, into the alcove. The Gray Monkeys behind me see that I'm not stopping.

I let go of the roller just as I feel myself entering the alcove. The momentum carries me, flying feet-first toward my target.

Gray Monkey warns, "Watch out!"

Too late, the Red Monkey tries to dodge but my left foot crashes into him, right in the stomach, throwing him sideways and into the wall of the corridor. My legs scissor open painfully and I deflect off-angle, my shoulder smashing into the side wall behind Trin with a white flash of pain.

The GoStick is thrumming and adrenaline soaks everything. I jump up, facing the Red Monkey, but he lies still.

"Stop. Now!" the Gray Monkey says, voice stern.

I look back. They're halfway down the wire, coming onto the platform.

Trin shuffles toward me on her knees, jerking herself in small jumps to get closer.

She shouts so I can hear. "We have about twenty seconds, Bard. I need his keys. Breast pocket."

I take four quick steps, crossing the distance between me and Red Monkey. He lies motionless, knocked out. I reach into his breast pocket and find a disc-shaped magnetic key. Trin rotates to face away so I can unlock her.

The first Gray Monkey has started braking. He's almost on us.

"We're going to have to jump, follow me." Her eyes are fixed on the three monkeys coming down the wire as I hold the disc to the center of the cuffs. They open with a snicking sound and clatter to the floor.

She moves fast, dropping to one knee beside her helmet. She

picks up her earpiece and twists it into her ear, clips on her helmet, and stands and looks at me.

I hear her voice through the earpiece. "Follow me."

"You have nowhere to go," the first Gray Monkey replies as he passes through the arc in the line, seconds away from the landing. "Surrender and we'll make it easier for you."

Trin sizes up the edge, rocking back on her heels for a second. It's just long enough for me to take in what she's planning, and what that means for me. I haven't parachuted since the war but I hope it's like riding a bike. Luckily any fear of heights has been drowned out by the GoStick.

She sucks down a huge breath before she leans like a sprinter into three long strides, arms pumping, leaping out and away from the ledge. She throws her arms and legs wide and plummets out of view.

"STOP!" Gray Monkey says, feet about to hit the deck beside me.

No time to think. I lean away from his reaching hands and go.

Four quick strides and a leap and I'm out over the empty air. The streets and buildings below are like aerial images, steadily zooming in. I'm spread-eagle, falling, then screaming: "FUCK!"

Trin's voice in the earpiece. "Stop screaming. Count to twelve, pull your chute, and follow me."

I shut my mouth and pull it together. Start counting.

Twelve.

My chest tightens as fear reasserts itself. Air rips around me, tearing at my exosuit, buffeting my helmet. I recall the scant training they gave me in the forces before they pushed us out of airplanes, trying to hold the falling position.

Eleven . . . Ten . . . Nine . . .

The Inner Sectors rush up underneath us, sketch marks zooming upward and resolving into streets and alleyways traversed by small dots of color. I reach my right hand behind me to feel for the shuttle and the shift in position instantly changes my course, left shoulder dipping closer to the city as I veer to the left. I can't see Trin. In my peripheral vision, the glass and concrete monoliths of the Outer Sectors look less like little concrete bricks and more like huge fucking buildings.

Eight . . . Seven . . . Six . . .

A multicar Airtrain slides through the air below, following the arc of the Outer Ring boulevard between the Shield Support Towers. I suddenly perceive the city as a spiderweb: a vast, man-made trap, filled with watchful Guardians. And I am a fly, plummeting toward death. I'm alone. I still can't see Trin.

Five . . . Four . . . Three . . .

The streets stretch wider. I make out the colors and clothes of people flowing through the streets below. To my right, a rectangular chute blooms, a bright orange against the Shield structure and its towering citadels. Trin.

Two . . .

I reach back, hand flapping to grab the toggle flying from the tail of my chute. My position shifts in the air. I can't get a grip on it.

One . . . .

The city rushes up. My hand closes around the cord and I pull the toggle to the right. The guide chute exits the pack with a rushing rustle of fabrics, and seconds later I'm pulled upright. Trin is floating to my left. I grip the steering handles on either side of the parachute and point my way toward her. We're close to the ground, a few hundred meters at most.

Trin speaks in a clipped manner, as if through gritted teeth. "Follow, but don't land on top of me." She steers her chute to the right, toward Central Tower, flying over Sector Eight. I pull on my right cable and follow.

We glide for a few minutes, descending toward the gracefully curved eaves of the Inner Sectors, punctuated by splashes of court-yard gardens.

I'm surprised Trin is steering us inward. I expected us to head toward the Outer Sectors, where I assumed there'd be more places to hide and more people willing to hide you. Here, the alleys are quaint and clean and filled with aristocratic types, fat from Syndicate profits or Temple tithes.

Trin's voice breaks in. "Shit. We have company below. Listen to me, keep quiet and follow. Remember this line is tapped."

I glance down. We're gliding above a wide boulevard running between two Sectors. People in the streets below are pointing up at us. Then I see the Guardian, running fast to keep track with us. He threads the crowd, shoving people out of his way mercilessly, his silver visor flashing the colors of the mob. His black uniform and red striped shoulders streak as he sprints, arms working like pistons.

We're coming down fast now. On either side, buildings line the boulevard, their sloping roofs creating a kind of ridgeline running parallel to the thoroughfare.

"Now!" Trin commands, suddenly veering to the right, tucking her feet up close to her chest to clear the crest of the roof next to us. I pull hard to follow, just in time to see her glide over. My feet barely clear the ridge. She continues, sailing over a thick gray wall. The wall is about two stories high and seems to extend hundreds of meters in both directions, running parallel to the boulevard. Beyond it is a field of smaller buildings and homes, their roofs almost touching, only the tiny shadowed gaps between them suggesting that a warren of alleyways runs beneath.

I suddenly see the genius of her tactic; we now have a long wall between us and the Guardian on the boulevard, and we're deep in the Old Sector. I just hope she knows her way around.

A purple tiled roof comes up fast beneath us. Trin touches down gracefully, one foot then the other, and she walks off the remaining speed along the ridge of the roof.

I follow much less gracefully, nearly crashing into Trin as my first foot hits the ground. I yank to the right to avoid her and touch down on the sloping section of the roof, tripping and stumbling before landing hard on my knees. The chute flaps down and around my head, muffling a minor commotion from below us—probably people wondering what the hell just crash landed above them.

"Unclip, leave the chute," Trin says from somewhere I can't see.

I roll over amid a tangle of wires and material and start to detach the pack from my harness. The material lifts and Trin's face appears. Her helmet is gone and her brown hair is slicked with sweat and stuck to her brow.

She plucks her earpiece out and throws it over the roof.

"Ditch yours too. If they've cracked it, they can track it," she says as she helps untangle me from the chute.

I stagger to my feet, unclipping my helmet and lobbing it over the other side of the roof. My earpiece follows. There's a clatter and shout of protest. I take a deep breath, noticing the musk of the city: the scent of jasmine blossoms, burning incense, and street vendor spices.

I shrug and stretch. I'm still sore, but the drugs are still working. "That was pretty good flying," I say.

"Thanks," she says, then looks me up and down. "You too, especially if you're injured. Can you run?"

"I think so."

"Okay, we'd better move," she says, then turns and walks to the edge of the roof. The tiles clatter under her boots. She crouches, grips the edge of the tiles, and vaults down into the shadowed crevice. I trot down the slope and see her standing below in the half light, waving me down.

I drop down beside her and we set off at a jog. The alleys are tight and curving, just wide enough for two people walking abreast. Doorways line the alleys, each with a small step up to a gold-banded door, richly decorated and framed with red lintels. I'd never been to this part of the city before, but Trin seems to know it intimately, regularly making turns, choosing dark alleys over bright, narrow over wide.

She stops at a T-junction, where the alley runs onto a curving street wide enough to see a bright band of sky running between the roofs. The flagstones seem newer, well kept. Trin clings to the corner, scanning each way.

"This your old haunt?" I ask, crouching behind her.

She turns back to answer. "That's Grandma's house," she says, pointing across the junction to a black door, banded in iron and set in a lintel of gold.

"Can your gran get us out?"

She nods. "She has access to the Undercut. We can find our skimmers and get out."

"So why are we waiting here?"

"It's too quiet. Maybe everyone's inside. Or out in the square, gawking at the Shield." She squints, looking up at the sky. "It's too far to see anything, though." She clicks her tongue and resumes scanning the alley.

"Do you know how it broke?"

Trin just shakes her head. I want to ask her why she left me there. How she got caught. But it doesn't seem like the right time.

"We shouldn't wait anymore," she says, "you stay on this side, under the eaves in the shadow. I'll see if Gran is home."

She dashes across the alley toward the black door set in gold, then hammers on the door with the heel of her fist in a distinctive pattern: three times fast, three slow, three fast.

I slip around the corner, staying under the eaves across the road, back against the wall.

Trin keeps knocking, then stops, turning back to look where we came from. Her eyes go wide and she shrinks against the door.

A figure steps onto the street from the narrow alleyway, moving with deadly grace. His uniform is almost entirely black except for his shoulders: two pointed red epaulets. A thin red stripe runs down his sleeves. His hands are gloved in black. He wears a black helmet with a FluxVisor concealing his face, reflecting the alley like a pool of mercury. He looks at Trin, then back at me. He speaks and his voice makes ripples on the visor's surface, flowing where his mouth should be, tiny wavelets of sound.

"You are under arrest."

"*Kao*," Trin swears.

I step away from the wall, turning toward the Guardian.

"Stop. Or you will be stopped," he says.

I raise my fists like a boxer and step into a light stance, bouncing on my toes. I expect to be beaten to a pulp, but I know that Guardians are forbidden to kill, and I'm not going to the mines without a fight.

I see my reflection in his visor, body distended by its curve. I look like a cartoonish boxer wearing a harness.

My reflection quivers as he speaks. "Don't be a fool."

I've already decided to be a fool.

I charge. I keep my head low and arms wide, going for the Guardian's knees. He drops into a stance and darts to the right so quickly I have no time to adjust my angle. He launches a powerful thrusting kick and his foot cannons up into my shoulder, driving my body backward into the alley wall. The air whooshes out of my lungs as I fall to the ground. I gasp, squeezing my eyes shut through the chorus of pain that completely overpowers the painkillers.

"Amusing," the Guardian says, "but tackling is for brawlers."

I open my eyes to see him standing in the alleyway, head swiveling from Trin at the door to me cowering by the wall. Trin steps toward the Guardian, lips tight, eyes narrow with concentration. She rolls her shoulders then steps into guard, square on, palms open like a kung fu fighter.

"Ah," he says, clapping his gloved hands once, "your girlfriend wants to have a turn? Maybe both at once? Come. Let's dance."

I need to pull myself together; if I'm going out, I'm going out in style. I get my hands under my body and push myself up onto my knees, then stagger to my feet, one hand holding my ribs.

"How about we use boxing rules?" I call out. "No dirty kicks."

The Guardian chuckles. It sounds like sandpaper on wood. "Only if you both attack at once."

Trin rushes in. I follow, coming in from the side.

The Guardian waits.

I reach him first and throw a quick combo—jab, punch, hook. He seems to read my mind, moving faster than seems possible—a palm pushes my jab aside and down, the same palm comes back up and across. His forearm whips into my punching arm with a crack so forceful it spins me to the left. My hook sails through empty air. The Guardian closes in again and shoves me back into the alley wall so hard that light flashes in my eyes as the wind rushes out of me. I lean against the wall, blinking.

The Guardian pivots toward Trin. She shapes up for what looks like it's going to be a quick jab-punch one-two. The Guardian moves to intercept with a palm block. At the last instant Trin's fist opens and twists, catching the Guardian's blocking arm. She wrenches down on his wrist, pulling him off balance, lifting her knee to snap a kick straight upward toward the Guardian's neck—

—and he slips the kick flawlessly, moving his head just enough for her boot to sail past his visor.

The Guardian closes instantly. He catches her kick midair. His right foot whips out to sweep Trin's standing leg out from under her. She crashes to the ground. The Guardian takes two steps back and laughs. The silver visor swivels back toward me.

"Your girlfriend is a far better fighter than you. You should ask for lessons." The Guardian tilts his head as if listening.

"Enough games. You are both under arrest for damaging the Shield."

"We didn't damage the Shield. It just shattered."

The Guardian grunts. He reaches behind his back, pulling two sets of cuffs from his belt.

I shake my head at the obvious setup. They just need a scapegoat.

I consider our options. The painkillers are wearing off and everything hurts. Pain pulses through my head, my ribs, and my back. Trin is struggling upright. Her face crumples in pain and her ankle wavers under her weight.

Then I hear the creak of a door on old hinges.

Behind Trin the black door opens, swinging inward within its golden lintel. An old woman emerges from the shadow, her back hunched under a gray shawl, a metallic walking stick rattling with each step.

"*Gou le*," she drawls in old Mandarin. Enough.

Trin shouts, "*Nainai!* Not now! Go back inside!"

The Guardian turns toward the old woman. "Listen to your granddaughter, old meddler," you can almost hear the snarl on his face, "or I'll arrest you too."

"Eh," she grunts, easing herself off her doorstep and into the alley. Her stick clacks as she hobbles toward him. "You have many to arrest today, it seems. Perhaps too many."

The Guardian stands deadly still, watching.

"*Nainai*, please," Trin says.

The old woman is closer now, almost next to Trin. She stops, smiles and then she . . . unfurls, her hunchback somehow dissolving as she straightens, standing up with her shoulders back, staring at the Guardian with hard eyes. Her grip shifts around the walking stick and she steps into a wide, stable stance, like someone riding a bus without something to hold on to.

She is transformed, suddenly powerful.

"I—we—have had enough of you. Guarding nothing but yourselves and your greedy syndicates."

The Guardian drops back into a fighting stance and his uniform begins to vibrate around his body, pulsing across his chest and torso. The vibrations traverse his arms and legs before falling still. Flux-Armor. I'd never seen it up close; this kind of nanotech armor, fully flexible when moving and yet impenetrable to attack. He hadn't bothered to activate this to fight us. I have no idea why he's activating for the old woman.

We all stand still, as if waiting for a wave to break. A light breeze runs down the alley, ruffling the old lady's hair. The alley is silent; I realize the klaxon has stopped. Even the usual sound of human activity is absent.

The old woman moves first. She swings her metal walking stick up and holds it like a shotgun.

The Guardian sees it sooner than I do. He leaps toward the old woman so fast that my eyes can barely track him.

A flash fills the alley accompanied by two deafening booms, one after the other. The Guardian seems to hang for a moment in the air, mid-leap, before landing on his feet. He sways for a moment, silent, then falls upright onto his knees in front of the old woman, head level with her shoulder.

The Guardian's clawed hand rises slowly toward the gun, reaching.

The old woman adjusts her aim, moving the barrel of the gun to point at his visor. She pulls the trigger. Another deafening boom. His helmet shatters under the point-blank impact, and in its place a red cloud of blood and shining shards blooms. His body jerks and he collapses backward, his knees bent unnaturally beneath him.

I try to process and fail. Trin's grandma just shot a Guardian. With a contraband weapon. In the center of Sankar City, ground zero for Guardians and their allies.

I look at her victim. The scene is as gruesome as my repressed memories of war. Blood pools around his body and what was head is now a gaping mess of blood, pinkish flesh, and bone.

I start walking toward Trin and the old woman. Each step hurts, forcing me to go slow. Trin winces as she takes a step toward her Gran. That takedown must have wrenched her ankle. She limps over to the old woman, who has shrunk back to her original size, and wraps her arms about her gran's thin shoulders. The old woman lets the gun rattle to the ground. She returns the embrace, smiling.

"I was so worried about you. Silly to come here! And parachuting, no less!" The old woman shakes her head. I wonder how she is so well informed. She looks down the alley, past me, and steps away from Trin. I hear it too: the sound of combat boots striking on flagstones.

"Sounds like we have company," I say.

She nods. Her face is lined and leathery, framed by straight, shoulder-length white hair, and her eyes are dark pebbles. They excavate my soul and find me lacking. She breaks eye contact and bends down to pick up the gun in one smooth movement, like someone half her age. She leans on it again, like a walking stick, then looks back to me and winks. "Come, let's go."

Two more Guardians appear from around the curve of the street.

They wear silver visors and tight-fitting black uniforms, moving toward us at a steady jog.

"*Kao*," I swear.

I hope the old lady has a few more bullets in that gun.

"What's our plan here? That's two Guardians," I say, trying to keep the desperation out of my voice.

The old woman looks down the street.

"Not Guardians," the old woman says. "Friends."

I'm skeptical, but she has the gun.

The "friends" approach with a steady stride, steps in unison. The one on the left stands slightly taller and looks female by the fit of her uniform. I notice their epaulettes and stripes are a saffron yellow, not the blood red of the Guardian. She speaks, FluxVisor shimmering. "I see that you . . ." she pauses as she looks at the bloody mess on the ground, "took care of your emergency, Lady Fang."

Lady Fang shrugs. "I had to. You're late."

"We were engaged," the tall woman says as she steps forward. "At least fifteen Guardians remain at large, including Guardian Six."

Lady Fang inclines her head. "All's well that ends well. And the Council?"

"We secured them first."

"Good. So it goes to plan."

"Apart from the break in the Shield, yes."

I can't help but interject. "What happened to the Shield?"

The tall woman doesn't respond, silent behind her mask, until Lady Fang nods.

"Our agent in the Sixth Sector Market misfired his gun while being arrested by Guardian Six. We think his bullet broke the Shield. These weapons we've equipped our people with may be antiques, but they can wreak havoc."

I can't help but look at the body on the flagstones. The blood glows ruby-red under the sunlight, and I feel sick.

"Indeed," the old lady says. She inclines her head. "Thank you for responding to my beacon."

They move in unison to bow, raising both hands and placing their left palms open against clenched right fists.

They speak in one voice: "For the everlasting dawn."

Lady Fang responds, "And dawn everlasting."

They turn and run.

Lady Fang, unperturbed, turns toward her door.

"Come inside," she says, "you're both hurt."

Trin doesn't move. "Wait. What's going on? The council, Guardians . . . is there some sort of battle? An uprising?"

Lady Fang looks at Trin and stands a little straighter. Her eyes narrow as she nods slowly, pursing her lips. "It was time."

Trin frowns, squinting in disbelief. "And you're with . . . them? You killed that Guardian like it was nothing . . ." She trails off, shaking her head.

Lady Fang puts a hand on her shoulder. "Let's not talk here." Her eyes flick to the dead body. "Come inside."

She threads her arm through Trin's. Trin takes a breath and follows her grandmother's lead, limping across to the doorstep and through the door.

I walk across the yellow flagstones, rounding the pool of seeping blood before stepping up and into the doorway. I move slowly, letting my eyes adjust to the soft, Earth-spectrum light inside. We're in a hallway lit by Enviropanels, the kind that simulate any type of sky scene. These are set to a gentle cloud-gray, the colors of a summer storm.

On either side of me, ornate wooden carvings depict the colonization of Darmani. Trin and Lady Fang pay no attention, but I can't help but stare, ogling the depictions. A flotilla of Ark Ships traversing the stars. The construction of the first Orbital Station and Starport, the first failed landing at Stormside, and finally the building of Sankar City under the Habitat Shield. I walk past them carefully, hands tight by my side; if they're carved from Earth wood, they would be worth a small fortune.

Trin and Lady Fang pass the carvings and stop next to two beautiful wooden doors, glowing amber. At the end of the corridor lies a stone garden surrounded by tiny green Earth trees. The color of their leaves betrays their nonnative status. I realize my mouth is hanging open; the sheer wealth in this hallway alone is staggering. After our conversation up on the platform, I had imagined Trin's family was rich, but this was uncommon wealth.

The door on the left glides open and is silently inhaled into the wall.

"We can talk and rest in here," Lady Fang says.

We walk into the room. Inside, the room has two halves, one with couches and soft furnishings, the walls covered in yellow and red drapes in a mixture of silk and velvet. Bowls of sweet cloned fruits—bananas, apples, and peaches—sit on a handsome wooden table near the couches. The other half opens onto a lush Earth garden of green foliage, growing under Enviropanels showing a blue simulated Earth sky. In the corner, a fountain burbles on cool stones.

We cross the room and sit on the couches. The cushions are blessedly soft yet supportive. I close my eyes and breathe. The adrenaline and fear drain away, replaced by pain and fatigue.

"Now can you tell us what's going on?" Trin asks. I open my eyes. She's leaning forward, elbows on her knees, looking at her grandmother intently.

Lady Fang speaks. "Yes, but I must be brief. Today the Acolytes of Sankar are taking back the city. We will return to the teachings of Maryam Sankar, and rebuild our society as our colony's founders intended. Unfortunately, overthrowing power requires power. And in some cases, death."

"So your Acolytes are killing the Guardians?"

"Only when necessary. The Acolytes are ex-Guardians, neurally recalibrated for our goals. Guardians are elite soldiers with a lifetime of training in nonlethal enforcement. We don't want to waste them. But my hand was forced today due to your misadventures."

Trin's eyes widen as she speaks. "You're their leader?"

Lady Fang chuckles. "Dear girl. No. The Temples are taking the lead. I am something of an investor, a sympathetic civilian."

Trin looks at her knees, frowning.

Lady Fang speaks again. "I must go. You two have caused enough trouble for today. The city is on a knife's edge. If the Acolytes fail, we will be hunted and arrested. I will take my chance here, but you must get back to Stormside."

"I won't leave you," Trin says. "If you're fighting, I want to join."

"You will leave," Lady Fang says, backing out the door. "I will be back. Rest. Have something to eat—those fruits were picked yesterday."

She rattles through the door and it glides shut behind her.

"Your grandma is badass," I say.

Trin laughs ruefully. "I had no idea."

She shuffles closer on the couch, takes my hand, and looks me in the eye.

"I was trying to come back for you," she says, squeezing my hand. "That Shield Monkey in the red suit? He was my contact. Usually he rides a desk. I asked for his help and he turned on me. Alerted them to our presence. I think he told them we blew up the Shield so he wouldn't get in trouble for letting us up there in the first place. And then that Guardian. I'm so sorry. This all went so wrong."

In all that had happened since I'd rescued Trin, I'd forgotten she left me alone. I'd forgotten she hadn't told me she was a wanted woman, that she'd hidden her background from me.

Some fucking mystery date.

"What did you think was going to happen? Red Monkey would just come and help carry me? You're on the city watchlist! He probably decided he could collect some reward for turning you in." I shift on the couch, turning to face her. "This is not the place to bring someone you," I make air quotes with my right index fingers, "care about. I trusted you. I was really into you. But I didn't realize you were so reckless, so willing to put people in terrible situations."

She sits for a moment, looking at the floor, then back at me. "Was?"

I don't know if she's tired but there's a sheen in her eyes.

I start paying close attention to the fake blue sky on the Enviropanels across the other side of the room. I hate seeing people cry, and I'm too mad to comfort her.

She sighs. "I've done this before, so many times, usually alone. I guess I'm used to the danger. And the Shield breaking was just a freak accident, a total surprise—"

"Yeah maybe not so surprising if you'd bothered to ask your Warlord Grandma."

She stops for a second, then suddenly laughs.

I can't help but smile. I still love that sound.

Trin knuckles at the corner of her eye. "I had *no* idea. She'd got an access way to the Undercut. I thought we'd escape that way . . ." She trails off, and then almost whispers, "You hit that cable pillar real hard . . . and then with that Guardian . . . it scared me so much." She looks skyward, and exhales heavily.

I straighten up, one hand lightly roving over my head, feeling for sore points. "Well I'm not dead yet. But I definitely need to see a doctor."

Her eyebrows furrow. "Can you make it back to Stormside? You can drive?"

I enjoy seeing her concerned about me. "I think so."

"The way you took out Red Monkey . . . what was that? Missile mode?" She asks, grinning.

I sense the admiration in her voice. A smile tugs at the corners of my mouth.

"What can I say. I'm tough."

"So I've learned. I like it." She threads an arm behind my back and rests her head on my shoulder. I'm trying to hold onto my righteous anger, but a colony of butterflies has sprung to life under my ribcage.

We sit like that, resting, waiting for Lady Fang to reappear. The fountain burbles in the corner and the fake Earth sky glows a for-gotten shade of blue. It's been so long since a woman has held me like this.

She murmurs into my shoulder. "If we get out of this, what are my chances for a second date?"

She puts her other arm around me and nuzzles at my neck. My face heats up. The butterflies jostle for pole position.

"Depends," I say.

"On what?"

"Can we just go bowling?"

She laughs. Still my favorite sound.

Ambiguous Loss

J. L. Price

JOSIE WATCHED THE NUMBERS on the digital clock mounted above the whiteboard in the seventh grade science classroom tick away the seconds. The numbers on the far right of the digital display cycled through in rapid succession in a repeating sequence of 60—01, 02, 03 . . . 59, 00. Each cycle leading to a change in the minute column, which in fifteen minutes would thankfully lead to a change in the hour from two to three. Normally she liked science class and had little trouble paying attention, but today she was anxious to go. They were having a party tonight, well, really just a small family dinner because Danny, her older brother—Dan, she quickly corrected herself as ever since he came back he got pissed every time anyone called him Danny—wouldn't let their mother throw him a real party. He'd barely agreed to the dinner.

Josie winced at the thought of the fight Danny and their mother had had when their mom insisted that they at least invite over a few friends and family who had been dying to see him.

"Why, so they can come over and feel sorry for me, and gawk at my fucking leg, and thank me for my service when you know they don't give a shit?" he'd yelled.

Josie had been hiding out in the den at the time, with the door shut, and the TV up loud, but she could still hear him yelling loud and clear. Just like she could hear him slam the front door when he left, and gun the engine of his truck as he peeled out of the driveway. Granted, Josie had been young when Danny first joined up—she being only six and he eighteen at the time—but she didn't remember him and Mom fighting like they seemed to do all the time since he'd gotten back. She didn't remember him cussing as much as he did now, either. Josie tried to tune back in to Mr. Flintock and what he was saying. She tamped down the uneasy feeling that always clenched her gut when she thought about Danny and how much he'd changed in the six years since he'd been gone.

"Most animals do not raise their young for years, like humans," Mr. Flintock explained to the class. "Some do not raise them at all, such as certain snakes and other reptiles who abandon their eggs to the wild as soon as they are laid." Mr. Flintock pressed a button on the controller he held in his hand, causing pictures of the animals he'd just mentioned to appear on the whiteboard.

Josie shifted her attention from the board to the clock, which had only moved a minute, and then looked out the window. Thankfully in this class she had been able to get a seat on the far side of the room next to both the window and the heater. For the first time in weeks the sky was blue instead of gray and the sun shot rays through the branches of the big tree that grew out of the hole in the cement in the school yard two stories below. The tree had just finished blooming a few days before, and a light breeze made the leaves look like they were dancing in the sunlight. A bird with red on its head and its chest hovered outside the glass, staring Josie in the eye before it swooped off to some better place.

Josie looked back at the clock. Only two more minutes had rolled by. Her mom was going to take off early and meet her at home after Josie got off the bus. She had talked her mom into letting her make giant chocolate chip cookies tonight for Danny's birthday instead of a cake. She didn't have a lot of memories about her and Danny before he left home, but she remembered baking cookies with him and eating so much dough it made her sick.

"There are a few animal groups where the young will stay with their families for many years . . . ."

As Josie looked back toward the board, trying to concentrate on what Mr. Flintock was saying, she caught Amanda, her best friend since second grade, signaling her from across the room to check her phone. Mr. Flintock, like nearly all their teachers, didn't allow them to use UEDs (unapproved electronic devices) during class, which included their phones. In his case he made them put their phones on their desks where he could see them. Early in the year, she and Amanda had figured out that he had a tendency to lecture to only the right half of the room, often turning his back to the side Amanda sat on. Consequently, Amanda was free to text regularly in science class. Josie hardly dared.

Mr. Flintock clicked the button on his handheld device, changing the picture on the screen. As he did so, he activated the red laser dot and used it to circle the picture of the two Orcas he was discussing. Josie took the moment to hit the home button on her phone and see what Amanda had written.

Dan's party tonight? Amanda had texted. Josie glanced at Mr. Flintock and quickly tapped *yes*.

Am I invited? Amanda texted back. Josie gritted her teeth. She had already told Amanda earlier this week that they weren't having anyone over for Dan's birthday. Plus, why would she think he'd want her there? But then Josie knew why. Another thing that had been annoying the shit out of her lately. Ever since her brother had come back home for good, more of her friends kept asking to come to her house and stay the night. They were always asking where her brother was. Having conversations about him, about how cute and hot he was, like Josie wasn't even in the room. There were times where she felt like screaming at all of them. *He will never have anything to do with you, and don't let those looks fool you—he came home a first-class jerk.*

As soon as those thoughts ran through her head, she felt the guilt that always accompanied them. Especially because she knew they weren't entirely true. Yes, he was angry a lot and sometimes, well a lot of times, he yelled. But almost never at her. And sometimes he was still nice too, and if she caught him at the right time when he was in a good mood, he'd even be like she remembered him. And she understood why he was angry. She didn't know what he had seen; he never talked about it. But she'd watched a few shows about war. She had some idea it could be bad. She knew too that the guy he'd been best friends with in his unit, who he would sometimes bring home with him when he came back for short visits and holidays, died in the same explosion that had taken Dan's leg. She sucked in a deep breath, checked that Mr. Flintock's back was still to her, and wrote Amanda back.

No. No one is, remember?

A few seconds later, Amanda wrote back, *Yea, sorry, forgot. Want ride home.*

Josie sat and thought for a minute. Since Amanda's older brother, Andrew, had gotten his license a month earlier he had been using every excuse he could find to drive. His parents still weren't letting him have free reign, but they let him drive to school if he promised to take and pick up Amanda. He often gave Josie a ride home too, just so he could stay behind the wheel a little longer. The problem was, Amanda often stayed at Josie's once Andrew dropped her off, giving Andrew an excuse to come back later and get her. Amanda could probably stay until the party started, since that wouldn't be until dinner time, but Josie didn't want her to. She wrote back.

Yes, but U can't stay, have to work . . .

"Ms. Johnson!" Mr. Flintock shot her name across the room, causing Josie to jump and knock her phone to the floor.

"Would you like to share with the class what is so important that it can't wait, the three minutes we have left in class before you send that message."

Josie shook her head. She felt the color rise in her cheeks as the entire class turned to look at her.

"What was that?" Mr. Flintock continued, crossing his arms, and raising his eyebrows expectantly. Josie couldn't think of anything to say, since she didn't think the truth was a good option, and a plausible lie didn't immediately present itself. Instead she silently prayed he wouldn't give her detention, at least not for tonight.

At that moment the bell thankfully chimed, leading to the usual bustle and rush out of class. Grateful for the distraction, Josie let out the breath she'd been holding, quickly picked up her phone off the floor, and grabbed her books.

"Ms. Johnson, will you please come here?" Josie stopped her eyes from rolling, just barely, and headed toward the front of the room.

"You know I do not allow cell phone use of any kind in this classroom."

"Yes, I know. I'm sorry. It's just that my mom was texting me about tonight. She's been bugging me all day, since it's my brother's birthday and it's the first time he's been back for his birthday since he went in the Army. She was just making sure I was going to be home on time." Josie stopped, a little surprised at how easily the lie rolled off her tongue. Her heart pounded as she hoped Mr. Flintock didn't ask to see her phone to verify her lie.

Mr. Flintock gave her a funny look, then asked, "Danny Johnson is your brother, right?"

Josie nodded, inwardly cringing and wishing she hadn't included Danny in the lie.

"You know I had him several years ago. He was a good student. I'm very sorry to hear about what happened to him in Afghanistan."

Josie nodded again, now wanting to melt into the floor.

"Well, tell your mom to quit sending you messages during class. And please thank your brother for his service for me."

Josie nodded one last time and rushed from the room. She nearly collided with Amanda, who had been waiting for her in the hall, clearly eavesdropping.

"Well aren't you lucky," Amanda said as they started down the hall toward their lockers.

"What do you mean?" Josie responded.

"Playing the brother card to get out of detention, smart."

Josie stopped in the hall, a rock in the sea of kids flowing around her, glaring at Amanda. "If you wouldn't have sent me that stupid text in the first place I wouldn't have had to play the brother card," Josie stated, louder than she intended, but not caring.

"Whoa," Amanda held up the hand not holding her books, in a gesture of surrender. "Didn't mean to offend, I was just saying well played. And sorry about the text. But do you want a ride or not?"

Josie relaxed a little and continued down the hall, merging back into the sea of kid traffic. Amanda followed by her side. "Yeah, I'd still like a ride, but you can't stay. My brother doesn't want any visitors, just family."

"Got it, no problem." Amanda pulled out her own phone, likely texting her brother. She moved down the hall, deftly evading others as she multitasked.

"So, he's been kind of a loner lately, huh?" Amanda asked, as they arrived at their lockers.

"Who?" Josie asked spinning her combination and opening her locker.

"Your brother, Danny. I mean Dan."

"It's not that he's a loner." Josie could feel her defensive hackles rising. "He just gets sick of everyone asking about his leg and stuff."

"Yeah, I guess I get that, although cute as he is, I don't know that anyone is paying much attention to his leg."

"Really, Amanda?" Josie said, slamming her locker door and slinging her backpack over her shoulder and her jacket over her arm. "He's my brother for fuck's sake."

"All the more reason to invite me to the party." Amanda shut her own locker, draping her arm over Josie's shoulder as they headed toward the exit doors.

"Not gonna happen," Josie replied.

"A girl can dream, can't she?" Josie shoved Amanda playfully and half-heartedly, then ran for the exit.

Amanda ran after her. "Hey, wait up!"

TWENTY MINUTES LATER, JOSIE and Amanda were singing the latest Taylor Swift song at the top of their lungs, as Amanda's brother made the left-hand turn off the main highway onto the long dirt road that led to Josie's house. They sang not because they were big Taylor Swift fans, but because it drove Andrew nuts. He let them get away with it in exchange for Amanda not telling their mother about all the times he drove to places he shouldn't, usually with girls he had been told to avoid.

Josie's family lived ten miles out of town in the farmhouse that had been in her family for generations. They still owned the nearly five hundred acres that surrounded the house, but all but the fifteen acres closest to the house were now leased to others to farm on their behalf. As they made their way down the quarter-mile drive, Josie saw several migrant workers in the distance, appearing and disappearing between the large tree trunks that lined the drive, like actors in a poorly drawn flip animation book. Josie pushed the button to lower her window and let the breeze and the outside smells into the car. She always liked this time of year best. The days were getting warmer and sunnier, everything was starting to bloom, and the smell of fresh earth hung in the air as all the dirt got turned for spring planting. Although she hadn't told anyone, she planned to take over the farm when she got older. She liked having acres and acres of open land all her own; she loved growing things and was already good at it. Plus, she liked the idea of being in charge, just like her grandmother had been up until she died a few years ago.

As they neared the house, Andrew spun the wheel and hit the brakes, sending the car into a sliding halt in the gravel apron in front of the porch. Stopping just inches away from Dan's truck.

Josie reached forward and punched Andrew on the shoulder.

"Ow, what the hell did you do that for?" Andrew asked, rubbing his shoulder like it actually hurt.

"For nearly hitting my brother's truck, you dumbshit. If he saw you do that he'd probably come out here and kick your ass. Plus, if my parents saw you do that they'd never let me ride with you again."

Their eyes locked in the rearview mirror and Josie felt a funny warm wave ripple through her stomach. It was rather pleasant.

"I guess I better not do that again, because you'd miss me too much," Andrew replied, smiling and keeping his eyes locked with hers.

"Yeah, you wish," she retorted, but couldn't help but smile back.

"Tell Dan I said hi and happy birthday," Amanda cut in, breaking the moment.

Josie grabbed her backpack, slid out of the car, and slammed the door.

"Text me and let me know how it goes," Amanda called out rolling down her window.

"I will," Josie replied over her shoulder not bothering to turn around as she headed toward the house. She could hear Andrew complete the U-turn in another swirl of gravel as he and Amanda headed back down the drive.

In a few short seconds, the noise of the speeding car gave way to the quiet bustle of late afternoon in the country. Josie stood before the steps of the front porch, closing her eyes and taking a deep breath, letting it all sink in. The song of a meadowlark fluttering in the distance. The buzz of a bee nosing around the flowers that were starting to bud in the front flower bed. The sound of a pickax out in the fields. Some vibration coming from in the house. Josie opened her eyes, looking around, noticing that only Danny's truck was in the drive. Both of her parents' cars were gone, so they still weren't home from work yet. Josie followed the vibrating thump up the front stairs, across the porch, and to the front door.

As she opened the door, the assault of loud harsh rock music made her blood run cold and her heart start to pound. Lately when Danny cranked his music up like that, it was a sign he wasn't doing well.

Josie dropped her backpack and jacket on the floor by the door and bounded up the stairs to the second floor, hoping she might be able to talk to Dan and get him in a better mood before their parents got home. She turned right at the top of the stairs, making her way across the landing that overlooked the two-story entry. Danny's room was the first door on the left as she entered the hall. She found herself tiptoeing across the floor, even though with the blasting music there was no way he could hear her coming. As she approached Danny's door, she lifted her hand to knock and noticed that the door was cracked open. Thinking that he wouldn't hear her knock anyway,

Josie pushed the door slightly wider and stopped short on a sharp intake of breath.

It had been a few days since she'd been in his room, but the normally neat space had stuff strewn all over it. Clothes mostly, but other things that looked like they had been smashed, covered the floor. His prosthetic leg and foot lay on top of a clothes heap that resembled a pile of smelly garbage. The drawers in the dresser were half open, with more clothes hanging over the side, as though he'd been frantically looking for something he couldn't find. Dan sat on his bed with his back to her, looking out the large window above his bed on the wall opposite the door where Josie stood. This was the first time Josie had seen him without his shirt on in the four months since he'd been back. She felt tears sting her eyes as she looked at him. Raised welts and tracks spread all over his shoulders and torso in a web of scars that looked like the tentacles of some creature trying to take over his body. She took a step back, making sure he couldn't see her, thankful that he hadn't seen her initial reaction to his back. From her vantage point, Josie could see his face reflected in the full-length mirror propped against the wall by the right side of his bed. There was a star in the middle that sent two cracks running in opposite directions. It had clearly been hit with something, although Josie had no idea what.

Danny sat still as the angry music with the yelling singer swirled around him. He seemed to be tapping something against the stump of what was left of his right leg, but from this distance she couldn't tell what it was. His face looked serious and angry, but his eyes looked a million miles away. Josie wasn't sure he'd see her if she walked right in front of him and danced. At any rate, it didn't look like the talk she had planned would work, and the last thing she wanted was to accidentally make him mad. She had just decided to leave him alone when he raised the thing he'd been tapping on his leg and put it to his temple. Now Josie could see the gun clearly reflected in the mirror. Danny pulled the trigger. Josie's hands flew to her mouth smothering the scream that nearly escaped.

Tears streamed down Josie's face as she nearly collapsed in relief over the fact that the gun hadn't gone off. For a moment she froze, paralyzed in shock, then she found herself running down the hall to her room, fueled by adrenaline and fear. She shut the door, louder than she meant to, and locked it.

She stood in the middle of her room, as heaving sobs took her breath away and she shook uncontrollably. She bit down on her index finger to keep from screaming and to stifle the noise from her crying. She reached in her pocket for her phone and then realized she'd left it in her backpack by the front door. What the hell was she going to do? Danny had turned off the music in his bedroom, and she could hear him moving around through the wall. Had he seen her? Josie looked around frantically for a place to hide. She wedged herself behind her large papasan chair and her bed, rolling herself into a ball, trying to make herself as small as possible. Her heart pounded as she listened to Danny moving. She clutched her arms around her knees trying to make the shaking stop.

She heard a loud thump and then several cuss words. She clutched her knees tighter. She heard Danny coming down the hall with the funny-sounding uneven gait he now had when he walked with his crutch. Josie pushed herself against the wall, trying to disappear behind the chair as she heard him pause at her door. She held her breath, trying not to make any noise, waiting to see what he might do. He knocked on her door, rapping so softly she wouldn't have heard it if she hadn't been listening. She kept quiet. He knocked again, a little louder this time. She buried her head between her knees, still holding her breath.

"Josie, are you in there? I thought I heard you come in?" He jiggled the door handle, causing her to jump and let out the breath she'd been holding in a squeak.

Just then she heard her mom yelling from downstairs, "Daniel, Josie, I'm home. Are you here? Daniel, Josie?" Josie could hear Danny move away from her door, his uneven stride moving back down the hall toward their mother's voice. Josie sat there, by the side of her bed, tears running down her face, soaking her jeans. Now that she felt safe, she sucked in several deep, shuddering breaths trying to calm down.

Josie heard her mom banging around in the kitchen below, opening and closing cabinets. That motivated Josie to move. It would only be a few minutes before her mom came looking for her. How could she explain why she was lying on her floor crying? What would Danny do if he knew she had seen him? Josie made herself get up and move quickly. She rushed over and unlocked the door. If her mom came up and found her door locked, she'd ask a bunch of questions Josie wasn't sure she could answer. She then went into the bathroom, which thankfully adjoined her room, and splashed cold water on her face. Luckily, she wasn't an ugly crier, and although her face looked a little red and blotchy, it wasn't horrible. Just as she was getting ready to put on a different pair of jeans, there was a loud knock on her door.

"Josie, are you in there? I saw your backpack and jacket by the door, which you know you aren't supposed to be leaving downstairs," her mom yelled as she turned the handle, pushing open the door.

Josie turned her back to the door, burying her head in her closet and replied, "Yeah, sorry, I just got home, I spilled something on my jeans in science class and had to go to the bathroom, so I just rushed up here. I'll go down and get it in a minute." She hoped her voice sounded normal. Her mom was way too good at picking up on when something was wrong.

Josie made a show of taking off her jeans and looking for another pair in her closet, as a moment of silence stretched across the room. She could feel her mom's eyes boring into her back. She prayed she didn't ask her what was wrong. Part of her wanted to turn around, run to her mom, and tell her everything. But how could she tell her she just saw Danny trying to commit suicide in the room next to hers? Her hands were still shaking. But then she thought back to seeing Danny, sitting there with only one leg and all those scars. Danny not knowing she saw him like that. Like she'd snooped on the most private of moments. She wanted to tell, but she knew she never would. She would keep that secret for him.

Josie took a deep breath, pulled up and snapped on a clean pair of jeans. She forced a smile she hoped looked real and turned to her mom. "I'm coming. We're making cookies, right?"

Her mom tilted her head to the side and gave Josie a weird look before she smiled as well. "Yes, you're right, let's get going. Danny is already downstairs in the kitchen." With that she turned and walked out of the room. Josie followed slowly behind, wondering how the hell she was going to get through the evening.

JOSIE WOKE THE NEXT morning with a start, rolled toward the nightstand that sat to the right of her bed, and clicked the home button on her phone. She needn't have looked: 6:35 a.m. right on the dot. Although today was a Saturday and she didn't have to get up, like usual she was up at the crack of dawn. That was one thing she hated about herself, the way she was like a walking atomic clock. Once she woke up consistently for a few days in a row, you could set your watch by her.

She flounced her head back on her pillow, closing her eyes, trying to force herself back to sleep, but instead memories from the night before flashed through her head, like a trailer for a bad film. Her coming home and finding Danny, her watching him almost kill himself. Making cookies with Danny and her mom, pretending everything was normal. Which actually hadn't been all that hard, now that she thought about it. It was almost like Danny knew or suspected she might have seen him. He was nicer to her last night than he'd been in weeks. There were moments when he almost seemed like himself. Laughing and joking, giving her a hard time. But she didn't trust it. They had all pretended last night like life was just fine, and maybe that's what you did. Fake it 'til you make it, like Amanda was always saying.

Giving up on more sleep, Josie got up and walked to the window. As much as she wished she could sleep in, she did have to admit her favorite time of day was early morning. The time when everything sat in quiet anticipation of the coming day, and when she got a front-row seat to the world waking up. She kneeled on the bench in front of her window, resting her head on her forearms, gazing over the trees across the acres of land that lay behind the house. Right now the fields lay brown and fallow, but in a little over a month they would sprout green as far as the eye could see.

As she watched the pale morning light brighten, she caught movement out of the corner of her eye and looked down to see the swing on the back porch moving forward and back at a leisurely pace. She peered closer, and realized it wasn't the wind, which almost never blew here anyway, but a person sitting there rocking the swing back and forth. What the hell was Danny doing out there this time of the morning? Had he slept at all? He'd left the house around ten last night, and still wasn't back by the time she went to sleep around midnight.

From up where she was, he looked lonely and small. He wasn't wearing a jacket, just a T-shirt and sweatpants. Josie felt her heart ache and her eyes sting. She got up from the bench, shoved her feet into her slippers, put on the robe that hung on the hook by her bathroom door, and swiped the quilt from the top of the bed. She tiptoed down the hall in a zigzag pattern, careful to avoid the planks that creaked so she wouldn't wake up her parents. She held her breath as she snuck past the door to their room. She took the stairs slowly, then picked up the pace as she crossed the vestibule and slid out the front door.

Once outside, she hesitated. She looked back at the door and took a deep breath, steeling her resolve. Although she'd been scared yesterday when she saw him with the gun, she had also been mad at herself later. She had just sat there frozen, staring at him, trying not to scream. Had the gun actually been loaded, he would have killed himself right in front of her and she would have done nothing. She wasn't ever going to do that again. She curled the blanket up in a ball, clutched it to her chest and made herself walk to the end of the porch, heading toward the backyard.

Danny looked up at her as she opened the short metal gate, causing the hinges to squeak, then he turned and looked off into the trees as if she wasn't there. Josie's heart started pounding, but she made herself keep moving toward the swing. As she got close enough that her shadow fell over him, Danny looked at her again. This time he didn't look away. His eyes were red from crying. He wiped his nose with the back of his hand and looked down by Josie's toes.

Josie stood there for a breath not knowing what to say. So she did the only thing she could think to do. She sat next to him on the bench seat, threw the cover over both of them, and then put her arms around his waist and held on. He stiffened at first, and she thought he was going to pull away or maybe even hit her. But then she felt him take a deep breath and relax. He put his arm around her shoulder, pulled the blanket up higher, then kissed the top of her head. And there they sat, swaying gently back and forth, watching the sun tip over the top of the house, waking the world for another day.

Memory Lapses

Julia Parmentier

I

It hadn't been one of the good days. The male aide had nicked Harry's face while shaving, then contradicted him on the choice of clothing for the day. If Harry wanted to wear shorts and a T-shirt, why shouldn't he? He wasn't going to go outside, and she could turn the heat up inside. She had brokered a compromise, khakis and the T-shirt, with his fleece-lined flannel shirt on the edge of the chair in case he got cold. Then the aide left, thank goodness. She would have to call the agency and see if they had a replacement, which would be the fourth that month, and the agency was threatening to charge an overtime fee. She'd almost rather do it herself, but she couldn't manage the showers, and dressing Harry on the days when he'd forgotten that a person needed to wear clothes was beyond her strength, let alone her patience.

She left Harry watching TV, telling him she was going into the kitchen to get him another cup of coffee. She sat down at the kitchen table with her own coffee cup, taking just a few minutes for herself. How did other people cope? There was an Alzheimer's support group in the next town over, but she couldn't really leave Harry long enough to attend the meetings. He got so anxious whenever she wasn't there; often it led to a physical standoff between the aide and himself, and before the agency sent male aides, Harry would just push the women aside and rage throughout the house or rush out the door. He had pushed one woman so hard she had fallen and injured her back; that could be a lawsuit waiting to happen, though Madelaine had warned the agency that her husband was difficult to control, and they had to send staff that could handle a 180-pound man with the self-control of a two-year-old.

"Maddy, where are you?" She braced herself.

"I'm right here, honey, just getting you your coffee. Do you want a muffin?" She had made muffins that morning. The aides liked them and sometimes Harry would eat half of one and smile at her, like old times. She would do almost anything to see that smile.

"No, god damn it! I want my coffee. Now." Not a day for smiles.

"Coming." Madelaine levered herself out of the chair and fetched the plastic thermal mug with the flip top lid which held his coffee, lukewarm, so he wouldn't burn himself if he tipped the cup over. She walked back out to the living room holding his cup in one hand and her own in the other.

Harry was agitated. He was holding the remote, aiming it at the TV, only he was holding it backwards, pointing the beam at himself, and nothing was happening as he pressed the buttons.

"I can't get this damned thing to work."

"What do you want to watch? There's a nice travel show. Or we could watch a cooking show together."

"I want to watch the news."

The news was a bad idea. Harry couldn't follow the rapid-fire delivery, and the photos of car accidents, house fires, and other disasters upset him. But he seemed to know that the news was something that marked days and time, and he kept asking to watch.

"Let's see," Madelaine put the mugs on the coffee table, took the remote, and started flicking through the channels. "How about this? It's a golf tournament. You like watching golf. Here I'll watch with you." She handed him his coffee and sat down on the edge of the couch closest to his

recliner. They both watched, mesmerized by the endless green fairways with the arc of the ball tracked in slow motion by the camera, lulled by the peaceful voice of the announcer. Harry's eyes started to droop. Madelaine continued to sit, drinking coffee, alternately watching the golfers setting up for their next shots and her husband as his breathing slowed into the rhythms of sleep.

MADELAINE THOUGHT ABOUT THOSE days, in retrospect, not the worst of days, as she changed out of the jeans and fleece she'd worn to go apple picking with Catherine, and into a pair of wool slacks and a turtleneck. She packed her discarded clothes into her suitcase and zipped it shut, then slipped on her new blue cardigan.

Catherine called from downstairs.

"Lunch is almost ready, Mom."

"Coming." Leaving her suitcase and a flowered shoulder bag by the door, she headed downstairs.

She entered the kitchen just as the kettle started whistling on the stove. Steam rose from a saucepan of soup on another burner. Catherine was standing next to the stove reaching into the overhead cupboard for teacups and plates to match the flowered teapot on the counter. She turned and carried these to the kitchen table. Then she returned to the stove to pour boiling water into the tea pot. It all looked so warm and welcoming; Madelaine was sorry to leave.

"You look nice, Mom," said Catherine. "I see you changed." Catherine, herself, was still wearing the track pants and sweatshirt she'd had on earlier in the day and was padding around in red-striped socks, having left her muddy shoes at the front door. Her short light brown hair curled around her face, which was slightly flushed from their morning in the sun. "You didn't need to, you're only driving to Gloria's house."

Madelaine pulled out a chair from the table. "I know," she said.

"I just felt the need to take a little trouble with my appearance. And you remember Gloria, she always looks so put together." She slid sideways onto the chair and rested her elbows on the table's polished surface, catching wisps of gray curly hair in her fingers and pushing them back from her face. "I caught a glimpse in the mirror as I went upstairs, and oh my goodness, I can't imagine what the people in the apple place thought of me, a chubby old lady in baggy jeans with wrinkles and crazy hair. And then I had to start pontificating about the best late apples."

"They probably thought you were dressed appropriately for picking apples," said Catherine. She walked over to the table with the teapot, but stayed standing. "And I'm sure the owners enjoyed talking with someone who actually knew what she was talking about." She poured a half an inch of tea into one of the cups. "Needs to steep another minute." Then she looked at Madelaine. "Why are you so worried about your appearance? You never used to care very much. You've been buying all these new clothes. Don't get me wrong, I love them, and they look great on you, but when Dad was alive, you didn't dress up much at all."

"Your dad didn't care about clothes; I looked the same to him, whether I got dressed up or not, and there were always other things we could spend that money on. But since your dad died," Madelaine stopped, rubbed her hands across her face, "I worry more, I guess, about what other people think of me. I feel like if I take more care with my clothes, people will take me more seriously."

Catherine poured the tea carefully into the two mugs, then slid one over to her mother. "Is that what you were thinking about on the way home? You seemed awfully quiet, distracted even."

"Not really, mostly I was thinking about your dad, and if I'm honest, dreading this trip to Gloria's."

"Then why go? You're welcome to stay here for as long as you like.

Madelaine gave a short laugh. "I appreciate the offer, really I do. But I feel like I need to work a little harder to maintain friendships, and I haven't seen Gloria and Mike since they came to your dad's funeral. We used to be such close friends before they moved to Cooperstown to be close to Annie. She just had a baby, you know."

Madelaine sat back in her chair, cradling her cup in her hand.

Catherine had walked back to the counter to take the soup off the stove and, ladling soup into bowls, had her back to her mother.

"Yeah, I know, I saw the baby pictures on Facebook."

She turned and brought the bowls over to the table, returning to get a plate of cut-up apples and cheese. With the plate in her hand, she turned to her mother. "But we wished you could stay longer; this is your first long visit. Since Dad died you've only come up for a few weekends, two days, max." Madelaine winced at the disappointment in Catherine's voice as her daughter returned to the table and set the plate down. It rattled as hit the surface. "Is it something about being with me, with us? Or is this about Dad?"

Of course, it was about Harry. But she couldn't tell Catherine that.

"You can't sit around your house and mope forever, Mom," Catherine continued, still standing, looking down at her mother, one hand on the back of her chair. "It's been almost a year since he died. I thought when we were out today that you were coming out of it. You were finally talking about him, remembering the fun we used to have on our expeditions, as he'd used to call them." She sat back down and took an apple slice from the plate.

"They were fun times, and I enjoyed remembering them with you." Madelaine smiled, but she couldn't maintain it. She couldn't tell Catherine about the bad times. And Catherine, busy with a new job, building a life with her husband in Vermont, hadn't been home those last six months. The longer Madelaine stayed, the more likely she might inadvertently say something. She couldn't do that to her daughter; it would be like losing her father all over again. She picked up her spoon and started in on the soup.

"This squash soup is good. I like it with the apples and cheese."

Catherine pointed to the edge of the counter. "Comes out of a box. I'm not the cook you are. But it tastes pretty good and it's quick. I knew you wanted to get going so you get there before too late. How long a drive is it to Cooperstown, anyway?"

"About three hours. If I leave by two, I'll get there just in time for a glass of wine before dinner." Madelaine picked up a piece of cheese and layered it on a slice of apple. "But I'm glad I stayed to go apple picking this morning. It did feel like the old times."

Catherine had her head down, ladling soup into her mouth without looking at her mother. Madelaine wondered if she might be crying, but just as she was about to ask, Catherine put her spoon down and looked up, picking up her napkin and wiping her face, all business.

"I guess that means you need to get going pretty soon, it's quarter to two now. It's too bad David isn't home yet. That's the problem with real estate. The only time people have to look at houses is on the weekends. He'll be sorry he missed you."

Madelaine laughed. "You can give him my love. He's probably happy to have his mother-in-law out of the house." She got up and headed out of the kitchen to get her bags.

When she came back downstairs, she found Catherine in the hallway, holding a freshly filled travel mug and her purse.

"I found your purse in the kitchen," said Catherine. "Do you have your car keys?"

"They're in the pocket of my coat," said Madelaine, putting down her suitcase and carryall, and picking up her coat off the rack by the door. She felt in the pockets. "They're here with my phone."

She gave her daughter a hug and a kiss. "I love you, you know, and I've had a lovely time. Next time, I'll try to stay longer. I am getting better; it just takes time."

Catherine returned the hug, handing her the mug and purse, then picked up Madelaine's bags while shoving her feet into a pair of Crocs.

"Next time," she said. "No excuses. And call me when you get to Gloria's."

II

MADELAINE HEARD THE BLARE of a truck horn at the same moment that her car hit the rumble strip. She opened her eyes, swerving back onto the highway, almost over-correcting into a black SUV passing on her left. The truck behind her was flicking its lights, high, low, high, low. Adrenaline rushed through her system, hot and cold at the same time, as her heart beat a panicked rhythm in her chest. She shook her head to clear it. She was awake now. She focused on the road, speeding up to a steady sixty-five and settling her car into the center of the lane, scanning for exit signs to tell her where she was. She knew she was on the Mass Pike, but she had lost track of where. A sign loomed, announcing the Charlton Service Plaza in two miles. Thank goodness, she could stop there and get more coffee and rest for a while. Though she had assured Catherine it would be no problem, she had been worried. It was a long drive home, especially this late in the day. But with Gloria sick with norovirus, there was no way she could have continued her trip to Cooperstown.

As she drove, the taillights of the cars ahead of her receded into the distance and a steady stream of traffic passed her on the left, but in her rearview mirror she could see the lights of the the truck behind her matching her speed, maintaining a steady distance. The arc lights of the rest area were visible now, so she slowed and took the exit, noting that the truck was pulling off behind her. Hopefully, she wasn't going to have a confrontation with an angry truck driver. She parked her car as close as she could get to the building, directly under one of the overhead lamps. Truck parking was on the other side of the building. She shook her head to clear it of paranoid thoughts. How did she know the truck wasn't planning to stop here anyway?

She gathered her shoulder bag and her keys and stepped out of the Subaru, thinking that perhaps it was time she got a new car, one with all the auto driving bells and whistles, and a hands-free cell phone system. She felt in her pocket for her phone, then brushed down her wool coat and buttoned it against the chilly wind blowing across the parking lot. Locking the car, she dropped her keys into her other pocket, and headed for the travel plaza. She had stopped thinking about the truck, so she barely noticed the man hanging out by the trash barrel, until he stepped up and opened the door for her. She looked up at him briefly, as she passed, thanking him, noting a bearded face beneath an orange trucker's cap with some logo on it. He followed her into the central space of the plaza, coming up beside her as she stopped to survey the food court options.

"I sure was glad to see you stop at this rest area," he said, a faint southern lilt to his voice. "I thought for sure you were going to go off the road back there. Hope I didn't scare you too much."

Confrontation, but not anger. He sounded concerned. Madelaine turned toward him, seeing a tall, heavily built man, with a middle-aged face. His beard, black threaded with gray, was topped by a large nose, high cheekbones, and dark eyes. He was wearing a short navy blue jacket, unzipped over a light blue T-shirt advertising the Blue Ridge Mountains. The start of a trucker's belly protruded over his faded blue jeans, and he was wearing a pair of battered sneakers, worn at the edges. He didn't look very threatening.

"Was that you, in the truck behind me? I have to thank you, then," said Madelaine. "I guess I started to doze off."

"Sure did. You'd been wavering for a couple of miles, and slowing down. At first I thought you were drunk, but then when you swerved off the road, I realized you were having trouble staying awake. It's happened to me on some long drives. You want my advice, you take a good long break and get some food as well as coffee."

"Thank you," said Madelaine, "that's just what I was going to do. I'm debating between the healthy Subway or the unhealthy Big Mac. I'll probably get MacDonalds coffee, however. I actually like it better than Starbucks. What about you?" She stopped. Why was she babbling?

"Subway for sure, but I'm with you, I don't like Starbucks coffee either."

"I'm going for the Big Mac," said Madelaine, "and fries, since my daughter's not here to disapprove." She started walking toward the MacDonald's counter.

There was a line, it being the tail end of dinner time, but eventually she got to the counter and placed her order. She noticed the truck driver with his Subway sandwich in a plastic bag, joining the end of the line for coffee. She waved at him, pantomined getting him coffee and he nodded, indicating a large with his hands and mouthing the word iced. She raised her eyebrows, but gave him the okay sign. "And a large iced coffee," she told the bored young server taking her order, as she handed over her credit card. Within minutes she had her meal and the two coffees in a cardboard holder.

The man took the coffees from her as she walked over to him. "My treat," she said, as he tried to hand her a five-dollar bill. "It's the least I can do, given you probably saved my life. Though I can't believe you drink iced coffee in November."

"I always drink my coffee iced. Want to eat together?" he said, pointing toward an empty table. "I get lonely for conversation when I'm driving."

Madelaine's eyes crinkled. That would be a great pickup line, except she probably reminded him of his mother.

"You remind me of my mother," he said. "My name's Jimmy."

"I'm Madelaine, and yes I'd be happy for the company."

"Why are you driving by yourself so late?" Jimmy asked after they had settled at the table and unpackaged their food. He took off his cap and set it on the edge of the table, then ran his fingers through salt-and-pepper curls that were several weeks past the need for a haircut. Madelaine read the logo on his cap: Summer Transport, letters in green with a bright yellow sun. She set her container of fries between the two of them, indicating he should help himself, then shrugged off her coat, letting it drape over the back of the plastic chair.

"Last minute change of plan," said Madelaine. I was heading to New York to see my friend Gloria." She picked up her coffee cup and took off the lid to let it cool. "I had been visiting my daughter in Vermont, and it was a three-hour drive or so from her house to Cooperstown, that's where my friend lives. Anyway, Gloria called me when I was about an hour out, and told me she'd come down with a stomach virus. I'd better not come. She was sure it was norovirus as there was a lot of it in the school where she volunteers."

Jimmy nodded, his mouth full of meatball sandwich.

"I had a choice of going back to my daughter's or driving home. I thought it would be easier to go home. It's all highway driving. I would have to drive back roads to my daughter's house, not to mention that she and her husband have had to put up with me for the last five days, and they both work. Home's a little bit further, but I thought I could do it." She stopped to take a sip of coffee. "Only it's been a long time since I've driven so far by myself."

Jimmy wiped his mouth, carefully removing tomato sauce from his beard. "I'm surprised your daughter didn't give you more grief. I wouldn't have let my mother drive so far alone." He squeezed a package of ketchup onto the edge of the sandwich wrapper and took a french fry.

"Oh she gave me grief. Made me 'share my location.'" Madelaine made air quotes with her fingers. "I suppose you know all about it, but she had to walk me through setting it up on my phone. Now she's tracking my every move." Madelaine laughed and started eating her Big Mac, savoring the greasy, salty-sweet flavor. "Tell me about your mother."

"Not much to say. She passed away about two years ago. Cancer. I miss her though." Jimmy took another french fry and dipped it in the ketchup, stuffing the whole fry in his mouth.

"So she didn't do much driving?"

"Oh no, she drove a lot. But she and my dad drove together. They got an RV after they retired and took off to see the country. They had those senior passes for the national parks, Yellowstone, Zion; I think they were trying to see them all. I don't know how many they got to, maybe thirty or something like that, before my mother got too sick to travel. But they had a good time. I own my rig, so I'd meet up with them sometimes when I was headed cross country and we'd spend a couple of days together."

"My husband and I talked about doing that. It sounded like a lot of fun. We were going to rent an RV and see how we liked it, but we never got around to it."

"Your husband died?"

"Yes, not quite a year ago; he had a heart attack. What about your father, is he still living?"

She saw his face change, a creasing of the forehead, a pinched look around the eyes, signs of stress. "Yes he's still alive, but he's in a memory care facility. He went downhill fast after my mother passed."

"Oh I am so sorry. My husband had Alzheimer's too."

Jimmy looked at her, his eyes focusing directly on hers, nodding.

"So you know what it's like. I'm on the road, there's no way I can take care of him as I'd like, and the place he's in, well, it's okay; it's the best he can afford. I pay some too, but it's bleak. Imagine living with a whole bunch of demented people.

"I stop by and see him whenever I get back home, but he doesn't recognize me anymore," Jimmy continued, sitting back and swirling the remaining ice cubes in his coffee. "The staff there seem to take good care of him, but he's always trying to escape. They called me last week. He'd climbed out his window—his room's on the second floor—slid down the porch roof into the bushes, so he didn't hurt himself. Luckily all the memory care rooms look out on an enclosed courtyard, so he couldn't get lost. The people who work there, they have to be saints."

"He's lucky."

"I guess, but I know he really wants to be on the road. I guess it runs in the family."

"Was he a truck driver too?"

"Lineman for the electric company. Always said he had the best job in the world. He could be his own boss when he was out in his truck." Jimmy crumpled up the wrappings from his meal and took a last slurp of his coffee. He stood up, holding out his hand for Madelaine's trash. She handed him the box, but held onto her coffee.

"I'll keep this for the road," she said, replacing the lid on the coffee, placing her elbows on the table, watching Jimmy as he walked over to the counter with the trash bin. She felt much better after the food and talking to a stranger had restored her to some semblance of calm.

———

"Chainsaw," Harry had said that morning when they were eating break-fast. He had just finished a plate of eggs and was drinking his coffee. He put the cup on the table. "I have to fix the chainsaw today. It's a good day to cut wood." It was a good day for cutting wood, October, the sun shining, the temperature a comfortable fifty-five degrees, with a slight breeze.

"That's a good idea," said Madelaine, taking their plates over to the sink. She turned back to look at him. He seemed energized today, rising to his feet with his old grace and finding his own coat in the closet. He stuck his arms down the sleeves of the old barn jacket, tan twill, frayed at the collar and cuffs, stained by many years of projects. She saw him look at the buttons and decide to leave the coat hanging open. No matter, it was warm enough. "Give me a shout if you need anything."

He unhooked a battered old PawSox cap from the back of the closet door and stuck it on his mostly bald head, gave her a cheery wave, and left the house for his workshop in the garage. Madelaine followed him out to the back steps and watched him as he bent over and hauled up the garage door, leaving it open for the extra light. He seemed okay; she'd take him out some hot coffee in a little while and see how he was doing.

The project had kept him busy all morning. Madelaine spent the time cleaning her kitchen and baking brownies. She needed to go to the market, but she couldn't leave Harry alone anymore, and if he was happy with a project, she wanted him to have that opportunity. She had just started making sandwiches for lunch when she heard the whine of the chainsaw starting up. She winced, put down the knife, and headed out to the garage.

"Hey, that's fantastic," she said. But he had his ear protectors on and didn't hear her. He was fiddling with the gas feed and revving the motor. Madelaine walked around until she was in his field of vision and waved at him. He let the motor die, the blade slowing to a stop, then he placed the chainsaw on the stand he'd built to hold it. "It's lunchtime," she said. He nodded and followed her back to the house. He wasn't walking as steadily

as earlier, and he wasn't talking, but he still seemed to be energized by the completion of the project.

"HEY." JIMMY'S VOICE BROKE into her thoughts. "Where did you go? You didn't fall asleep again, did you?" He had come back from disposing of their trash, and was standing on the other side of the table looking down at her. It took her a second to cycle back to the present, remember who he was, and register what he was saying.

"Oh, I'm sorry." She shook her head back and forth several times as if to shake away the memories. "Just lost in thought, remembering." She pushed back from the table and started to stand up.

"About what?" Jimmy asked, taking her coat and holding it for her.

Madelaine laughed. "Chainsaws."

"Chainsaws." His eyebrows disappeared under his curls. "That's a bit macabre."

"Oh, not like massacres, more like cutting firewood. One of my husband's favorite activities. I was thinking about your father, happiest out on the road. For Harry, it was all about the woods, maintaining the forest, trimming trees, cutting firewood. I was thinking about the time he went to fix the chainsaw. You know all the books and articles on Alzheimer's and other dementias, they don't get into the real hazards that are out there for active people who forget how to do an everyday task." She slipped on her coat. "Thanks."

He stepped away, picking up his cap from the table and settling it back on his head, a few unruly strands sticking out over his ears. "So what happened with the chainsaw?"

"He went out to fix it one morning, got it running by lunchtime. But after lunch he'd forgotten that he'd fixed it and went out to fix it again. Only this time he got it all taken apart and couldn't figure out how to put it back together. He was so frustrated. He kept saying that he didn't have the right part. Finally, I convinced him we should take the chainsaw to Tony's shop, a place he'd used before."

"Did he go for it?" asked Jimmy.

"Yes, sort of." She thought back to piling all the pieces strewn across the workbench into a box, and into the car, then realizing, as she buckled Harry's seatbelt, that he wasn't registering anything she was saying. He had gone away to whatever that place was where he wasn't really Harry anymore. She squinted her eyes, feeling tears welling up, and smiled shakily. "It didn't really matter. By the time I got him in the car, he'd forgotten all about the chainsaw, which was a good thing, as I had no idea where Tony's shop was."

His eyes crinkled, but a quick touch on her arm conveyed his sympathy and understanding of the situation.

"So did he ever go looking for his chainsaw again?"

"Only once, and I told him that it was at the shop, since it needed a part. He never asked again."

Madelaine picked up her bag and the coffee cup.

"I don't have too far to go now," she said, "I'll get off at Auburn and take 395 south. Thank you for the company, and for watching out for me on the road."

"I'm headed into Boston, so I'll follow you to the exit."

Madelaine looked up from her shoulder bag, where she had been digging around for her keys, then remembering, stuck her hand in her pocket, and drew them out. "Thanks, I'd appreciate that, but not if it holds you up. I'm fine now, really."

"I'm not in any rush. I have a delivery time of four a.m. Should get there in time for a short nap first."

An excerpt from the novel-in-progress, *Emergence*.

The Mad AI

Andrew Hinshaw

0: The Mad AI

GUNNERY SERGEANT KATE DESEO knew a drive topside through snow and ice in a ten-ton vehicle wouldn't be smooth sailing, but she hadn't expected so much chop. The armored personnel carrier was as short as it was wide, somehow making the vehicle feel cramped at only half capacity. The interior was dark, except for some yellow lighting that ran along the center of the ceiling. The light strip above the crew was long past its operational life, casting a flickering, murky glow through its weathered glastic coating. Deseo looked up to see the smattering of scrapes, cracks, and scratches caused by countless soldiers entering and exiting the old APC and imagined them hunched over to avoid banging their heads as their rucksacks dragged across the low ceiling.

Deseo checked the sights of her MC Assault Rifle, ensuring they were in sync with her standard-issue Monocle, a triangular device just behind her right ear. For the umpteenth time, the holographic red crosshair appeared just where the iron sights would be. The synced data between her Monocle and the gun also produced a visual readout, listing in small, red, capital letters wind speed, distance, and ballistic arc, none of which was useful given that she was pointing the barrel at the APC's rusted metal floor.

"Something wrong with your gun?" Moss asked to her right, his husky voice full of friendly snark. The man had a permanent, stalwart grimace on his face, giving his ebony skin a lackluster appearance, particularly on his forehead, which was compressed into three permanent ridges. Moss had seen nearly as much combat as Deseo; one could see that fact just from the relative ease in his eyes, despite their unpleasant quarters and ominous mission. With his rank of staff sergeant, he was also the highest-ranking soldier beneath her.

Deseo shrugged him off and chewed her mint-flavored stim-gum. It was a poor replacement for coffee, but the gum helped mask the sour smell that seeped up from the grates of the narrow, rusted walkway that separated her and Moss from the other two members of her squad, McCarthy and Gormley. Brackish water sloshed around on the floor, somehow seeping into her "waterproof" boots. She attempted to adjust her right boot, moving it just enough to not be stepping directly on McCarthy's foot. It was as if they'd all sat down for dinner, then removed the table and shoved their chairs together. She couldn't complain too much, knowing the reason for the cramped quarters and bumpy ride was due to a two-inch thick layer of depleted uranium walls surrounding them.

Both McCarthy and Gormley's faceplates were partially fogged up due to the sauna-like conditions inside the APC, despite the sub-zero temperatures outside. The APC lurched again, hitting a chunk of rubble as it plowed through the ice and snow. Deseo could see enough past their foggy faceplates to see the whites of their eyes. Wide-open and alert. She'd seen that look many times before; the double-edged blade of fear and excitement.

Moss leaned over a few inches, putting his weight on his rifle as he rested the butt of it on the floor, uncaring that it was sitting in dank water. He switched to a private channel. "You up for this, Gunny? Sure you're okay?"

"It's nothing," Deseo said, rolling her shoulders. "Just antsy to get out of this hotbox." She wrinkled her nose. The acrid smell of stale sweat cut through the mint fragrance of her gum. Her suit's scrubber was good at keeping her oxygen mixture balanced and neutralizing most toxins, but odor control was low on the designer's priority list. It didn't help that it was a shared suit, composed of more replacement than original parts.

"You and me both," he agreed with a commiserate sigh. He leaned away from her. A second later, he asked, "You're not worried about me, are you? You know I'm solid." He knocked his gloved knuckles against his armored right leg, the flesh and bone of which had been regrown from the thigh down. A few months back a depth charge had struck the *Audacity*, their home and the flagship submarine of the One World Alliance. Moss had been in the wrong place at the wrong time, though Deseo was starting to wonder if there was such a thing as the *right* place anymore.

"I know you are, Moss," she said with a small smile. She looked over at Corporal McCarthy and Private Gormley. McCarthy, while being older and outranking Gormley, somehow managed to look younger. He had a narrow face and full lips, and his skin was a smattering of white and pink, suggesting someone who wasn't fully cooked yet. He looked younger than anyone in the whole platoon, which was four squads totaling sixteen soldiers. Deseo and the other three that shared the cramped sardine can masquerading as an APC were Requisition Squad, which was the last one to be dropped off, closest to the fuel depot and tasked with the primary mission to secure the cargo. Deseo was also captain of the entire platoon, a position command had *voluntold* her to take.

Both McCarthy and Gormley were dependable soldiers. Even if

they hadn't seen much combat, they had performed well in the past and she felt like she could rely upon them. She was a bit more worried about McCarthy, as his young face was turning green and she suspected it wasn't just from all the jostling around. She pulled up his biometric data using her Monocle. It brought up a small window on her faceplate, appearing as if it was projected just a few feet away. Accelerated heart rate, increased respiration, increased galvanic skin response. Nothing out of the ordinary, given their mission.

A mission she hoped would be uneventful, but a knot in her gut told her that was unlikely. Command had given her very little, other than stating that a Priority One package was their target and that her platoon was to acquire said package *at all costs*. The package in question was four pill-shaped cases roughly the size of coffins. When she asked what the cases contained, she received an expected, but annoying, out-of-your-paygrade response. She'd thought about pointing out to her commanding officer that she didn't get paid, but sarcasm was often seen by top brass as insubordination. Her mission was to run willy-nilly into a known Secular depot to complete a snatch-and-run with no knowledge of the packages' contents or enemy preparedness. What could go wrong?

McCarthy, apparently aware she was still looking him over, gave her a small grin full of white teeth, making his pale face look even younger. A second later, he batted away Gormley's hand, who had been trying to draw something blatantly phallic with a white marker on the side of McCarthy's helmet. Gormley, seeing he'd been busted by Deseo, held up his hands, comically tossing the marker behind his back. A look of mock guilt washed over his freckled face.

"Private Gormley," Deseo said, leaning toward him with a curling finger. He leaned forward and Deseo could see the orange mustache above his lip, which looked like a thin, unkempt eyebrow. "When exactly are you going to shave that shit off your face?"

"Regs say I can grow anything on my body that doesn't exceed one inch."

"I'm not interested in your privates, Private," Deseo said, unable to pass up such an easy joke. "And I don't give a shit about regs. Grow your hair *ten* inches for all I care. What I do care about is the fact that I'm forced to look at a man-child with knuckle fuzz for a mustache all day."

Gormley's visor faded black, concealing his face. "That better?"

The APC hit another bump, this one hard enough to cause a small compartment to open to her right and above the small hexagonal door that led to the driver's station. Several silver morphedra tubes spilled out and clattered on the rusty floor.

"I think I'm gonna be sick," whined McCarthy.

Moss, looking as though there was no other place he'd rather be, said with an amused frown, "Forget your aspirin?"

Deseo chuckled, knowing Moss was citing the military cure for any illness, ranging from a stubbed toe to a sucking chest wound: two aspirins and a glass of water.

"I think he means mentally," Gormley said, twirling a finger at the side of his helmet.

McCarthy sighed in irritation, shaking his head. "You were trying to draw a dick on my helmet."

"It's for your call sign," Gormley said, putting a gloved hand to his chest as if wounded.

"Therapy is for civvies," Deseo said, referring to Gormley's joke about McCarthy's mental state. She leaned forward and stared at both of them. "You guys are military. PTSD stands for something different."

"Psychological Training for Superior Discipline," Moss, McCarthy, and Gormley all groaned in unison.

"Oorah!" Deseo said, trying hard to muster enough enthusiasm to hide her reservations about the mission.

Gormley leaned toward McCarthy and spoke in a hushed voice. "I don't suppose the fact that there are no civvies anymore makes any difference to her?"

Deseo grinned in spite of herself. She tried to think back when "civilian" was even a thing. She thought of vague memories of people in white coats treating injuries or orange overalls fixing control junctions. She was five when mandatory conscription was enacted by Admiral Kudrat. Those jobs never went away, but the people performing them may have to put down a wrench or syringe and pick up a gun at some point.

Deseo switched again to a private channel and leaned toward Moss. "It's not you I'm worried about, Marcel. It's them. They're still pretty green."

The APC hit some rough terrain and jostled around again. Moss lazily swayed with the motion and cocked a thick black eyebrow. "Weren't we all once?"

"That does not make me feel any better," Deseo said, sighing. She switched to a global channel, knowing a live picture of her face was sent to the entire platoon. She did her best to portray confidence. "Okay guys, I want to make this mission as short as possible. Brass wants these containers, nothing more. Intel says the Secular transport will be doing a pit stop at a hidden fuel silo in thirty mikes. The facility is reportedly unmanned, so whatever resistance we get will come from the transport itself. Switch to active camo. If you come across a patch of quicksnow or snirt, just trust the tech; don't try and get fancy and fuck with your Monocle."

Gormley raised his hand. "What if we come across some yellow snow?" His faceplate was still as black as his small, tubular MTGB rocket launcher that sat across his lap. One of his hands rested on it as if it were a pet. Deseo couldn't recall what the actual acronym stood for, but colloquially everyone called the launcher *Make Things Go Boom*. It certainly lived up to that.

"If it's you, Gormley," Deseo responded without missing a beat, "I say chow down." She heard a few chuckles on the global channel, probably due to nerves more than in response to her lame joke. "Now remember, we're here for the cargo, not a firefight. If we can disable or kill a few of these *bleaks*, that's frosting, but we're not going out of our way to do that. We've got about a fifteen-mike hump to the abandoned silo. That means we'll have an extra fifteen to dig in once we arrive. Once the Secular transport lands, we snatch the goodies, hitch them to our UGV and provide cover as it heads back to the APC. Resistance is supposed to be light, so with discipline, we should be back aboard the *Audacity* in time for lunch while the Seculars are still trying to figure out what the hell happened. Intel gave us the Secular's sensor frequencies, which should be good for the next thirty hours, so we'll be invisible to them as long as none of you do anything shitbrained. And switch to IRCOM," she said, referring to infrared line-of-sight communication. "It's going to be radio silence once we arrive. Keep your heads on swivels and message me securely if you see anything. Questions?"

She got thumbs-up from McCarthy and Gormley, and a gentle, double hammer fist from Moss against her shoulder. A green OK symbol appeared in the upper right corner of her faceplate, indicating a copy from the other squads. The floor vibrated as the APC's brakes kicked in, whining as they strained to slow the heavy vehicle. It came to an abrupt halt, making them all sway toward the driver's station.

"Sergeant Moss," Deseo said, pushing her stim-gum into the space between her gums and cheek. "Take it from here."

Moss nodded, stood up as much as he could, his helmet banging against the ceiling and his back bent at an angle. He barked out his orders, sounding more like a drill sergeant than a staff sergeant. "McCarthy, take up the rear. Gormley, you take point."

The back door opened by sliding from the top downward, converting it from a door into a sloping ramp. The interior of the APC was bathed in bright, white light as flurries of snow flooded the cabin. Deseo squinted, despite her faceplate auto tinting to handle the excess illumination. She waited as Gormley and Moss exited the APC, then stood up and shuffled the few steps it took to get to the exit. It was even brighter outside, whitewashing the view like a floodlight pointed directly at her. Deseo held up a hand, but it didn't help. She focused instead on the small, thin lines of snow cutting across the ramp as she made her way down. As she stepped onto the ground, her boots crunched against the top layer of ice just before sinking at least a foot in. Her suit's motors whined to keep her upright as a powerful gust of wind struck her body, producing a shrill howl around her. Small red text blinked in the corner of her vision, indicating a temperature drop just short of negative one hundred degrees.

After a few careful steps, the flurries died down and her eyes finally adjusted. A desolate white landscape stretched out before her, much of it sparkling in the sunlight. Miles of snow that covered the sweeping terrain were pockmarked with a scattering of rocky upgrowths. Remnants of structures from the old world long eroded by the powerful winds speckled the landscape. Much of them were weathered down to sharp edges and looked like monstrous, brown fangs jutting up through the frozen earth. Snow flowed around them and over the ground like a fast-moving stream. Topside always looked like this, a frozen wasteland hostile to life. Deseo had to admit though, there was a certain kind of beauty to it all.

The wind picked up again, dusting up the air with snow and reducing visibility. Deseo kept her eyes on Moss, who stood directly in front of her, his camouflaged suit bending the light like a warped mirror as he moved. Due to the platoon having individualized transponder beacons, she was able to keep tabs on him despite his camouflage. Deseo's suit was doing its best to maintain an even temperature inside her armor, but after a few minutes, the tips of her fingers were burning from the cold despite her armpits sweating. Time stretched out as they wordlessly trudged to their destination. The terrain was becoming rugged, and a trickle of sweat ran into Deseo's eye, stinging it.

They came across a small hill with a chasm cut through it, its uneven edges suggesting it was naturally created. Lining up single-file, they entered the crevasse. The walls were a mixture of sediment, snow, and ice. As they made their way to the deepest part, the narrow walls bulged with permafrost. The strange, layered formations looked like the soft white gills of an oversized, alien fungus. At one point, an odd, circular white rock with a hole in it caught Deseo's attention. She zoomed in and realized she was seeing a child's pelvic bone, frozen in ice. Her unease worsened as her Geiger counter began ticking, registering a small spike in RADS. She wagged a closed fist between her thigh and shoulder. Her Monocle interpreted this and messaged the squad to move double-time. The four of them increased their pace, jogging in lockstep.

Emerging from the chasm, they entered a clearing and the silo came into view. Deseo held up a closed fist and the squad stopped. The four of them took a knee, which offered some coverage as they sank into the snow a few feet. The silo, around two hundred feet in front of them, looked like a rock cylinder shooting up to the sky with layers of ice covering its walls like melted candle wax. It was taller than it was wide—she estimated it would take less than thirty seconds to walk around it. It also appeared to be half its original height, its top uneven and crumbling from a partial collapse. The walls were covered in a few holes, likely caused by erosion. They were makeshift windows and could offer a hide site for recon and a wide view of the surrounding area.

The building was unremarkable, just another remnant of a long-forgotten era, eroding as the past distanced itself from the present. No wonder the Secular had used it as a disguised fuel depot. It looked completely abandoned and unstable enough to make anyone, even if they were stranded, leery about stepping inside.

Deseo noticed crumbled rock around the silo's base and magnified the image. In some places, she could make out the vague shape of broken concrete and twisted rebar. She sent the image to Moss via IRCOM and received a message a second later.

> SSGT MOSS: What am I looking at?
> GS DESEO: See how little snow there is? It's like it recently came loose.
> SSGT MOSS: Natural erosion?
> GS DESEO: Not a fan of coincidence.
> SSGT MOSS: Think they're onto us?

Deseo didn't respond. She switched her Monocle to detect multiple EMF wavelengths, granting her a much wider visual range beyond that of the typical visible spectrum. Waves of white energy pulsed out and away from her, glazing the world and flowing like flat, slow-moving shockwaves. She scanned the area, first looking to the ground surrounding the silo and then to the silo itself. Nothing registered. No characteristic blots of red, yellow, or green indicating heat sources; no patches of violet fog indicating microwaves or golden flares indicating radio waves. She disabled the scan and opened squad messaging.

GS DESEO: McCarthy, go and check the interior of that silo. Report anything funky, I don't care if it's a swirl of snow that looks like the Virgin Mary. If A.C., make your way to one of those windows facing east for overwatch. Moss, Gormley, and I are going to dig in and wait for the transport.

McCarthy responded with a "wilco" and partially stood up, keeping a forward lean as he crouch-ran toward the silo. Deseo held out a knife-hand, palm facing down. She spread her fingers. Fan out.

Moss moved fifteen feet to her right and Gormley to her left. Deseo lowered her body into a slightly raised plank position, flattening against the snow but giving her just enough elevation that she could aim her weapon at any target in close proximity. She glanced left and right to confirm Gormley and Moss had done the same. She felt a touch of relief as she noted how difficult they were to see, despite their transponders. They looked like a discolored patch of snow, blending in seamlessly with the various other shades of gray. The Secular sensors were considerably more robust, but intel had insisted they would not be able to see her platoon until they cycled their frequency.

McCarthy disappeared into the silo through a large, dark gap. It was covered in knots of ice and looked like an opening at the base of a giant tree, one that had been polished and bleached white. Deseo checked the time: just short of ten minutes before the Secular transport would stop to refuel. She looked at the ashen sky beyond the silo. Visibility had dropped. Fat snowflakes were starting to shoot past her visor, some skating across the icy earth like tufts of cotton.

Deseo took in a few slow, controlled breaths and forced her shoulders to relax, trying her best to lower her heart rate and manage her adrenal response. She waited for McCarthy's all clear, the sound of her breath amplified in the claustrophobic confines of her helmet.

After another moment, she tongued her gum from the inside of her cheek and started chewing again. She checked the time again. Five minutes had passed.

"One fucking job, McCarthy," she hissed to herself. She waited another fifteen seconds, praying the damned all clear message would pop up on the general channel, but nothing came. Her Monocle chirped twice, informing her that an unknown vessel was inbound. She glanced up to see a single pinprick in the gray sky, bracketed by a red reticle. Apparently, the *bleaks* also abided by the military's version of on time: early.

GS DESEO: McCarthy, acknowledge.

The message just hung in her vision. She checked McCarthy's biometrics. He was conscious and his heart rate was elevated. That didn't tell her shit other than he wasn't dead. If he hadn't suffered some sort of miraculous stroke that cut his ability to communicate but left him otherwise unharmed, she was going to forcibly insert her foot into his ass. She messaged her squad, telling them the mission still stood and to fire on her command only.

The transport was in sight. Utilitarian in design, it had been designed for quick takeoffs and landings with the ability to leave or obtain cargo on a dime. It looked like a giant horseshoe with a rectangular shipping container crammed in its gap. The vessel had four vase-shaped turbines spread out evenly along its crescent shape. The turbines collectively roared, ejecting sharp, blue flames as the transport descended toward its landing zone, roughly thirty feet to the right of the silo.

Deseo kept her body still and trained her rifle on the descending transport. Despite its cumbersome shape, the vessel moved with precision, the turbines whining as the pilot throttled them down.

Time seemed to slow as the transport inched its way closer to the ground. The moment was almost here, Deseo could practically taste it. Disable the ship, kill any passengers, hitch the cargo to the UGV and bug the fuck out.

Mere feet from landing, the pitch of the turbines increased, crackling in the air as the transport started to gain altitude again. Exhaust kicked up snow and caused flurries of the white powder to rotate into sideways vortices.

PVT GORMLEY: Sir, it looks like they're not going to land.

"No shit!" Deseo said over the global channel, breaking radio silence. She scanned the vessel, looking for a weak point. She eyed one of the turbines, watching how they articulated small movements independent of one another to keep the vessel stable. "Gormley, take out one of its engines. Fire two missiles back to back. I have a feeling this transport is more heavily armored than most."

"Firing," Gormley replied without hesitation, taking a knee and lifting the launcher to rest on his shoulder. He angled the launcher upwards, sighting the transport.

"Make sure to enable shock charges," Deseo added at the last second. "We want to cook its systems, not turn the whole thing into mulch."

"Wilco," Gormley said. "Blast area clear!" A second later, the weapon kicked on his shoulder and two white vapor trails cut a line from the end of the launcher to one of the transport's turbines. The dual missiles fired so fast they almost appeared as one. On impact, thin, jagged lines of electric blue bolts branched across the side of the ship, followed by the audible crack of superheated air. The electrostatic discharge was powerful enough to cause Deseo's vision to flicker a few seconds before her Monocle could recover.

The transport began listing to the right. As the pilot attempted to keep the vessel level, the damaged thruster crackled as if broken glass was being ground through a metal combine. One of the four thrusters hit by Gormley's deadeye shot was blowing out yellow flames and twitching like a mangled limb trying to realign itself. The transport was still flightworthy, but the shock charges were playing havoc with the vehicle's guidance and stability systems. Despite this, the stubborn pilot, apparently refusing to accept that the craft needed to be landed, gunned the damaged thruster in a desperate attempt to regain altitude. Doing so sealed the vessel's fate; the thruster let out a high-pitched whir that raised several octaves just before exploding with a loud boom that Deseo felt rattle in her chest.

Smoldering shrapnel and bright sparks rained down and the transport swayed sharply to the right, its remaining three thrusters roaring like dragon's breath as the pilot tried to keep the vessel's attitude in line with the horizon as it descended. Deseo couldn't help but feel grudging admiration as she watched the pilot handle the crippled ship with some measure of grace. The vessel crashed into the snow cockeyed, sending up a plume of white powder that was rushed away by the powerful crosswinds.

They had a small window of time. The pilot could potentially restore the transport to flight, and even if it was permanently downed, there was a good chance the pilot sent a distress call before communications were fried by the shock charges.

"Gormley," she said. "Disable your cloak and take aim again. But this time I want you to fake a misfire. Fuck with your MTGB as if it's jammed up."

Deseo tried to put herself in the headspace of the Secular pilot. If she were inside the transport and fell for Gormley's bluff, the next thing she'd do would be to fire any possible countermeasures she had. Even with the ship's fried electrical system, she knew they'd have some sort of last-ditch emergency backup. One they likely couldn't aim, like chaff firing from a jet after being painted by a missile.

Gormley did as she commanded. In fact, he doubled down and cycled his suit's camo, darkening it just enough to make him stand out against the gray-and-white terrain. He aimed the launcher and pulled the trigger twice, then smartly turned to look at a blank patch of snow away from Deseo or Moss, as to not give away their position. He made a chopping motion at his neck. Technically he'd radio the entire squad to report a malfunction, but for all the Seculars knew, if he was having weapon difficulties and failed camo, his coms could be down, too.

"Hug the ground and blacken your faceplates," Deseo ordered, "and cut external mic—"

She was cut off by the sound of the transport's countermeasures. Black, golf-ball-sized cartridges ejected from all sides of the transport, detonating before they hit the ground. The last thing Deseo caught from her periphery was Gormley being knocked back on his ass from a concussive blast. His launcher fired up at a wild angle, sending a streak of smoke sailing off into the sky. Deseo hugged the cold earth as she felt the shrapnel from the grenades thud against the ground in front of her, while her Monocle unhelpfully warned to take cover.

She messaged Gormley to change position and reactivate his camo. She hoped he'd done this already but was unable to visually verify. The barrage lasted around ten seconds, but even for emergency countermeasures, it seemed weak. Then she mentally smacked her forehead, realizing the Secular hadn't wanted to risk blowing up the fuel depot and their precious transport along with it.

Deseo checked the biometrics of her squad, all still in the green, including the silent McCarthy. She did a quick glance, confirming Gormley had reactivated his camo and changed position about five yards away from his previous location. She made a mental note to recommend him for a promotion when they got back aboard the *Audacity*.

For nearly a minute, nothing happened. The transport remained cockeyed, half-dug into the snow, its left wing curving around behind it like a giant sickle. The wind died down enough that Deseo could see smoke rising from the damaged thruster. She was about to try to message McCarthy again when a hidden door on the side of the craft spiraled open like a camera's aperture. Deseo watched as two soldiers exited the vessel, their bodies appearing crystalline and semi-transparent in form. Her eyes struggled to interpret the strange sight of something moving with a vaguely human shape but appearing to be solid glass with the shifting surface of the skin of a bubble. She wasn't about to complain, though; she shouldn't have been able to see them at all. Intel was right for once, allowing her suit's inferior sensors to pick up just enough of their integrated electronic frequencies to paint a strange, but suitable enough to target, image.

Deseo did just that. She pushed herself up to a kneeling position, raised her rifle, leveled the red targeting reticle center mass on the nearest Secular soldier, and fired.

"Weapons free!" she yelled before squeezing the trigger on her gun. Armor-piercing ammo in two-round bursts ejected from her rifle, a firing arrangement they'd all been briefed on beforehand: one to cut through their armor, and the second to cut through their flesh.

She heard Gormley and Moss firing in conjunction, the clicking of their rifles blending into a cacophony of sound as her own kicked into her shoulder. The Seculars began dropping, splattering gray blood onto the snow and leaving strange, ghostly imprints as their compromised armor bent and refracted light at odd angles.

"CS Alpha," she called over the global com. Counteroffensive

Squad Alpha was meant to stay put and offer cover while Deseo's squad hauled the package back to the APC. No longer. Deseo had learned there are times to double down and hammer a target hard, and she wasn't about to allow whatever Seculars were left inside that transport to catch their breath. "Alpha, I need you to flank the transport. Bravo, move to Alpha's previous position and keep an eye on the silo. Charlie, move to Bravo's position and wait for further orders. Everyone slide up the line; I want to expedite this before they send reinforcements."

Two Secular soldiers fired, their weapons' muzzle flares flaming blue inside the transport's dark interior. The rounds struck the snow nearby, but it looked as though they were "spraying and praying" instead of having identified any specific targets. They drew their weapons back and forth on full automatic to cover the widest area possible. She heard Gormley cry out and in the periphery saw his torso twist as he stumbled back into the snow.

Deseo aimed at one of the Seculars inside the transport and fired, watching a smattering of gray blood eject onto another Secular soldier, making it look as if a moving ice sculpture had paint splattered onto it. The blood coated, half-camouflaged Secular fired several shots that kicked up snow in increasingly close shots in front of her. She took the better of two bad options, diving to the right to avoid the inevitable round but sacrificing her camouflage as she impacted the snow. The Secular's weapon fire followed suit, but just before the rounds closed in on her, more blood splattered the interior of the Secular's transport.

Deseo glanced to her right to see Moss, knowing he had landed that shot.

"Always gotta one up me?" she asked, breathing heavily.

"You know it," Moss said.

She turned her gaze back to the transport, then over to Gormley.

He had gotten to his feet and was holding his shoulder. "You with me, Gormley?"

"Yeah," he replied, voice pained.

"Then stack up," she said, nodding to the transport's open door. She did a quick check of her mini-map. It showed the members of Alpha squad had dug in on the other side of the transport, awaiting further orders.

She, Gormley, and Moss ran toward the transport's entrance, guns raised. Gormley stopped on the left side of the opened door, Moss on the right. They faced one another, hugging the outer walls of the vessel. Deseo stopped just far enough that she could see a few seats inside, but nothing more.

"Do it," she said.

Moss and Gormley turned and fired into the transport, this time their guns only firing two rounds that traveled in a slow ballistic arc before making a dull popping sound. Thunder-flash rounds. Upon detonation, they crackled angrily, lighting up the cabin like a strobe light as they released a powerful discharge of electricity. Secular or not, whoever was left inside that vessel was having a very bad day.

Deseo pointed with two fingers toward the entrance and her Monocle sent the order for Moss and Gormley to enter. Moss leapt up, his powered armor allowing him to jump several feet in the air and land inside the transport with ease. Gormley followed just as Moss disappeared from view.

"Cabin's clear," Moss said, "except for the entry to the pilot station. Door's locked."

"Think it's automated?" Deseo asked.

"I'm doubtin' it," Moss said. "I'd bet the next year's worth of green-room time that one of these *bleaks* is on the other side trying to get the transport going again."

Deseo started walking toward the transport again.

"Or waiting to detonate the thing once we're all inside," Gormley said.

She stopped walking and frowned. "Moss?"

"I doubt that too," Moss said. "They'd have detonated it by now. Plus with our thunder-flash rounds we'd have cooked anything requiring a more complex detonation system than a fuse and a match. Still, I'd recommend you hang back until we open it up."

"We're short on time," Deseo said with a touch of ire, "so how about you just ask them real nice like?"

"Wilco," Moss said.

Deseo chewed her stim-gum and glanced around her surroundings, seeing nothing but a desert of ice and snow. She eyed the crumbling, ice-covered silo. It looked nothing short of ancient, frozen ruins, long since abandoned. While listening to Moss finish explaining in no uncertain terms what a breaching charge would do to whoever was on the other side of that door, she pulled up her messaging window.

GS DESEO: CS Alpha — Go find McCarthy. P.W.C.

McCarthy's malfunctioning monocle cutting his coms wasn't entirely out of the realm of possibility, given that much of their equipment and armor was a patchwork of materials in various states of disrepair. Still, she told CS Alpha to proceed with caution, as the kid should've at least visually signaled his coms were down.

"Door's open," Moss said. "We have one Secular pilot. No explosives that I could identify."

"Outstanding, Sergeant Moss," Deseo said, walking to the transport again. "Your talent for persuasion is unrivaled."

"Must be my pretty eyes," Moss said.

Deseo smirked as she looked up at Gormley. He stood to the left of the opened door, gripping a metal bar that ran along the inside of the entryway. Deseo attempted to hop up the six feet to the opening, but one of the legs of her powered suit jammed. She came up just a few inches shy of the step, and had Gormley not reflexively reached out and snagged her arm, she would've fallen back into the snow again. Gormley sucked in a breath, hissing in pain as he helped pull her up. She grabbed the lip of the opening and climbed inside the transport, then took a second to acclimate to the floor being at a slight tilt. She stomped her right leg a few times, unsuccessfully trying to get the motors to unbind. She cursed under her breath and looked up at Gormley. Even through his faceplate, she could see his pale skin was glistening with sweat. She tilted her head to check the black scoring on his ribcage, where a glancing round had burned through his armor.

"You sure you're solid?" she asked. She completed a biometric scan and saw an area of deep red under his suit. Cracked rib for sure, but mostly tissue damage. His suit had sealed itself and released some local analgesics, but it didn't look like he'd taken anything else. She felt around on her hip for a tube of morphedra.

"I'm good, Gunny," he said, holding up a hand and grimacing from the movement. "I don't need it."

Deseo cocked a questioning eyebrow.

"It's keeping me sharp," he said, wincing. "Ask me when we're back aboard the *Audacity* and I'll gladly take two hits along with a stiff drink."

"I'll bring you the drink personally," Deseo said, grinning. "Even with that silly mustache. Now let's have a look around, shall we?" He nodded and she took a few careful steps around him, running her hand along the metal support bar to keep upright against the uneven floor.

Two large Secular bodies lay inside the entrance. Even knowing they were dead, they were still intimidating. Their shoulders were broad, their bodies heavily muscled. They were easily close to seven feet in height. One was leaning against an arming station that contained a range of weapons magnetically locked to the back wall at the tail end of the ship. The second was in the main walkway. The downed soldiers' active camo had not been disabled upon their death, leaving the parts not covered in gray blood partially transparent, bending the light as if she were looking through slightly murky water.

After glancing at the arming station again, she looked left again to see the vehicle's main cabin, which contained a row of seating along each side of the ship with a wide walkway in the middle. Each seat was oversized and the height of the ceiling was tall enough to allow Deseo to walk upright with ease. Toward the front of the vessel, the seating ended with another opened door, round just like the external hatch. Moss stood to the right of the entryway with his gun aimed inside the cockpit, pointed up.

Deseo stepped over the dead Secular and walked the few steps to join Moss. She raised her gun and peered into the cockpit. The pilot stood only a few feet away, his large hands held up and narrow fingers splayed. The cockpit had a large, one-way window that wrapped around in a slight curve. The rest of the space was barren, save for a seat, one small screen, and two closed-grip handles below it, likely mechanical backups. The Seculars had Cortical Meshes that communicated directly with vehicles, weapons, and other technology.

Deseo traced the form of the Secular pilot. He had wide shoulders and a narrow waist. He wasn't the biggest Secular she'd seen, not by a longshot. Still, she had to angle her rifle upward to point it at the pilot's head. Her eyes first connected with his strange, square pupils. Pupils that appeared mildly holographic, as if she were looking into the opening of an inky black void. Unlike Deseo's smooth brown skin, the shade of the pilot's skin had a dark bluish tinge to it, like polished iron. She recalled learning when Seculars enter an area with minimal to no radiation, that their skin gradually turns transparent, losing nearly all pigment. Not peach or white like an albino, but see-through, like clear rubber or nylon. She shivered at the thought of seeing what sort of technologically enhanced muscles, bones, and organs would be revealed within.

This particular Secular was lanky and thin, but still had solid muscle underneath his black clothing. Clothing that resembled a three-piece suit with miscellaneous utilitarian pockets and a holster at the hip. Despite the strange union of the formal and tactical, the material was finely stitched and fit the pilot as if custom tailored. The pilot's face was round, and he wore no helmet over his shaved head. His narrow lips trembled, and despite his looming form and alien eyes, he looked afraid.

"Disarm it," Deseo said, half-tempted to briefly open her faceplate to the subzero temperatures just so she could spit on the ground in disgust.

Moss stepped toward the pilot and pulled the pistol from his holster. Moss flipped the oversized gun and clamped it on the back of his utility belt.

"So," Deseo said, raising her eyebrows. "Where's the goodies?"

The pilot opened his mouth then closed it again. He shook his head, his bizarre eyes wide with confusion. She raised her gun and fired two shots through his right hand. Silvery blood coated the inside of the curved windshield behind him. It had the consistency of clotted motor oil. He screamed out in pain and grabbed his wounded hand, doubling over. Deseo snorted derisively. His voice was higher than she expected.

She stepped around Moss and used the barrel of her gun to lift the pilot's chin, forcing him back upright. "Redundancies," Deseo said, leaning in and locking eyes with the Secular. "It's what makes you guys so hard to kill." She looked behind her, making a show of looking back at his dead comrades, before turning back again. "Moss, how many holes do you think it will take before this *bleak* bleeds out?"

"Huh," Moss said, his face forming a contemplative frown. "That does sound like something we could test fairly easily."

"Okay!" the pilot said. He looked past her, just over her shoulder. "I have to unlock it."

Deseo turned her head to follow his gaze and her eyes landed on the arming station. The racks containing rifles and ammunition were stuck to a hidden door. She lifted her chin at Gormley and he caught her drift. He reached over to pull the door open.

"Slow down, Private," she warned. "Work your corners."

Gormley took a deep breath and nodded, then walked to the other side of the door, just next to the opening of the transport. Deseo raised her rifle, pointing directly at the door. Gormley reached for one of the racks and pulled, swinging the door open.

Inside were four slick, black objects stacked and held in place by black netting. They looked like giant black pills, longer than they were wide. They reminded her of polished cocoons. Or coffins. That thought was unsettling.

"Restrain this thing," she said. Moss plucked a pair of cuffs from the back of his belt and walked toward the pilot, ordering him to turn around. Deseo headed back to Gormley, who had one hand covering his ribs while he examined the four polished boxes. Her Monocle estimated their weight to be around 120 kilos. It was manageable, but not ideal. They'd have to cut the net, then drag out each one by one. Even with the UGV's help, it was going to take more time than she wanted. She received a ping from CS Alpha and checked her mini-map. They had surrounded the silo and were requesting clearance to enter and figure out what was going on with McCarthy. She messaged him and once again received no response. Part of her considered telling them to retreat. She didn't like the idea of leaving a soldier behind, but something was off.

DESEO: Do it. Stay alert. Something's hinky.

She brought up her command screen and connected to the UGV. She was about to command it to come to them when she had a thought.

"Moss," she said, looking back at him. The pilot was on his knees, arms bound behind his back. Even kneeling, the pilot's head was practically chest high on Moss. "Think you can fly this thing?"

She saw his dark face frowning through his faceplate. "If we had more time, maybe. As it stands now, it's pretty corked."

"*Time* is the reason I'm asking," Deseo said. "It doesn't even have to be pretty. Hell, you can crash the damn thing if you can get us back to the APC with the cargo intact in less time than it would take to unload and haul this shit back with the UGV."

"Well," Moss said with a half-smile and a crooked eyebrow, "when you put it that way."

As if punctuated by the end of his sentence, gunfire popped off in the distance. It sounded wrong. Uncontrolled, sporadic. She pulled up her weapon fire locator and saw an overhead topographical map of the silo. Multiple red flashes lighted up its interior. She eye-clicked to check McCarthy's biometric readout. It was in the red. He had flatlined.

"Fuck!" She jogged toward the transport's exit, leaping over the soldier. She grabbed Gormley and pulled him out of the way so she could look outside. A powerful wind pressed against her, howling as it blasted over the transport. White snow flurries dirtied the air.

She saw the silhouette of the depot, a vague outline of its nearby crumbling structure enhanced by her Monocle, but nothing with any clarity. It was like trying to look through smoke. She flicked on infrared but it told her what she already knew. "CS Alpha, report."

More gunfire. Some static over the coms. Biometrics for all three Alpha members were in the red. She checked Bravo squad, still in the green. "Bravo, advance on our position."

No response.

"Bravo, copy!" Deseo said.

"What the hell is happening?" Gormley asked.

"We've been hacked," Deseo said. "Someone has been cutting us down, blocking coms and feeding us false biometric data." She hammered a closed fist into the metal railing, then walked toward the Secular pilot and pointed her rifle at his face. "Talk!"

He gave her the silent treatment again, though she had his attention, given the look of fear on his inhuman face. Deseo brought the rifle back and cracked the butt of the gun into the Secular's mouth. His head snapped back from the impact but he recovered quicker than she expected. He stared up at her, his eyes narrowing in defiance. She kicked him in the chest and he fell backwards against the bulkhead, arms still pinned behind his back. She shoved the gun down into his crotch. "Come on," she said, looming over him, "I know you things still like to get down, even if you don't do it for procreation. How many are there?"

A devilish smile grew on his face, revealing crystalline teeth and pronounced canines, a few of which were clouded from Secular blood. "Does it matter?"

"What the hell does that mean?" Gormley asked from behind her.

Deseo checked the ammo on her rifle, then glanced at Moss. He stared at her with a look she'd never seen on him before. A cold, distant gaze. Resignation of a dark fate to come. "There's an Auditor here," Moss said, reading her mind.

"Oh fuck me," Gormley said, his voice rising on octave. He grabbed the sides of his helmet and started pacing. "We're not equipped to handle this."

"Hey!" Deseo yelled, half-barking the word. She walked over and shoved him against the wall with the side of her gun. "Knock it off!

Deseo's hot breath blew back into her own face. Gormley's eyes were wide, and his freckled face was nearly as white as the snow outside. He looked young. Too young.

"The boy's right, you know," said the pilot, his words slow, as if he were savoring them like a fine wine, clearly enjoying the turn of fate.

"He *is* right," Deseo said after a moment, slowly stepping back from Gormley. She turned to the pilot, who looked momentarily perplexed that she had agreed with him. After holding his gaze a moment, she started walking toward him, taking strong, purposeful steps. The pilot's eyes widened and he got half a word out before she raised her gun and fired, the barrel blazing orange as she emptied half her magazine into his chest. He fell back, his head slumping to the right, the look of shock frozen on his now lifeless face. "See if you can survive that, you *bleak* sack of maggot shit!"

"Oh god," Gormley said, voice shaking.

Moss grabbed her arm. She could tell by his expression that he was concerned she was losing it.

"We're getting out of here," she said, eyes narrowing. "Fuck these crates."

"Our orders are at *any* cost," Moss said.

She jerked her arm away from his grip. "Fuck the orders!"

"I don't like it either," Moss said, "but for all we know, whatever is in those crates could end this war."

She studied his face a moment, thinking of their history. Moss had been with her on so many OPS. He always had her back. She thought of the times they laughed, both in the field and back home. Times they spent mourning in the Greenroom, times they both drank a little too much and razzed each other about it the next morning. Moss was an excellent soldier, but he was an even better friend. And she wasn't about to let him die because Brass wanted them to secure some shiny crates.

"Gormley," she said, turning back to face him.

His expression was blank and he seemed frozen in place. She snapped her fingers at him, her armor clicking as she did so. "Private Ashton Gormley!"

He looked at her, partially snapping out of it.

"You got any rockets left?"

Gormley nodded. He swallowed. "Two with me, I think."

"What are you thinking?" Moss asked.

Deseo took a deep breath. "We're hitting that silo."

Moss looked away a moment, his eyes dancing back and forth, as if he was considering other options. Finally, he looked back at Deseo, pursed his lips and gave her a single nod.

"Gormley, you know what to do," Deseo said. She walked over to him, grabbed a carabiner from her belt, and unspooled the nanocord attached to it. She attached the hook to a notch on Gormley's belt, then grabbed the lip of armor above his chest and pulled him close to her, his faceplate clanking against her own. "You've got this. And we've got you."

Gormley nodded again. She let him go. He took the few meager steps toward the exit, moving like a man walking to his death. Snow had started to collect on the floor of the transport and he left footprints as he got into position. He crouched, reaching down for his MTGB launcher. Deseo sat back into one of the oversized seats, grabbed one of the harnesses, and tried to pull it over her shoulders. The harness was too big with too much slack, even when it was clipped into place. Instead, she wrapped some of the extra material around one wrist and grabbed a support post separating the seats with the other. She looked over at Moss who had used some of his own nanocord to anchor himself to a handhold sticking out from the wall. He had placed his back against the entryway between the cabin and the cockpit, pinning himself with one foot pressed into the opposite part of the doorway.

Moss nodded to her. She looked to Gormley. "Do it."

He hoisted the MTGB over his shoulder and took aim.

Deseo swallowed her gum so she didn't choke on it. She clenched her teeth and held her breath, gripping the harness over her chest with both hands.

Gormley never got the shot off.

The M8 battle armor was designed to handle various impacts, both from direct shots, such as from ammunition or melee strikes, or indirect blasts, such as from fragmentation grenades or shrapnel. When damaged, the armor had self-healing capabilities that consisted of microscopic gel filaments that branched throughout it like tiny capillaries. When these became severed or damaged, they oozed a nanogel into the damaged areas, similar to blood clotting on a wound. This gel would harden in seconds, sealing the opening. This was particularly useful in sub-zero temperatures, or in areas that contained toxins or low levels of oxygen. This corrective ability did have a downside: if struck by something large, such as a spear-shaped object or piece of shrapnel that impaled a soldier, the object would become bonded to the armor, generally requiring some sort of additional mechanism to remove a soldier pinned to something, or remove something too awkward or oblong to transport along with the soldier back to medical.

That's why, when what looked like a makeshift pickaxe attached to an old chain swung down from above the transport's opening and struck Gormley in the face, his visor began to seal itself, despite the hunk of metal lodging itself into his brain and killing him instantly. His arms fell and the launcher sagged off his shoulder but didn't reach the ground. It was still mag-locked to his hand, dangling as if he were holding it in a death grip.

Deseo looked in shock as she saw the savage, archaic-looking weapon still buried in his faceplate. Several cracks ran through the visor, already starting to bubble from the suit's attempt to seal the damage while battling the change in pressure and subzero temperatures. The chain attached to the weapon slackened, dropping from the top of the exit to the bottom, clanking against the floor. It then tightened again, pulling taut like a fish hooked on a line. Gormley's body shot out of the craft's exit a second later, vanishing into the gray world outside, as if he'd been sucked out due to explosive decompression.

The small amount of slack in Deseo's nanocord snapped straight, pulling her along with him. Her body was yanked from the seat. She traveled only a few feet before she was snapped to a halt, dangling midair. The cable twanged, straining under the tension. Her right arm, tangled in the harness, kept her connected to the transport. Her suit's mechanical assist let out a low, whining groan as it attempted to resist being pulled apart. The mechanical joints around her shoulder let out a crunching sound just before they gave way with a loud crack. She felt the rush of supercooled air flood her suit. Warning sounds blared in her ears and angry, red text flashed in her vision, warning her that her suit was compromised. She sent the command to disconnect the cable attached to Gormley's body only to receive a message that it malfunctioned. She scrambled with her other hand to try to disconnect the cord, unable to bend her neck enough to see, feeling around on her belt for the manual release. The armor in her suit crunched again and she felt her entire body move several inches before stopping again. A sharp, burning pain radiated from her shoulder as the ligaments and muscles began to tear from the socket.

A gun blast boomed to her right and the wire snapped. She hit the ground and looked to see Moss kneeling to her right, the end of his gun's barrel smoking. His eyes, laser focused, caught hers. His words were half choked up, a mixture of fear and sadness. His eyes softened. "Get out of here, Kate."

He stood up and ran, leaping over her toward the exit of the transport.

"No!" she screamed, trying to grab him with her good arm but missing entirely. He leapt out of the craft, his rifle roaring as he fired a steady stream of bullets.

Only seconds passed before the sound of his gun stopped. Deseo forced herself to a kneeling position, groaning in pain as her injured right shoulder and wrist protested the movement. She stood up, falling into the side of the ship, and pulled her sidearm with her left hand. She peeked around the corner, looking outside. Dense snow flittered and dashed through the air. In the fog of snow, she caught a glimpse of Moss. He was on all fours, crawling toward her. He coughed and a splatter of red blood coated the inside of his faceplate. One of his arms was under his body as if he were holding his chest. He reached out and grabbed the snow ahead of him, pulling him a few feet closer.

They were being played with.

The Auditor was using Moss as a lure. Deseo didn't care. She holstered her gun and grabbed the corner of the transport's exit with her injured arm. It had started to go numb from the cold or from shock, maybe both, but her forcing it into action brought it back

alive, pain burning bright and jolting through her shoulder and bicep like an electric bolt. She reached out to Moss, hoping to pull him
inside the transport. He was only feet away.

"Marcel," she said, "take my hand."

He looked up to her. Eyes bloodshot, blood running from his
nose. He reached out again, crawling a few more inches toward her.

"It's going to be okay," she said. She leaned forward, trying to
grab his hand.

A great, looming shadow appeared behind him. Snow whipped
around the massive body, its shape only visible by the snow's inability
to permeate it. It seemed to Deseo she was seeing death itself, the
massive dark form of a wraith materializing behind Moss.

The Auditor cut its cloak, clearly unafraid of Deseo seeing it
without camouflage. It was a woman. As Deseo drew her eyes up the
hourglass shape of the Auditor's massive, muscled form, she traced
the finely stitched, blood red clothes that waved as gusts of wind
blew past her. Underneath the clothes was a skin-tight, dark green
undersuit, one that Deseo could see peeking from the sleeves of the
Auditor's wrists and out of the square, low-cut collar. The undersuit came to points over the back of the woman's hands, like partial
gloves, and clung to her like a second skin. She took another step
forward, straddling and standing over Moss's body. Her size made
him seem so small, like a demon standing over a child.

The wind died down. The Auditor had the typical jet-black skin
of a Secular. She had a shiny braid of black hair that ran along the
top of her head and behind it; the rest was shaved. The sides of her
head, just above her ears, were tattooed with arcane symbols that
glowed gold, as if fueled by their own light source.

The thing that stood out to Deseo the most was the woman's eyes.
They had the same, strange square shape to their pupils, but with a

vibrant, emerald outline so sharp, it caught the light like a cat's eye-shine. They had a subtle slant, and the skin in between was creased, like the eyes of a snarling tiger. They were wicked, as wicked as the smile on the Auditor's face. She was a predator that had cornered its prey, savoring the moment just before the kill.

"Let me help you," the Auditor said, in a deep but feminine voice. Her thick lips almost appeared sensual as they twisted into a look of amusement. She looked down at Moss and unsheathed a vicious black knife from behind her back. Deseo screamed as the towering woman rotated the blade and brought it down in a savage thrust, penetrating Moss's body armor in between his shoulder blades. She rotated her grip and lifted Moss's body, using the blade as a handle. She held him out to Deseo, as if offering a piece of meat at the end of a skewer.

Moss's eyes blazed with pain. They looked animalistic, mad. Dark blood spurted from his mouth.

Before Deseo knew what had happened, she looked down to see that she had been handed a heavy, round object. It was the MTGB launcher, she knew by its weight and balance before her mind could even process what it was. Thank god for the Core's obsession with reflexive training.

Moss had somehow retrieved the launcher and concealed it as he crawled back to the transport. The Auditor's face shifted from amused to calculating, as if she'd just realized what had happened.

Deseo swept the launcher up, pointing it directly at Moss. He deepened his gaze and nodded.

Just as Deseo fired, the Auditor dropped Moss's body and dove to the left, moving with preternatural speed, as if she were much lighter than she appeared. Her movement was so sudden it was like seeing a small animal jetting away in the periphery of one's vision.

The missile erupted from the end of the launcher with a chemtrail of white smoke, sailing in a straight line past the Auditor's shoulder, missing by inches.

The Auditor hit the ground, tucked her body, and rolled. She landed back on her feet. The suggestion of a smile returned to her face, but vanished as quickly as it appeared. She had only managed to turn halfway to look back at the frozen walls of the crumbling silo just as the building erupted in a swollen orange fireball.

Deseo threw a hand up to shield herself as a series of bone rattling explosions detonated, causing the ground around the silo to erupt as if some massive beast were under it, attempting to unearth itself. Her body was lifted from the ground and she was weightless a moment, just before she collided with the transport's opposite wall. For a split-second, she caught sight of one of the black crates sailing toward her along the roof. She only had a moment to process that the transport was tumbling when she bounced again off something and saw the ceiling coming at her face. She tried to lift her arms to brace the impact, but wasn't fast enough. Her faceplate slammed against the immovable material and her world flashed white.

As consciousness returned, she heard a steady, shrill, high-pitched ring hissing in her ears. She worked her jaw and tasted blood. At first, she thought she had been blinded, only seeing a dull gray blob in front of her. She blinked several times, focusing to see a warning flashing her vision, showing a generic outline of her suit, most parts outlined in red. Her faceplate was cracked. That, paired with her suit's torn shoulder, had caused the inside of her faceplate to frost. Though she couldn't see it, smoke lingered in the air; the sickly sweet smell of burned electronics seeped into her helmet. She started to cough.

The damage to her shoulder was most critical; the sleeve had been nearly pulled from the seam. She felt around on her beltline until her hand landed on a sealing gun the size of a large syringe. She plucked it from its sheath and brought the tip of it to her shoulder, squeezing in sealing foam, doing her best to aim. The foam expanded upon contact with air, filling in gaps too large for the suit's ability to self-repair. She used the entire tube. A second later, the alarm shut off. Her eyes and throat stopped stinging, as the suit's scrubbers were no longer overwhelmed by having a massive hole in a closed system. She'd have little use of that arm, but at least she wasn't going to suffocate or freeze to death.

As the frost cleared away, she lifted her head, causing a sharp pain in her neck. She let out a groan. Her vision started to clear through the faceplate. She saw a dusting of snow or ash covering her body and most of the interior of the cabin.

She tried to sit up and felt something pressing on her legs. She looked down to see the limp body of the dead pilot, jaw slack and gray blood oozing from his open mouth. She pulled one of her legs free and kicked his body off, grunting as she did so. The pilot was heavier than he looked.

She reached for her belt again and pulled out a tube of morphedra. She popped the cap, rotated the small tube, and jammed it into a port on her belt. She felt the chemical burn as it traveled through a small tube connected to her femoral artery on the inside of her thigh. Her heart rate slowed and the pain in her body faded. Her bones felt warm and her vision cleared further. She tossed the spent bottle and took in a deep breath, laying her head back. Every stitch of her being wanted to rest. Rage and sadness sparked inside her. Moss was dead. Her whole crew was gone. She was out of time. She may have taken out the Auditor, but Secular reinforcements had to be en route given the shit-show the mission had turned into.

She lifted her head again, looking around to see that most of the transport appeared intact. At least the interior, anyway. The black crates had fallen, but the net in front of them had held them all except the one she dodged when the transport was rolling. It likely had spilled out of the transport's door. The door remained open, and a fine dusting of snow drifted in. Deseo didn't know why, but found she couldn't look away from it.

A blackened hand grabbed the bottom of the entrance. Two fingernails were missing and parts of the skin were peeled off or gone entirely. For the briefest of moments, she thought it might be Moss, that he had somehow survived his grievous injuries despite the explosion, but then the twisted, dark face of the Auditor peeked above the flooring. One of her eyes was damaged, its surface covered in a mercury-like sheen. The other stared at Deseo with seething hatred. Half of the Auditor's scalp was burned, its flesh bubbled and peeling.

Deseo's heart rate doubled. She looked around. No sign of a rifle. She reached for her holster. It was empty. She rotated her body, forcing herself onto her chest, all the while clenching her jaw as several more new pains burned bright in her back, hips, and neck. She forced herself to move, despite the pain making her dizzy. Then she saw her gun a few feet away. It was lying among the broken glass on the floor of the cockpit.

She crawled toward it. Her entire body protested, her lungs inflamed from the cold and toxic smoke. Her shoulder was dislocated for sure, if not worse. What little it moved felt wrong somehow, like bone against bone. She suspected she had a broken ankle as well. She continued her crawl, relying on her left arm, the only thing on her body that felt mostly unscathed.

She slammed her hand down on the gun and twisted onto her back in nearly the same movement. She used her good leg to press her body into an upright position, her back leaning against the doorframe of the cockpit. She checked her gun. Other than being covered in snow, the magazine was full and the gun appeared scuffed, but otherwise undamaged. She leveled it at the transport's opening.

The Auditor nimbly jumped up, landing on both feet inside the transport. She took a step toward Deseo and stumbled, catching herself against the wall, head tucked slightly under the ceiling. Her mouth was half-open, as if she'd lost her ability to breathe through her nose. Her clothes were shredded, smoldering, and nearly in rags, but her undersuit seemed intact, except for the material on her left arm, which had melted into her flesh.

"Ow," the Auditor said, grunting the word out while sounding half-drunk, glaring at Deseo with one good eye as she did so. Had the situation not been so grave, Deseo might have even found the comment funny. The Auditor spat gray blood onto the floor and wiped her mouth with her burned arm. Tendrils of white smoke drifted off the flesh as she did so.

The Auditor stepped toward her. Deseo fired three shots, one connecting with the Auditor's shoulder, one with her hip and the third glancing off her forearm. But as each bullet impacted, the Auditor continued to advance, her body twitching as if she'd only been struck by a rock.

Deseo was about to fire a fourth shot at the Auditor's head, but then she kicked Deseo's wrist and sent the gun flying away from her. She then reached down, grabbed Deseo by the neck, and jerked her to her feet. Deseo tried to resist but the Auditor's vice-like grip lifted her off her feet and slammed her against the wall.

Deseo reached behind her, grabbing on the hilt of her combat knife tucked into its sheath on her belt. She thrust the blade toward the Auditor's neck, but she caught the sharp edge of the blade with her free hand. Deseo tried to hang on to the knife, but the Auditor rotated the blade and wrenched it away from her grip. She then moved her face within inches of Deseo's faceplate. For a moment, Deseo thought she saw some sort of strange admiration in the beast's ghastly eye.

Then a wicked grin grew on the Auditor's face and she flipped the blade, catching the hilt. She leveled it with Deseo's neck, her elbow bent with precision, like a scorpion aiming its stinger. "I'll make it quick," she said in a slow, cool voice.

"Go to hell, bitch," Deseo said, her voice raspy from her throat being compressed. She braced for the thrust of the blade, readying her mind and soul for the brief moment of pain before the final release.

It never came. The Auditor cocked her head and stared at Deseo with what looked like fascination. She turned to look behind her and Deseo realized she must have heard something.

Deseo tilted her head just enough to see past the Auditor's muscled, broad shoulder, and saw Moss standing only feet away.

His suit was mostly undamaged; apparently having hugged the ground caused most of the blast to pass him over. But a mess of frozen blood ran down from a hole in his chest, where the knife had stuck through him. His faceplate was shattered, a fractured mess of jagged edges, exposing his face to the cold. The blood on his nose and chin was frozen as well, the striations of red ice looking like frozen woodgrain. His eyes were clouded, as if both had formed cataracts.

He should have been dead. But he stood there, his shoulders out, back straight, as if he felt no pain whatsoever. For a moment, they stood there, the three of them unmoving. Deseo questioned if she was hallucinating, suffering from hypoxia.

Moss reached for the Auditor, which caused her to spring into action. She grabbed his wrist, halting his movement. For a moment, Deseo thought she saw a golden glimmer flash in the man's frosted pupils. Moss continued to press into the Auditor, as if they were doing a standing arm-wrestling match. The Auditor, to Deseo's surprise, was losing. She resisted with all her might, but Moss was somehow overpowering her.

The Auditor let go of Deseo, causing her to crash to the floor, choking as she sucked in air. Transparent veins throbbed in her vision and she fell forward, catching herself with her hands. She looked up to see the Auditor had now brought her other arm around, and Moss was somehow controlling the giant woman, having grabbed both of her wrists. He then twisted with surprising power, throwing the Auditor face-first into the wall. He kicked the back of her knee, causing her leg to buckle at an odd angle and crack. She snarled in pain, sounding more like an animal than a woman. The injury made her lose her balance and she fell to one knee. Now behind her, Moss wrapped his arm around her throat and locked the chokehold by crossing his other arm behind her head and grabbing his own wrist. He squeezed.

Veins stuck out in the Auditor's temple as she clawed at Moss's arm, spittle foaming from her lips. Moss turned his head to stare at Deseo with dead eyes, then looked down at her feet.

Deseo followed his gaze and saw her gun. She picked it up and pointed it at the Auditor's face. She attempted to step to the right to get a clean shot at the Auditor, but Moss mirrored her movements.

"I'll hit you," Deseo said, confused.

"He is gone," Moss said, his voice mechanical and raspy. His pupils shimmered golden again. "I am just using his body."

Deseo stared at Moss, finally realizing what she was seeing. She had heard stories, knew of the thing in front of her, but had never actually seen it. "The Mad AI," she said, her words a slow whisper.

Moss stared back at her like a standing corpse. The Auditor struggled again, somehow lifting Moss up one-legged, causing him to leave the floor a few feet while clinging to her neck. He kicked hard into the back of the Auditor's thigh, causing her to yell out in pain and fall to her knees again. "You must act quickly," Moss said. "She is powerful and this body will soon be of no use."

Of no use. Deseo sucked in air. No training she had ever received was directed on how to interact with one of your recently deceased friends having been possessed by a deranged artificial intelligence. She focused on the real and looked down at the Auditor. Deseo pointed the gun at the Auditor's good eye.

The Auditor stared back at Deseo, her one eye burning with pure hatred. Her lips peeled back in a grimace. "You know what to do—"

The gun kicked as Deseo squeezed the trigger, the dual-firing solution creating a near perfect hole to form in the Auditor's eye socket. She released Moss's arm and her body went limp. Her hands fell to her sides. Moss let the Auditor go and she fell forward, crashing facedown on the ground.

Gold mist drifted from the hole in his chest, pouring out from it like heavy smoke. It landed onto the floor of the craft, lingering for a moment before disappearing into the small cracks as if sucked in by some sort of vacuum. Moss walked toward the craft's exit, telling Deseo to follow.

Deseo stumbled behind him and made her way to the entrance. She grabbed the edge of the doorframe and looked outside. The clouds had cleared up and the blizzard had passed. The sun was setting, partially eclipsed by the horizon, casting an orange glow on the snow-covered landscape. There were mountains in the distance, ones she hadn't noticed before.

A second later, she heard the familiar whine of the transport's three functioning thrusters. Snow flurried around the ship. She was about to turn around when she felt a powerful thrust in the center of her back. Her neck snapped back and she fell forward out of the vessel, crashing into the snow below. She rolled to her back, looking up at Moss, who stood in the exit of the transport, staring down at her.

"Where are you taking the transport?" Deseo yelled.

"Away from you," Moss said. It was his voice, but it was mechanical and full of disdain. It sickened her to see him used as some sort of puppet. "Away from *all* of you." Moss turned away, disappearing inside the craft.

As the transport gained altitude, a missile streaked past, causing the vessel to bank hard to the right to dodge it. Deseo watched as the Auditor's limp body spilled out of the transport along with one of the black crates, landing a few feet away from her.

The transport's thrusters rotated from pointing down to behind the craft, and they fired hard, turning a bright blue and rumbling Deseo's chest. Snow blasted past her, some sticking to her faceplate. The transport bolted away at the breakneck speed of a fighter jet, but stayed low to the ground as it moved. Two cloaked vessels suddenly appeared, the front of their invisible noses creating a white cone of air as they rocketed past her. Secular reinforcements.

Her com crackled in her ears. It was Command, asking her to report. The death of the Auditor, or something the Mad AI had done, lifted the communications blackout. The voice repeated twice more. It was a request for her to respond.

"Deseo here," she said reflexively, as if she were in a dream. She looked around, seeing the remains of the silo, now a smoldering stump of rubble and ash, with streaks of black soot encircling it. She saw Gormley's body not far away, the Auditor's makeshift weapon stuck in his face, a smattering of red snow around his head like a poorly drawn halo.

The body of the dead Auditor was in a fetal position, with one burned arm draped over her face. She made her way toward the Auditor, knelt down, and scanned the body. To her surprise, the Auditor's heart was still beating, about once every ten seconds. Secular bodies had the ability to go into hibernation after suffering damage, but a round point-blank to the skull was catastrophic. She fought the urge to shoot the Auditor again for good measure. Not a few feet behind her was one of the slick black crates that had fallen out during the explosion. Deseo forced herself to her feet again and limped toward the crate. Part of her wanted to destroy it; a thing so important to Brass it caused the death of her entire platoon. But as she got closer, she noticed some sort of window that had gone transparent. She made her way over and wiped her hand across it, clearing the thin layer of snow. Inside was the frozen corpse of a middle-aged woman.

"Repeat last?" the voice crackled in her ear. "Did you secure the package? How many for pickup?"

She shook her head, staring at the dead woman. It was so bizarre; she couldn't help but let out a desperate laugh. She turned around and half fell down, sliding her back against the crate. A warm tear trickled down her cheek as she thought of Moss, of Gormley, of all the men and women that had died on her watch. "Three," she said finally. "Three to pick up."

Love in the Time of COVID

Bennett Gates

Day 1
Sunday, January 25, 2020
First case of COVID-19 in California.

A man in Orange County tests positive for the novel coronavirus—now known as COVID-19.

IN HIS TINY HOUSE in San Francisco's Marina district, Walter Evans, forty-five and divorced, shakes his head, a little worried about his sniffles.

Day 32
Tuesday, February 25

San Francisco Mayor London Breed declares a local emergency. There have been no confirmed cases of the illness in the city yet.

Day 43
Saturday, March 7

The city and county of San Francisco ban all nonessential group activities in city-owned facilities, such as city hall, the piers. And libraries.

AT FIVE THIRTY P.M., in a walk-up studio apartment in the Marina District, Eleanor "Ellie" Reedy, thirty-four and divorced, is watching TV news. She gasps, then grabs her cat and lifts it so their noses touch. "God, Wiffles, they're closing the library!" She pauses a moment, staring at the cat. Finally, she drops Wiffles on the sofa, pulls her long coat off a hanger and heads for Joe's Bar.

Day 47
Wednesday, March 11. Four days later.
4 deaths reported
202 cases reported
> **Governor Newsom recommends gatherings not to exceed 250 people and extends paid family leave and disability benefits to those affected by the coronavirus.**

> **WHO declares COVID-19 a pandemic.**

AT FOUR P.M., WALTER EVANS gives thanks his sniffles are gone. He shuts down his work-from-home computer and walks to his bay window. He watches the drifting fog fold around the little Monopoly houses across the street, turning them into homes for ghosts. He grabs his old denim jacket and a scarf and heads for Joe's Bar.

It's busy on Chestnut Street, even with the fog. For a Wednesday, the sidewalks are packed. Earlier, it was the first warm day in months, and the predatory females are still everywhere, like spring buds on a thorny rose. It's barely sixty degrees, but some are braless, with nipples like gum drops. Cleavage abounds. Excited girls in short-shorts walk in safe huddles, making sexy eye contact with stunned boys. He winks at an attractive young woman as she passes, glances back in time to see her turn and look at him. He keeps walking. If men are hunters, women are trappers. His old anger catches up with him, biting at his heels. He shakes his head. Trap me once, shame on you. Trap me twice, shame on me. Never again. So why is he hurrying to see Ellie?

Finally, he's there, in front of the big oak door with stained glass letters that shout JOE'S BAR! The glass is wet with fog; it squeaks when he wipes it with the side of his hand. She's not at the bar. He takes a breath and steps into his refuge.

The huge old bar runs along the right wall, halfway to the back. It's an 1850s masterpiece of carved and polished wood--black Philippine mahogany, Joe insists. All the cushioned-leather, high-backed stools are occupied. He studies each patron carefully, just to be sure.

Opposite the bar, the wall is hung with etchings of San Francisco's bawdy gold-rush days, pictures of old and new earthquakes, and the Golden Gate bridge under construction. He walks past them all into a noisy area in back, crowded with captain's chairs and wooden tables. Baskets of popcorn and tortilla chips and unshelled peanuts cluster under warming lights in the far right corner. The smell of spilled beer reaches him, then the stronger smell of roasted beef. It's an aroma that usually heralds Tanya's arrival, hefting a tray of Joe's famous hot Italian beef sandwiches. Walter closes his eyes, imagining one, dripping with juice, peppers on the side. He sighs and thinks of Tanya. Beautiful, blond, with a smile that pulls you right into her world. An ambitious girl with the sharply defined morals of a nun—in the words of her doting father, Joe.

On cue, a smiling Tanya stiff-arms through the kitchen door, balancing a tray of steaming sandwiches. She's wearing baggy sweatpants and a Forty-Niners jersey, but the way the clothes move on her body holds the eye of every man in the bar. She lowers the tray and deals out the sandwiches to a full table of beer-swilling workers, laughing as they pound the table and shout her name. Then she comes over to Walter, giving him that little pat on the chest that cute girls save for their grandfathers. She stands on tiptoe and whispers.

"She'll be here, promise. It's Wednesday."

A construction worker stands, faces Walter, and holds out his arms. "Dude, she *touched* you!" He bows, then claps, and the room bursts into laughter, hoots, and applause.

Walter, red-faced, bows in return and heads for the bar, suddenly aware of the peanut shells crunching under his shoes. His old friend Joe is behind his bar, both hands on the polished copper top, guarding an empty stool for Walter. Joe's a huge, round man, Forty-Niners front line huge. Thick-featured, with a crooked nose and a high forehead. His slicked-back gray hair is always in a short ponytail, pinched by any stray rubber band, sometimes a bag tie. He's on the far side of sixty years and three hundred pounds, with the red, sweaty face of a screaming baby. Walter loves the guy.

Walter rests his elbows on the bar's copper top. Joe has left as-is a century and a half of dents and scratches, but he can slide a beer over its polished surface with the accuracy of an Olympic curler. Walter's always loved this bar, with its carved mahogany cabinets and bottles of every kind of alcohol lining its glass shelves, arranged in mysterious ways that only Joe and his fraternity of tenders understand. Around the mirrored shelves, light reflects through bottles of bourbon and pomegranate juice, Aperol and Amaretto, flooding the bar with a happy orange glow. From above, where the cabinets meet the ceiling, carved demons stare down at him with amusement.

When a new customer walks up and pulls out the empty stool next to Walter, Joe leans his six-foot-six-inch frame over the wide-eyed man and holds up his hand.

"Couples therapy," he says, pointing to Walter. The man backs up. Joe points toward the kitchen. "One table left in the back, any beer you want. Tell Tanya it's on the house. We good?"

"We're good," the man says over his shoulder. Joe, as his daughter Tanya likes to say, is a pussycat. Joe moves away and Walter sips his Perrier, thinking about Ellie.

Six months ago, when he first saw her, her hair had been long, brown, and wavy. Now it's short and straight with brown and gold streaks in a medium bob. With bangs that make her look French. The hair on the sides of her face curves forward, hugging her cheeks. She likes to move the hair around with a little toss of her head or a brush of her fingers.

Three months ago, he'd been sitting at a table in back, staring at her while she sat at the bar. When some player made his third approach, she whirled on him and screamed, "Just *go away!*" The place went silent for a few seconds, then back to noisy. Joe walked over and put a hand on her shoulder, and from the way his hand shook, Walter could tell she was crying. She left, and he'd gone up to the bar to speak to Joe.

"Wow, I guess she's little tense," Walter said.

Joe nodded. "Spring-loaded." He dropped a twist of lemon into an old fashioned and set the drink on a tray. "Self-hater. Bit of a man-hater, too—can't trust them. Like you not trusting women." Tanya slid the tray off the bar as she glided past.

Walter nodded toward the back, where two guys were hustling two girls at the next table. "Does she ever—"

Joe shook his head. "Only talks to me. Walks in alone, walks out alone." He leaned close. "Tea. Earl Gray. Perrier water. Sometimes a glass of champagne." He stood back. "She's no drinker."

"Divorced?" Walter leaned against the bar, stared at the big man.

"Yep. A nasty one." Joe shook his head. "Damaged goods, the two of you." He stared at Walter. "Chat her up sometime. Might do you both some good."

About a month ago he'd sat next to her at the bar. Again the week after that. Tonight—if she comes—will make three.

He thinks about her face, her bright, intelligent eyes. And—his favorite—the smile lines that crinkle when she laughs. A face with the fierce determination of a bomber pilot or the vulnerability of an orphan. A face he finds beautiful. Last week, at a table near the peanuts, he'd told her so.

She had stared, unblinking. "What makes a woman's face beautiful, Walter Evans?"

He'd stared back, stayed silent for a while. "The absence of extremes."

"You've thought about this before."

"Yes," he said.

"And?"

"Face not too round, not too narrow. Eyes not too wide, not too close together. Nose not too long or wide or flat. Teeth not yellow, no gaps—"

"Okay," she said, and held up a hand. "Got it. Now I know why I find you handsome." She touched his forehead. "Not too bald." She used a finger to push up the tip of his nose. "Not too many nose hairs." She laughed and went back to sipping her Earl Gray. He couldn't tell if she was flattered or annoyed. He had changed the subject.

Now Walter looks up when the bell jingles. He recognizes the coat first, then her hair. He takes a breath and wipes his palms on his jeans. She stops by the empty stool and nods, then raises a shoulder, struggling with her coat. Walter helps her out of it and Tanya hurries over to carry it to the racks. He's never seen Ellie without her coat. On her way back, Tanya pauses, leans close to Walter's ear, and whispers, "Wow!"

Joe brings her tea and she lifts and lowers the tea bag in and out of its little silver pot. She reaches for the cream. Next will come the sweetener. A chance to study her coatless body. She's wearing silver heels, a short, tight skirt the color of—he glances at the bar—pomegranate juice. Her bare legs are perfect. He can tell she's fit by the way her nicely curved hips press down into the leather seat without spreading. A shimmering silver blouse hangs loosely but clings just enough to show off her full breasts. A choker of white beads circles her neck, sparkly silver earrings peek through her hair.

She catches him looking. "Hello again, Mr. Evans."

He nods, red-faced. "Miss Reedy."

It's their little ritual greeting. They clink, teacup to glass, then sit quietly side by side, staring at each other in the mirror. Joe lumbers by, managing to top up Walter's Perrier as he goes.

"Isn't he wonderful?" Ellie says, nodding toward Joe's back. "And so *huge*."

Walter nods. "If Hollywood needs an Irish sumo wrestler, they'll go straight to Joe."

"Did you ever see a Harry Potter movie?"

"Yes," he says. "Why do . . . of course! *Hagrid!*" He glances at Joe's ponytail. "With more hair control."

Ellie tosses her hair and laughs. "Exactly!" Suddenly serious, she asks, "Do you know Joe's story?"

"That he used to be a marriage and family counselor?"

"Yes. But do you know why he opened this bar?"

Walter nods, sips his Perrier. "Not opened, really. It was his father-in-law's bar. He married Helen, took over the bar when her dad died. Had more fun counseling from behind the counter and gave up his license."

Ellie puts her face next to his ear. He smells her perfume and his face grows warm. She whispers. "Do you know how he met Helen?"

"No."

"He helped her after a bad divorce."

Walter stares toward the kitchen where the invisible Helen is making sandwiches. She is a tall, handsome woman who was probably as gorgeous as Tanya back then. "Well, I'd say things worked out pretty well." He nods at Joe. "Maybe he can help *us*."

Ellie pours tea into her cup. "Not me," she says. "Nobody can."

In the mirror, he watches her sad eyes close. He sighs. If he had to pick a mission in life, it would be to make this lovely girl smile.

As he stares at her in the mirror, her eyes stay closed. What has he learned about Eleanor Reedy? Divorced for three years. She just celebrated her thirty-fourth birthday, home alone with her cat, and that's *just fine*. She loves to read and goes to book clubs at the library and does some creative writing *as therapy*. And no, he could *never, ever* read it. She likes his straight black hair and doesn't mind that it's gray on the sides and thin in front, calls his tired face *rugged* and thinks his big nose is alternately *Roman* or *funny*. She likes his wide shoulders and narrow waist and asked once *do you work out* but turned red because it was such a *cliché* and made her sound like a *bar whore*, so he made her laugh by pulling up his sweatshirt to show his love handles. He knew she'd earned a business degree from San Francisco State and now she's a buyer for Macy's. She used to take trips and go to fashion shows and touch *real clothes* but got promoted to an office and now she looks at sketches and pictures all day and sorts them into piles and *totally hates it*. And he knows she was married for five years to *that bastard Henry*. He has to be careful. She is, as Joe said, spring-loaded.

He glances at the mirror just as she opens one eye and stares at him. Her lips slowly form a smile and it's like a long, sexy wink. And then she's gone again, eyes closed.

And what does Ellie Reedy know about Walter Evans? He takes another sip of his Perrier. That he's forty-five and divorced for almost nine years from *that bitch Lisa* and has no interest in a relationship with a woman *ever again*—but a friend might be okay. She'd leaned closer after he said that. She knows he grew up in Los Altos and got a law degree and an MBA from Santa Clara University, knows he got a dream job and got married and lived in a big house in Silicon Valley. He throws back his Perrier and waves to Joe for a refill. He glances at eyes-closed Ellie and wonders if he'll ever tell her what really happened with his job and with Lisa and how he came crawling to San Francisco and bought his miserable one-room Monopoly house. He shakes his head, afraid he might finally cry after all these years and have to run out of the bar. Her eyes are open now, staring back at his, and she looks scared; she reaches over and barely touches his hand. Suddenly he knows why they're both so wary, so afraid; one more rejection could crush them forever. Their hearts, for sure. Maybe even their souls.

Walter waits for Ellie to finish her tea. Finally, he asks, "Did you ever talk to Joe about divorce? Feeling like no one can help you."

She stares at her empty cup. "Some. He gave me his rules for getting along." She looks up. "Do you know them?"

"Tell me."

"Okay, his Rule of Three. Say we're a couple—" Color rushes to her face. "—and we need to decide what to do tonight. You start with three things you'd like: Giants game, dinner out, movie. I choose dinner, give you three choices I'd like: Scomas, Il Fornaio, Ruth's Chris, and you choose. You can take it as far as you want, but we always wind up with something we both like."

"Genius. Are there others?"

"Rule of Ten. It's about money. If it doesn't cost more than ten dollars and it won't matter in ten years, screw it, just do it. The dollar figure goes up with income."

"I love it. More rules?"

"Well, it's not really a rule." She holds up a fist. "Rock, paper, scissors."

"Have you used any?"

She stares back at her cup. "They're meant for couples."

He clears his throat. "Did you ever talk more about . . . divorce?"

"He got busy. Said I should talk to you."

"Really?" He turns to look at her face. "Well, here we are."

She shifts around and puts her face close to his. "So is this some rescue fantasy of yours? We talk our way into my pants?"

He shakes his head. "No, I don't think it's a . . . rescue fantasy. But if I'm wrong, it's as much about rescuing me as you. Okay?"

She stares at him without blinking and says nothing.

"And about your pants." He sees she's fighting a smile. "That would spoil everything."

"Because?"

"I'm not ready," he says. "And I don't think you are."

"Right," she says, not smiling. "You'd be wasting your time. This candy store's closed." She slides off the stool and stands.

He stands next to her, whispers, "Don't go. Please."

"You're a nice man, Walter. But still a man, so I'm not comfortable. And I'm an awful person." She walks to the racks, grabs her coat, heads for the door. Then she stops, comes back. "Here, Friday night? Same time?" Her small voice. Her vulnerable look.

He nods and she's gone. He shakes his head. Women.

Day 49
Friday, March 13
5 deaths reported
320 cases reported

    Schools across the state close in response to coronavirus.

    President Trump declares a national emergency.

"Social distancing" becomes a household phrase.

FOUR THIRTY P.M. WALTER sweats a little as he hurries along Chestnut Street. A scattering of the colorful shops are dark now, some of the always-packed bistros are closed. No one is double-parked, and he sees metered spaces without cars, unheard of a month ago. The crowds, always thick on Friday nights, are thin. A few people are wearing masks. An evening fog is trying to form. He stops in front of the door, peers through the glass. In back, half the tables are empty. She's at the bar, leaning forward, an elbow resting on the counter. He sees black heels, a short black dress riding high on her thighs, a near-naked back. A necklace flashes in the bar light when she flips her hair. All that's missing is a diamond-tipped cigarette holder. She's alone in a clear space of empty stools, an unapproachable sophisticate, too good for the likes of Joe's Bar. An Audrey Hepburn, waiting for her lover. He takes a breath and pushes through the door.

She turns when she hears the door jingle, pats the stool next to her. "Hello again, Mr. Evans."

"Miss Reedy."

He sees her long raincoat hanging on the back of her stool. Ready for flight. He pulls out his stool. "Waiting long?"

"A few minutes."

"Where's Joe?"

She nods toward the kitchen. "Getting my Earl Gray."

An awkward silence. They stare at each other in the mirror.

"Friday the thirteenth," she says. Are you superstitious?

"Not at all." The silence is painful.

She clears her throat. "Don't you just love these old leather barstools?"

He nods.

She leans back. "Little easy chairs on stilts."

He nods again.

Joe arrives with her tea. "Hey, Walter. Great to see you again." He nods at Ellie. "Both of you." He leans close to them and winks. "Together again." The counter trembles as he clumps away.

"You don't drink?" she asks, pointing to his Perrier.

"I do, sometimes." He points to her tea. "What's your story?"

"Sometimes. It's just a control thing."

"Me, too."

Ellie leans forward to doctor her tea. Walter gasps—her black dress is all cleavage and not much else. She catches him staring. She turns to him, still not smiling. Suddenly she stands.

Walter takes her arm, his face hot. "Ellie, I'm sorry. Don't go."

She pushes his hand away, lifts her coat off the stool, and slips it on, standing close to him as she buttons it, bottom to top, very slowly. Her breasts disappear, like a reverse strip tease. She sits back on the stool.

"So, Walter." She stares at him, her face expressionless. "How long since you've had sex?"

"Long enough I'm not sure I'll remember what to do when—"

"They say it's like riding a bike. Complicated, but it all comes back to you."

"A bike. You think?"

She nods. "So I've been told. How long?"

He still feels the warmth in his face. He clears his throat. "Well . . ." He closes his eyes. ". . . about nine years."

"Nine *years*?"

"I've been angry," he says, and tries a smile. "Nine years, plus or minus."

"Plus or minus what?"

"A couple of times, near the end. When she wanted me to think things were okay."

"So she could do what?"

"Ah, you've been there," he says.

"Yes."

"My last sex was the night before the bitch cleaned out our joint account."

She touches his arm. "Joint accounts should be banned." She sighs. "And marriage, possibly men, too." Her hand squeezes his arm. "But not you. I like being here, sitting next to you."

"What about you?" he asks.

"What about me what?"

"Last time you had sex."

She sips her Earl Gray, then lowers the cup. "Three years ago next month. The night before he left."

"Because he wanted what?"

"Just me. To use me. He hadn't loved me in a long time. I was just too stupid to notice." She shakes her head. "That's what you men do, right? Just—" She squeezes his arm again. "Sorry, not you. *Most* men use love to get sex until they get bored . . . and then they find another girl or just move out."

"Ellie, you don't have to—"

"And in my case, Henry did both." She's speaking too loudly now. "Left for LA with that *bitch* from his office and—"

Joe appears in front of them, a glass of champagne in each hand. He holds one out to Ellie. "On the house," he says. "Got to use up the open stock—governor's going to shut us down any day now."

Ellie takes the glass, her hand shaking. Walter knows Joe has been keeping an eye on her from down the bar. Joe hands him the second glass and fills one for himself. "A toast," Joe says, raising his glass. "To recovery. From pandemics. And divorces." He gestures toward Ellie. "It always happens."

"Promise?" Ellie's hand has stopped shaking.

"Promise," Joe says.

They raise their glasses. "To recovery," they say, and clink.

Joe pours refills, raises his glass again. "And to love," he says.

They don't move.

A customer waves and points to an empty mug. Joe steps away to draw the beer.

"Tell me," Walter says. "Why do you think you're an awful person?"

Ellie's cupping her champagne glass with both hands, staring into it like a crystal ball. She looks up. "Why do I think I'm *what?*"

"Last time, before you left, you told me you were an awful person." He stares at her, demanding eye contact. "Tell me why."

She rocks her glass back and forth. "Because men frighten me, make me angry. Because I wreck relationships." Her face has taken on its vulnerable look. "Because I ruin love, make it a nagging contest." She turns away from him. "First, the little things, you know— he stops opening doors, I stop saying thank you. Then it's pick, pick, finally drip, drip, like little drops of acid . . ."

He touches her shoulder. "Like fighting over dumb things?" She turns to stare at him. He makes an angry face. "Well? Are you going to leave the freezer door open *forever?*"

She wags a finger. "Drink from the box one more time and I'll poison the milk!"

He points at her. "No, it is NOT cold in here. Take your socks off and get your thyroid checked!"

She's bright-eyed now, points a finger at him. "You love tools . . . squeegee the fucking shower once in a while, okay?" She waves her fist. "And *we* bought the TV, so how come it's *your* remote?"

Down the bar, a couple is laughing, waving their glasses at Ellie. In front of them, the counter trembles. Joe is standing there, applauding. "Forgive me for listening," he says. "It's what I do."

They nod. "So look," Joe says. "Everybody fights over dumb things, okay?" He reaches for an orange, picks up a knife and starts slicing. "But when a marriage is sick, those moments are poison." He flicks out orange seeds with the point of his knife. "People stay together too long after the marriage dies." He wags a finger at Ellie. "And the people they turn into aren't themselves."

"Thank you, counselor," Walter says.

"On the house."

Ellie shakes her head. "I'm not so sure. Maybe that's who they *really* are. You know, like the happily married days were just play-acting." She looks up at Joe. "Is there a way to find out?"

"I've got an idea," Joe says. "Lemme think about it, get back to you." He turns and walks toward the kitchen.

"What was your reason?" Walter asks. "Divorce, I mean." They're talking to each other in the mirror, over the corks and bottle caps. "Want to talk about it?"

"I've talked more tonight than I should have." She stands.

He stands next to her, grips an arm gently. "Ellie, please don't go."

"Here," she says. "On Monday. Okay?"

"Three days."

"We'll survive. We've come this far." She pats his shoulder, and he watches her walk to the door and push out into the fog.

Day 52
Monday, March 16. Three days later.
11 deaths reported
588 cases reported

> Governor Newsom requests that restaurants use to-go orders only and gyms, health clubs, and movie theaters close. Seven Bay Area counties including San Francisco declare shelter-in-place orders through April 7. The move orders 7.6 million

residents to not leave their home unless it's for "essential business" like buying medicine or groceries.

SIX P.M. ELLIE AND WALTER sit side by side, wearing jeans and sweatshirts; she's still in her long coat. Joe stands in front of his two friends.

"This shutdown!" Ellie speaks, full of concern. "Joe, what are you going to *do*?"

He flips a towel over his shoulder, rests his hands on his hips. "I'm luckier than most, I guess. I own the building, my tenants have solid pensions. Still, there's insurance, utilities . . ." Tanya glides past with two beers on a tray. "But the help's cheap, so—"

"Heard that, Dad," Tanya shouts back. "Theater's closed. I'm thinking med school." She delivers the beers and disappears into the kitchen.

"When does it start?" Walter asks.

"Midnight tonight. Tomorrow, we'll be takeout only. For sandwiches." He shakes his head. "Nothing's clear. Not sure I could even pull you a beer while you're waiting."

"Joe, could we wait at the bar? I mean . . . next time?" Ellie glances at Walter. "Together?"

"Of course," Joe says. He nods at Ellie. "God forbid you'd have to meet at *your* place. Who knows what hanky-panky *that* might lead to." The bell jingles and he steps out from behind the bar to greet a party of four.

Walter can see the glass front door reflected in the mirror. It's black outside. They've been quiet for a while.

"Leaving your coat on?" Walter asks her.

"It's chilly in here."

"It's not. Get your thyroid checked."

She pulls back, stares at him wide-eyed. Then laughs. "For a minute, I thought you—"

"Bad joke," he says. "You want to talk? I mean, last time, you said you talked too much."

"I know." She pulls at her bangs. "But we have some stuff we should probably get past, put to rest, you know, like—"

"Like what killed your marriage?"

"Kids," she says, meeting his gaze.

"Okay. And?"

"We both wanted them, couldn't have them. We had a big workup, I was fine. Turned out he had no sperm. Azoospermia, it's called. Nice name, huh?"

"Could be worse. What then?"

"It's like I'd castrated him. Cheated on him. Somehow—"

"So did you? Cheat on him?" He hates himself for asking.

Her eyes flash. "No. Never!" She takes a breath. "Somehow he turned it all around and blamed me. I wasn't sexy enough, you know. Stuff like that. He was angry all the time."

"But what about adoption? A sperm donor, maybe?"

"I tried to talk about it but it made him crazy. Another insult to his manhood." She sighs. "Somewhere in all that, the marriage died and I turned into an awful person and started hating men."

"So you said." He clears his throat. "You wanted kids. What about now?"

"Absolutely. Two." She sighs. "A boy in a little sailor suit, a girl in a ballerina skirt. But—"

He leans toward her. "But what?"

"But that would involve a man." She turns away. "And I'm thirty-four. That ship's about to sail."

"Adoption? A surrogate?"

"And raise a child alone?" She shakes her head. "It must be hard enough for two. Doesn't seem fair to the child." She swivels her stool to face him. "What about you, Walter Evans?"

"Kids? Sure, I wanted them. A boy I could teach to pitch. A girl I could help grow up, walk her down an aisle someday." He reaches across the bar, steals a swizzle stick, starts playing with the lime slice in his Perrier.

"And now?" she asks.

"Kids mean relationships," he says, and stabs his lime.

"And Lisa? Did she want kids?"

"Yeah. Pre-meds and soccer stars, straight-A students she could brag about at club luncheons while the au pair did the work."

"Trophy husband, trophy kids."

He looks at her and nods. "Exactly."

Joe arrives. "Any of that champagne left?" Ellie asks. Joe turns away for a few seconds, turns back with two brimming flutes. She faces Walter and they raise their glasses. "To recovery," she says.

Joe splashes some into another glass and holds it up. "To a quick recovery—from divorces *and* shelter-in-place." They all clink.

Ellie's watch chimes. "Oh no!"

"What?" Walter asks.

"I forgot. Work. A Zoom conference—Macy's in Honolulu." She stands. "In thirty minutes!"

He stands next to her. "I'll walk you—"

"No!" She puts a hand on his shoulder, pushes him down. "Sit, stay." She laughs. "Tomorrow, same time?"

He sits. "Tomorrow." He can see her running before the door swings shut.

Joe eyes him. "Special, isn't she."

Walter nods. "Special."

Day 53

Tuesday, March 17. The next day.

14 deaths reported

732 cases reported

> **Even more counties declare local emergencies, and many adopt bans on gatherings larger than ten to fifty people.**

FIVE THIRTY P.M. WALTER'S walk down Chestnut Street is surreal. *Apocalyptic* is the media's buzzword. All the restaurants are empty. Most of the stores are dark, with loopy closed signs taped to their doors. He spots a few customers in a dimly lit Walgreens, a half-dozen in the Marina Supermarket. The sidewalks are empty. A single car rolls slowly past.

She's at the bar when he walks in. She turns and pats the stool. He sits.

"Got some left," Joe says, and hands Walter a glass of champagne before he moves down the bar.

Ellie skips their ritual greeting. "Your turn," she says. "*How Money Killed my Marriage*, by Walter Evans. A short story or a novella?"

"A tragedy either way," he says, and takes a sip of champagne.

"May I listen?" Joe asks. "Professionally speaking. My old profession, that is."

"Sure." Walter faces Ellie, takes a breath. "I had my law degree and my MBA and some connections in Silicon Valley. One day they hooked me up with this red-hot international company and pretty soon I was heading up the California operation and the bucks were rolling in. So I—"

"You must have been so *young*," Ellie says.

"Late twenties. Hey, that's Silicon Valley. I went to all the Valley parties—where I met Lisa. She screwed me silly, then cut me off until I married her. We—"

"A founder-hounder," Ellie says.

"A what?" Walter asks.

"Founder-hounder. What you call a predatory hot babe in the Valley." She pokes his shoulder. "You know, a trophy-wife wannabe."

He laughs. "Yeah, that's Lisa. A bitch by any name. So we got the big house and the fancy car and joined the country club and talked about kids and nannies and boarding schools and then . . ." He finishes his champagne.

"Jesus, come on." Joe waves his hands.

Ellie's eyes lock on Walter's. "Then *what?*"

Walter throws up his hands. "Poof," he says.

"Nah, come on," Joe says. "Not *poof.* What *happened?*"

Walter sighs, shakes his head. "Netflix." Walter pushes his glass across the counter. "Netflix happened."

Joe tops off Walter's glass, holds the champagne bottle up to the light, pours what's left into Ellie's. "Hey, wait a minute," he says. "Lemme guess. Your hot company was that . . . what was that video rental outfit called—"

Walter nods. "You got it. Blockbuster. Blockbuster Video, the darling of Wall Street. Until it wasn't." He sits back in his stool, closes his eyes. "Netflix changed the game."

Ellie turns, touches his arm. "Oh no, Walter. What did you *do?*"

"Legal stuff. I stayed on with Blockbuster, untangling our franchises, cutting them loose." He sits forward, elbows on the counter, head low. "Lisa saw the light and cut *me* loose—"

"*Because?*" Ellie was staring at him.

"Money. The stock tanked, I waited too long to cash in my options, our mortgage was a killer, so—"

"She just *left?*"

"Not exactly *just* left." He sits up straight, counts with his fingers. "Left with our car, cleaned out our joint account." He clears his throat. "Left with good ol' Bill, our senior vice president. A bozo smart enough to cash out early, sneaky enough to hide his insider trading, dumb enough to steal Lisa."

"Lisa," Ellie says. "Did you love her?"

"No, I don't think so. Looking back."

"You're not sure?" Ellie touches his shoulder.

He shakes his head. "Sex blinds." He sighs. "I haven't been sure about love in a long time."

Ellie squeezes his shoulder. "Hey. What happened to her?"

"Lisa? Divorced again. She cleaned him out in six months. Last I heard she's in the Bahamas, probably screwing in place with her next victim. Good ol' Bill's back in the Valley, begging for scraps."

"Hell of a bar story." Joe leans over Walter, slaps him on the back. "I'll change the names. No friend will be harmed." A customer waves and he walks away.

Ellie pokes his shoulder. "Walter, how come you wound up in San Francisco?"

"Yeah, sorry. Blockbuster hit bottom in 2010, and Dish Network bought us out. Dish kept me and brought me to San Francisco to tie up some loose ends with Blockbuster." He sighs. "I hate it."

"Could you quit?"

"I still have lawyer friends in Silicon Valley who'll throw me a bone if I need one." He clears his throat. "Lots of bones, actually. I'd be okay."

She gives his stool a shake. "But what do you really *want* to do?" Another shake. "I mean, lawyering, sure, but there's something else, I just *know* it."

"You do?"

"Just look at you." She puts her hand under his chin and lifts. "Sit up straight, Walter."

He does. "Is this you being a nag?"

"No, it is NOT. This is me demanding you be *honest*. With yourself and with me. Okay?"

"Okay, but—"

"No buts, Walter Evans." Her face is inches from his, her eyes blazing. "*Tell me.*" She has the bomber pilot look.

"It's our secret, yes? I've never told anyone—"

"Tell *me.*"

He takes a deep breath. "Okay, lawyering, half-time. Back in Silicon Valley. But for the other half, what I really want to do is *write*." He leans closer to her. "Legal thrillers," he says. "I have my main character, plots, a setting—"

She claps her hands. "In San Francisco?"

"Bay Area. Silicon Valley stuff. You know, corporate pirates, stabs in the back, trade secrets, murder for hire, drug parties—"

"And founder-hounders, yes? I love it already." She sits back. "Wait. Have you written anything? Published?"

"I've outlined two thrillers, half of a third." He shakes his head. "But I need to be a better writer before I start, so I—"

"So just write a bad thriller. You'll be a better writer when you're done."

"Maybe." Sharing makes him want to reach out and hug her; he hasn't felt this good in years. "But I want to be *great*."

She has a look he's never seen. "I haven't been exactly honest. About writing, I mean." She stares at the counter. "I have a book contract on my desk at home."

"Really? That's great!"

"It's not threatening? That I'm . . . ahead of you?"

"No, never, I swear. Fiction or nonfiction?"

Her face relaxes. "Kind of a mix," she says. "A thinly disguised exposé. The fashion industry. What goes on behind closed doors, what models do when they're not modeling. Other stuff you'd never guess."

"Hot!"

"Definitely." She sighs. "But that's the problem."

"A contract offer? How could that be—"

"I haven't signed it."

"Jesus, Ellie, why—"

"I hate my job sometimes, but really, it's great. A job I *need*. If I publish—whether it sells or not—I'll be out the door in a flash." She shakes her head. "No one in the industry would touch me again."

"So use a phony name."

"I've interviewed too many people. They'll ID me as soon as they read the book."

"Such a first-world problem," he says. "But fun to think about."

"Yes." Her eyes are bright again. "Do you think we could ever—"

Joe trudges over and stops in front of them; he waves an upside-down bottle. "Open stock's finished. If you'd like some more champagne, I'll pop a cork."

"I'm good," Ellie says.

"Me too. But thanks, amigo."

"Any time." Joe puts down the bottle, leans close. "Hey, remember earlier, when I said I had an idea about you two?"

Ellie and Walter bob their heads yes.

"I'm going to share it with you now. One at a time." He wipes his forehead with his apron. "Trust me?"

Again, heads bob.

"Great." He speaks to Ellie. "Okay, young lady, say good night to Mr. Evans here and follow me."

She looks at Walter with wide eyes. "But I—"

"It'll be okay," Joe says. He motions with his hand. "Come."

"Go," Walter says. "Might be fun."

She follows and sits at the end of the bar. Joe leans over her and they talk. At one point they play rock-paper-scissors. Joe laughs when she pulls him toward her and plants a kiss on his forehead. When she comes back to her stool, she grabs her coat, says, "Good night, Mr. Evans," and keeps walking. He jumps up when she reaches the door.

"Let her go," Joe says, putting a hand on his shoulder. "I'll explain."

They talk for the next fifteen minutes, sometimes arguing, finally agreeing. Joe ends by saying, "Hey. We're all going to be sheltering-in-place, right?"

"Looks that way," Walter says.

"So why not?"

"Yeah, why not." Walter looks up at Joe. "But writing a story—"

"Don't be nervous," Joe says. "It's just a *virtual* shelter-in-place."

Walter stands up. "But together, right?"

"Yeah, virtually. You'll both be writing your own stories. Hey, like I told Ellie, just be yourselves, be honest. Make it natural." He turns to the calendar stuck on a cabinet door. "Stories done in five days."

"Five days? Jesus, Joe—"

"Hey, you wanna be a writer, learn to live with deadlines." He takes a pencil from his apron pocket and circles a date. "Saturday, March twenty-first." He pockets the pencil. "I told Ellie we'd all meet here, eleven a.m. Can you make it?"

Walter pulls out his iPhone, makes the entry. "I'll be here."

Joe wags a big finger. "And above all, remember: No hanky-panky."

"Got it," he says, and heads for the door, not at all sure he can do this.

Day 55
Thursday, March 19. Three days later.
19 deaths reported
1,067 cases reported
Gov. Gavin Newsom declares a statewide shelter-in-place.

TEN A.M. WALTER SITS outside in the morning sun, at the top of his stairs, his coffee cup on a step. He rests his laptop on his thighs, opens it, shifts his position so the screen is shaded by his neighbor's Italian cypress. *Just write the story,* Joe had said. Finally, he starts writing.

Chapter 1

He knows she won't come, but he wants her here, leaning against him, like an addict wants his fix. Wants her close, so he can laugh, something he hasn't done in years. He's desperate to know her favorite books, her secrets, the things that make her laugh, places she dreams of going. He longs to find out what she wants most from her life.

Mrs. Sharma is in her tiny yard, deadheading her geraniums. He waves until she waves back, then heads down the stairs and across the street.

"Good morning, Mrs. Sharma." He bows and puts a palm on his chest. "You're as slim and radiant as a Bollywood star." They keep their social distance.

She shows her perfect teeth. "Not bad for eighty-three, isn't it?" She waves her clippers. "And you're as full of beans as our President." She walks unsteadily toward her roses, turns back. "Yellow or red?"

"A couple of each?"

She bends over and her snipping sounds fill the air, exciting the birds on her feeder. When she turns, he sees an armful of long-stem roses. She moves slowly across the yard and leans them against her front gate, then moves away.

"So many, Mrs. Sharma. You shouldn't—"

"Any lady worth you, Walter, is worth a dozen." As usual, there's mischief in her wrinkled face.

"Who said anything about a lady?"

She waves her clippers again. "You've been perched on your top step for days, watching for her, yes?"

He shakes his head. "Mrs. Sharma, you're such a mystic. Why do you think—"

She shows her teeth. "It's in your face, Walter Evans. Your eyes." She wags a finger. "Like a teenager's." She looks at him with obvious concern. "Is she coming or not?"

"We'll see."

She shakes her head. "You know, arranged marriages are much safer. I can—"

He waves the bundle of roses. "Thank you, my dear friend. Again."

"Watch those thorns," she says, waving goodbye. "They're ever so prickly, you know. Like love."

He strips off his Giants windbreaker, wraps it around the roses, and cradles the bundle in his arms, then walks across the street. He turns and waves a last time to Mrs. Sharma, carries the roses up the stairs to his kitchen sink. He rinses his old coffee pot, fills it with water, drops in the roses, and arranges them, yellow here, red there until he's happy. Finally, he places the bouquet in the center of his little kitchen table. Perfect. Now she has to come.

But will she? *No hanky-panky,* Joe had said, and that might do it. Clearly, they like each other's company, and they aren't quite ready for the rest. And they're veterans of the same war. He steps outside and looks down the street. Nothing. He glances at his watch. Almost noon. She's not coming.

His cell rings. It's Mrs. Sharma.

"Your lady," she asks. "Bangs, bob hairdo? Bolly-body?"

"Yes to all three." His heart is racing. He glances down the street, sees nothing. He looks across the street.

Mrs. Sharma is standing at her bay window, waving to him as she speaks. "She's coming!" She points. "From the other direction, foolish boy." She chuckles. "I've always told you, life is unpredictable."

"Yes, thank you, I—"

"She's pushing a bicycle."

"Thank you so much, Mrs. Sharma. I—"

"Her bike is loaded—a gentleman would run help her. She's moving in, yes?"

"Not exactly. It's complicated. She—"

"We were cheap with the roses, you know."

"I'm sorry, why were—"

"She's three-dozen sexy." He hears her musical laugh. "I'll close my drapes." They hang up and he rushes for the door.

He slides his hand down the railing as he takes the steps two at a time, hits the ground running. She's to the right, half a block away, pushing her bike slowly in his direction. As he runs, he wishes he'd put on something nicer than jeans and a T-shirt. Reaching her, he turns and walks slowly alongside, catching his breath.

"Hello again, Mr. Evans."

"Miss Reedy. May I push your bicycle?"

"Thanks, no. I might need it any second."

"To?"

"Bolt, ride away. Push away, actually." She's white-knuckling the handgrips like a paratrooper clenching the jump-hatch.

"Scared?"

She nods, stares straight ahead. "Immersion therapy. With a man. Who wouldn't be?"

"You trust Joe?"

"Yes," she says.

"We swore no hanky-panky."

"I wouldn't be here if we hadn't."

"Okay." They walk on a while in silence. She's wearing a baggy gray sweatshirt, thin black tights. She has the legs of a dancer. A model's walk. Her sparkly pink cloth shoes look like they were dipped in glue, then in crushed diamonds. "Where's Wiffles?"

"At my sister's, in Marin." Finally, a smile. "She'll spoil her to death."

"Her? I thought Wiffles—"

"She *is* a boy. I just . . . think of him as a girl."

"Because?"

She stares at him. "Because I couldn't stand having a man around the house."

"You could have brought him," he says. "Her."

"Wiffles? Seemed a little too much, too soon, don't you think?"

"More than sheltering-in-place together?"

She stops walking. "Tell me, Walter. Why are we doing this?"

"Simple. Two broken people, helping each other heal."

"Nice," she says.

"Joe says we've been sheltering-in-place since our divorces."

She nods, starts pushing her bike again. "If you're okay, I'm okay."

"Okay with what?" he asks.

"Trying this . . . one day at a time."

"I'm okay," he says. "Now can I push your bike?"

He checks out her bike as he pushes. A black computer case rests in the handlebar basket. She's bungeed a lumpy, blue duffel under the crossbar. And she's used a belt to cinch a makeup case to the carrier over the rear tire. Overall, she's traveling light. He takes a breath. She *is* ready to bolt. They push on slowly.

It's a perfect April day, clear and fresh. There's a warm breeze, full of ocean smells and the shrieks of gulls. They stop by Mrs. Sharma's gate and Ellie is fascinated by her flowers, by the bees, so busy pollinating.

He takes her arm, tugs. "Wait," she says. "I love watching the birds hop around her feeder."

They cross the street and she cables her bike to the post by his house. He starts to carry her stuff upstairs.

"I'm good," she says, and tries to grab it all. He takes her duffel anyway, and they climb the stairs up the right side of the house and stop by the door to his apartment. He unlocks it, holds it open.

"Why, thank you, sir," she says. When they step inside and put down her stuff, he watches as she starts a slow, clockwise survey of her new shelter, like she's planning an escape in the dark. She looks at the door to the left of them.

"Coat closet," he says. "A place to hang your stuff."

"C'mon, a guy's closet? It's full of junk." She opens the door, stares at the neat row of empty hangers, shakes her head. "You're too good to be true."

"I tossed the junk yesterday."

"Men," she says, smiling. "Always so much to confess." She looks out the bay window.

"East facing," he says. "Great sunrise views."

"Why doesn't the sofa face the window?"

"It did when I got here. My early, monkish days. I turned it around, away from the world."

"It's still turned around, Brother Walter." She walks past the window to the front corner of the room, studies his easy chair, the brass stand lamp, the small bookcase. She bends to read some titles.

"Grisham, Turow, Rankin, Connelly." She looks up at him. "Mystery writers—your inspiration?"

"Guilty."

She continues her clockwise survey. His queen-sized bed in the far back corner, the bathroom door on the back wall, and next to that, facing the sofa, his big-screen TV. Along the rest of the back wall and half the entry wall, an L-shaped kitchen. Just to the right of the entry where they stand, a small table for two with a coffee pot in the center. She gasps.

"Roses! Such beautiful roses!" She bends over to smell a red one. "And the coffee-pot pitcher. It's so . . ."

"Eclectic."

"Yes. Nice. Are the roses Mrs. Sharma's?"

"They are."

"They're so *perfect*. Walter, I have to tell her."

"We will. Soon."

"What's with the shower curtains?" she asks, pointing to the walls on either side of the bay window.

"Privacy."

"To do what? Privacy how?"

"Shelter-in-place privacy. I'll show you." He walks first to one wall, then the other, draws the curtains almost together in the middle of the room. "Two halves." He points. "You get the bed, bathroom, TV, the kitchen. I get the sofa, coffee table, my easy chair and books."

She studies the white cloth shower curtains on hooks. "You knew I'd come."

"I hoped you would."

She picks up her duffel and tosses it on the sofa, puts her computer case on the coffee table. "Keep your bed. You're six-two, I'm five-ten. Plus I sleep on my sofa all the time. With Wiffles. Watching TV."

"Wiffles isn't here."

"I'll hug a pillow." She steps into her half of the room and pulls the curtains closed, claiming the space. He hears her clap her hands. "It's like a big tent! We could have just gone camping."

"Parks are closed. By the way, you seem a little livelier here than at Joe's."

Her head pops out between the curtains. "Joe said be honest, right?" She stares at him with her full smile. "I haven't felt this comfortable . . . alone with a man . . . for a long time."

"There's something about you that makes me comfortable, too. It's like we're . . . war buddies."

"Exactly," she says. "Now show me how to make tea in your kitchen."

He shows her where everything is, makes them each a cup of Earl Gray. They finish their tea sitting outside on his top step, then he shows her around his apartment.

He's proud of the bathroom. "Plenty of room for your stuff on those shelves."

She nods. "I don't have much." She steps over to the shower, studies the rack. "Are you the bar soap or the liquid soap person?"

"Bar. I can open another one if you—"

"No, I like the liquid." She looks at him. "It's sweet you have both."

"Something you should know," he says. "The exhaust fan's not much—it can get really steamy in here after a shower."

"And?"

"Sometimes you have to come out, leave the door open, read a book or something until it clears."

"Got it."

"Wait," he says. "I just realized. If you take the sofa, you'll have to come out from behind the curtains to use the bathroom."

"Do you have a robe I could use?"

He shakes his head.

"A big towel?"

"A beach towel, yes." He clears his throat. "Look, I remember my wife coming in and out of our bathroom a *lot*; why don't I just take a walk, go for a run when you—"

"Let's try the towel, see how it goes." He can tell she's trying hard not to laugh.

He points. "There's a lock on the door."

She punches his shoulder. "We're grown-ups, Walter, we'll be fine."

She's having fun, and it makes him happy. She stares down at the coffee table, noticing the remotes for the first time. He's surprised to see her wipe her face with the back of her hand.

"Jesus, Walter, two remotes." She clears her throat. "When did you get the second one?"

"Yesterday."

"What man ever does that? For a woman." She closes her eyes. "You're working so hard at this . . . relationship." She shakes her head. "I will, too, I promise." She sits down on the far end of the sofa, quickly looks up. "I'm sorry," she says. "Does it matter which end of the sofa I—"

"Definitely." He tries a stern voice, points. "That's your end, this is mine."

"Really? Because?"

"Your remote doesn't have batteries."

For the first time, he hears her full and happy laugh and he loves it.

"Where's your pantry?" she asks.

"It's half my closet."

She opens the door, takes a box from a shelf. "So many pastas. Do you cook?"

"Sure. Italian—as you can see. Spaghetti with meat sauce, linguini with clams. Lasagna—"

"What else?" she asks.

"Well, I grill steaks sometimes. Burgers—"

She looks at him. Anxiously. "Rare, medium? Don't say *well*—"

"Medium rare."

She sighs. "Thank god. Breakfast?"

"Eggs, usually. Omelets, sometimes. Toast. Waffles or pancakes on Sundays."

"You haven't mentioned a vegetable."

"What are those?"

She shakes her head. "And you probably bake, too."

"Well, I can whip up a mean *pâte à choux*."

"A what?" Her worried face.

"*Pâte à choux*. A French puff pastry. I use it for profiteroles."

She looks ready to cry. "You make *profiteroles*?"

"It's all about how you get the ice cream inside." He can't hold back and bursts out laughing.

She thumps him on the chest; he loves the contact. "Exactly how much of that was true?"

"Everything but the profiteroles," he says. "My idea of baking is warming a cheese Danish in the microwave."

She's suddenly serious. "Lie to me for fun—that's okay. Just never lie to me for real, Walter. Ever. Promise?"

"I promise."

Day 55

Thursday, March 19. That same day.

Governor Newsom announces his shelter-in-place order is legally enforceable. Violation can result in a misdemeanor with up to one thousand dollars in fines or six months imprisonment.

THEY'VE BEEN WATCHING Newsom on TV.

Ellie gasps. "A thousand dollars! You won't catch me out on the street."

"Another reason to stay here," he says.

And so she settles in, bathroom first, flitting from duffel to shelves. She's done in under five minutes. "There," she says. "Your bathroom has been *feminized*." She stands next to him. "Now, when the investigator in your thriller bursts in to search for evidence, he'll take one look in your bathroom and say, 'Hmmm, he has a *woman*.'"

"He wouldn't have to see the bathroom."

"Oh?"

He points. "My investigator would spot your makeup case by the sofa."

"Of course! You'll be a *great* thriller writer." She gestures toward the kitchen. "Meanwhile, what about dinner?"

They decide to try Joe's rules for dinner. She sits on the sofa, pats the cushion next to her. He sits.

"You start," he says.

"Okay, the Rule of Three." She holds up a hand, counts with her fingers. "One, Chinese curbside. Two, DoorDash brings us fish tacos and Dos Equis from Pedro's. Three, we cook at home."

"Three," he says. "My turn, yes?"

She nods.

He skips the fingers. "Chef's choice, pasta, or steak?"

"Chef's choice. So who cooks?"

"Rock, paper, scissors," he says. "Loser cooks." He waves at her. "Ready?"

She nods. "One, two, *three.*"

"Rock breaks scissors," he says. "You cook."

"Jesus, Walter. This really *works!*"

"Joe's our man."

She goes back to the pantry, speaks into her phone as she rummages, then checks the refrigerator.

"I'm going shopping," she says, and holds up a hand when he tries to join her. "I want to surprise you."

By the time she gets back, it's late afternoon. He reads on the sofa; she works in the kitchen, chopping furiously. They've thrown open the door and windows; the sea air blends nicely with the aroma of beef bourguignon. Minutes later, the room fills with the smell of sizzling bacon. He watches as she pours French Merlot over the meat and covers the pot. She finds two glasses, fills them with wine, and joins him on the sofa. They raise their glasses.

"To recovery," she says, and they clink.

"To us," he says. They each take a cautious sip.

She says no when he asks if she wants to watch the news. They talk of their families, about her parents, retired on the coast of Oregon, a sister in Marin, a brother in France. "The beef bourguignon," she says, waving at the stove. "It's his recipe." Walter admits he's an only child, with a sister who died young, his parents gone. She gets up, puts another pot on the stove, and comes back. They talk for a while about music, sports, searching for common interests, laughing when they find a few. Suddenly there's the sound of water dripping on an open flame. "The noodles!" She jumps up and turns down the gas. An alarm sounds on her iPhone. "Dinner's ready!"

They move the roses and he helps her set the table. She pours the

French Merlot. They chat over dinner, comparing favorite restaurants, sharing stories of trips they've taken. Later, still at the table, they lean back, gently waving their glasses.

"No dessert," she says. "I thought we'd be too full."

"That was wonderful," he says. "And that's the absolute truth."

"It's the buttery garlic mushrooms. You have to cook them separately, add them just before serving."

They clear the table together. She pulls open the dishwasher, sits on the floor next to it. "Show me how you load this."

"What? I mean, it's just a dishwasher. You—"

"Near the end," she says, "our worst fights were over how I loaded the dishwasher."

He starts to protest, and she raises a hand. "Okay," he says, bending over. "The little bowls go in a line across the front. The saucers and salad plates in a row behind them." He loads as he talks, trying not to laugh. "And across the back, the plates." He stands. "I wash the big stuff in the sink. As for the top—"

She crosses her ankles and rises up like a geisha. "The top's easy. And I love these little clip-thingees for the wine glasses." He wants to hold her, reassure her somehow, but he doesn't. "You are trying hard, aren't you?"

"Like you," she says, and moves to the sofa. "Let's finish the wine."

They sit on opposite ends, talking comfortably about books and movies. Later, their glasses empty, she stands up. "I need a shower."

He finds the beach towel, hands it to her, then tosses folded sheets, a pillow, and a blanket on the sofa. "I'm going for a quick run, back in half an hour."

"Walter, you don't have to—I mean, it's dark *and* foggy."

"Best time," he says, and leaves. He jogs lazily, crossing the empty streets without waiting, and still finishes in record time. He pauses halfway up the stairs to his door. Someone waiting on the other side makes him smile.

He knocks, hears her laugh. "Come in, my prince."

She's sitting on the sofa, perfectly wrapped in his beach towel, combing her hair. The curtains are still against the wall. "Any chance you've got a sleeping bag? It's what I use at home—when I sleep on my sofa." She points to the folded sheets. They get all tangled, you know?"

"Sure." He stares at her, then the sheets. He pulls the bag from under his bed. She stands up, one hand clenching the towel as he unrolls it, unzips it, lays it out on the sofa so the head faces his side of the room. He tosses a pillow on the bag, picks up the sheets and blanket. "There you go." He pulls the curtains closed between them. "Good night."

He sees the bulge where the towel falls to the floor next to the curtain, hears her zip the bag. She must be sleeping nude.

"Good night, Walter." She's giggling. "A sleepover. This is fun."

He strips, hangs from the bar over his closet door, and manages a dozen slow pull-ups. He takes a quick shower, kills the bathroom light, and slides into bed. The apartment is pitch black but for the oven clock and his USB hub. He can hear her breathing. She coughs.

"Sorry if the bag's a little dirty," he whispers. "I hiked Angel Island last week, camped overnight."

"Angel Island, I love it. Did you take your bike on the ferry?"

"Yes."

"The bag's perfect." She makes a happy, humming sound. "It smells like you."

He's wide awake, wondering. She was just sitting half-naked on his couch, talking about tangled sheets—where did she learn this? From her mother? Other girls? Who teaches women those happy little hums, the words that slide into a man's cells and pluck his cave-man DNA like a harp? *It smells like you,* she'd said. He'd better stay on guard.

He hears her breathing. "Walter?" she whispers.

"Good night, Ellie."

Day 56
Friday, March 20. The next morning
24 deaths reported
1,283 cases reported

Governor Newsom deploys the National Guard to help distribute food, as need grows and volunteer forces dwindle.

Connecticut, Illinois, and New York join California in telling nonessential workers to stay home.

SEVEN A.M. THE SMELL wakes him. He sits up, sees her holding a spatula over his skillet. It's a cool morning, and she's wearing blue sweatpants with a matching top. She's singing, too softly to make out the words. He studies her face. No makeup yet, but still beautiful.

She turns. "Good morning!"

He realizes she has a clear view of his bed from the kitchen and pulls the sheet around him. "Turn around, don't look." She laughs while he darts naked into his closet to dress.

"Bacon," she says. "The last pack in the store, can you believe it?"

He joins her at the table for a bacon and cheese omelet, fresh orange juice, and coffee. They put away the dishes and read on the sofa until lunchtime, then use Joe's rules to decide on PBJs from home and a walk to the beach. They laugh as they chase each other down the stairs and head for Marina Green.

She jogs ahead, then turns and walks backwards, studying him. "You're really fit. Did you do sports in college?"

"Soccer, mostly. Some rowing." He laughs. "No medals or anything."

She lets him catch up, turns, and walks beside him. "And now? To stay in shape?"

"Jogging, biking," he says. "Some exercise stuff at home. What about you?"

"Same. Ride my bike a lot, walk, jog a little." She points across the bay. "We could ride together, bike across the bridge, down to Fort Baker. Take some wine, have a picnic, you know—"

"Perfect."

They decide to turn south on Baker, away from the beach. They find a wide, grassy place in the park by the Palace of Fine Arts and sit on the lawn, stretch out their legs, and open their sandwiches. Later, they lie back on the warm grass, arms outstretched. Their fingertips touch, no one pulls back. They doze.

She wakes up first. "It's so warm!" She stands up, raises her arms and slowly pulls her sweatshirt over her head, then drops it on the grass. She's wearing a pink T-shirt, cut short to show off her tight midriff. Before he can catch his breath, she tugs her sweatpants down over her hips and lets them fall to the grass. He gasps—her white shorts are tailored and high-cut; the stretchy fabric clings to her body as she walks to her backpack. She finds her sparkly cloth shoes, tugs them on, stuffs her sweatsuit into the pack. "Let's go home," she says, casually, unaware of her transformation, blind to the raw sexuality that radiates from her like a beacon. He stands up, but waits, watching her walk away, hypnotized by the maddening way her hips move. He shakes his head. She pulls him with a magnetic force that could lift a bus. And whose fault is that? Hers, a trap-setter? Or his, a sex-hunter? Her innocence is reassuring. Maybe they're both just pawns in life's game, victims of their DNA.

She's smiling. "You like?"

He laughs. "You think?" He stares. "You might as well be naked."

"I know it's a little . . . risqué. I've been afraid to wear it." She looks down as they walk. "You know, without an . . . escort."

"So today's outfit is about . . . confidence building?"

"Sort of, I suppose. Mostly, it's just *fun!*" She holds her arms straight up, turns in a little circle. "And skimpy feels so great in the sun, in a warm breeze."

"Have you worn it before?"

"Once, on a beach, with my sister and her husband." She holds her arms out to the sides, skips along for a few steps like a ten-year-old. He hurries to stay beside her. "She got it for me in Sausalito." She looks at him. "I'd never wear it . . . alone."

"Well, you wouldn't be alone for long."

"Are you okay, being my—"

"Bodyguard? I'd feel better if I was armed."

A cyclist breezes past, wildly ringing his bell, laughing. He looks back too long and barely misses a parked car.

He nods toward the vanishing cyclist. "See? He's helping you confidence-build."

She sighs. "It has its risks."

They continue down Baker, turn left on Francisco. "You're quiet," Ellie says. "Can you tell me?"

"No."

"Joe says we have to learn to trust."

They reach a bus stop and sit on the bench for a while. Finally, he takes a deep breath. "Okay. Lisa, my wife—"

"The founder-hounder."

"Yes, the very one." He stares at the asphalt. "She was a model."

"Oh, no," Ellie says.

"Used her body to set the hook, the sex to reel me in."

She touches his shoulder. "And ruined your life."

"Exactly."

"Like you said, sex blinds."

He nods. "Well, it sure kept me from seeing what a snake she was."

They both stare at the pavement. "Joe was right," she says.

"About?"

"Hanky-panky." She unzips her pack, starts pulling on her sweatpants. "Even the appearance of."

"Ellie, you don't—"

"It's okay, the fog's coming."

He doesn't protest.

"But this outfit." She wiggles her chest. "was for *fun*, not—"

"Fun, yes. But men are from Mars."

She pulls on her sweatshirt and zips her pack. He wonders if he's lost her forever.

They're almost home. A free-roaming neighborhood dog appears, tail wagging, following along and licking her hand as she pets him and laughs.

"Must be the sandwiches."

"Or maybe he just loves me," she says, and looks up at him. She stops in front of his house. "Well, here we are. Home." They wave at Mrs. Sharma's closed drapes as they climb the steps.

Later, Uber Eats brings Chinese with Tsing Taos and they eat outside on the steps, side by side, facing east, watching the clouds over the city catch fire. She leans, ever so slightly, and the gentle pressure of her shoulder makes him close his eyes. It's dark when they go back in.

She clears her throat. "Do you have any candles?"

He starts rummaging in a kitchen drawer. "A few, in case the power goes out." He finds three.

She gets up, lights one from the stove, drips wax, and sticks them onto saucers. She lights the rest—one for the kitchen, one on the coffee table, one on his bedside table. After turning out all the lights, they sit quietly together on the sofa. Finally, she gets up and walks to the window.

"What do you see?" he asks.

"I'm searching for stars." She turns to him. "Going for your run?"

"Think I'll pass tonight."

"Okay if I use the shower?"

"Of course." He takes his laptop to the kitchen table and she pulls the curtains closed between them. By the time she reappears, he's sitting on the edge of his bed.

She stops in front of him. Inches away. "You're almost out of bar soap," she says.

He stares. "Either you're taller or the towel's shorter."

She nods toward the bathroom. "Sorry. Your beach towel's wet. This is just a bath towel."

The candles are still burning, but she's all he can see in the room. Somehow, she's pulled the towel tight in a way that makes it ride too high on her hips, too low on her breasts. He wants to rip it off with his teeth and shake it like a dog. "Looks great," he says. She disappears into the bathroom.

Once she leaves the bathroom and darts between the drapes, he strips, carries his clothes to the closet, and tosses them in the hamper. He grabs the bar over the door and does his pull-ups. After he finishes his shower, he uses a spoon to snuff the candles and slides into bed. He listens in the darkness until he hears the soft sounds of her breathing.

"Walter?" she whispers.

"Yes, Ellie?"

"The hanky-panky thing—God, I wish we had a shorter word. It—"

"To Joe it means sex, don't you think? We could just use *sex*."

"The sex thing, then." She sighs. "Do you think it would be okay if we just . . . held hands?"

"Ellie, we're both naked. That would definitely be—"

"No, not now." Another sigh. "I mean, like when we're walking? You say something nice and I just squeeze your hand, hold it for a while?"

"Sounds safe enough."

"What if I just hug your arm when we cross the street?"

"Should be okay." He shakes his head. She's good. He wonders if she can hear his defenses cracking.

"Walter, you know, if you made your bed so the head was by the sofa, it would be easier for us to talk."

"We'll try it tomorrow."

"I'd like that." He hears shuffling sounds as she turns over in the bag.

"Good night, Walter."

"Good night, Ellie."

He closes his eyes tight, shakes his head to clear his thoughts. Earlier, on the steps, when he'd felt the touch of her shoulder, he just wanted to put his arm around her, to keep her safe. To rescue this wonderful girl. And maybe rescue himself. And now? Everything's changed. He can't forget she's just a few feet away, naked. He wants to unzip her bag, slide his arms under her, and carry her back to his bed. His heart is pounding like an animal's. His desire is gut-clenching, his cave-man DNA's on fire—

And then she coughs. And again, dry and raspy. Desire's gone by the third cough. He listens closely to her breathing and thinks he can hear wheezing. "Ellie? You okay?"

"I'm okay." Another cough. "Would you mind bringing me a glass of water?"

He stops by the closet, pulls on his sweatpants, and runs to the kitchen. He helps her sit up in the bag, hands her the glass. "Ellie?" He tries to hide the concern in his voice. He touches her forehead and it's warm.

She looks up at him. "I'll be fine." She clears her throat, takes a sip of water. "Just allergies. They always flare this time of year—usually it's mountain cedar." Another cough, another sip. "Don't worry. Go back to sleep."

Back in his bed, he stares wide-eyed at the ceiling. Surely it's not COVID. And if it is, she's young and healthy—eighty percent do fine. He clings to the eighty percent like a drowning man clings to a log. Allergies maybe, possibly the flu. She's right, she'll be fine. He tries to sleep. He wakes up later to a muffled cough. She's standing by the open door, breathing roughly, silhouetted by the glow of a streetlamp. He can see she's naked, so he says nothing. She pads back behind the curtains and he hears her zip the sleeping bag. She needed air. Not a good sign.

Day 57
Saturday, March 21. The next morning
28 deaths reported
1544 cases reported
> Newsom issues an executive order increasing capacity of healthcare facilities. He also says that Tesla CEO Elon Musk will help the state get more ventilators while Apple CEO Tim Cook has pledged one million medical masks.

EIGHT THIRTY A.M. SHE coughed all night. Now, her face is wet, her forehead hot. She denies it, but he can tell her breathing's worse.

"Okay," he says. "Let's go to the ER."

"Don't be silly. Look at me, Walter. I'm young, healthy . . . and

I'm not that sick. They'll just send me home, tell me to come back if I'm worse." He wants to argue but she puts up a hand. "It'll cost a fortune and I'll probably catch COVID while I'm there."

He brings her more water and a cool washcloth for her forehead. Yes, eighty percent do fine, but he knows when the young get COVID, they can go downhill fast. He sits on the floor for more than an hour and reads to her from her thriller. And then she's not listening. He touches her forehead; it's cold. Her breathing is shallow.

As he types, his fingers tremble over the keys. He stops. How can he write her death, no matter what purpose it serves in his story? He wants her here, with him, alive. He looks around the empty room and marvels at the power of a story to transform the characters, the reader, and—especially now—the writer himself. It's incredible she's never set foot in his house. He wants their shelter-in-place to have been real, not virtual. More than a product of their imaginations, more than just the stories Joe convinced them to write. Even so, the writing has changed him. Especially at this moment, when he almost wrote her out of his life. It's like he glimpsed some great truth. Is it an epiphany if you can't find the words to describe it? He knows the right words will show up, during a run, in the shower, like they do for so many writers. He checks his phone—it's time to end this story. So he stops searching for words and simply types, *As he kneels next to her and holds her hand, with sudden, amazing clarity, he understands everything.* He hits return twice and types:

~The End~

He checks the time and makes the call. Joe answers on first ring.

"Hey, Walter," Joe says. "Right on time. Story finished?"

"I just typed the last line," Walter says. "Is Ellie there?"

"In back, reading your story. Waiting."

"Tell her I'm on my way."

"Good. Send her the latest before you leave."

So he highlights what she hasn't read and sends it to her. He grabs his laptop and runs for the door. At the bottom of the steps, he sees Mrs. Sharma and waves. He turns and jogs down Alhambra, then turns left on Pierce and stops to catch his breath at Chestnut. He walks east on Chestnut, stops in front of Joe's Bar. He pushes through the door and Joe looks up when he hears the jingle.

"In the back," Joe says, but holds up a hand, motions Walter to come closer. "You made her cry," he whispers. "Good work, I think."

Walter sees her at a table by the tortilla chips. Her laptop's open. She glances up, sees him, and scrapes back her chair. She rushes through the tables like a slalom skier. They hug and he lifts her up and turns a circle before setting her down. "I missed you," he says.

She touches his cheek. "Me too. It's like I've known you my whole life!" She looks toward the bar. "Isn't Joe an absolute *genius*."

Walter shouts. "Joe! We both think you're a genius!"

The floor creaks as Joe walks over to the front door. He hangs the closed sign behind the clear glass and walks back to the bar. "You okay with a beer to celebrate?"

They nod their heads. A beaming Joe comes over and sets four mugs on the table at the same time Walter smells the beef. Tanya bursts through the kitchen door and sets her tray in the middle of the table.

"Four sandwiches?" Walter asks.

"Lunch," Joe says. "Join us?" Walter and Ellie nod and they all pull up chairs.

"Where's Helen?" Walter asks.

"Home. Looking for stuff. You know, birth certificate, social security card." Joe nods at Tanya. "For her med school application."

"All right, Dr. Tanya!" Ellie reaches across and they smack a high five.

"Obstetrics, I'm thinking. Maybe I'll deliver your grandchild." Ellie stares at the floor; Walter looks out the window. "But hey, tell us. Did it work? You know, your stories, the virtual shelter-in-place?" She's wide-eyed and breathless. "Walter?" His mouth's full and he nods, then puts down his sandwich and holds two thumbs-up.

"Worked *perfectly!*" Ellie laughs and grabs Joe's hand. "It was brilliant. Joe, how did you get such an idea? Did you ever use it before when you—"

"No, never. First time." Joe takes a sip of beer. "But you're a couple of angry, scared rabbits when it comes to relationships. And you're both writers, right? So getting each of you to write a story about sheltering-in-place together seemed like it might be, you know . . . an icebreaker."

"And was it?" Tanya asks. "Are you going to shelter-in-place together . . . *for real?*" No one speaks. "Okay, awkward," she says. "Walter?" She pokes him on the shoulder.

He ignores her and stares at Ellie. "I'm ready," he says.

"That's *great*," Tanya says, tossing her blond hair. "Because your willowy sex-bomb here has her bicycle parked out back." Tanya's green eyes flash. "And it's *fully loaded.*" They all applaud and hoot while Ellie blushes.

Joe stands. "Don't forget—the real thing might not be so easy." He wags a finger. "But I'm counting on you."

Joe goes back to the bar. Tanya wipes up, sits down again, elbows on the table, chin in her hands. "One thing I don't get. I mean, you've known each other for a while. But Walter, how did you write stuff about Ellie in your story? How did she write about you in hers?"

"Okay, everything I wrote about myself was true. What I wrote about Ellie came from getting to know her here at Joe's—and some really fun guesses."

Ellie nods. "It's amazing how much he got right!"

"We *both* got right," he says.

"And we shared our stories online while we wrote. So we learned more stuff from that."

"Like she loves to dress skimpy," he says.

"Like he got me my own remote for the TV."

"Oh my," Tanya says, clapping her hands. "You two belong together!" She's suddenly serious, leans toward them. "But for sure you'll be sheltering together, right?"

"Shelter together," Ellie says. "What a perfect way to put it."

They all stand up. "So exciting," Tanya says, waving her fists.

"We'll come for sandwiches," Walter says. "And keep you posted."

"Good luck with med school." Ellie gives her a thumbs-up.

They wave goodbye and Ellie and Walter head for the back door. He laughs when he sees her bicycle. He pokes the lumpy blue duffel bungeed under the crossbar, spots the computer bag and the makeup case. "Ellie, it's all the same stuff."

"I thought it would be fun." She lets him push her bicycle. "And I know where to put everything."

"Did you pack a nightgown?"

"Don't you have a beach towel?"

They walk slowly down Chestnut. She hugs his arm when they cross the street. "Nervous?" he asks.

"Definitely," she says.

"We should play by the same rules, don't you think?"

She sighs. "Yes." She looks up at him.

"Of course," he says.

"Don't stare too long at my towel."

"Don't ever wear the short one."

"Deal."

By the time they turn and walk down Alhambra Street, it's a clear and sunny day. Mrs. Sharma is tending her roses. She sees them coming and stands just inside her gate, socially distanced. Walter makes the introductions.

"Mrs. Sharma, this is Ellie. Ellie, meet Mrs. Sharma."

Mrs. Sharma beams, makes a slight bow. She holds her hands against her chest, palms together, fingers pointing upwards. "Namaste, my dear. I've heard so much about you." She shoos Walter away. "You're as beautiful as a movie star." She laughs. "His words exactly, you know."

Ellie blushes, returns the namaste. "I've heard so much about you, too." She points. "And Walter loves your garden."

She tilts her head back proudly. "He loves me, too!" She winks. "I'm your competition."

As the two women chat, Walter pushes her bicycle across the street and locks it to the post. He carries her things upstairs and puts them in the places he'd imagined in his story. He finds the old coffee pot, fills it with water, and sets it on the dining room table. After they'd started writing their stories, he'd hung the real curtains across the room, almost certain she would come. He pulls out his sleeping bag and drops it by the sofa. He finds the beach towel and puts it next to the bag. He glances out the window. Ellie is standing by the gate, and Mrs. Sharma is cutting roses.

He strips his bed, remakes it so the head is close to the couch. He smooths the spread, and he's making her tea when she walks in.

"Don't you just *love* her?" She carefully puts the roses in the sink, then waves at him. "Shears? Scissors?"

He finds some clippers, and she trims the stems and arranges the flowers.

She finishes her tea and unpacks. He can't stop smiling. "It's like watching an instant replay," he says.

"Isn't it weird?" She laughs. "I know where everything belongs!"

By midafternoon they're sitting on the sofa, a bottle of French Merlot from her duffel open on the table in front of them.

"I brought you a couple of books," she says. She holds up one. "Janet Burroway's *Writing Fiction*. It's all about the craft." She holds up a second. "*Bird by Bird*, by Anne Lamott. It's all about motivation. And it's funny. Bottom line? Just write a shitty first draft."

They sit on opposite ends of the couch, the books between them. She has a sip of wine, then picks up *Bird by Bird* and starts reading him her favorite parts. Outside, the fog builds, the light in the room fades.

She looks up. "Do you really have three candles?"

"Of course."

She follows him to the kitchen. "And the saucers? Like your story?" He finds them for her. She drips the wax, stands up the candles, lights them and puts them around the room.

They use Joe's rule to choose Grubhub, Greek, and moussaka. She claps her hands because the moussaka goes so well with the Merlot. They eat slowly in the candlelight, watching each other. Later, they clean up and go back to the sofa; she reads to him again. She puts down the book. "You're already a very sexy writer, you know?"

"Really?"

"I liked your sofa fantasy. Unzipping the sleeping bag, carrying me to your bed."

"I thought maybe I'd gone too far."

"Well, some readers might say not far enough."

"In your story," he says, "you had Lisa call me, ask me for money."

"And ask you over for a drink."

"And I told her no, try another ex-husband. I was firm but never lost my temper."

She looks at him over the top of her wine glass. "Was I close?"

"Perfect," he says. "I'm not angry anymore." He stares back at her. "Why'd you write it?"

"A trust thing. To get it out there, deal with it." She sips her Merlot. "In your story, at the end. If you hadn't run out of time, were you going to let me die?"

"Of course not. I just needed you sick enough to clear my head."

"So you could think about me? Without the distraction of—"

"Yes."

"Sweet." She sighs. "As you said, sex blinds." She waves her glass. "The last words of your story. Your epiphany. The feelings you couldn't explain. Have you—"

"I still don't have the words. I'll tell you the second I do, promise."

"I know you will," she says. She stands up, refills her glass, moves to the window. "You can barely see the streetlamps in this fog." She stands by the window until she finishes her glass. She moves back, sets the empty glass on the coffee table. She squeezes his shoulder. "Move, please. Time for my shower." She closes the curtains across the room and disappears.

"Perfect time for a run," he says. He hears her soft laughter from behind the curtain.

He changes clothes, puts on his running shoes, then remembers the fog and grabs his windbreaker. Wrapped in her towel, she pops out from behind the curtain just as he's leaving. They almost collide. He smells her hair, her skin, feels his face get hot. Her shoulders and chest turn red as he stares. "Sorry," he says, "I didn't expect you to be . . . ready so soon."

They stare at each other quietly for a while. She has a new look on her face and she's breathing deeply, her breasts straining against the towel. "I didn't expect to be ready so soon, either." He feels the warmth of her breath on his neck. Her hand moves slowly across her breast to the little tuck holding up her towel. "You know, one of these days," she stares at him, "we should try that bike ride."

He clears his throat. "You mean the one across the Golden Gate to—"

"I mean the one where we find out if we still remember what to do."

"Ah," he says. "That one." He clears his throat again, nods at her towel. "The one where we shower before the ride."

Her eyes never leave his. "And after. If we get sweaty."

They stand, face-to-face. He's mesmerized by her pouty lips. They're both breathing hard. She moves her hand away from her towel, rests it against his chest. No one speaks for a long time. Finally, she says, "Walter, please do something for me."

He nods.

"Go for your run. But the whole time you're gone, promise me you'll try to think about just one thing."

He nods again. "And what would that be?"

"Us. Your epiphany." She moves her hand from his chest to hers and back to his, gives a tiny push. "What matters. What it's all about. See if you can find an answer before you come home. Please?"

"Promise," he says. He steps back, takes a deep breath, lets it out, and heads for the door.

It's dark, the fog's thick, and he's happy to slip on his windbreaker. He uses the fuzzy glow from the little houses to trot down the middle of Alhambra Street, alert for the sounds of other joggers, of cyclists. As the fog starts to thin, he picks up his pace. With each slap of his running shoes, he whispers her name—*Ellie, Ellie*.

The fog is wispy when he reaches Marina Boulevard. He jogs across, turns left, and heads west along Marina Green, past the yacht harbor, past the darkened Palace of Fine Arts, all the way to Crissy Field. He stops and leans forward for a moment, hands on his thighs, breathing hard, still thinking about Ellie. When he reaches the path, he walks to the beach, finds his familiar bench, and sits down. He looks up. The Golden Gate Bridge, wonderfully close, always humming with traffic, is eerily silent. He braces, knowing what's coming.

The fog on the ocean side of the bridge is thick and billowy, barely visible in the tower lights, as black as the night it fills. On the bay side, it's like gauze, and thinning, as though the bridge really is a gate, holding back the dangerous fogs. Suddenly, in a ground-shaking blast, one of the bridge foghorns lets out its long, sad moan. Soon after, farther away, the second foghorn answers, in a different pitch but just as sad. Two old basso-profundos, marooned on the rocks, trying to keep other men on the right path, out of harm's way. He shakes his head. He needs them tonight.

An orange cloud appears under the bridge, mid-span. Slowly, a giant cargo ship, lights blazing, moves out of the fog and into the bay, probably heading to Oakland. As it comes into focus, he sees the steel containers lashed to its decks. He wishes Ellie were here to watch it pass. And then he thinks of all the containers, what they might hold. Beds and table lamps and dishwashers, tricycles, pool tables, and swing sets. The stuff of life. Of families. The first foghorn sounds a low farewell to the passing ship. Walter closes his eyes. Thank you. He stands up and heads back.

Walking slowly, he reaches the yacht harbor and stops. A slight breeze carries nostalgic sounds of halyards whip-smacking their masts. He remembers a marina, a boat. He remembers Lisa, remembers swearing he'd never trust a woman again. He thinks of Ellie, and her story. He remembers all the things he asked her, and her simple, honest replies. He walks on, and by the time he reaches Cervantes, he's smiling.

As he walks down Cervantes, between the little houses with their cozy window-lamps and candle-lit rooms, he wonders if anyone can really define love. Experts laugh and say you know it when you feel it. And then he remembers what he felt when he made her sick in his story, sick enough to lose. The epiphany he couldn't find words to describe. He has words now, words he'll share with her when he gets home: *When life hangs in the balance, it brings everything into focus. You know what matters and what doesn't.*

And of course she'll ask, *So what matters?*

He'll simply say, *You. Without makeup, with all your clothes on. Just you.*

Ahead of him, in the light of a streetlamp, a police cruiser is parked along the curb. Two policemen—a young man and woman in crisp uniforms—stand side by side, leaning against the driver's door. Walter watches as they laugh, brush shoulders, bump hips. On and off duty, secretly, he's certain they're partners in every way. They come to attention as he walks up. They all keep their social distance.

"Good evening," Walter says.

"Evening," the young man says. "Out for a run?"

Walter nods. "Gotta love these empty streets." He points. "I live a block down Alhambra. Is there a problem?"

The young woman steps forward. "Oh, no. Not at all, sir." She makes a circling gesture. "Command has us scattered all around, you know? To see how this shelter-in-place thing's going to turn out."

"Are they still talking weeks?" Walter asks.

"Weeks, maybe months," the boy says. "Got a good TV series to watch? Any plans for the time off?"

"I do have plans," he says, and glances down the street. "I'm going home and do my best to make a baby."

"Woo hoo!" the young woman claps her hands. The young man steps away, as though he just heard something frightening. "You go, Daddy!" She raises an arm and he raises his and they air-smack a COVID high five. As he turns, she reaches through the cruiser's open window and gives him a little *woop-woop* with the siren. They're all laughing as he starts jogging. The fog is gone, not even a ring around the streetlamps, and the way ahead is clear. He thinks of Ellie, waiting, and he sprints.

Day 60
Tuesday, March 24. Three days later.
52 deaths reported
2,646 cases reported

> Governor Gavin Newsom suggests the shelter-in-place order could last until mid-June.

Contributors' Notes

LYNN BEMILLER is a retired physician and Navy veteran. She holds a certificate in novel writing from Stanford. This is her second published story. She has two grown sons and lives in Southern California with her husband.

JANE BOULDEN is a Canadian and a professor of international relations. She has been a member of Seth Harwood's workshop for three years. She has written and published extensively in the academic world. This is her first published piece of fiction.

NELL PORTER BROWN is a long-time journalist—and new fiction-writer—in Cambridge, Massachusetts. Her work is guided by fervid curiosity, a deep love of craft, and the simple, sweet act of letting the imagination run free. A staff writer/editor at *Harvard Magazine*, she focuses on alumni profiles and New England-based arts/culture, history, gastronomy, and travel. Recent features include: The Emily Dickinson Museum, tracing America's industrial roots in the Blackstone River Valley, and the joys of Provincetown in the dead of winter. She is also earning a master's degree in creative writing and literature—and is available for freelance editing and writing projects.

KATE M. COLBY is the author of the Desertera steampunk dystopian series and forthcoming paranormal fantasy novels. Her writing has been published in regional magazines, won local awards, and been taught in college courses. In addition to pursuing a master's degree at Harvard Extension School, Kate enjoys wine tasting, playing video games, and doting on her feline familiars. Learn more at katemcolby.com.

ELIZABETH COLEMAN is an attorney and writer based in San Francisco. Her work has been featured in *Art Animal Magazine* and *Swoop Magazine*, among others. This is an excerpt from her third novel, *City of*

Sevens. Connect with her at elizabeth-coleman.com or on Twitter, @thelizcoleman.

VICTORIA FERENBACH is a retired interior designer. She lives in New York City.

RICH FERRI is a soon-to-be-retired software engineer and inventor who spends his free time attending creative writing classes and workshops. He's published stories in *Aethlon: The Journal of Sport* and online at literallystories2014.com. He's an avid baseball fan and lives in upstate New York with his wife and their fierce Corgi, Nellie. He has a wide collection of plaid shirts.

JENNIFER FICKLEY-BAKER lives in Florida with her husband and has been a writer for more than twenty years. She focuses on thrillers and ghost stories for adults, as well as middle-grade fantasy (to the delight of her two children). Her first novel, *The Widow of Harteforde,* was written under the mentorship of author Seth Harwood. Follow her on Twitter @ JennFickley.

BENNETT GATES, once an engineer, now a retired physician, struggles to reinvent himself as a writer—with the patient support of his fellow students and coach. He lives in Silicon Valley with his beagle, cat, and beloved wife Joan, who in COVID days has become a formidable writer of honey-do lists.

ANDREW HINSHAW resides in the Midwest with his girlfriend, two cats, and a honey badger masquerading as one. Once a trance DJ and dog food lineman, he now works in a field more suited to his background in psychology. He spends his free time rereading the Darth Bane trilogy, looking stoic in grayscale photographs, and participating in online workshops hosted by author and instructor Seth Harwood. He's published short stories in *The Scarlet Leaf Review* and *Oyster River Pages* (the second of which, "Abigail," was nominated for the Pushcart Prize). "The Mad AI" is the prologue to his novel-in-progress, *Emergence.*

JEANNIE HUA has been a criminal defense attorney for twenty-plus years and a genius writer in her own mind since birth. While awaiting her genius to be discovered, she's attending the School of the Art Institute of Chicago and living off of her husband.

JULIA PARMENTIER is a retired geologist/environmental scientist who has gone back to writing after years of consulting and teaching. She has published occasionally in the past in the *Providence Journal* and the *Foster Home Journal*. She lives with her spouse in western Rhode Island, sharing the woods with the tree frogs, barred owls, foxes, and far too many deer.

ANDREW PETERSON is a writer currently working on his thesis for a master's degree in creative writing and literature at the Harvard Extension School under the tutelage of author Seth Harwood. He is a frequent lecturer at the annual Tolkien at UVM conference. Andrew is an avid reader, writer, and possible book hoarder who lives in Boston with his wife, a dog, and two cats. Andrew reads and writes about heroes because he's always wanted to be one himself. He's not. However, his daughter thinks he is and that's good enough for him. This is his first published work.

J. L. PRICE has recently made the move to fiction writing after spending most of her work life writing academic pieces and teaching. When she isn't working and writing, she loves to spend time with her husband and two kids enjoying places of natural beauty. She is particularly fond of the mountains of Wyoming, where she loves to hike, bike, camp, and fish (which for her means reading a good book on a nice rock by the water).

ALYCE WERDEL lives with her husband in San Francisco, where they raised three children. In a former life, she was a partner at the international law firm Baker & McKenzie, and was a frequent speaker and author on global equity compensation. She is a graduate of the University of Notre Dame Law School and Stanford University, where she played on two NCAA Championship tennis teams. Her husband always told her she had an active imagination, so she decided to try fiction writing. This is an excerpt from her first novel, *Vengeance*.

B. R. WELCH is a professional dilettante and writer of speculative fiction. He is currently working on a novel expanding the universe of "Shield Monkeys." B.R. is fluent in Mandarin Chinese and is an avid student of Tiger Crane Kung Fu. He likes to dress up as a poet on the weekend and is often mistaken for a houseplant. He tweets sporadically at @b_r_welch and can be reached online at brwelch.net.

Made in the USA
Middletown, DE
19 August 2021